BLUE SHOE

By the same author

LYING-IN
A FLESHLY SCHOOL
LINSEY-WOOLSEY
PARADISE
A PILLAR OF CLOUD
THE GOLDEN VEIL

GERARD MANLEY HOPKINS
A MOST UNSETTLING PERSON:
PATRICK GEDDES (1854–1932)
BARNWELL

POETS' LONDON

BLUE SHOE

by

Paddy Kitchen

HAMISH HAMILTON LONDON

HAMISH HAMILTON LTD

Published by the Penguin Group
27 Wrights Lane, London W8 5TZ, England
Viking Penguin Inc., 40 West 23rd Street, New York, New York 10010, U.S.A.
Penguin Books Australia Ltd, Ringwood, Victoria, Australia
Penguin Books Canada Ltd, 2801 John Street, Markham, Ontario, Canada L3R 1B4
Penguin Books (N.Z.) Ltd, 182–190 Wairau Road, Auckland 10, New Zealand

Penguin Books Ltd, Registered Offices: Harmondsworth, Middlesex, England

First published in Great Britain 1988 by
Hamish Hamilton Ltd

British Library Cataloguing in Publication Data

Kitchen, Paddy
Blue Shoe.
I. Title
823'.914[F]   PR6061.18

ISBN 0–241–12184–1

Typeset by Butler & Tanner Ltd
Printed and bound in Great Britain by
Butler & Tanner Ltd, Frome and London

121315

For Dulan

1   He meets Lydia in the British Museum shop

No one interrupted his stumping, rocking progress back from the tavern. Other midnight pedestrians, drunk and sober, stepped out of the path of such a bulky man. Dingy Tottenham Street was lit only by the slight lustre from the deep grey sky. In other surroundings that light might have been mysterious or romantic; here it was depressing.

He sniffed the air. It was flat, warm. Stale, late summer. He had not drunk enough. He should not be bothering with assessing the quality of the air. He should be five minutes away from absolute oblivion. If he was sober enough to be dissatisfied with the air, he was sober enough for insomnia.

Kenneth stopped writing. 'Insomnia'. Was the word invented by 1780? He swivelled his chair left to face the reference books and pulled out the *Shorter Oxford*. Evidently it came into use in 1758; before that, 'insomnie' had been followed by 'insomnium'. He liked insomnie. Perhaps he could use it – it might still have been around in 1780. But it would sound deliberately archaic, which he didn't want. And really he shouldn't be bothering with looking things up – he wasn't attempting to keep the language strictly within the period, just trying to make it sound natural. He wasted too much time with reference books: burrowing trails through dictionaries, companions, atlases, until often he forgot what his original quarry was.

He looked at the words he had just written, words which were meant to describe Richard Wilson, landscape painter, returning from the pub after too much porter. Returning to rooms whose furniture was nearly all in hock, and where unsold canvases glimmered in dark corners. Rooms that contained no further supply of porter. Just a rickety bed, a chest, a couple of chairs, a mirror, his easel, a few jars of colours and mixing agents, and one brush. Rooms to which, six months before, a posse of self-important members of the self-appointed Committee of Taste had deigned to come to deliver their resolution '*That the manner of Mr Wilson was not suited to the English taste, and that if he hoped for patronage he must change it for the lighter style of Zuccarelli.*' It had been Edward Penny, author of such canvases as 'The Virtuous comforted by Sympathy and Attention' and 'The Profligate punished by Neglect and Contempt', who had recited that resolution – no doubt in the full satisfaction that he was doing a fellow founding-member of the Royal Academy a gracious favour. Happily, Richard Wilson's customary robust manner of address had not been disabled by the committee's outrageous presumption and, within four minutes of clattering up the wooden stairs to his squalid first floor rooms, they had found themselves clattering back down into the street.

Kenneth had told this anecdote to Lydia over lunch in a sub-standard Italian restaurant just before they had been to see eight Richard Wilson paintings in an opulent, stand-offish gallery in Bury Street.

'Why don't you write about him properly? Not just art critic-ism.' She had cut her too-soft spaghetti into lengths easily contained in her spoon, and was shaking on a thick, sawdusty layer of parmesan.

He sucked manfully at the untidy hank spiralled round his fork. 'Biography, you mean?'

'No. Properly. A story. Like you've been telling me.'

'I don't like fictions about real people.'

'Not a whole book. A story.'

So he was writing the story for Lydia because a few hours after their lunch the editor of *Art London* had told him over the 'phone that he did not want a discursive piece on Richard Wilson – 'It sounds so bellettrist' – and was looking forward to a 'critical, decisive' piece on the Kandinsky exhibition which had just opened at the Tate. The rejection had made Kenneth want to launch into a barrage of exaggerated apologetics defending the significance of Wilson and the value of belles-lettres. But he just said resentfully, 'I'll contact you when I've seen the exhibition,' and put the phone down. Kandinsky. He didn't *feel* like having to think decisively about the direct appeal of abstract form and composition; he wanted to write affectionately about the man who had stood by the Terni falls with Joshua Reynolds and murmured to himself, 'Well done, water, by God! Well done!'

Now it occurred to him that 'pedestrians' didn't look right. He opened the *Shorter Oxford* again. Just as he thought. 1793. Bugger. He pushed the dictionary, pen and manuscript paper away.

His curving work-surface was built into a robust Victorian bay window that overlooked a shrubbery strip. A few pale November rosettes of a laurustinus pressed against the curtainless glass, but everything beyond was invisible. After dark, reflections of the room – and himself – became the view. He swivelled right to face objects that indicated he was about to begin an illustration for a William Trevor short story: the art editor's letter – margins now thick with doodles – giving colour supplement format details; a finished sketch of a fishmonger's and several rough ones of women's heads; coloured inks in chunky bottles that looked like a litter of dwarf robots; a blue plastic cutlery tray filled with pastels and crayons; a jug, shaped like Windsor Castle, of pens and pencils; several Xeroxed typewritten sheets with the lingering chemical smell that still reminded him of America because it was in New York that he had noticed it for the first time – sheets with corrections that gave him glimpses of William Trevor's handwriting. Kenneth noticed that he had crossed out 'brill and dory' and substituted 'saithe and snapper'. He wondered if Trevor minded being illustrated.

3

Sitting could no longer alleviate his urgent need to pee. In a continuous movement, he stood up, walked to the door, turned the handle and stepped into the middle of the hall – where he halted abruptly. He had not made his habitual check for sounds, and footsteps and animated voices were about to materialize into people at the top of the first flight of stairs.

Frances came first, followed by a stranger who Kenneth presumed was Serena Stein. But, despite mild curiosity, his gaze did not linger over her, because on the next stair Ronnie appeared with Alastair Faraday's hand on her shoulder. The rest of Faraday loomed thin and tall behind her, and for a split second Kenneth caught the familiar, lost expression on the actor's famous face. He had been about to respond to Frances's smile and gentle 'Hullo', but his mouth closed obstinately, and he completed his progress across the hall to the bathroom with just a vague wave of his hand.

He peed fiercely, and when he had finished stood indecisively by the bath. He could still hear them talking; the front door had been opened and the noise of the midnight traffic on the Old Brompton Road forced their voices to an even louder pitch of after-party self-importance and excitability. The tenants on the two floors between his and Ronnie's would be justified in complaining again, he thought smugly. Since he neither wished to re-cross the hall while they were still there, nor lurk silently in the bathroom until Ronnie was on her own, he slammed the plug in the bath and turned on the taps. The roar of the plumbing would obliterate all other sounds for at least ten minutes.

The conversion of the house into flats had been done in the Fifties with as little alteration to the structure as possible. His bathroom had once been a study, and the long room in which he lived was the old dining-room. He had bought a lease on the two rooms three years before, when Ronnie was already living at the top of the house and their relationship was six months old. It had seemed a sensible arrangement. It still seemed a sensible arrangement – only he was perhaps getting too old to parade across a public passageway each time he needed to pee.

When he emerged after his bath into the empty hall, wearing a towel and carrying his clothes, he could smell an unfamiliar perfume. It verged on the over-strong and over-sweet. Neither

4

Ronnie nor Frances, her partner, wore heavy scents. Serena Stein? It wasn't what one would predict an American feminist painter's taste to be. Ditto, he supposed, Alastair Faraday – who, according to the arts gossip columns, was supposed to be in Los Angeles about to sign up to star in a film based on Isherwood's *The World in the Evening*. Though that wasn't why he shouldn't have been with Ronnie. No man should have been. She had said quite clearly last night that the supper for Serena would be all girls. And how on earth had she suddenly got to know Faraday?

He stood inside the door of his room and looked around. Richard Wilson would have had to light a candle or fumble in darkness when he got home – no sudden snap of the light-switch to connect three wall-spots, or desk-lamp left burning in the window. This room would most likely have seemed a curious mixture of prosperity and poverty to him. Even in his Tottenham Street days of decline, the inclusion of kitchen appurtenances (be they old pine and stainless steel units as Kenneth's were) in a gentleman's living quarters would have been most odd, while the fluorescent green blind which covered the street window under which the units were built, would have shrieked outlandishly to eyes innocent of chemical dazzle. The junk shop Edwardian leather settee and chair might possibly have appeared luxurious – if monstrous, and the blue-and-white striped duvet thrown over a foam rubber platform a somewhat outlandish form of bedding. (Kenneth remembered the little sketch Wilson had made of a two-handled chamber-pot under a dishevelled bed in Rome. No place for a jerry here ... Though perhaps one might alleviate his hallway problem.) The melamine storage units and the block-board work-surface would presumably seem just makeshift, but the adjustable swivel chair – an expensive design in chrome and pale blue leather – might that seem a wondrous invention? As for the blue fitted shagpile, a bright summer ocean of wool lapping up to the edges of the thirty-foot-long room, surely that would be a consummate luxury to someone used to bare boards and decorated oil cloths? He walked appreciatively across it, and sat in the swivel chair. He might as well continue to ponder the beginning of the story until Ronnie phoned.

No one interrupted his stumping, rocking . . .

'Stumping, rocking'? It sounded like Long John Silver.

It occurred to him that he no longer felt sheepish about having lied to Ronnie, ages ago, when she'd asked him, 'Why is there so much pale blue in your life?' and he had replied, 'I don't know. Perhaps colours become a habit.' It was only the second lie he remembered telling her, their lives being deliberately arranged to avoid any need to deceive. But he had found it impossible to answer the apparently innocuous question that probed at a secret like a steel pin at a winkle.

His carpet and his chair were blue because he'd once, on the spur of the moment, painted a pair of old shoes cobalt blue for a party. Hard to believe now that they could have caused such a sensation, and that in the subsequent months, when he wore them about his business as a student at the Royal College of Art, so many people could have admitted, in their different ways, that they found them sexy. It wasn't long before coloured shoes were commonplace, but those summer weeks, when he had the most conspicuous feet around South Kensington, were halcyon. He hadn't deliberately stuck to pale blue ever since because of that, but he had little doubt it was why he was drawn involuntarily to it: pale blue jeans, pale blue paint, pale blue carpet – even pale blue Edding pens.

'Habit?' Ronnie had said. 'You mean from *baby* days?' And he had laughed.

Why hadn't he explained about the shoes? She wouldn't have disparaged – they'd shared dafter memories with sympathy. But he didn't want to share that one. He supposed he was perpetuating some dreadful narcissistic streak, framing himself in blue in memory of days when, even though he was short, he could make an entrance with effect. Days which had passed before America, that great iceberg of an experience, had touched his life.

When Richard Wilson got back to his rooms, would he have taken the candle close to a painting and looked at it, trying to resurrect a flicker of the glory he had felt when he used to stand on the hillsides near Rome and survey the magical evening light? Or would he have turned his back on the golden perspectives that nobody wanted – unless they were tricked out with groups of frolicsome figures à la Zuccarelli – and meditated darkly on death? What he would not know, Kenneth flicked the dates back and forth in his head, was that there was a five-year-old boy living in a barber's shop in Covent Garden, and a four-year-old boy living in Suffolk, who would grow up to be England's most exalted landscape painters, and who would both revere him to –

The trimphone made its 1940s Rose Murphy trill.

'Kenneth.' ('Ken-nethh.')

That was one of the things he still noticed about the American voice, even when it was tempered by several years of living in Britain as Ronnie's was: it made such a soft, gentle-surf-on-sand sound out of 'Kenneth'. He hated the name in its sharp, emphasis-on-the-first-syllable, English manifestation; but he positively liked the American version.

'Hullo.'

'You ignored us.'

'Not really intentionally. It just happened that way. I had a very full bladder.'

'Angry?'

'No.' Irritated, yes.

'Alastair Faraday was a complete surprise. I want to tell you about him tomorrow.'

'When?'

'I'm meeting Serena at the gallery at ten. How about lunch?'

'It would break up the day rather. I've got to go to the Tate to look at Kandinskys. How about the evening?'

'Mm ... I'm not sure.'

'Shall I come up at nine for coffee?'

'Yes ... yes ...'

'Buona notte, then.'

'Goodnight. Goodnight, Kenneth.'

A few minutes later he had a sense of unease. He had been very brusque. He should have asked about Serena. It was going to be a coup if she agreed to show at Ronnie's and Frances's gallery. He dialled. The number was engaged. Two minutes, four minutes and ten minutes later, it was still engaged.

Ronnie's door was unlocked when he reached the top of the

stairs at three minutes past nine.

He called out, and she replied from the kitchen. He walked across the cool beige and stone and white room, past the dining alcove rather perfunctorily cleared of dinner, to the archway. Ronnie, her cerise kimono belayed firmly round her small waist, was endeavouring to make the dirty dishes look orderly. On the edge of the draining board, a jug was ready with filter and coffee, and the kettle was beginning to sing.

She turned and smiled, her dark, deliberate-disarray-style hair not yet brushed. The kimono was too large – most things were too large for Ronnie – and her narrow, friendly face might have been overpowered by the tousled hair and ballooning robe, if it weren't for her granny glasses, rimmed with amethyst plastic, that magnified her deep brown eyes.

He kissed her gently but unhurriedly on the lips, then sniffed her hair.

'So it was your perfume.'

'What was mine?'

'In the hall last night.'

'Do you like it?'

'Bit sweet.'

'Mm. I felt like a change.'

'How did it go?'

'Very well.'

'Would you like some help?' He nodded at the dishes. It was unlike her not to have done them before she went to bed, no matter how late.

'No. But thank you. Go and sit down, and I'll bring the coffee in a minute. If it's not too early, there's some slides of Serena's by the viewer. Stuff I hadn't seen before.'

'Okay.'

He went to the long, cream-tweed settee and sat in front of the viewer on the coffee table. Beside it was a small box, that had once contained vitamin pills, with 'American painters (m.)' written boldly on it. He opened it carefully and took out a dozen transparencies.

When he pressed the first slide down into the viewer, he got a mild shock. The painting was jewel-like and intricate, reminding him of a narrative stained-glass window. At the centre, quite recognizable, was Mark Rothko, sitting hunched on a stool in front of a black and bruised-magenta chasm of a painting, his arms held out towards the onlooker, vermilion pouring from their slashed veins. Around him were painted scenes connected with his life, some of which Kenneth could more or less identify, some not. Curiosity aroused, he quickly fed the other slides into the viewer, one after the other, like childhood pennies into a slot machine. Each time he pressed with expectation, and each time he experienced a mild disappointment. The faces and fragmented lives and works of Jasper Johns, Robert Rauschenberg, Franz Kline, Jackson Pollock, Kenneth Noland, Robert Motherwell, Morris Louis, Willem de Kooning, and Barnett Newman lit up before him, stirring memories of exhibitions, articles, reproductions and gossip.

'Well . . .?'

Ronnie stood by him with a tray, and he made a space on the table.

'Quite a surprise.'

'What do you mean?'

'Not at all what I'd've guessed from those earlier reproductions you showed me.'

'And you taught me never to predict an artist's development.'

'Touché.'

'So . . . what do you think?'

'What size are they?'

'Four feet square.'

'I think they'll attract attention. I'm not sure if they'll sell.'

'They don't grab *you* much?'

'Can I wait till I see them in the flesh?'

'*If* you see them, Kenneth.'

'Yes, sorry. Let me think.'

He picked one of the slides at random and put it back in the viewer. Jackson Pollock, in the middle of what looked like a desert, was flicking a narrow ribbon of black paint from a tin with a stick. The paint already on the sand looked like leaks from an asphalt tank. From the top right-hand corner, Peggy Guggenheim smiled approvingly. In the top left, an American-Indian woman swept litter off a holiday beach. Kenneth remembered that Pollock had likened his work to the ritual images Indians made by trickling sand onto the earth. He stared at another image: the white and grey diagram of a brain into which a bottle of whisky dripped, dispersing in fragmentary swirls palely reminiscent of a Pollock painting. The reason he was finding it difficult to marshal his thoughts and give a proper reaction was a jarring mixture of genuine doubt and selfish jealousy: had Ms Stein perhaps found a better way of telling stories about painters than he?

He looked at Ronnie, hunched at the other end of the sofa, her hands curled round her mug. She didn't even know about the Richard Wilson story yet – and there wasn't time to explain before she had to leave. What she needed was his opinion. It would cost a lot to ship the twelve paintings over – and Stein would no doubt expect a considerable sum to be spent on publicity. The gallery could not afford a flop.

'Why isn't she showing them first in New York? That is – I presume she hasn't.'

'No. She's kept them under wraps. She says she wants to have the first reaction in London.'

'Oh. How do you feel about that?'

'Well, I have some sympathy. There's one element in New York that will say, "Jeez, those boring old Fifties and Sixties million-dollar painters just aren't worth the effort. And Tom Wolfe's said it all anyway."'

'They'd expect someone like her to have more topical targets?'

'Maybe. She suspects they might ignore or dismiss the meditative quality. That she's meditating on her student days.'

'When these men were the gods?'

'That's right. And for some people they still are the gods. They'll hate them.'

'They're well put together, as far as I can tell. And the gallery will suit them.'

'Yes. I thought that. I'd like to include three or four of her earlier paintings in the space by the desk, and then have these in the main area.'

'How do *you* like the theme?'

'Oh – I think it's brilliant. I can't wait to see them.'

'But I detect a worry?'

10

'Mm. I'm a little nervous that the art establishment might find their sheath knives again.'

Ronnie and Frances's gallery showed exclusively women artists, and it had taken several years for this exclusiveness to be accepted. Until recently, many critics had felt it necessary to include some light-hearted anti-feminist jibe in their reviews – though they always claimed privately to Ronnie that the jokes were meant to be affectionate. However, as she pointed out, the uninformed public did not have the benefit of their friendly little reassurances, and therefore found it all to easy to dismiss the gallery and not bother to make the journey to Covent Garden to see new exhibitions.

'I'm worried that a prospectus of their recent heroes, warts and all, might be thought "rather boorish".' She assumed an exaggerated Oxford accent for the last two words.

'Or they might love it.'

'You sound doubtful.'

'I'd better be honest.'

'You certainly had.'

'The thought that flashed across my mind was that they'd probably find them more persuasive if they were by a man.'

'God – you really mean that, don't you?'

'I think so. They'd feel more comfortable.'

'That clinches it. We're showing them.'

She'd put her mug down and was sitting very upright, her pointed chin jutting into the air.

Kenneth had seen that stance hundreds of times, and it still touched him. Little Ronnie Max from New Jersey against the rest. Only she was thirty-three and shrewd – not the frail high-school tussler a first glance suggested.

'I want you to meet Serena,' she said.

'I should like to. When do you suggest?'

'Will you need tomorrow free to write about the Kadinskys?'

He ought to say 'Yes'. But he realized he had not envisaged writing about them – just going to see them. Which meant that he had already decided, but not acknowledged, that he was going to resign from *Art London*. What he had pictured was writing more of the Richard Wilson story. And seeing Lydia. He'd pictured himself with Lydia again. Nowhere definite. But

11

probably among paintings. And Ronnie didn't know about Lydia yet.

'I'm not sure. I may not write about them.'

'Oh?' There was an instant tone of sharp concern in her voice. 'I assumed, from what you said, you were doing a piece for *Art London*.'

'That's what Richard Mafeking wants.'

She was staring at him, the serious eyes behind the jokey glasses trying to find out what he was really saying.

'But I'm not sure *I* want to. Adrian always let me select my own subjects. He didn't interfere.'

'Don't you think Mafeking will ease off? He's an ambitious man. He's bound to overdo the new broom bit at first.'

'Well – that's his concern. I don't think I want to be involved.'

'You're not thinking of resigning?'

Kenneth put on a smile in an attempt to block further probing. 'What were you going to suggest we do tomorrow?'

She gave a quick sigh, expelling her frustration and accepting the change of subject. 'Have lunch? The three of us.'

'Fine.'

'Okay. Well – I'd better dress.'

They both stood up, and he stepped to hold her, stroking her silk kimono with gestures of warmth and reassurance, and slipping his hand to her breast. She took off her glasses with the quick movement he knew so well and tilted her face. (When they'd first met he'd said, 'I'm not used to having to bend over to kiss people – we usually meet head on.') Her tongue touched his.

'Off you go,' he said. 'You'll be late.' She felt vibrant in his arms. 'Shall I call you up tonight?' He detected a slight hesitancy, resistance even. 'No – sorry. You're not sure what you're doing.'

'No.'

'You call me. To fix tomorrow. Or whatever.'

Her head still rested on his shoulder, the unfamiliar perfume lingering on her neck.

He waited. He realized he had no idea what she was thinking.

Their bodies, touching, seemed at ease; secure in the expectancy of intimacy soon.

'Yes, I'll call,' she said. 'And ... don't be too hasty with

12

Mafeking. Perhaps we should talk first?'

He went downstairs feeling irrationally irritated.

He decided to walk to the Tate. It was the sort of day that always reminded him of Canaletto's bright Venetian views of London: white masonry, blue sky, and sharp perspectives diminishing towards a glowing horizon. He liked walking; it filled in time in a virtuous but untaxing way.

As he cut down narrow Thistle Grove, where what looked like a nonagenarian Gaiety Girl – ankles still good above bunioned toes – walked her pekingese, he remembered that Alastair Faraday had not been mentioned. It was unlike Ronnie not to explain. Though she might have forgotten – he'd certainly forgotten to ask. And it was no good her frowning over *Art London*. He knew she liked him writing that column, liked the pieces themselves indeed, but it was not an indispensable part of his working life, and not one that he had sought out in the first place.

He crossed the Fulham Road into Elm Park Gardens, glancing across, out of habit, to the house where Elisabeth Frink and Laurie Lee once had flats. Why he looked, he did not really know. But the older he got, the more his walks across London became encrusted with memories and bric-à-brac information. When he came to the Kings Road, he hesitated. Should he walk up it, or go straight down to the Embankment? He decided to eschew the riverside abodes of Rossetti and George Eliot, and the moorings where the young Dorothy Tutin had lived in a houseboat, and do some cursory window-shopping. He did not strive to be fashionable, but he liked to take a sideways look at themes and trends.

There'd been a time, in his late twenties, when he'd joined in the chorus that the Kings Road had 'gone down', and that you could no longer buy necessities like half a pound of nails or a ball of string because of the bloody boutiques. But, now he was thirty-nine, he found he didn't mind at all. He was glad that ravaged-looking boys with mohican hair-styles, and soft English girls made up to look like Thirties German tarts, paraded there,

13

and that he could discretely witness their excesses from a distance.

An airforce-blue sweater caught his eye. Neat welts, extra-wide crew neck. Then he saw its price. Forty-nine pounds fifty, dear God, for just a humble jumper!

Lydia had been wearing a dusty-pink sweater which had a huge flower finely knitted in down the back. It must have cost a fortune. That had been the first time he met her, the day before yesterday. Yesterday it had threatened rain, and she'd worn a bright blue plastic mac over dungarees. The first time, he'd been in the British Museum shop. He'd just delivered a piece on contemporary portraiture to *Art London*, leaving it with the girl at the switchboard together with a note saying he'd do Richard Wilson next, and had gone on to the B.M. to replenish his postcard supply. He liked sending picture postcards; enjoyed selecting the image for the occasion and not having room for many words. He found letter-writing usually took far too long and increasingly made him feel self-conscious. He'd selected a fistful of cards, and was lingering over a little Richard Wilson drawing of an Italian wine flask and its shadow. But he'd bought that so many times, and could now no longer remember which people he'd already sent it to – it was particularly useful for saying thank you after parties when he'd drunk too much. Reluctantly he started to replace it in the rack, finding the fit rather tight.

'Whelks?' said a quiet, questioning voice.

With the card still not properly in its pack, he turned to see a girl with bright grey eyes, blushing.

'Sorry?' He saw she had, despite the blush, very pale, creamy skin, and pale curly hair, and thought she might be a Scandinavian whom he had misunderstood.

She shook her head.

'Can I help? I didn't catch what you said.'

'Whelks,' she repeated in a reluctant, unmistakably English, voice.

'*Whelks?*'

'I know. I'm sorry. It's what my father always used to say to me when I touched things in shops. And then I said it to Arthur when he was little. And it just came out – habit, I suppose.'

14

He stared at her, the uppermost part of his mind deciding she was mad, and the subterranean part thrusting forward the answer to her clue. *If you don't want the whelks, don't muck 'em abaht.*

'Billy Cotton,' she said sadly.

'Yes. I've just remembered.' He glanced back at the postcards.

'I'm sorry,' she said again.

'You're right. It's maddening when they're all dog-eared.' He took the Wilson wine flask out of the rack.

'No – don't. You obviously don't want it.'

'Well, I do really.'

She smiled tentatively.

'I'm not usually quite that indecisive,' he said. 'I had a good reason for putting it back.'

Concern replaced the smile. 'You can't afford another one?'

That jolted him. When had he last considered the cost of postcards? 'Just about.' He noticed she had one postcard of a Paris fashion plate. 'Come and have a drink with me across the road, and I'll explain why I put it back.'

Which led to him explaining who Richard Wilson was and asking her to meet him at the Bury Street exhibition the following day.

He'd got as far as Habitat along the Kings Road without even thinking of Edna O'Brien living in Carlyle Square, or the times he'd gatecrashed parties at Chelsea Art School in Manresa Road, and he crossed the road to the Town Hall and would have gone up Flood Street only he remembered the Prime Minister's home was there. Mrs Thatcher did not fit into the wide territory he regarded, after twenty-one years, as 'his'. It wasn't so much her politics as her individual unsuitability. She seemed to represent so many of the things people came to Chelsea to get away from.

The bright rectangles of fruit and vegetables in Safeways cheered him. Viridescent Granny Smiths, tortoiseshell pineapples, glaucous avocados, Tyrian purple cabbages – none of those adjectives was quite right, but, he felt, properly celebratory of his love of such abundance, of there being so many beautiful provisions to arrange in bowls, to draw, to cook, to eat.

'Kenneth Flete. You haven't changed a bit!'

Nor had the voice. He recognized it instantly. But not the person.

'You don't know who I am, do you?'

He had to look up to her, a big woman with grey hair flowing over a long black cape. She smiled, and behind the unfamiliar extra flesh, the tired eyes, he recognized – because of the quality of the smile – Rosemary Nene.

'Rosemary!'

'Oh . . .' She reached out and took his hand in hers. 'You do remember.'

For a few seconds they held their stance, like children about to whirl into a bout of playground twizzle. Then, awkwardly, they disengaged.

'How *are* you?' he said.

'I'm surviving. How long must it be? I haven't seen you since I left the College.'

'Twenty years. You left after my first year. I'm amazed you recognized me.'

'You still walk in exactly the same way. I remember it used to make me think of Rat in *Wind in the Willows*. And your hair's the same.'

He ran his fingers through the short, silky thatch. Yes, it had been short in those days too. And there was no grey among the brown.

'And – most important of all – you've still got golden eyes.'

He felt absurd under the inspection of this large, tented woman, yet faintly gratified too.

'I think they're supposed to be hazel.'

'I remember Anne Lingfield coming into the liferoom and saying, "One of those new kids has got eyes like topazes."'

'Good heavens!' He looked down at his feet. 'Do you still see her?'

'No, not for a long time.'

In his mind they had remained permanently linked, Rosemary and Anne, even their diploma shows displayed side by side; Anne's fierce black paintings of crows and cornstacks and broken barns, and Rosemary's soft, browny nudes and quiet interiors with the baby's crib.

'Darcy?' he questioned. 'How's Darcy?' It was crass stupidity,

16

he thought, to ask about a baby after twenty years, hornet thoughts of road accidents, borstal, Moonies, the National Front, swarming in his head.

'Oh, Darce!' she laughed. 'He's at Cambridge doing physics.'

And he laughed too. The infant Darcy had been the scandal of that year. Fathered, so he had gathered, by a lorry driver while Anne and Rosemary hitch-hiked to Cornwall, and of whom so many people had said: 'Poor baby, what can his future be?'

'Is he happy?'

'I think so. He's got the gifts he needs to do what he wants.'

'Are you painting?'

'A little. I teach mainly now. Have done for years. In a special school for kids with problems.'

Someone had once said she painted like Gwen John. 'Sounds interesting.'

'It's absorbing. I think I need that. But you ... you wrote a book, didn't you?'

'Yes. A novel. A long time ago.'

'Someone told me. I meant to look for it in the library.'

'I still do illustration mainly.'

She nodded. 'Family?'

He shook his head.

They stood, embarrassed, with nothing more to say.

'Well ...' he said.

'Oh, I am glad I've seen you. You haven't changed a bit. That must prove something.'

Their hands touched again, and they smiled nervously into each other's eyes across the twenty-year gap. Then they continued in their opposite directions, Kenneth selecting his route automatically for a while, not seeing the places that he passed.

Rosemary Nene! Nobody could have brought back more potent images of his first year at the College. With her long fair hair, and long dark skirts, and fine bones, and old silk flowers, she had seemed the archetypal female art student. He could remember the first time he saw her at the end of the long corridor in the Painting School. She was talking earnestly to one of the tutors, and the warm sound of her voice vibrated towards him. He would have shyly caught her eye if ever he met her after that,

17

and tried to smile, had it not been that invariably she walked with Anne Lingfield, their arms often linked, and Anne terrified him. Privately he called her Medusa because of her curling, matted black hair and staring eyes.

Then several weeks later he stood next to Rosemary in the mid-morning tea queue. Anne was not there, and the long line of students waiting in the corridor for the brew dispensed from an urn by a formidable cottage-loaf called Mrs Bucket moved exceptionally slowly. He had looked at his watch.

'Are you in a hurry?' Rosemary had asked. 'I'll get yours if you like. Where are you working?'

And from that small kindness had grown a secret, and very limited, friendship. Its only expression was that whenever they coincided on College territory, and both were unaccompanied, they would stop for a conversation, and these conversations had helped Kenneth to express doubts about what he was doing, and to be guided by Rosemary's gentle counsel into an alternative. There had probably been no more than five or six of them.

He had been eighteen, one of seven students who were part of an experiment the College was undertaking to see whether a strictly limited number of gifted students straight from school could take their place beneficially alongside the normal post-graduate intake. After three weeks, Kenneth had realized he would never be a painter, would probably never want to be a painter, and felt intensely uncomfortable and unhappy with this knowledge bottled up inside him. But he could find no way to communicate it. On the odd occasion he saw a tutor, his life-drawing was highly praised, and one of them remembered most favourably the landscape water colours he had submitted for the entrance examination and said that he looked forward to seeing stronger landscapes on canvas in due course. He couldn't say to anyone, couldn't convey it, that the two private times he had come in very early in the morning and prowled round the studios, sneaking into the barricaded cubicles built up by the second- and third-year students, had filled him with a kind of terror tinged with horror. He didn't hate *them* doing what they were doing, but he couldn't think of anything he might want to do that would entitle him to be a member of their species. It was a matter of scale. He neither wanted to fill large canvases, nor to spend months developing a theme. What did he want to do? He had fled the empty old building, and run up Exhibition Road to the park. The only way he could think of, as he wandered down the Flower Walk and circumnavigated the Round Pond, to describe how he wanted to work, was that he wanted to *fly*.

And somehow Rosemary had opened up a way that had led him, in the middle of the summer term, to ask quite confidently whether he might transfer to the illustration department, and there, once the dust of bureaucratic objections had settled, he had been both successful and happy. He couldn't remember now exactly what they had talked about, and knew that she had never given him any hard-and-fast advice; but she had enabled him to trust his instincts. He should have thanked her when they met just then. He had wanted to thank her before she left the College, but she and Anne had disappeared a week before the end of term, scorning (so he had heard) the Principal's elaborate Convocation ceremony, amd making tracks for Penzance. 'So I suppose there'll be a brother or sister for Darcy next Easter,' one of the tutors was overheard to remark.

He had never seen her again, never heard news of her. Nor sought it. His mind had occasionally verged near to a recognition of her role in his development, but never completely. It had needed her actual presence, with its air of generosity, yet still retaining a residue of the mystery she had once held for him, to do that. 'Thank you,' he said, quietly but clearly, as he left Chelsea and crossed into Pimlico Road.

A huge japanned – what was it, sideboard, chiffonier? – in an antique shop caught his eye, and he stood in front of the window marvelling. For some time now, he had been gradually building up a lust to own one vast piece of old furniture. Something monumental and exotic. This one glimmered darkly, its satiny facets black and bloody. 'I want that,' he thought. He almost went in to ask the price, but realized that would be time-wasting. While having no real knowledge of its value, he surmised it would be at least eight hundred pounds. Probably more – after all, that was only the equivalent of sixteen jumpers.

Further along was the shop with the pretty fanlight that had once been Anthony Armstrong-Jones's studio. Or so he'd been

19

told by the conductress of a Number 11 bus during his first year in London. The information had chimed with newspaper articles he vaguely recalled from the time of the royal engagement, and he had been curious because the event had to some extent briefly coloured his own life. He was in his last year at grammar school when the engagement was announced, and his normally reticent father had fulminated – there was really no other word for it.

'Armstrong-Jones!' he had snorted. 'Armstrong-Jones! A snapshotter with divorced parents.'

Taken aback, and with really no interest in royal affairs as became a sixth-former with pretensions to sophistication, Kenneth had said mildly, 'He's quite a good photographer.'

'Good? Good! What's that got to do with it? Good heavens, Kenneth, don't you get mixed up with notions that every little snapshotter or commercial designer is some sort of artist. And don't get mixed up with romantic ideas about artists either. Or actors. Wastrels and troublemakers. The Queen should have put her foot down. Once bohemianism infiltrates the royal family we're done for.'

The outburst amazed him. While calmly accepting his father as a philistine, he'd never known that he harboured such passionate views on the practitioners of art and allied skills. Even so, he might have relinquished any memory of the occasion of the royal engagement had it not been that the next day was when his headmaster had sent for him and said, 'Flete, Mr Cremorne thinks this might possibly be of interest to you,' and handed him a handsomely-produced circular letter, die-stamped with a small red crest, describing the Royal College of Art's experimental recruitment from schools. He'd known that Mr Cremorne thought he was good, but he hadn't known he thought he was that good.

In the subsequent muffled quarrels with his father, Anthony Armstrong-Jones's name had been mentioned, quite irrationally, two or three times. But Mr Flete's fire soon petered out. He ended by putting the blame – without telling him – squarely on the shoulders of Mr Cremorne, and became reticent once more.

Kenneth crossed Ebury Bridge into Sutherland Street and wondered whether to turn off down to Alderney Street and see if Jos and Pete were in. In some ways, they were his best friends –

which seemed to mean they didn't see one another often; they didn't make demands, and the older they all three got, the more time they spent being solitary. Perhaps he'd call there later, after he'd been to the Tate.

He completed the rest of the journey briskly, passing the three separate post-war styles in Lupus Street – towerblocked Churchill Gardens, supine-brutalist Pimlico School, and brick-and-slate vernacular Lillington Gardens – without his usual speculation as to their fitness. Finally, rounding the corner of John Islip Street into Atterbury Street, he thought of the pink blossom that covered its trees in spring and how, after the Kandinskys, he'd be able to look at the Tate's Wilsons.

He was uneasy about the public element of being a critic. On press days he always tried to get there early, hoping to avoid the half-familiar faces of the other journalists; and on occasions like today, when the exhibition was already open, he felt embarrassed at making himself known at the entrance so as to get in free and be given his complimentary catalogue. In private galleries he quite often paid for catalogues to avoid arousing the attention of the owners. It was, he had found, acutely discomforting to be observed looking critically at pictures, and sometimes this made him skimp his notes and leave before he had really looked his fill. On this occasion, the man at the exhibition desk made him wait while he checked a list to confirm the existence of *Art London*, an action Kenneth found he preferred to smooth-tongued recognition – or perhaps that was just because it served his own need to undermine the journal.

The exhibition, not a large one, occupied an L-shaped space in the new wing. It was laid out, with accompanying panels of text, to provide information and insight into Kandinsky's development. A teaching exhibition. Art historians would be urging students of painting throughout London and the suburbs to come to see it. Kenneth stood in the middle of the space and tried to empty his mind of preoccupations and preconceptions. The few other spectators walked slowly round, reading the panels and scrutinizing the pictures, like doctors checking medical reports before examining X-rays.

He could not change the reaction he had formed long ago to Kandinsky – that he was full of energy but was not exhilarating.

The restlessness of the paintings irked him; it was all journey and no arrival. And biography would seep back. He couldn't forget that Madame Blavatsky was mainly responsible for Kandinsky's endeavours to paint the spiritual matter behind material form, and that he had once claimed to sense a secret soul in 'a patient white trouser button looking up from a puddle in the street'! It was no good, he was not going to be able to make himself look at the paintings properly, to search out the strands of relevance and inconsequence. It was as though a handcuff prevented him reaching up to his inside pocket to take out his pen.

He swivelled on the balls of his feet to face the exit, and had walked out before he had consciously articulated to himself a wish to leave. By the time he reached the sculpture hall, and had decided to go down to the basement for a cup of coffee, he knew definitely he would not write for *Art London* again. His imagination would not take on Kandinsky, and without its involvement he grew stale and panicky.

He started to skip through the catalogue while he drank his coffee, but grew bored. Instead he took out his notebook and opened it at the page where Lydia's large handwriting – some of the letters the shape of miniature television screens – stood out against his own crabby debased-italic.

> Lydia Forsyth
> 6 Rosewharf Close
> SW6

That was so he could send her a copy of the Wilson story when it was finished.

She had already been standing up in the restaurant, about to put her mac on, when he'd asked if she'd like to see the story. He remembered looking up from his seat at the side of the bib-top of her dungarees pulled taut by their brace over the curve of her grey-sweatered breast. He had glanced guiltily under the bib at the shadowy tunnel running between her breasts and waist.

'Yes,' she'd said.

'Shall I ring you when it's finished?'

22

'We haven't got a 'phone.'

'Send it to you?'

'Would you?'

'If you give me your address.' He had held out his open notebook together with his pen.

He was fairly sure she had found the exhibition boring, though she had not said so. Only a small Italian landscape, with the classic ingredients of tree, lake, golden evening light and distant hills, had seemed to absorb her. Several of the others had been what he called 'tampered Wilsons' – ones where little Zuccarelli-type figures had been added later. She would barely look at these. He had taken her to the one drawing – a sketch of the Salute with moored gondolas in the foreground.

'The irony is,' he'd said, 'that, when he did this, he was visiting Venice as a virtually unknown painter, and Zuccarelli befriended and encouraged him. Then, when Zuccarelli himself came to England and was hugely successful, people somehow expected Wilson to emulate him. It must have made things very awkward between them.'

'Will you have that in the story?'

'I don't know. I'll have to make up my mind which relationships are important. But I'll be tempted, because I so love Venice.'

'I thought it was overcrowded and smelly?'

'Not between October and May.'

'Did he marry?'

'No. Though he might have had a son. Some years after his death, a young man claiming to be his son came to the Academy and was given a couple of guineas.'

She had looked at him in silence while she absorbed this information. Then she'd gone back to the Italian landscape and he had followed her.

'He seems to have wanted to exclude people,' she said.

'How do you mean?'

'It reminds me of a theatre set, when they dim the lights and merge day into night. Before any actors come on and you can think your own thoughts.'

He'd been surprised. To him, the golden light was palpable, you could almost smell the soft air; not at all like the electric illusions and dust-motes of the stage.

'Do you think he knew he had a son?' she asked.

'I hadn't really thought about it.'

'So he won't be in the story?'

Her question had seemed to be tinged with anger.

'It might make it a bit complicated.'

She had not replied. There was an awkwardness between them. He'd looked around at the trappings of art dealing – linen wallpaper, tracked spotlights, deep beige carpet, leather-bound visitors' book, tall young man in good suit at Sheraton writing-table – and had suggested they leave.

She'd headed for the door like a child let out of class. Looking at her hair from the back, he'd noticed it was permed and it had occurred to him that the craze for all-over curls ended some time ago. He'd wondered how old she was. They had parted on the pavement outside the gallery. She made no mention of her plans, but walked off quickly towards Jermyn Street, her shoulders squared and her hands in her pockets. She did not carry a bag. He had watched her for a few seconds, feeling a mild urge to run after her; then he'd patted his left pocket – checking that his notebook was safe – and turned in the opposite direction to go to the London Library.

When he left the Tate coffee-shop, running up the stairs from the basement two at a time, he did not, after all, go to the Eighteenth Century rooms. He needed to keep Wilson in his head, he decided, imagining the pictures as they'd been described by Constable in their prime – 'solemn, bright, warm, fresh'. The ones in the collection, he remembered, had a slightly tired air, echoing rather than contradicting Wilson's ill-fortune. Hanging in their heavy frames, with areas of foliage cracked like lizard skin in one Roman scene, their delicate light could seem lack-lustre, and they were ignored by visitors advancing towards the glowing Turners in the next room. Only his portrait of Zucca-relli, painted during the Venice visit, retained an obvious immediacy, and he did not feel like facing that at the moment. He'd sense too strongly what he imagined would be Lydia's disapproval of the Italian's rather self-satisfied expression.

He hurried towards the revolving doors. He needed to get out of the gallery.

24

2 He drinks wine and talks with Jos

The door at the foot of the basement steps opened, and Jos, a floorlength patchwork jerkin swinging out from her shoulders, held out her arms.

'Oh, *Ken*!'

He hugged her, his arms sliding under the jerkin around her shirt. She felt at least twice as solid as Ronnie. He kissed both her peony cheeks.

'Jos!'

'I know. We don't usually do this, do we? But when I saw you at the top of the steps I suddenly thought there wasn't anyone I'd rather see.'

'Gee ... lady ...' He stepped back smiling.

'Come on in. You have come to see me haven't you? Not just passing by? Pete's at the Poly.'

'If I'm not interrupting.'

'I'm stuck.'

He followed her along the corridor to the sitting-room door. He noticed that Pete had renewed the cork tiling in the places where it had begun to wear.

'Can I get you a drink?'

'Wouldn't say no.'

'Red or white? Oh – sorry – it's November.'

They laughed. It had long been established that he liked white wine in the summer and red in the winter. The changes took place, instinctively, around Lady Day and Michaelmas.

He watched her walk towards the kitchen at the end of the corridor – ample Jos, who had once been bony and glittering and who carried memories of shared pasts – his and hers and Pete's – on loosely anchored chains that he felt would never be broken.

He did not immediately sit down, but wandered round the room glancing briefly, almost unseeingly, at familiar things: the brown-and-white tiled fireplace, with fire laid but unlit; two of Jos's Tuscany paintings; the collage of images of Sky when she was an infant; Pete's small wrought-iron table set with tobacco tin, green packet of Rizlas, roller, ashtray, matches, toothpicks and dictionary.

The bookshelves that clung to every apparently available wall-space had spread to the narrow strip under the window, and the old wood, rescued no doubt from a builder's skip and now immaculately sanded and polished, was already almost obscured by the alphabetically-arranged army of Pete's fiction collection. A thought slid into Kenneth's mind and, after checking a spine, he left the new shelves and went to one of the alcoves beside the fireplace which were filled from floor to ceiling with novels. *Goodbye to Berlin . . . Down There on a Visit . . .* ah! *The World in the Evening*. He was taking the rather faded blue book from its shelf when Jos came in with a bottle and glasses.

'Do you think Pete would lend me this?'

'I'm sure he would.' She didn't attempt to see what it was.

'I'll make a note of it for him so he knows I've got it. It's a first edition – I hope it's not worth a fortune.'

'Well, he'll never sell it, even if it is. He keeps poring over catalogues and discovering things he bought for half a crown are selling for twenty quid. But, as he won't even turf out books he doesn't like to make room for new ones that he does, I can't get particularly excited.'

'The books versus picture battle still rages?'

'It always will. I've stopped fantasizing we'll ever get a place with room for both.'

'You've got the cottage for overflow.'

'The ceilings are under seven feet high. Anyway, we're vaguely

26

thinking of moving there altogether – and it's already awash with books and drawings and God knows what.'

'You're not!'

'Vaguely. Do you think we're mad?' She had poured the wine and gave him a glass before sitting at one end of the sofa whose dark velvet had bare patches, partially covered by a marigold shawl. He sat at the other end before replying. He sensed he ought to tread carefully.

'Of course not.'

'But ... ?'

'You must have discussed all the buts.'

'Yes, I think we have.' She sighed, crossing her black-trousered legs and shaking her thick black hair before resting her head on the sofa's back. 'I'm bored with talking about it really. We've done the lists – pros and cons.'

'How do they come out?'

'They don't. My pros are frequently Pete's cons, so everything ends up in a column called "unresolved".' She suddenly roared with laughter. 'Middle age is the most extraordinary thing.'

'How about Sky?'

'How indeed. She obviously won't want to move down there.'

'Could you leave her in London?'

'Technically and morally no – she's still only sixteen. But given that if we did move it would take at least a year to organize, and that she hardly spends any time here anyway, I should think we probably could.'

Kenneth decided to put off asking for up-to-date news of Sky's storm-tossed career. 'So Pete's decided to negotiate for redundancy?'

'Well, he hasn't actually *said* so, but I *think* so.' She glanced at Kenneth, and her tone became subdued. 'He's fifty next year. I think he privately regards that as a kind of watershed.'

'God, is he really?'

'Well, I'm thirty-seven, so he must be. Even *you'll* be forty next year.'

'What do you mean, even me?'

'Oh, I don't know. I just don't connect you with growing old. My image of you is stuck back in the Sixties. When you came to Steayne.'

27

'Yes.'

He'd been harking back to Steayne recently as well. For a decade it had simply been a teaching job he'd once had; but now it started to flash up images – primarily the image of the broken stone walls enclosing the space full of weeds and garden flowers run wild. That space lay between the run-down villa where the senior painting students worked, and the three prefabricated huts that housed the graphic design department. It was in that space, on his first day as part-time tutor in illustration at Steayne School of Art ('Six minutes walk from the station, trains leave Victoria at thirteen and forty-eight minutes past the hour, the journey takes thirty-three minutes,' Logan, the Principal, had informed him) that Kenneth had met up with Pete again. The September sun had been streaming down, and the dun autumn grasses in the abandoned garden harboured sheaves of mauve michaelmas daisies. Pete had come striding through a broken arch to where Kenneth was nervously wandering – taking stock of his new surroundings. His first thought had been, 'That must be Pete Brown's brother. He's so like him, but so much more vigorous – so handsome!'

'Kenneth! I hoped I'd see you today.'

'You ... knew I was here?'

'Why, yes. When you applied for the job Logan asked if I knew you. So of course I said he'd be mad not to grab you.'

Kenneth smiled. Pete's extrovert confidence was so unexpected. 'I'd no idea. Even that you were here, I mean.'

'I run the General Studies. A sort of one-man band.'

'Oh – I didn't realise ...' He remembered seeing the name Peter Brown in the school's brochure.

'Why should you? I was studio dogsbody when we last met. And it's a very common name.'

'It is good to see you.'

It was almost as though Pete had *grown*. Like Kenneth, he was then wearing his hair – which was fair – down to his shoulders, and with his faded denims, alert blue eyes, and angular tanned face, he looked quite different from the black-clad, over-thin, taciturn young man Kenneth had known at the Royal College of Art. There he had worked as studio assistant in the print-making and illustration department, tending the

28

equipment, and showing the students how to use it. He began to become popular, and some students started to turn to him for more general advice on their work, but this led to criticism from the tutors, and Pete quickly withdrew into a shell of resentment, loosely disguised as reserve. He was in fact using the job – for which his innate resourcefulness qualified him as much as his diploma from the London School of Printing – to take an extramural degree in philosophy: a fact which Kenneth was the only person at the College to discover.

'Steayne seems another world,' said Jos. 'I know we used to moan at the time – say it was parochial and provincial – but, my God, give me a run-down little Surrey art school any day of the week, compared to a couple of corridors calling themselves an art department in that vile Poly.'

'And it's beginning to get Pete down?' Unlike Jos, Pete had not been totally averse to the closing of Steayne and transfer to a job near Richmond.

'Hard to say. His hopes of building up peace studies as a general studies option for the whole Poly have collapsed. He has to confine that to the art students, and just do the industrial revolution and America for the whole lot.' She smiled and filled their glasses. 'In fact he's been infringing your copyright.'

'How's that?'

'He uses an extract from *Who's Vineyard?* for his America lectures. He used to read it out, but people asked to see the book so he's had several pages copied. As it's out of print.'

He did not respond. It was odd to hear his novel mentioned for the second time that day.

'You don't mind?' Jos said.

'Good heavens no. It was just strange to hear about. To think of students reading a little gobbet.'

'Pete says they find it hard to believe we used to be romantic about America.'

'Yes.' Had he been romantic? He'd found romance there, certainly. Followed the charter-flight trail set by older College students – Hockney, Bowling, Bates – two years earlier, and gone to America in 1963. When he came back, his plans for the future revolved around Aline Verseck of Boston. He'd done little drawing, but he had kept a diary.

'Has Ronnie been over to the States recently?' asked Jos.

'Not since last January.'

'Will she go this winter?'

He smiled. 'At the moment, no. But we'll see when her father sends her a ticket.'

'It's weird. In one way she seems enviably independent. Yet ...'

'Enviably? But you're the most independent of all, Jos.'

'Do you know why I can't work today?'

'Why?'

'Because I've had a letter from my bloody mother.'

'Whatever did it say?'

'Nothing really. It just burbles on as usual about my brother and his family.'

'Well that's not surprising, considering she lives with them.'

'I know. I'm being stupid.'

'Show it to me.'

She got up and took a letter from the mantelpiece. After handing it to him, she refilled their glasses. As soon as she'd sat down, she shivered. 'The heating's too low. I'll light the fire.'

He started to read the letter.

My dear Jos,

I thought you would like to know that Tom seems to have got on very well with his two early 'O' level exams. As usual he does not say very much, but he has seemed very relaxed when he arrives home after each one. Naturally Theo and Elizabeth are very glad, although they had no real fears for him.

They are planning a little celebration for him on Saturday ...

The once familiar, and now almost exotic, scent of smoky paper suddenly reminded Kenneth of childhood and made him look up. He watched the kindling catch and flame, and waiting for the coal to fall as the loosely-screwed paper burned away and the supporting sticks collapsed into the vacuum. He remembered how sometimes, when the wind had been in the wrong direction, that point had marked the beginning of the demise of Mrs

Pennington's fires, and how miserable he had felt in the chill, smoky sitting-room, waiting for her to come through from the kitchen to put it right in time for his father's arrival home. Jos's fire, with smokeless fuel that looked like small cindered cakes and seemed dull compared to shiny coal straight from the earth's belly, burned warmly. She was looking at it too.

'I think it's the one thing about home that still completely works for Sky,' she said. 'The fire. Thank goodness I didn't succeed in stopping Pete from uncovering it.'

'Did you want to?'

'I was impatient at the idea of shovelling coal and raking out the cinders in those days.'

'But – '

'Quite! Pete does most of it anyway.'

He returned to her mother's letter.

Kiss Me Kate has opened in Birmingham and they have got tickets for the matinée and will come back here for a buffet supper to which several of his friends have been invited. Elizabeth will leave it all prepared, and I will set it out just before they return – half an hour before the guests are due. Theo of course saw the original London production of *Kiss Me Kate* while he was up at Cambridge – we worked out it must have been about thirty years ago. We agreed it was much more sensible that the Arts Council should help good productions of popular shows like this along the way, than waste money on stupid bricks and unpleasantnesses. Though I suppose you will feel you have to disagree. They are taking Jonathan with them of course. But I'm afraid he is being most ungracious both to his parents and to his elder brother at the moment.

I wonder if Sky is still trying out restoration work and still intent on finding some kind of a job abroad? I only hope she knows what she is doing. But I'm sure that you and Peter have every confidence in her.

My love to you both,

Mother

31

'Does she always call Pete Peter?'

'Always.'

He realized that was probably why Jos had always called him Ken. For some reason he did not mind, though he hated anyone else to do so.

'Poor Jonathan,' he said.

'Yes, it is unfair that Tom's so perfect. He also looks terribly like Theo did at that age, so of course mother thinks he's even more perfect. I can't imagine how Elizabeth copes.'

'The remarks about Sky have riled you?'

'Oh, I'm used to those.' She emptied her glass. 'Well, I suppose I am. No – it was the buffet supper. Knowing days in advance the exact moment when it will be set out.' She gave a big sigh. 'And those damned bricks. I think they're just as boring as everyone else does.'

'But you won't be able to admit it.'

She laughed. 'No.'

'And does Sky still want to do restoration work?'

'Well, I think so. A furniture-maker and restorer Pete knows has taken her on for a few weeks. But she's not sure what area she wants to specialize in. And she'll have to decide before she goes to restore the cathedrals of Europe single-handed.' Her tone verged on the sarcastic.

'It's not a bad thing for a sixteen-year-old to want to do, Jos.'

'I know. If only I felt sure she did. And that she won't mess people about.'

'How did your mother react to her exam results?'

'Well, since she refused to admit that she's ever heard of the C.S.E., just like one of those judges who used to ask what Elvis Presley was.' Her face relaxed. 'It was rather funny really. I don't know if you remember, but Sky got grade ones in woodwork and metalwork, and grade twos in photography and social studies, and she deliberately bunked off for the English exam. So mother's publicly convinced she's illiterate – particularly as she never writes thank you letters – and privately convinced she must be a lesbian.'

'There was a time when you said you rather wished that she were.'

'When she was going round with that ex-borstal Irish boy.

32

It's a bit better now. She's found a monosyllabic economics student who likes cathedrals too. It's just that she will stay away for days at a stretch. It would be all right if she were a bit older.'

'She soon will be.'

'True.' She lifted up the bottle and found it was empty. 'Have you had lunch?'

He shook his head.

'Then I'll make us some.'

'No ... honestly ...'

'Please. I'd like to.'

'I feel quite tight.'

'I'll give you a refill and complete the job.'

He didn't bother to demur. He'd drunk too much with Jos over the years to pretend to be moderate now. He followed her from the room towards the kitchen, but outside her studio door she stopped and turned.

'Would you like to see what I've been doing? While I open a bottle and start the food?'

He felt, briefly, a frisson of flattery. Jos was a very private worker. He could count the occasions he'd had the run of her studio, alone, on the fingers of one hand.

'Please.'

She opened the door for him. 'The one on the easel is what I'm stuck with.'

He stepped in, and she closed the door behind him. His first thought was: 'How can they move to the country? Jos has painted here for over fifteen years.' The matting around the old easel was spattered with paint the way the ground under a long-established roosting tree is splashed with bird droppings. The old familiar studio smell, and the familiar lineaments of stone jars with brushes, chipped saucers and mugs to be used as mixing vessels, tins and tubes of paint, beloved objects (dried flowers, bottles, fossils) furred with dust, and brightly-stained rags from a newly torn sheet, enveloped his senses. After the wine, he could have lain down in this consoling place and been wholly happy. This was the atmosphere of painting which, after his early recoil from the strained ambitions of some of his fellow students, he had grown to love – to admire, too, for he knew he would not have had the stealthy patience to deepen and perfect traditional

33

themes as Jos had done over the years.

But the painting on the easel was not of a piece with the two on the walls and the many in his memory. The image of a car shocked him. Jos paint a car? Jos of landscape and flower and human face paint a – he walked up to it and peered – a Standard Vanguard, circa 1955! There was a shadowy figure in the front passenger seat, and a man standing behind the car by the driver's door. In the foreground the back of a girl's head was barely sketched in – she seemed to be staring at the car. A boy, also barely sketched, was striding towards it. Trees, a cedar and a monkey-puzzle among them, filled the near horizon. It was an awkward, eery composition.

He stepped back and looked around, trying to discover if there were any drawings connected to the painting. He could not see any, but his curiosity was aroused by three handwritten notes pinned to the wall and he went to read them.

The low sun making the leaves coated with dew glitter, and every blade of grass carries minute shiny drops. There is a slight, hanging mist everywhere, which the sun turns to pale gold broth.

When there is a low grey sky, but it's quite bright, a little damp, the birdsong seems closer, louder; as though we are all sharing an invisible grey-silk tent, the size of the county.

There are horrible moments, in littered streets, when people have been sick and you get jostled and heavy metal blares from an arcade. BUT, there are also bleak moments in a cold field, when the freezing wind stiffens your fingers and you take food for the animals and break the frozen water, when the camaraderie of jostle, and litter, and even closing-time vomit, seems near to heaven.

When, some minutes later, he went to the kitchen, the first thing he said was, 'You haven't always written notes like those on the wall, have you?'

Jos was stirring a small saucepan of sliced mushrooms, garlic and cream. Green fettucine writhed in boiling water. Fresh gratings from a lump of parmesan were ready on a board. He remembered Lydia and the stale, sawdusty parmesan.

He thought she blushed.

'No. Just recently. I suddenly find I enjoy keeping a notebook as well as making colour notes on sketches.' She pointed to the dresser. 'There's your wine.'

'I think they're lovely notes.' He wanted to ask her about them, but knew he must mention the painting first. 'Tell me about the car painting. I never,' he made his tone gentle, 'thought I'd find you painting a Standard Vanguard.'

'Well, at least you recognized it.' She dipped a thumb and forefinger into the boiling water, nipped off a bit of fettucine, and put it in her mouth.

'Jos – you'll scald yourself.'

'Not if you do it quickly enough.'

He thought of Ronnie's battery of saucepan-holders and oven-gloves. He watched Jos drain the pasta, shake it vigorously with the cheese, then serve it smothered in mushrooms.

They drew up their chairs to the table. He bent over and sniffed his plate. 'San' Stefano.' He named the restaurant in Venice which she and Pete had once recommended to him.

'Oh, don't!'

'It's a compliment.'

'I know. But don't. It just makes me want to be there.'

'Those Sunday lunches, when huge familes seem to eat continuously for three solid hours.'

'And look so *happy*. That's what the car painting's about. Sundays.'

'Sunday outings?'

'After lunch. In the summer. We would go for what my father called "a little run". I always felt carsick. My mother always chided me for taking too long to get ready. The places we visited never came up to my parents' expectations. They would criticize them all the way home.'

'No wonder that letter put you off. Sort of the same territory thirty years on.'

'It's odd. Last year I was privately getting very worried that I'd dried up. I had a sudden panic that I couldn't go on painting the contours of the land and people's faces for ever. Then the

35

notes started. And then suddenly I was thinking in terms of compositions. All to do with my childhood. I've never done that before.'

'Writing sometimes releases things.'

'I suppose. Are you still writing for *Art London*?'

'I don't think so. I think I'm doing something else. I'll tell you later ... I was interested in your town and country note. The Armageddon one.'

'Oh ... yes. Well, of course that's to do with this whole cottage thing.'

'Perhaps thinking about the move sparked off the paintings. After all, you spent your childhood in the country. Doubts, perhaps, about returning, linked to doubts about family.'

'Oh God, Ken, it's all so *complicating*. Other people just seem to move house. With us – or, to be fair, with me really – it's like contemplating emigration.'

'Doesn't Pete have doubts about giving up his job? I don't really mean money, but just missing the teaching – the company – the general carry-on.'

'I don't think so. He thinks he's sufficient unto himself. But *I* think he'd miss it.'

'He always seems to get a kick out of his special courses and lectures.'

'I know.'

They both took forkfuls of pasta, and Kenneth decided he'd better ask the crucial question. When he'd swallowed, he said: 'Presumably he intends to write his book?'

She nodded, her mouth still full.

'Has he ever shown you any of it?' he asked.

'There's nothing to show. It's all in loose-leaf notebooks, box-files and card-indexes.'

'I thought those articles in *New Society* were fragments from it.'

'No. He wrote those specially. He's never actually started.'

'Oh.'

'Quite.' She reached for the bottle and filled her glass. His was untouched.

'I didn't mean – '

'I know you didn't. But it poses a problem.'

'Whether he'll be able to get it all together?'

'Well, there's that. But I've got quite a lot of faith in his powers of synthesis. No – it's the sentences. The actual sentences.'

'What do you mean?'

She hesitated, then took a deep breath. 'Well, I don't actually think he writes very well. The sentences are so unwieldy. And that wouldn't matter if it was to be some academic tome. But he wants it to be a sort of popular classic.' She pulled a face. 'Of course he doesn't actually use that phrase: but I know that's what he wants. You know – like *Small is Beautiful* or something. Still, as my father used to say, nothing ventured nothing etcetera. And I'm probably just erecting problems out of selfishness.'

He put on a joky tone. 'The wife should be positive about the move, and supportive of the book. Not jealously guard her solitary days so that she can prowl through her childhood and erect private worlds in paint?'

'Something like that.' She paused. 'It really is a prowl too. I sort of feel I want to start charting my life like Turner charted the topography of England.'

He nodded. It sounded so unlike Jos.

'Sorry. That's incredibly pompous.'

'No. I understand . . . Is the car painting the first?'

'Not really. There are others. But none is properly finished. Or remotely right yet.'

He wondered whether he should ask to see them.

'If and when I get them more complete, perhaps you'll come and have a look?'

'Of course.'

He hoped very much it was going to prove a rewarding path for her. If she could bring it off, could fuse her psychological memory with her sensitive technical skills, it might be wonderful. And just the kind of thing that Ronnie would be interested to hear about.

'I must tell Ronnie about this development. It's just the sort of – ' He broke off abruptly, embarrassed. 'God, how can I be so stupid? I'd simply forgotten.'

'Don't be daft. There's no need for *you* to feel bad. Anyway, it was ages ago. I'd like Ronnie to see the paintings, if I can finish them. I want both of you to.'

37

'Thanks.' Their eyes met, and they smiled.

'Cheese? Apple?'

'No. I couldn't.'

'I'll make some coffee.'

Not very long after Kenneth had introduced Ronnie to Jos and Pete, she'd rung Jos up, without first consulting him, and asked if Jos would consider exhibiting with her. Up till then, Jos had concealed her views on the concept of an all-female gallery for Kenneth's sake, but the abrupt intrusion of the 'phone call, as Kenneth was to discover, had caused a bald disclosure of her disapproval. The breach was smoothed over but, on the few occasions when the two couples met up together, Ronnie and Jos were uncharacteristically wary of each other.

'Jos is one of those English women who enjoys being in a man's world,' Ronnie had remarked to Kenneth, somehow indicating that was the end of the subject. So he had not said that, unlike most Americans, Jos hated the telephone and would never have dreamed of using it to make a business proposition.

He had also quelled a comment along the lines that anyone who showed regularly at Humphrey Lamborn's gallery in Cork Street, as Jos did, would be mad to switch to a then virtually unknown gallery in Floral Street, be it feminist or not. He knew Ronnie would have said that was not the point, and that there must be trust to start with, and that anyway soon she would have commercial success parallel to Lamborn's and take only half the commission. Which was, more or less, proving to be true. He had never tried to explain to Ronnie about his deep, comfortable affection for Jos, just as he had never described to Jos the emancipating sense of buoyancy and opportunity that Ronnie had embodied for him when he met her.

He drained his glass with sudden urgency and when they went back to the sitting room to drink their coffee, Jos brought in the wine as well.

He told her about Richard Wilson and *Art London*, and his inability to look at the Kandinskys.

'I have to confess,' she said, 'I feel rather the same about Wilson. Not long ago I tried looking at that pair that hang either side of an archway in the National Gallery but they seemed awfully brown and dead.'

38

He nodded. 'I'm becoming dangerously hooked on seeing things through biographical eyes. It was sort of latent – but then something brought it to a head.'

'What?'

'A girl called Lydia in the postcard shop at the B.M.'

'Ken, *really*!'

'I don't think it was quite like that.'

'That's what they all say.'

He wondered whether Pete's intense but brief involvements with students were still a thorny factor.

But she was smiling. 'I don't recollect the B.M. figuring in the league table. The boys at Steayne used to have arguments about whether the Tate or the National was best for picking up crumpet. Except it was chicks then, wasn't it?'

'The ones in the Tate were more interesting and therefore more bother.'

'You didn't . . . ?'

'Only for coffee and a chat about kinetic art.'

'You're sending me up.'

'Myself, more like.'

'Well, here's your coffee. Now, chat to me about Wilson.'

He leaned back with a feeling of satisfaction. It had been a good idea to come. Now the wine was making it easy for him to slip back into the happier aspects of the Wilson story, and for his mind to conjure up romantic visions of eighteenth century evenings on a summer hillside by a lake near Rome.

'That phrase in one of your notes, about the sun turning the mist to a pale gold broth, reminded me of something a fanatical Wilson enthusiast called Colonel Grant wrote.'

'Colonel Grant!'

'Maurice Harold Grant. Currently my favourite writer about art. The sort that would send Richard Mafeking screaming for refuge into a gallery of Agnes Martins. Shall I read it to you?'

'If you like.'

He took out his notebook. 'He's talking about Cuyp's effect on Wilson. He writes, "His air is the very golden breath which enwraps Cuyp's lush meadows and hazy hillocks. Beside Cuyp and himself, Claude gives Nature paralysed; Monet Nature drowning; Cézanne and Van Gogh, Nature drunk".' He looked

39

up, happy, and saw that Jos was frowning. 'No?'

'No! I hate writers sometimes. They're so pat and clever. I don't want to be dismissed in one descriptive word – paralysed, drowning, drunk. I suppose your Colonel Grant would say *I* was "frozen".'

Immediately he saw the harm of that one, not totally inapposite, word. He jerked his mind back to the present, away from the perpetual golden evenings. 'Sorry. I get carried away by the Colonel's grandiloquence. I don't take him too seriously.'

'You know what you said earlier? About the wife being positive and supportive?'

'That wasn't meant very seriously either.'

'I realized that. Though you'll have to get used to the fact that your words may affect people seriously – however they're intended.' She emptied the bottle into their glasses. 'Anyway, it brought up something that I've been thinking for some time.' She clutched her glass into her body, and bent one leg under her on the sofa.

'What, Jos?'

'That Pete would be better off without me. If we separated.'

Kenneth felt pure fear. 'No!'

She looked startled. 'Why are you shouting?'

'I ... sorry. I didn't mean to. You ... frightened me.'

'*Frightened* you?'

'Yes.'

'Well, I certainly didn't mean to. It's just I have this idea that Pete might make more of a success of a work change if we changed too. My routines, my painting, are an insidious ball and chain.'

He remembered the accumulation of paint droppings by her easel.

'But he's ... he's – I was going to say, "so proud of your work", but that's such a cliché, and not right anyway. But involved in it – *glad* of it ... about it.' He paused. 'Isn't he?'

'As much as ever he was. Yes.' She lifted her glass, found it empty. 'Oh – I don't know. I just feel ... he may need a *chance*.' She stared at him.

The ghost of the words 'last chance' seemed to hover between them.

She got up. 'It's no good, I'm going to have to open another bottle.'

'Let me go round the corner and buy a couple.'

'There's absolutely no need.'

He knew that would be true. The wine racks in Pete's study were never ill-supplied.

He heard her first go along the corridor to the bathroom. He tried to concentrate, to think constructively about what she had just said to him. But he found he couldn't. A plaintive, almost desperate, scream inside his head cried, 'No, please no, no, Jos!'

He hadn't met her that first day he went to Steayne but, just before he left the wild garden to return to his teaching duties, Pete had said quietly: 'There's something I want to tell you. I got married two years ago. To Jos Shepheard. She was a student here. She's a painter.' Kenneth had been surprised. His memory was still full of Pete the taciturn loner, and secretive philosopher; marriage had seemed so unlikely. Then, on his next teaching day, Pete had sought him out and invited him home for lunch, and he'd met the twenty-two-year-old Jos and the infant Sky. In their sparsely-furnished, sun-filled flat over a hardware shop, with a philodendron that grew like a vine right across one wall, and bread, beer, a runny brie and ripe peaches set out on the wrought iron table that now stood beside Pete's chair, Kenneth's first sight of the marriage had been, for him, paradisal.

Black curiosity insisted that the image be pushed back to where it belonged – the over-and-done-with past – and prompted a string of stark questions. Had Pete's flings with students killed the relationship? Was Jos bored with him? Was she in love with someone else? Did Pete want the marriage to end? Had he even, at some time, suggested that it might? And what effect would a split have on unpredictable Sky?

'Ken?' Jos's head was round the door.

He started guiltily. 'Yes?'

'Come and look at the wine. That was the last of the Côtes du Rhône, and I'm not sure which of the others you prefer.'

He followed her to Pete's study next door. While she held out, one by one, three alternative bottles, he took furtive glimpses around the narrow room. Books – philosophy, architecture, planning, sociology, anthropology – were shelved ceiling high, and Pete's desk was surmounted by lines of box-files and ring-folders. He knew that these were filled with notes and comments and cuttings and quotations, the raw material for his book.

They decided on a wine, and then Kenneth said, 'Perhaps now isn't the right time for major decisions. Perhaps you should wait until he's got into the writing of the book.'

'But change might be even more dangerous once he's begun.'

As she closed the study door, he said, 'I can't imagine you both moving. Either to the country or apart. Your work places seem so – so entrenched.'

'I know. But that's supposed to be dangerous. Rigidity.'

'Oh, Jos.' Briefly he put a hand on her shoulder.

'It's all right, we won't talk about it any more. It won't get anywhere. Just like it doesn't when Pete and I talk about the cottage.'

'But ... if you want to. If talking will help?'

'There was a line in a play on the box not long ago. "A trouble shared is a trouble drawn out till bed-time".' She laughed, briefly. 'And it's not even a trouble – just a notion.'

He remembered his list of stark questions. He didn't want talk that might lead to answers.

'Come on,' she said. 'I want to hear more about Lydia.'

They returned to the fireside, the bottle was opened, and Kenneth had one last pang of guilt that he was letting Jos down before he followed her lead into less fraught waters.

Once she'd heard about the British Museum encounter, and the Italian lunch and the exhibition, she said, 'And will you see her again?'

'Oh, I don't know. I shouldn't think so. But I got her address so I could send her the story.'

'Where does she live?'

'Fulham.' An idea occurred to him, winging in on the wine. 'Have you got an A to Z?'

'Yes. Here.' She fetched it from some shelves by the telephone.

He studied the index. 'Is this up to date?'

'Yes. I bought it in the summer. Our old one dropped to pieces.'

'Maybe I'm too pissed. You see if you can find Rosewharf Close.'

42

She took the book from him. 'Rose Walk, Roseway, Rose-wood ... no, there aren't any Rosewharfs.'

'Well, I'll be ... bloody girl!'

'You're really cross!'

'Yes, I *am* really cross. There was no need for her to throw me off with a cheat.'

'She obviously didn't like Richard Wilson.'

'That's the worst part. I've been jilted because I'm a bore. Not because she suspected my motives.'

She grinned, and got up. 'Remember this?' She went and pulled out a record, keeping the sleeve hidden from Kenneth, and laid it on the player, placing the stylus gently on a particular track. The adolescent, lachrymose voices of the Everly Brothers changed the mood in the room.

Bye bye love, bye bye happiness ...

'Why are you playing that?' He found he was singing along despite himself.

'Because it cheered you up once before.' She turned the sound up a little, and filled his glass.

As the song anaesthetized the niggling veins of guilt, uncertainty and irritation in his mind, he remembered how shocked he'd been as a sixth-former to read, one Orpington Sunday, that a painter called Peter Blake was exhibiting paintings of the Everly Brothers and other pop idols at somewhere called the Institute of Contemporary Arts.

'You still don't remember?' she asked, as the song ended.

'No.'

'It was a party we gave. When we first came here. You were very down because some girl had refused to come with you, and you insisted I kept playing this. You were all mournful at first, but by about the sixth time you started dancing, and you were leaping about all over the place by the end.'

'Pissed Flete as usual.'

'Nice Flete as usual. You never mope for long.'

She came and stood behind him and bent, briefly, to kiss his hair. 'Sorry I got heavy.'

He reached up and took her hand. 'Don't go away, Jos. Stay in London and paint.'

'Why do you want me to?'

43

'Because ... Oh – I don't know. I've got no right.' He laid his cheek against her hand before letting it go.

Then he stared into the fire. The cindered cakes were a hot, glowing conglomerate now. Would Wilson have had a fire? Surely? But, since he could not afford to replenish his brushes, how would he have paid for his fuel? Even now, people were wandering through the heated, air-conditioned National Gallery, past Gainsborough's feathered ladies and feathery foliage, and through the archway flanked by Wilson's two views of the River Dee – one in a threatening storm light, the other an afterglow of pale apricot – unaware that in the end their begetter had lacked brushes. Perhaps most who glanced at the paintings shared Jos's reaction – 'brown and dead'. Yet, really, compared to Gainsborough's soft branches, Wilson's trees were rooted with a firmness that made each leaf quiver with permanent life, as though their sap had been laced with liquid gold. Once he'd held sable brushes loaded with Naples yellow, Roman ochre, ultramarine, burnt terra di Sienna, and had painted that moment of hesitation – of heaven – before the light begins to seep from the evening sky. But few had paid for those images, and the brushes had worn out – or been lost in various debilitating moves – until finally there was only the skeleton, the shadow, of a studio in the two rooms in Tottenham Street.

'I just do, Jos.'

3   He receives a proposition from Ronnie

The alarm was set for seven, but the repetitive trills of the telephone hauled his mind out of a deep sleep fifteen minutes sooner. He reached to pick up the receiver, and wondered why he had all his clothes on.

'Hullo.' As he spoke, he remembered.

'Kenneth. How are you?' Ronnie's voice was at its softest.

'Asleep.'

'*Asleep*! Are you ill?'

'No. Too much wine, followed by very cold fresh air on the walk home.'

'Where were you drinking?'

'I dropped by at Jos's after the Tate. She offered me lunch, and we talked our way through three bottles of wine.'

'Oh ...' She sounded restrained.

'How was your day?' He remembered now: she had promised to ring him to arrange their lunch with Serena Stein.

'Very good. I'll tell you. I'm going to leave the gallery now.'

'You're not going out?' He remembered, too, that she had been vague about her plans for the evening.

'No.' She said the word lightly – nonchalantly.

'Good. Fine. Shall we have a meal down the road?'

'That would be nice. But I must finish clearing up the flat first. If I come down about nine?'

'I'll be here.'

He got up briskly then, feeling ashamed of his sleep; Ronnie's completion of a full working day made his own performance seem slack. But there'd been no way he could have kept his eyes open when he first came home.

After selecting a clean shirt and underclothes, he went to have a bath. As he lay in the water, he stared at the islands of wet skin that showed above the soapy scum. Women had said they liked his skin, beige in winter and cinnamon in summer, because it was smooth but not soft. Once it had caused him embarrassment, when the dry, goose-pimply skin of a girl had felt so alien to him he had baulked at an attempt to seduce her. She was the third girl whose thighs he had touched, and their horripilation made him recoil as abruptly as if she'd had tin legs.

When he was dressed, he would write to Mafeking. Get that out of the way. And he needed some soda water in case Ronnie wanted a drink. He could go to the off-licence and post the letter at the same time. He must make a space in the evening to tell Ronnie about Richard Wilson – and mention Lydia. And he must find out about tomorrow and lunch. It was time he worked out his countdown timetable for delivery of the William Trevor illustration; he had been procrastinating. Presumably Ronnie would explain about Faraday.

He thought he heard her come in just as he was sealing the envelope to Mafeking. Certainly someone had slammed the front door. He imagined her going upstairs, perhaps getting into her kimono, and then tackling the washing-up. This made him faintly guilty, despite his morning offer of help. He knew she would dislike doing it, though would not say so, and there seemed no way, within their framework, he could share it with her. And, to be honest, the last thing he wanted to do at that moment was to dry up her, or anybody else's, dirty dishes. He took a stamp from a drawer, pulled on his jacket, and went out into the street. When he came back, it was exactly eight o'clock. An hour to look at, and think about, the illustration . . .

He saw immediately why he had been avoiding it. It was a lazy composition, unconsciously echoing something he'd done before, and it did not suit the subject. He'd been concentrating far too much on the decorative aspects of the fish slab and not nearly enough on the woman's stance. He put the existing sketches aside – once he would have screwed them up, but he had grown more cautious – and pulled a clean pad towards him. As he tried out various ideas, he reflected on his attitude to visual repetition. Wilson, as was common then, had made many copies of paintings. Anything that was successful in his brief heyday was repeated several times. Was it only the existence of photography and increasingly efficient printing that made him feel he must avoid repetition?

He concentrated on a new sketch, and it began to go well. He forgot about Wilson. He forgot about the time, too, until, with a sudden lurch of unease, he looked at his watch and saw it was nine o'clock.

He had the door on the latch a minute before Ronnie arrived, and greeted her with a particularly close kiss. And in the seconds when he saw her, spoke to her, touched her, he realized how glad he was to be spending the rest of the evening with her, and not alone.

He went through the familiar ritual of getting a mixture of German wine, ice, soda and a slice of orange for her, and a glass of red for himself. They sat either end of the settee, he with his arms outstretched along the swollen hummocks of maroon leather, she poised upright, legs crossed, her skirt of Liberty wool dipping to the floor. They smiled.

'It's all arranged for tomorrow. Serena's coming to the gallery at one, and I'll book a table at Joe Allen's. She's looking forward to meeting you.'

'And I her. You've definitely decided?'

'Yes. And she's agreed. We had a good morning together.'

'When will you have the show?'

'May.'

'Will she come over?'

'Yes. And she's willing to do publicity. I think we'll be able to set up quite a lot of things.'

'She's striking looking. From that brief glimpse I had.'

'You haven't asked me about Alastair Faraday.'

'*You* haven't told me.' He said it exaggeratedly, teasing.

She replied quietly, and quite hurriedly. 'Serena met him three days ago at a party in New York. When he heard she was about to fly to England, he decided to come too.'

'Are they having an affair?'

Ronnie looked straight at him, and he could see her magnified eyes behind the glasses. She had very honest eyes.

'If they are, they haven't told me.'

'But he decided to come along on her dinner date?'

'She 'phoned to ask first. I couldn't really refuse. Anyway,' she smiled, 'I wanted to see him.'

'What's he like?'

'Mm ... edgy. It may be the situation. There are hitches in the Isherwood film deal. He's been hanging around in L.A. Then he decided to have a couple of days in New York. And meeting Serena suddenly made a few days in London seem like a good idea.'

'Okay. So he travels a lot – edgily.'

'But what's he like ... Let's see. Charming. Very into Thirties writing. Drinks a lot of vodka. And that incredibly beautiful voice is for real.'

'Is he going back with Serena?'

'That's the plan.'

There was a short silence.

'How's Jos?'

He felt the change of subject was rather abrupt. 'Oh ... muddled.'

'Really? That is unusual.'

'Yes.' He had a fleeting hesitancy about passing on all the ingredients of Jos's situation, but it went as quickly as it came. When he had explained about Pete's possible redundancy, the cottage, Jos's new paintings, and Sky, he added quietly: 'And then suddenly, out of the blue, she said she'd been thinking it might be better if they separated. That Pete might be better off without her.'

Ronnie looked really interested for the first time. 'Did you discover why?'

'Not really. Well ... something about giving Pete a chance. Freedom, I suppose. She seemed to think her routines were a drag on him.'

'There must be more to it than that.'

'I suppose.'

'Didn't she want to talk about it?'

'I'm not sure.' He weighed up whether to add, 'The main thing was I didn't want to talk about it. It momentarily frightened me.' 'I don't think I really wanted to talk about it.'

'You never want to talk about relationships.'

'No? I'm not sure that's true. But come on – we'd better go and eat. Rafi will be getting to the last orders stage.'

'You see.'

'No, I don't see. If I remember correctly, when it comes to talking about *our* relationship, you back off.'

'That's because you don't approach any discussion in the right way. You want to set out the conclusions before you begin the talking.'

He laughed, and went to fetch her jacket.

They ate regularly at the Golden Lotus. Rafi greeted them serenely, and pulled out their usual table. 'Do you wish to order?'

Kenneth looked at Ronnie, who shook her head. 'We leave it to you,' he said.

Rafi smiled. 'It will be my pleasure.'

He always remembered the things they had particularly enjoyed, and they liked the element of surprise in watching the little oval silver dishes set out before them and discovering the selection he had made. There was usually something untried – this time it was a sort of aubergine purée.

'Baingan bharta,' said Rafi. 'Very popular at my home.'

Kenneth tore off a piece of chapati and dipped it into the paste. 'Delicious,' he said.

'I still use my mother's recipe.'

Ronnie took a little. 'Please tell her, when you write, that we both enjoyed it.'

Rafi nodded, and before leaving watched them for a few seconds with an air of satisfaction.

'Strange world,' said Kenneth.

'Why?'

'My father thought India would collapse completely without British rule. And there was Rafi being fed these exquisite concoctions by his mother, while we sat like two dummies at table and allowed Mrs Pennington to place dishes of utterly disgusting food in front of us night after night.'

49

'Did your father think it was disgusting?'

'I suppose not. I imagine he just assumed that cabbage which had been boiled hard for an hour, and stew which was grey and sticky and gristly, and trifle with custard so thick it could be cut into squares, was normal.'

'Stop!' Ronnie lowered the fragment of pappadam she was about to put in her mouth. Then, with what seemed to be a slight challenge, she said: 'But he must have thought pretty well of her to leave her the house.'

'Mm.' He was taken aback by the remark. That was the second lie he had told her, beside the one about the carpet. His father had not left the house to Mrs Pennington. 'This aubergine stuff's good on the chicken.'

She did not pursue the matter. 'How was the Kandinsky?'

'Unappealing.'

'Oh.'

'I have in fact resigned.'

Ronnie added a generous spoonful of lady's fingers to her plate. He knew she would eat only about a quarter of them, and, though long reconciled to her tiny appetite, he was still puzzled by her habit of taking normal portions and then chasing them slowly around her plate, like a cat with an expiring prey.

He watched her trying to think of something truthful but tactful to say.

'I am sorry, Kenneth. I thought your pieces were valuable. What did Mafeking say?'

'I wrote to him.'

'I see.'

'I never set out to be an art critic. It all happened by chance.' He was irked by his need to defend himself.

'Most things do. But writing is very much part of your work.'

'Well – I've started something else.'

'What is it?'

'A story about Richard Wilson.'

'Story . . . ? A novel?'

'No. A story. Short story.'

'What is the significance of the name Richard Wilson?'

'Eighteenth-century painter.'

'Quite. But you're not making a fiction around a real person?'

50

'Yes.'

'How strange.'

'Why?'

'It seems . . . so unlike you.'

That was the cue to tell her about Lydia and, involuntarily, he baulked. He talked about Wilson instead.

She listened. When he had finished, she said, 'Will you send it to William?'

'I hadn't thought about it. I don't know how it will turn out.' William was the literary agent who had approached him when *Who's Vineyard?* was published, and who had subsequently handled his literary illustration work.

'What gave you the idea of Wilson in particular?'

'I talked to someone who knew nothing about him. Had never heard of him.' He waited for her to ask who the person was, so he could tell her.

'Yes, I see. He's generally forgotten now, yet – I am right, aren't I – the painters who came after him, Constable, Turner, worshipped him.'

'Yes.'

'It's very fascinating. Perhaps . . .' She looked away.

He waited for a time. 'Perhaps?'

'My mind's leaping around. Perhaps you could do a series. For some reason I thought of Fuseli. His episode with Mary Wollstonecraft.'

He did not much like Fuseli. And didn't think he liked Mary Wollstonecraft. 'I hadn't thought that far.' But he did like the idea of a series. Girtin, his mind thought greedily, and possibly Sandby, and – would he dare? – a glimpse of Turner. And *Bonington*. He loved Bonington. Bonington in Venice. 'It has possibilities.'

'I've got a biography of Wollstonecraft.'

'Yes.' He reached out and put his hand over hers. 'Thank you.'

'Why?'

'For thinking of the series.'

'Okay.'

'And I'm forgiven for not being an art critic?'

'I just worry when you give things up.'

51

They ate without speaking for a while, catching up with the food before it became too cold. He leant over and forked up two of the lady's fingers she would never eat. She seemed about to protest, but then she suddenly said, '*You* gave the house to Mrs Pennington, didn't you?'

They were too cold, the lady's fingers, slightly slimy in his mouth. He quickly scooped up some bharta and rice. 'Why do you say that?'

'That time, ages ago, when you were telling me about the death of your father, and coming back from America, and the whole thing with Aline, I asked what happened to the house.' She speared a small piece of saffron chicken breast and put it in her mouth.

He did not say anything.

'And you said Mrs Pennington lived in it. And I asked if your father had left it to her, and you said "Sort of" and changed the subject.'

Each time, in the intervening eighteen years, when he'd especially wished he had more money, he'd remembered that afternoon. The waxy begonias in the front garden bruised by October wind, the telephone receiver still in his hand, and the knowledge that Mrs Pennington was lurking in the kichen after explaining to him about her daughter. He had put the receiver back, walked quickly through to her, and just said quietly, 'You can have this house. I will be in touch.' When he saw the mistrustful incredulity on her face, he had added before leaving, 'That is true. You may count on it.'

'What did you mean, "sort of"?'

He sighed. 'Nothing, I suppose. A sort of obligation. Left unresolved by my father.'

'He hadn't left it to her?'

'No. I was his sole heir.' He gave a brief laugh. 'Heir. What a grand word.'

'Will you explain to me?'

'Yes. But . . .'

'But, "not now"?'

He nodded.

'So it does give you concern?'

'In a way, I suppose. A mild sort of way.'

52

'That's why I worry about you giving things up.'

'Darling, only you could equate Richard Mafeking with an Orpington villa.'

'Don't be so literal.'

'Occupational disease.' He caught Rafi's eye, and the bill was brought. He knew he had to say more. 'It's just that it would take rather a long time to explain it properly. I don't feel like the past tonight.'

'All right. Anyway, I have a future proposition for you.'

'Oh?'

'I'll tell you back at the flat.'

'Mine or yours?'

'Yours?'

'We'll have a brandy.'

'Mm.'

His room felt cold. Ronnie did not take off her jacket, and he turned up the heating before putting the kettle on for coffee and pouring the brandy.

'Time it was finished,' he said. 'It's nearly Christmas again.' An advertising agency gave him a bottle each year.

'Don't you think you might put a curtain or a blind at that window just for the winter? You lose so much heat.'

From the sink, he looked across to the black glass catching the reflection of the room. There the colours looked deeper, floating out into the unseen shrubbery. 'I'd feel hemmed in. I like living partly in a mirror.'

'I'll never be convinced that someone doesn't lurk there, watching us.'

'Only sparrows and pigeons. You'd need wings to get over the wall. Even cats don't.'

'Do you want to hear my proposition?'

'Yes.' He poured boiling water into the coffee jug and stirred. Then he carried the brandies to where she huddled in an armchair. 'Here.' He went and sat on the sofa.

'How would you feel about coming to the West Coast for two months?'

An image of surfers came into his mind, followed by a

53

Hockney swimming pool.

He stalled. 'Two months?'

'You once said you didn't want to go to the East Coast again, but that you'd like to see San Francisco.'

'Yes, I would.' He smiled at her. 'And Leningrad. And Nairobi. And Peking.'

'You're on the defensive.'

'Come on, Ronnie. Explain.'

'It's an idea I have for widening the scope of the gallery. London's still fairly in touch with what goes on in New York, but not in the West. I'd like to travel around, make contacts, look at a lot of work. And show slides of my main British clients. And talk about mutual print deals. Serena's very excited by the possibility of doing some print-making over here. It could work the other way round.'

'Finances for the trip?'

'If we went fairly soon, in the slack period, Frances could cope with the gallery. And father's already written to me about Christmas. It's a proposition I think would interest him.'

'Surely us having two months in California doesn't equal you being home for Christmas?'

'Well, we could stop by for two or three days. If you didn't want to come, you could stay with my cousin in New York.'

'I see.' It was a very unsettling idea – Christmas chez Philadelphia Maxes, or chez New York cousin Max. 'But that doesn't solve the problem of my finances. I can't afford to take two months off, let alone travel around America.'

'Obviously the gallery would pay a major proportion of your travel, because I want your advice. That's the whole point. And you would get a store of experience and images to bring back with you.'

'Did you dream all this up today?'

'It crystallized today – when I was talking to Serena. But I've had the possible potential of the West Coast at the back of my mind for a while.'

'Have you told Frances?' Normally Ronnie didn't like to leave the gallery entirely under Frances's control.

'Yes. I think she'd quite enjoy being in charge for a spell.'

'Could the gallery afford it?'

'Well . . . it depends how you look at it. There's a lot of money about over there. We were talking about that last night.'

Alastair Faraday materialized by the Hockney swimming pool. 'Yes.' Why should that image depress him? Wilson and Reynolds and Stubbs were all in Rome at the same time probably as much for the money and fashionable company as for the art. Los Angeles could be fun, just as Rome had been.

'Would you like to think about it?'

'Perhaps. Though I ought to be able to make up my –' He broke off abruptly. 'Oh – no, sorry. I can't.'

'Why, Kenneth?'

'Fox.'

'*Fox*?' The word had brought instant irritation to her face.

'The illustrations for Book Three will be needed in a rush.'

'Why?'

'Because Bernard should have delivered by the end of September and he still hasn't.'

'When are the pictures due?'

'End of January.'

'Well, surely if Bernard can be two months late, then so can you. Let's see. If we went third week in December to second week in February, you'd have six weeks to complete by the end of March.'

'No. Sorry. It's not like that. They must keep the press date. They'll want to publish for Christmas.'

'But why should you be inconvenienced by Bernard?'

'Partly because he's elderly and famous, but mainly because he's made himself, the publisher, and to a lesser extent William and me, a lot of money. You know that.'

He watched her frown.

'Honestly, Ronnie. There's too much at stake for other people. And, now that the Fox sidelines are building up, I can't possibly afford to jeopardize him.'

'You like doing him best anyway.'

'Best?'

She kept perfectly still and did not answer.

He got up and went to pour the coffee. She ought to have remembered he was waiting for Bernard's manuscript; it wasn't as though he hadn't mentioned it. William was setting up an

55

emergency plan to extract it, and he'd been vaguely planning to devote Christmas to Fox. Best? Ronnie read him too well. He had never properly admitted it to himself, but, yes, *if* Fox were to become ... well ... lasting... He suppressed the word 'classic'. Hubris. But Bernard's stories werę good, very, very good, and he was ... well ... not displeased with the look of Fox.

It was all a long way from the West Coast and the feminine art of the Eighties. And a few years ago he would have leapt at the idea of two months away. He'd hated settled routines.

He carried the mugs to the sofa. 'Am I getting too set in my ways?'

'I think, my darling, you're just becoming more you.'

'What does that mean?'

'Nothing and everything.'

'Couldn't you make the West Coast trip on your own?' Before he'd reached the end of the sentence he knew he shouldn't have uttered it.

There was a long silence. Then she said, very quietly, 'That's a kind of slap in the face.'

He didn't fully comprehend. After all, where did freedom end and rejection begin?

He watched as she became completely withdrawn, taking off her glasses, cradling her mug and rocking slightly. Then suddenly the coin of his thoughts flipped, revealing San Francisco sunny-side up. No longer were there any second-hand images, but a whole new blank terrain, exciting, and, suddenly, within his grasp. How dangerous to be swinging, at thirty-nine, towards longing for old-fashioned veneration as the part-perpetrator of bookshop Christmas-present Fox, and away from that slightly lightweight, but at least unique, image which his drawing style and the now faded contemporaneity of *Who's Vineyard?* had once given him.

He reached for her, sickened by his unsureness, taking the mug gently from her hands, and drawing her into his embrace. 'I know it can't be wiped away with a kiss. But I want to kiss you.'

He felt her light body relax against his chest with a sigh, and with urgency born of relief kissed her mouth. Her kisses were

56

never tentative, never sloppy, never hurried. They had strength, and sensuality; they had consideration – and sex. With Ronnie, precious Ronnie, for his immanent bed, San Francisco seemed quite natural.

'Ankles?'

'Please.'

'Take off your tights then.' He released her.

With her eyes almost closed, she bent to slip off her shoes, and then she stood and pulled up her full, soft skirt to reach the elastic at her hips.

When her legs were bare, she settled into the corner of the sofa and he took her feet into his lap. Then, teasingly slowly, he started to massage her ankles.

This ritual was one of the silver keys to their mutual castle.

After making love, he felt like an extended sea anemone floating loosely against the rock of the bed, surrounded by the soft swell of the duvet, and lit by the pale moon of the lamp. Everything was simple, and sure, and right; security conveyed through the brush of Ronnie's thigh against his, her slender hand outstretched on his damp belly.

'Things are always more complex in the end,' she said.

'Things?'

'America and London. Living here. Going there. Work. Commitments.'

'Yes.'

'I was hasty.'

'Perhaps I was too.'

'No. You were right. You can't be cavalier about Fox.'

'No?'

'I just wish it wasn't written by such a spoiled old queen.'

He smiled.

'But you really don't mind, do you? I mean, you celebrate Bernard.'

He saw the long South London hill past the allotments up to Bernard's house, its green paintwork peeling in contrast to his neighbour's gleaming white. He saw the laburnum and the unpruned lilac at the front, and Bernard with his untidy hair and dirty pullover at the door. He thought of the strip of waste ground, brambled and blackthorned, at the back of the houses, where Bernard had seen urban foxes for years before suddenly amalgamating them into Fox. He remembered his anecdotes about Evelyn Waugh, and the ones about Coward. He thought of his glee at becoming accepted into the nurseries of England almost fifty years after being banned from its drawing-rooms.

'I suppose I do.' He put his hand over hers. 'But I'm probably –'

He was about to say that he was probably being foolish, that to turn his back on San Francisco and, at any rate partially, on their sharing in the background of her work, and on the opportunity to replenish his mind-store, was not right; that a compromise should be considered. But the telephone rang.

'Hell!' He lurched over and picked up the receiver. 'Yes?'

'Hullo, Kenneth. Hope it's not too late – there was no reply earlier.'

'Of course not.'

'It's just that Jos told me about Rosewharf Close.'

'She did?'

'It's part of a new development by the river in Fulham. Not in the A to Z yet. Thought you might like to know.'

'Of course. Thanks, Pete.'

'Just off Lysia Street and Stevenage road, if you want to pursue it. Lysia runs off Fulham Palace Road, near the junction with Lillie Road. I know about the development because we've had a group at the Poly that's been monitoring that river site over the years.'

'Great. Thanks a lot.'

'Good night, then.'

'Good night, Pete.' He put the receiver down.

'Anything the matter?'

'No. Not at all.'

Ronnie said nothing further, and he felt impelled to add, 'Just an address of someone that Jos and I got muddled.'

'Mm.'

He lay down again and put his arm around her.

After a few moments, she murmured, 'You know ... I think I'm falling asleep.'

'Then I will too.'

He closed his eyes. He'd once been to a perfectly dreadful party in Lysia Street. He couldn't remember who gave it, or why he'd gone. Just the name. Lysia. Lysia – Lydia. Odd how the one sounded ugly and the other rather beautiful.

4   He is introduced to Alastair Faraday

Searching through a drawer of catalogues, Kenneth came across a small, black sketchbook. The instant he saw the splash stain on the front, he remembered what was inside. Gingerly, he parted the covers and turned the pages. Bottle after bottle, in various stages of completion, met his gaze. He felt a quick, convulsive twinge in his left temple.

The book was the nearest he had ever come to doing penance. After Steayne, when he was earning enough not to have to teach, he had – quite simply – drunk far too much. It hadn't seemed like that, not for a long time; headaches, fuzzy mind, six o'clock drinks that ended in someone's flat at four in the morning, had all been part of life as he and various friends, mainly male, married and unmarried, knew it. Then one day he'd been standing in the Fulham Road in the pouring rain, late for an appointment and cursing the non-appearance of taxis, and had noticed that the dull ache in his left temple had disappeared. Which made him realize that it was now normal for it to be there, and that he'd just had twenty-four hours without a drink because a dubious bouillabaisse had upset his stomach. He'd said out loud: 'Alcohol is eating my mind.'

It was always the left temple that hurt. Was the left side of the brain responsible for mechanics or imagination? It didn't really matter: he couldn't afford to do without either. Didn't *want* to do without either.

On his way home after the appointment, he had bought the sketchbook. And for six months, on the morning after every night when he'd drunk too much so that his temple hurt, he drew a bottle. Mr Cremorne at school had always said, 'If you can draw a bottle, you can draw anything', and he'd brought in light ale bottles for them to practise on. Kenneth drew the wine bottles he and friends had recently emptied. When his pencil came down the neck and curved out to the shoulder – sharply for claret, gently for burgundy – and the effort of co-ordination made his fingers clench and his eye cringe, so that the line jerked and created a misshapen non-bottle, he forced himself to repeat the passage, again and again, until through the cumulative marks a passably accurate bottle emerged.

The drawing checked his behaviour, halted a blind slide into alcoholic conformity. There were less pub sessions, fewer strange beds, and by the time he met Ronnie he was in no danger of being passed over as a reasonably charming man, but an impending slob. He, like her, was in control – and carried a faint aura of past venery which she'd once admitted, and regretted, she found attractive.

The sketchbook shouldn't have been in the catalogue drawer, but he returned it, not particularly caring to place it alongside his general sketchbooks on their shelf. He found the Southampton Art Gallery's catalogue that he was looking for, and opened it at the *Classical Landscape* by Wilson that had been identified both as a view of Lake Nemi and of the River Arno. He fed on the evening light: the passive gold and the faint blue. He pressed a thumb over the small foreground figures, obliterating them. Was that better? No; this time the figures were needed. This heaven had to be peopled. They were a couple, old enough to copulate, young enough to play. He on his stomach, fishing, she looking towards the camera so to speak, with a wicker basket by her side and a baby in her lap. But, hang on a minute, it was a funny-looking baby. He reached for his magnifying glass. It wasn't a baby, the proportions were wrong. It was a doll. And, magnified, the woman's heart-shaped, almost chinless face, looked decidedly odd.

'*Do you think he knew he had a son?*' '*I hadn't really thought about it.' 'So he won't be in the story?' 'It might make it a bit complicated.'*

A baby that was really a doll. Water that might be a lake or river. Muddles and mergings in the head, and on the canvas. That perfect light which passeth all understanding.

Had Wilson made the mother of his child pose with a doll in her arms, while the real child was either fretful, sick – or in an orphanage? Back in London, had Nemi and Arno merged with the ale, just as the woman – sitting, perhaps, on a dusty studio floor in November – had to merge with a remembered summer Italian girl, while the doll in her arms pierced her heart as she thought of their son? And all for art's sake. Or money's.

He returned to the writing of Lydia's story.

As he turned off the Strand into Exeter Street, and approached the unprepossessing doorway to Joe Allen's, he realized he was feeling angry. The interruption to the morning – Wilson left in the middle of his final meeting with his mistress; the irresolution of the conversation about California the night before: these were things which normally might have made him tense, easy to irritate, but not combine to create anger. That was caused by a still-full stomach from his meals yesterday. He did not want to enter the restaurant until he was really hungry and could enjoy the meal. He did not look forward to Ronnie spending money on over-feeding him as part of a public relations procedure – a patchwork made up of the fashionable eating-place, the visiting artist, the up-and-coming gallery owner, and himself as 'someone I *really* want you to meet'. What difference would meeting him make to Serena Stein?

She was standing by the bar with Ronnie when he entered, and the boy on the door – seeing him respond to Ronnie's raised hand – did not ask him if he'd booked a table, but gave him a casual, not-quite-off-hand 'Good morning'. Reaching Ronnie, he smelled her new perfume.

'Kenneth. How nice. You know this is Serena.'

He took the tall woman's hand, felt her bones grip his. She was more glamorous than the fleeting glimpse on the stairs had revealed.

'Hullo.' He smiled, rather than invent a more complex greeting.

'The phantom in the hallway,' she said.

He retained the smile for a couple of seconds.

'Preoccupied,' he said. 'Rudely, I had not legislated for people as I made my way to the bathroom.'

'You English position your bathrooms most oddly.'

'Lack of practice. But we're learning.'

Watching her eyes become bored, he understood that she had decided she need not like him, and after that there was no mechanism by which he could stop himself from beginning to dislike her.

At table, he asked the waiter for a very small Caesar salad. He sensed that Ronnie thought this was an expression of his lack of enthusiasm for Serena, and in an attempt to restore goodwill he launched into the explanation for his lack of appetite. When he realised he was being tedious, he compounded his gaucherie by saying he didn't see any point in emulating Ronnie and chasing a full portion of uneaten salad round and round one of the outsize wooden bowls.

By coffee, he knew Serena had him down as a dull lightweight, and that Ronnie was furious with him. His attempts – which really had not been crass – to talk to Serena about her work had been sharply deflected, and it was left to Ronnie to make conversation about the London art scene and answer Serena's questions on the function of the Arts Council. Kenneth refilled his wineglass and wondered what would happen if he contributed the only piece of inside information he had ever remembered about the Arts Council: that on the wall of one of its women's lavatories there had once been a piece of graffiti that read 'Open the box' followed, in another hand, by 'Oh no, no, Pandora'. Ennui at his own triviality made him look up and out across the tables to the entrance, a literal seeking for a wider horizon since Serena had denied him the chance to expand within the intimate circle of their table. For the second time in three days he found himself looking at the familiar face of Alastair Faraday.

With an apparently practised eye, Faraday was taking stock of the assemblage of actors, media people, image-makers and lovers dispersed through the garage-like informality of the restaurant. Kenneth noted that when he recognized Ronnie and Serena – who had not seen him – he did a fleeting double-take, which for one unguarded second made him look pettish.

Then Ronnie, who had her back to him, suddenly broke off in mid-sentence and turned her head. It was as though she had heard a familiar, long-awaited voice – though Faraday had certainly not spoken, and would not have been heard over the hubbub at that distance unless he had shouted. The blood rushed to her face, and with it, with its warmth, an extra breath of perfume was released, and Kenneth hated it, and knew that Ronnie was in love.

The actor came over to their table, his expression now one of surprise, and energy, and friendliness. He kissed both the girls, and shook Kenneth's hand warmly. As information was exchanged about what they were all doing, and why they were there, Kenneth remembered Ronnie saying, '*And that incredibly beautiful voice is for real*'. He was there to meet an old friend – a theatre director. There was a spare seat at the table, and he agreed to sit and have a drink with them while he waited.

Kenneth knew that Ronnie would want him to order the drink. That, despite the fact it was her lunch, her unexpected friend, and that she ran a feminist gallery and was entertaining a feminist client, she would want him to attract the attention of one of the waiters. Paralysed briefly by a surge of superficial resentment and the deep-seated fear that his intuition of Ronnie's feelings had implanted, he did not instantly attempt to meet a waiter's eye – but suddenly one was there, only too eager to find out what Alastair Faraday might require.

Kenneth watched as the pale profile of the actor tilted complaisantly upwards to hold the tired, knowing eye of the blond young man – who quite probably was an actor too.

'A large vodka and tonic,' Kenneth said, the words sounding strangely unreal. The waiter still did not look at him, but seemed almost to seek affirmation from Alastair that this insignificant hanger-on had given the correct order.

Then the profile was turned away, the order written down, and conversation resumed.

Alastair made a particular point of asking Kenneth about himself.

'Jack of all trades.' Ronnie was staring at him as he spoke. 'And probably master of none.'

'I remember your illustrations for that special edition of Edward Thomas's poems.'

Ronnie would have shown him those. She always kept a copy on the underneath shelf of her coffee table.

He heard himself saying, 'Sometimes – even when you've got plenty of work on – you can suddenly wonder what you really want to be. What you're going to be when you grow up, I suppose.' He began to push his chair back. 'Sorry – I must be off. Getting late.' They were all staring at him now. Looking over the tops of Alastair and Serena's heads, he said: 'So glad to have met you,' and, dropping his gaze to Ronnie's left hand which was agitatedly crushing a left-over roll to smithereens, he muttered, 'I'll see you.'

Then he raised his eyes to see the helpless expression on her face.

'Yes,' was all she said.

'Tomorrow morning.' His voice sounded so brisk. 'Around nine.'

He walked out of the restaurant feeling like an automaton that had been programmed to find the door, but if necessary would be capable of blundering through the wall to get out into the street.

When he reached the Strand, he had no idea where he was going next. He noticed a stationary number 11 bus on the opposite side, and a kind of homing instinct made him run for it. But, once he was sitting on the top deck, he knew he did not want to go home – did not want to get off when they reached Beaufort Street and then walk through to the flat. He wanted to sit on the bus until it reached a place where things did not come to an end. Ronnie had never fallen in love with him so deeply that she could hear him across a crowded restaurant when he hadn't even spoken.

He remembered how pleased with themselves they'd been when he'd first moved into the flat. He'd felt very secure in the ground floor room close to the door, with her upstairs near the roof. And free. But that was to begin with. Latterly, he realized with a jolt, both the freedom and the security had ossified into a kind of formality.

For a long time he did not look out of the bus window; the familiar sights made him feel too sad. How could it have happened so suddenly? She'd only met the bloody man once. One meeting, and they'd turned the whole of London sour.

The bus lurched round a corner, and he looked out. He did not recognize the garage with its citrine neon fascia bright in the dingy afternoon. Some children rushed down the gangway and pressed the bell, and he followed them on to the pavement. He felt let down when he looked over the road and saw the Greyhound pub and knew he was in the Fulham Palace Road. He had wanted to be completely disorientated, in body as well as mind. He walked back past the garage, and suddenly wished he had a car. He'd always claimed it was ridiculous to keep one in central London, but now he just wanted to be able to drive himself away at will, to have complete autonomy over distance.

A bus overtook him, and then slowed for a stop on the other side of the road by a small park. Boys with sports bags and girls with plastic carriers jostled out of the automatic doors, rushed round the back of the bus, and tried to cross the busy road despite the lights of a belisha beacon flashing at a crossing a few yards ahead. It reminded him of Orpington – the midwinter afternoons when schoolchildren had played dare against the traffic on the main road, before they separated into the various closes, ways and drives that led to their individual front gates. Two of the boys reached the pavement in front of him, swearing jubilantly at a driver who sounded his horn, and then walked along swiping at each other's legs with their bags before turning down a side road. He looked after them, struck by their self-enclosed world of trivial aimlessness, and, as he did so, he saw the road's name: Lysia Street. Calmly, with no hesitation, he followed them.

He did not remember the street at all, could not guess in which two-storey brick house with its tiled porch and pathway the party had been held. Towards the end the houses ceased, and on the left there was a tall primary school set behind a brick wall whose two arched entrances had 'BOYS' and 'GIRLS' carved in the fancy stonework. On the wall, someone had painted in letters as big as the carved ones, 'BA 4 BG'. On the other side, there was a small tenement block in the process of being given a face-life. Smooth aluminium frames had been set under the fancily-cut brick window arches, and there was a skip containing rubble that had been wheeled out along a plank through the heavy battered black door with its central brass knob shaped like a cupola. He stared at the knob and realized he was filling his mind with this detail to avoid thinking about why he was walking here at all.

In front of him, the old black road and grey pavement ceased and merged into a modern ground of pale roan-coloured, wavy-sided bricks. These bricks led him between dwellings of varying size, shape and aspect – their odd corners and spaces lovingly differentiated with low walls, brightly-painted rails, steps, public seats, and small plots of earth whose newness was emphasized by the lengths of rough chestnut paling that were temporarily tilted round them to protect young bushes. The buildings themselves had none of the rawness of most modern architecture; their brickwork was mixed and mellow, and every detail of the complex junctures and joins was congruent and neat. Their scale proclaimed them to be local authority houses; their intricacy and finish placed them firmly in the good tradition of dense urban building that includes packed harbourside cottages and the old dwellings that cluster around cathedrals and castles. Kenneth was so surprised by them he became genuinely distracted.

'Careful now, the river's just beside you.'

He started at the sound of the voice, and turned from the line of three little houses he had been studying so closely that he was walking half backwards, to find that the path he was on had formed a T-junction with a wider path edged by a knee-high wall over which was indeed the river – full and sombre, except where a pale sun, just escaping the huge black clouds above the trees along the towpath on the other side, was reflected in a gleaming slash. Continuing to turn until he faced the corner opposite the houses, he saw a man on a seat between two sapling rowan trees.

'Thanks,' he said.

'Don't suppose you *would* have gone over. But thought it best to be on the safe side.'

'It's a very low wall.'

'Expect there'll be a fuss about it. But, whatever they build, kids'll find their way to the river, and I expect they thought it best to make it as open to view as possible. Even for toddlers. But they weren't reckoning on you coming through sideways.'

'I must have looked daft. But I was so intrigued by the new houses.'

'Not seen them before?'

'No.'

'Looking for anywhere special?'

'Er – no.'

'Just out for a walk, like?'

'That's it.'

'It's a beautiful spot. Opening up the river like this.'

'It certainly is. Do you live on the new estate?'

'I do. We've been here a month. Like princes, I say.'

'It makes a change, doesn't it?'

'Rehoused. From a tower-block. Londoner yourself?'

'Pretty well. For over twenty years.'

'But not council.'

'No. I have a – a big room, on the Old Brompton Road.'

''Spect you wish you could come here.'

Keneth looked along the path at the houses with walled yards and french windows that faced the river. 'I certainly do.'

The man smiled and got up. 'The country may be going to the dogs. But for once I'm not grumbling. Good day to you.'

'Goodbye. And – thanks again.'

He watched him walk along the river path, a slight man with thin, grey hair, wearing a donkey jacket and heavy-duty jeans.

He realized the brief contact, however trivial, had made him feel better. And also that he did not want to risk bumping into Lydia, to be seen, like an adolescent, lingering in the vicinity of the home of a girl he barely knew.

As he walked back to the Fulham Palace Road, he remembered, with satisfaction, that he could catch a number 30 bus from there right to the flat, and while he waited for it he decided that earlier he had been foolishly melodramatic.

When he thought about it, Alastair Faraday really did not strike him as someone who would be desperately interested in Ronnie, so even if she *did* have a thing about him – well, such things do pass. It was up to him to be supportive. He must think about California seriously. And about his own performance that day. If he did not want his work interrupted, he should have rung up the gallery and told Ronnie he couldn't make lunch. That's what he would have done a couple of years back. Or, if he'd got a shift on, he would have had time to walk part of the way, so he'd have been hungry, and all that stupid rigmarole wouldn't have happened.

Except that Serena Stein still wouldn't have been impressed, and Ronnie would still have 'heard' Alastair Faraday.

Oh, *fuck* Alastair Faraday. He'd been, in his opinion, a lousy Mark Antony.

When he got back, he slammed the heavy front door of the house behind him and shoved his key hard into his own flat door. Normally he slid it in gently, careful of the lock's mechanism. Once inside, he took a deep breath and looked around. It was all right, he was on home ground. His territory. He was secure – he was. The story still lay on his desk, the white paper almost fluorescent in the dim light. When he'd finished it, he could have a drink.

He took off his jacket, turned up the heating, and went over to the big window. Before he sat down, he put his knuckles on the work table and leaned forward to peer out. Beyond three shallow steps, he could still just see the flagstones below the high wall, their surface almost totally covered with green algae stains.

He began to think of Ronnie, playing over again in his mind what had happened in the restaurant. Then he stopped himself, sat down and prepared to read over what he had written that morning. But, before his eyes had found the first paragraph, his mind returned to Ronnie and he was trying to remember how quickly it had been after they first met before they had acknowledged they were attracted.

Someone had introduced them at a private view, and they'd had a drink together in that tiny pub on Piccadilly. Then ...? She'd 'phoned him. The next day. That's right, to ask him to come to the gallery. And the invitation had stretched into a conversation – they'd talked and talked. Ronnie loved the telephone.

It clicked. When her 'phone was engaged that night, after her dinner party – she'd been talking to Alastair Faraday. He could see her, the instrument like a beloved cat on her lap, her glasses off, her voice light as she tentatively chose the first links of words that just might turn into the chain of a relationship.

The phrase 'call girl' flashed through his mind. Why did jealousy make one so crude?

He forced himself into the story. He'd already decided that Wilson had known about his son and that the child had been sent to an orphanage in the country, paid for with the sum received for the very last painting that he sold. And that the mother, as well as being poor, had fits, which was why she couldn't keep the child. And that the decision, which would have been perfectly acceptable in those days, had inwardly eaten into Wilson's morale, making him drink more, paint less, and become depressed. Then when he had finally been taken back to Wales, his birthplace, where he was sheltered by relations for the last year of his life, his recorded loss of memory had been, Kenneth also decided, caused by alcohol, not senile decay. The way the pieces slid together, documented and imagined, exhilarated him.

He finished the story with an epilogue, set five years after Wilson's death, in which his son, by then thirteen, started to walk to London with the intention of finding the Royal Academy, and discovering information about his father. He thought Lydia would like that.

It was nearly midnight. The events of lunch time had receded. Now, he was very hungry. And almost happy. He opened a bottle of wine, and cut some bread and cheese. Looking for something to read, he discovered *The World in the Evening* and began the first chapter.

It was about a man at a Hollywood party who discovers his wife cuckolding him in a wendy-house in the hosts' garden. He rushes home, rips up her clothes, and leaves for Pennsylvania.

Kenneth read on, with embarrassed fascination.

5 | He hears news of Bernard, and returns to Rosewharf Close

There was a smell of hot croissants. Ronnie was standing by the window. The table, covered with a new brown cloth, was laid for breakfast. There were a few small white chrysanthemums in a white jug.

'I had forgotten it was Saturday,' he said. When Ronnie was upset, she was extra meticulous; happy, and she could allow herself to be careless.

'I hope you feel like weekend breakfast.'

'Yes. I do. I'm very sorry about yesterday.' He had not gone automatically to kiss her, but was standing in the middle of the room, looking at her intently. She was dressed in a black cotton flying-suit, her hair hidden under a crimson scarf, and she reminded him of a tiny pirate. He expected her to rebuke him.

'I don't understand why you took against Serena.'

'It was fairly mutual.'

'She's very strong. But I thought you'd like that.'

'She made me feel highly dispensable.'

'I realize it was partly to do with our unresolved talk the night before.'

'Oh?'

'You were putting up a resistance to all things American.'

'Was I?' A touch of belligerence crept into his voice.

'I think so. But I'll get the coffee.'

He watched her cross the room to the kitchen and, when he could hear that she was busy, he called out, 'Perhaps it had something to do with Alastair Faraday as well.'

She did not reply immediately, and childishly he started to count the seconds of silence inside his head. '. . . Eighteen, nineteen, twenty, twenty-one – '

'He didn't arrive until right at the end.' She came in with the coffee.

'No.'

'And you were already fed up when you arrived.'

'True.'

'Why do you think he had something to do with it?'

'You don't?' He watched her. She looked miserable.

'No.'

He didn't pursue it, was relieved not to have to – that the conversation changed, and the croissants were produced, and their plans for the day discussed. He suspected he'd traded dropping the subject of Alastair Faraday for her postponing an analysis of his reaction to the California proposal.

'Frances and Jim have invited us to lunch tomorrow. Usual thing. About a dozen people. I'm going into the gallery this morning, and I said I'd let Frances know.'

He thought about it: the open-plan ground floor in Islington, lots of delicious food laid out on a round table, pleasant people whom he never could remember if he'd met before or not, Jim pulling corks and extolling the virtues of some new mechanical gadget, chicken bones being whisked from the reach of the omnipresent English setter, the minicab that didn't turn up until an hour after he'd decided he wanted to leave.

'Would you mind if I said no?'

There was the briefest pause before she said, 'Of course not,' and they both knew that she did. And suddenly he wondered if he wouldn't rather go anyway. It was very safe at Frances and Jim's on a Sunday – he'd never actually disliked being there.

'How's Richard Wilson going?' The tone of her voice was gentle, and she smiled slightly when she'd completed the question. Once, he would have said she was false. Once? – when

72

he was young, a decade ago. Then he would have said she was false: carefully finding a question that would interest him, and composing her voice and features to eliminate her own feelings of disappointment. She'd said they should be truthful to one another, but she'd also taught him that it was sometimes worth making the effort not to be. That to hide one's own pissed-offness wasn't necessarily the same as sycophancy.

'I've finished the first draft.'

'Will you let me read it?'

'I think I need to polish it a bit first.'

'How does it feel? Getting back to fiction?'

'Mm ... curious. Though I don't think it's at all like the last time.'

'Well – that was directly inspired by personal experience.'

He gave a brief laugh. 'I'm not sure "inspired" is quite the word – it sounds so lofty.' He could not stop himself adding: 'There's nothing lofty about being jilted.'

He couldn't judge whether she simply did not react to this last remark, or whether she suppressed a reaction.

'Do you really think that, if Aline hadn't broken it off, you wouldn't have written about that summer?' she asked.

'I've never thought about it that way.'

'Perhaps – forgive me for saying this, Kenneth, I know you don't like raking things over – but perhaps you should think a little about that time. About America. About relating to it ... to me. So we get our future plans right.'

How could she be saying this to him if Faraday obsessed her?

'We've never really had future plans before.'

'No.'

'Do we need to now?'

'I think perhaps I'm beginning to.'

He had a sensation of sadness. He'd never had plans other than those to do with his work. Without children and parents there'd been no need. He'd thought that was good. Was he going to be forced to have them now, forced to admit he'd been wrong, because without plans you do not build a life?

'Writing about Wilson is like building,' he suddenly said. 'Or sculpture. You almost physically take the pieces and struggle to get them in exactly the right place. Writing *Who's Vineyard?*

was like drawing from memory. The hand moved and the book gradually appeared.'

Ronnie jerkily picked up the almost empty coffee jug and looked inside it.

As shè got up to go to the kitchen, he thought she was about to cry. 'I'm sorry. I'm not avoiding what you just said. I will think about America. It's just that it suddenly came to me what writing about Wilson did feel like.'

She put the jug down. 'I've got something for you.'

Her voice was constricted, and – he thought – desperate.

She brought him Claire Tomalin's biography of Mary Wollstonecraft and a glossy Fuseli catalogue.

He took them and held on to one of her hands. 'Ronnie?'

She shook her head. 'I don't think I can talk any more now.'

He stood, put his arms round her, and held her tightly for a full minute. Over her shoulder the domestic prettiness of the breakfast table mocked him. He kissed her red scarf where it pulled tight at her temple. 'Thank you for the books. I'll take them downstairs now.' A lump in his throat prevented him from thanking her for breakfast.

Back in his room, he slumped on the sofa and looked up Fuseli in the index to the biography. The sentences he dipped into quickly conjured up the man. 'Like Mary, he was a born romantic. Byronic heroes yet undreamed of were to be built on his model: vain, sardonic, lecherous, treacherous, bisexual, given to much declamation on the subject of his own desires and feelings, bored by other people's. . . . Like Mary, he needed glasses; like her, he was too vain to be seen wearing them.' He sighed, and turned to the illustrations in the catalogue. Fuseli's self-portrait reminded him of Frank Finlay in one of his more mannered roles. Otherwise, pictorial flights of fantasy postured past his eyes and enervated his mind. Such demonic portrayal of the power of suffering eluded his imagination. He was, he supposed, being far too English, and proving Fuseli/Füssli right when he had said of his adopted countrymen, 'Their taste and feelings all go to realities.' He wanted a vision that floated him nearer to a glimpsed heaven, not one that nailed him into hell. Hell did not excite him. And, if he were honest, the relationship between Mary and Fuseli was far too complicated for him to tackle. Or was he being lazy? Oh, fuck it – that was only him worrying about what Ronnie would think. Fuseli was outside the vague, indescribable impulse that had set him on the Wilson quest.

He wanted Bonington though: yes, he did want Bonington: Bonington in Venice.

He stood up abruptly. California had got to be resolved one way or the other. He went to the 'phone and dialled William's number.

As soon as he heard Kenneth's voice, William said: 'You've heard then? Isn't it dreadful?'

'Heard what?'

'About Bernard.'

'No. What?'

'He's had a stroke. He's in hospital. He was lying on the kitchen floor for fifteen hours before anyone found him.'

'Oh, no!'

'They say he's pulling round. But they don't know how long he'll be there. Or whether he'll make a complete recovery.'

'Was . . . ?' He didn't complete the question, aware how selfish it would sound.

'No. It wasn't. He'd barely begun it. Just a few pages.'

'Oh.'

Fox, and the support Fox represented, was jerked away. He could see Bernard, fat and untidy and dead-looking, sprawled on the lino that attempted to imitate Italian tiles. The ghost of Fox disappeared with a leer through the brambles beyond the fence.

'I'm afraid there's nothing we can do about it for the moment, Kenneth.'

'No. Actually that was why I was 'phoning you. To find out if there was any progress. Ronnie and I are – were – thinking of going away around Christmas.'

'Well, you might just as well.'

'Where is Bernard?'

'The new Charing Cross hospital. In Fulham Palace Road.'

'You've seen him?'

'Not yet. I'm going this afternoon. He's allowed limited visiting.'

'I'll go tomorrow. Can you give me the times?'

75

At the end of their conversation, he replaced the receiver and went to sit at the work-table. So it was all resolved. They could go to California. But he and William had better rustle up a whole lot of work to replace Fox.

He felt, with an absolute certainty, that Ronnie had finished with him. But she did not know it yet – and therefore neither should he.

Doggedly, he took out his atlas and looked at the map of America. It was his old school atlas. His father had bought it in the Army & Navy Stores. He remembered he had used it when he needed to check the distances he and Aline had driven when he was writing *Who's Vineyard?* And he remembered that noticing then the little Army & Navy Stores label stuck inside the back cover had given a brief glimpse of the void that was his knowledge of his father. He'd probably bought the atlas on his way to Victoria Station after leaving the office early, one Friday afternoon: he always seemed to make purchases for Kenneth on a Friday. But Kenneth had put so much silent energy into disagreeing with what his father wanted for him, that he never found out what his own dreams had been, before he was born. During his birth, his mother had died; a fact which did not dawn on him until he was twelve. Until then, he'd just accepted his grandmother's gloss: 'Your poor mother died when you were a baby.' The truth had made him uncomfortable and angry. It implied somehow that he was uncouth and savage – like a member of one of those pillaging tribes in Julius Caesar – if his first act in the world had been to kill his mother. Yet, sometimes, when he looked at his friends' mothers, he was glad not to have one.

His father had wanted him to go to Oxford. 'You'll get in with the right sort of crowd there.' Kenneth had deeply resented such a crass view of his future. Now he saw it was probably simply a last attempt by his father to clutch at the unattainable, to get within vicarious reach of that social rung where, if like him you were a civil servant, you were never made to feel inferior. What he suspected his father would not have accepted was that Oxford by itself could not have sufficed, and that there had been other missing vital ingredients that made them both ineligible for inclusion in the favoured class corral.

Mr Flete had not come to the degree ceremony when Kenneth left the Royal College of Art. Kenneth's own derisive view of painters and designers suddenly donning academic gowns and receiving scrolls, coupled with his father's continued lack of enthusiasm for the world and practitioners of art, had meant there was little point. But he had probably been deprived of a morning's unusual pleasure. For the trumpet fanfare, the reasonably distinguished guests and reasonably witty speeches, the flock of graduates in their hired robes, perhaps even the salmon mousse, Sancerre, and strawberries afterwards, would have impressed him.

So Kenneth collected his first-class degree wearing his painted blue shoes and with a Robertson's golliwog brooch pinned to his gown, and left that evening for America on the cheapest charter flight. Within a week he had met Aline, and they borrowed a car and drove wildly up the coast of Maine, to make love on rocks, in surf, on pine-needles, in sand dunes, and under smooth, purple night skies. He was finally tracked down five weeks later in New York, when he was so brown and lean and exultant that everyone's eyes seemed to quiz him, and Aline kept her silver-bangled arm tight around him. Tracked down by a message at the airline office that said his father was dead. By the time he read the message, Mr Flete was both dead and buried.

Kenneth's glance hopped across the atlas from New York to Pittsburgh, St Louis, Kansas, Denver, Salt Lake City and Los Angeles. How exciting those mountains should be! But how unappetizing the names all suddenly sounded – even San Francisco.

What a coward he'd been about his father's death. He'd written and thanked the three relatives and two office colleagues who had arranged the funeral, but he hadn't seen or spoken to any of them. The only person he talked to was his father's solicitor about the will – and to Mrs Pennington, of course. She had been willing to supply the details of his father's death, but he had manoeuvred her to keep to a mere précis. Then she had started to try to tell him about her daughter, and he had realized there was a possibility that she might be about to say that his father was the father of her girl. And he didn't want to know; didn't want to know because of the suspicion that she might be

77

lying and because he didn't want to have to think about it if it were the truth. He chose, deftly, to concentrate on the one thing that he already knew was true: that Mrs Pennington's daughter lived in a home for the disabled. He thought he also knew, because he thought that that was what a conversation he had overheard years before had implied, that the daughter was a mongol. He was about to make a swift, and reasonably generous, financial offer, when the back-door bell rang, and Mrs Pennington went to see to the boy who came every week to mow the lawn.

Kenneth had left the kitchen, and wandered through the hall to the sitting room. There, he looked around the reproduction furniture, touched the rough maroon moquette of the three-piece suite, and stared at the genteel brass tongs, brush and shovel hanging on a little stand in the empty fireplace. He noticed the sunburnt skin peeling finely, like scurf, on the back of his hand. He would break the rule they had set: he would telephone Aline. Writing was not enough. He had not touched her, seen her, smelled her, for six whole days. He checked his watch. It would be ten o'clock there, surely not too early. He got through to the overseas operator.

By the time the operator rang back with his required connection, the boy had mown the front lawn and was pushing the green machine noisily round to the back. While he waited, Kenneth had not gone to the kitchen to explain to Mrs Pennington that he would resume their conversation once he'd taken a call. He'd just paced around the room, desperate for the 'phone to ring, and aware that she was probably waiting almost as desperately in the kitchen. Almost, but not quite. Disabled daughters, possible poverty, grief or whatever she felt over his father, they must all be subsidiary to what he felt for Aline. He could not do anything until he had spoken to her.

He had allowed the telephone to ring twice. In those days, three rings had been his habitual pause before answering, but he had not been able to risk assuming that a third would occur.

At first, no one had spoken. Then Kenneth said huskily, 'Hallo?'

'Yes?' A man's dry, East Coast voice.

'Oh ... please may I speak to Aline?'

'Who is it?'

'My name is Flete. Kenneth Flete.'

'I'm sorry, Mr Flete. But I am afraid you cannot talk to my daughter.'

'But I . . . Will she be there later?'

'She will. But not available. I had better explain something to you.'

There was a pause. Kenneth felt angry – and panicky. 'Why?'

'Because Aline is no longer free. She is betrothed.'

'Be-' Kenneth tried to make sense of this remark, and failed. His mind was plunging, like a rearing horse petrified of what was in front of it.

'I have to tell you, Mr Flete, that Aline is going to marry her lifelong friend, Benjamin Mayer.'

It was then that he particularly noticed the begonias. They were orange and lemon and vermilion, the colours of jellied sweets, except for the brown wind-bruises around the edges of the outer petals. Some of the flowers had been sliced off by the mower. They lay on the razed, damp grass, all effort to prolong summer terminally suspended.

Unconsciously, the hand holding the receiver was moving further and further away from his ear, until he felt the black plastic bang dully against the edge of the table. Then, vaguely, faintly, he heard the click of a receiver being put back at the other end. He looked back at the guillotined begonias, and replaced his own receiver. Then he walked through to the kitchen and told Mrs Pennington she could have the house.

He had left Orpington later that day and had never been back. He hadn't told Ronnie the full story because she would have been horrified at such careless charity, and she would have seen the gesture as proof that the Aline-affaire – as they sometimes referred to it – cut far deeper than he'd ever admitted. In *Who's Vineyard?*, the man was half-relieved to get shot of the girl at the end, and Ronnie had never questioned whether that resembled the truth or not.

'Ben' had been mentioned by Aline many times. The boy next door who'd been there all her life and whom her parents would like her to marry. 'But I never will,' she had said, 'not with the whole world out there waiting for me.'

79

He hadn't tried to contact her. Once, a long time after, he had wondered if he'd made her pregnant.

He put the atlas away, avoided looking at the pile of things connected with the unfinished Trevor illustration, and rather guiltily reached for the Wilson story. He began to read it, and was soon engrossed in the intricate engineering of testing, and sometimes changing, the correlation of word, punctuation and syntax. It was nearing noon when he had finished.

He stood up and stretched, with that pleasurable absence of guilt and feeling of comfort that a period of concentrated work can bring. Poor Wilson! Why shouldn't his vision of the natural rim of heaven have been enough? Why should he have been asked to kowtow to fashion and society? As a Welsh parson's son, with a birthright of independence and scenery, the whims of short-lived social conformities must have seemed so deeply ludicrous. Just for the moment, Kenneth felt he had perhaps done him justice.

He would go out. He would go to the pub. He would first take the story to Lydia and they would both go to a pub. If she could. If she wanted to.

That day, when he came to the river, the sky was clear, and the rays of the low midday sun were striking the water in a dazzling glare. They were emanating warmth too, and there were several people strolling, or sitting on the benches by the low embankment wall. Kenneth asked one of them, a straight-backed woman with a slight air of the warrior about her, if she knew the whereabouts of Rosewharf Close.

'I'll walk you there,' she said. 'It's so near, but hard to explain.'

She had got up and started forward before he could deter her, and from underneath the bench a slow black labrador and a purposeful tabby cat emerged to accompany them. Kenneth was so taken with asking about the cat, he did not properly notice the two quick turns that brought them into Rosewharf Close, a tiny street by a grass play area, with an angled view of the river.

'Do you know which number you want?' the woman asked.

'Four.'

'There you are.' She pointed to a red front door, gave a slight smile, and walked away. The dog lumbered behind her, while the cat – its feathery tail held level with the line of its backbone –

stepped out in front.

'Thank you,' he called after her, and went to press the bell.

For a long time, nobody answered. He wondered whether to ring again. He realised he had not considered what the make-up of Lydia's household might be. He had simply thought of 4 Rosewharf Close as her address. Yet a son had been implied. And she had not worn a wedding ring. There might be any combination of parental, marital, extra-marital relations behind the shining crimson paint.

The door in front of him emitted two smooth, well-oiled clicks, and was opened by a hand's breadth. Lydia had her thumb pressed against the door's edge, and her little finger stretched to touch the jamb. In the gap, he was mainly aware of her startled expression and the fact she was wearing the dusty-pink sweater.

'Hullo,' he said.

'Hullo.' She sounded uncertain.

'I can't really claim to have been just passing, but I thought I'd come and see if Rosewharf existed. You're not in the A to Z, you know.'

She just looked at him, and he wasn't sure whether she had understood what he had said. It reminded him of the first encounter when he had thought she might be foreign.

She stepped back, opening the door to its full extent, and pointed her arm into the house towards a wooden staircase. He went inside. It was like following the moves of a dance that he had never learned.

He did not like to look inquisitively around, and kept his eyes on the knitted flower on her back as she led the way up the stairs. The scale and contours of the house were closed, like a cottage, but not claustrophobic. Light from a half-landing window made the white painted stairwell seem airy.

By contrast, the room she took him to was like a cave. There was no natural light, and wall lamps made areas of brightness and shadow among the emerald and indigo satin dresses that hung down the walls on two sides. A large sewing-table filled the centre, and a third wall was lined with cork smothered with swatches of stuffs, picture cuttings, photographs, messages and drawings. There was a clearing in the middle of the cork containing a single postcard. The windows in the fourth wall were covered with drawn curtains of antique red velvet, and under them was a shabby black chaise which she indicated he should sit on. She sat at the table in an upright chair.

'I've brought the story,' he said.

He thought she looked confused. Surely she hadn't forgotten?

'Would you like to read it?'

'Oh yes.' She spoke very quietly, but emphasized the 'yes'.

'I hope you don't mind me coming?'

She shook her head uncertainly.

'Well . . . ' He pulled the folded pages from his inside pocket and held them out to her. She leaned forward and took them; her hand was shaking.

'What's the matter?'

She smoothed the pages against her sweater. 'I shan't have anything to say.'

'How do you mean?'

'About the story. I shan't have anything clever to say.'

'I just want you to read it. I wrote it for you. Because of you.'

She smiled. The troubled face, the lucid grey eyes, the pretty mouth, became transformed. He was certain he was briefly witnessing an expression of pure happiness.

'Must I read it now?'

'No. Keep it. Until we arrange to meet again.' He waited for her to say something. 'We will meet again?'

'If you say.'

'You have a say too.' He tried to hold her gaze, but she looked away. 'Lydia?'

Still not looking at him, she just whispered, 'Kenneth,' as though the syllables formed a talisman.

'Shall I come here to pick it up? Perhaps tomorrow. I've got to visit someone down the road at the hospital.'

'Could it be Monday? Could we – meet somewhere?'

'Yes, of course. Pub? Park? Or would you come to my place?'

'Yes.'

'What time?'

'Afternoon?'

'I'll be there. Anytime after two. I'll write down the address and telephone number. It's not far away.'

He went over to the table, looking for a scrap of paper, but could see only pieces of material. 'Give me the story, I'll put it on there.' As he leant over to write, his head was close to hers. He did not straighten when he had finished, but kept his weight on his hand and turned to look into her face. She seemed to be waiting for him, invisibly trapped. The narrow passage of air between them felt magnetized. He tilted forward, kissed her without pressure on the mouth, and the feeling of her lips settling naturally against his gave him a sensation of intense, almost inaugural, pleasure.

There was the sound of a door opening downstairs, and voices. Kenneth and Lydia snapped apart, he feeling absurdly embarrassed and ill-prepared.

He looked to her for guidance, and watched a sort of dreamy shine fade from her eyes and be replaced by an expression of wooden purposefulness. She stood up, saying quickly, 'That's my son. And father. They're back early.'

'Will it ... matter?'

'We'd better go down.'

Before she opened the door, he went up to the cork wall. Most of the images pinned up were theatrical – stage sets, scenes from productions, costumes. The postcard at the centre was the Paris fashion plate from the British Museum.

'Are you a designer?'

'Just a dressmaker.'

'For the theatre?'

'Yes.'

He remembered what she had said about the Wilson landscape being like an empty stage.

He came close to where she was standing by the door. He started to put his arms on her shoulders, when a penetrating boy's voice shouted: 'Mum!' He drew back, but she put her arms up and he resumed the embrace, holding her tightly until a second, more urgent 'Mum!!' forced her to break away.

When he stood behind her, at the top of the flight of stairs, he saw below a thin, muddy boy, with serious eyes that seemed to demand urgent reassurance, holding a huge dark green cabbage with mottled violet on its outer leaves.

'Look, Mum! Look!'

83

Then the boy saw Kenneth, and his eyes became puzzled and angry, and at the same time seemed in even more need of comfort. Behind the boy was a man whose donkey-jacket enabled Kenneth to identify instantly as the man who had spoken to him on the embankment the day before. He stared at Kenneth in pure disbelief.

'It's a whopper, Arthur,' said Lydia. 'And you'll have to learn to like it, if we're ever going to eat it all. Dad, this is Kenneth.'

'We met yesterday,' The man looked at him steadily.

Lydia turned and Kenneth thought she was afraid. 'Met?'

'By the river,' he said quietly. 'I came this way yesterday.'

'But – ' She broke off, leaving the sound of the brittle little word hanging in the air, making him feel cornered by a need for some kind of explanation.

Arthur intervened. 'Who is he?'

The rudeness stung Kenneth, but he spoke gently. 'My name's Kenneth Flete. I was going to send something I had written to your mother, but I thought I'd come and see if I could find Rosewharf Close and deliver it myself.'

They were all staring at him now. A small window threw sunlight onto a trug basket filled with newly-pulled carrots and parsley which stood on the floor by the man's feet. Kenneth wondered where the fresh vegetables came from and waited for someone to speak.

But Lydia just walked to the door and opened it, and, after scanning up and down the street, stood, apparently waiting for him to go. When he was level with her, he started to say, 'I'm sorry if – ' but she cut him short.

'Thank you for bringing the story.'

Then she gave him one brief, private look, as though willing him to trust her.

Once outside, he did not look back, and set off fast, unseeing of the few people whom he passed.

6 | He and Pete cannot see the Future

He knew it was Sunday and, the instant before he moved his arm to touch Ronnie, he knew she was not there. Like Saturday breakfasts, shared Saturday nights had become habitual. He kept his palm flat on the sheet where she might have lain, and missed her.

The day was already compromised. Early last evening they had spoken on the telephone, and he had told her about Bernard and had received no response to his remark that this could make a difference to his thoughts about America. Ronnie had just said she'd perhaps see him when she got back after lunch with Frances. She had sounded subdued, private – as though she were in hiding from him. He had said he would visit Bernard in the afternoon, and now felt apprehensive at what he might find. What would he do until then? The day ahead seemed very lacklustre.

A corrective rush of self-disgust had him out of bed, washed, dressed, making coffee, and informing himself that he must finish the William Trevor illustration before going out to buy a Sunday paper. He was at his work-table, everything spread out, full coffee mug in its safety bracket (an expensive accident accounted for this gadget), without further thoughts other than of the drawing.

He was shy of admitting, even to himself, that he was aware of his audiences, and that the Sunday colour supplement audience unnerved him the most. There was something theatrical about being seen by thousands of weekend people in bed, in the bath, in the garden. Millions of pairs of desultory eyes casting a glance at his image, as you might throw crusts to a duck. No ... not like that at all! He ought to be concentrating more on the text and less on the Flete impact. He re-read the description of the central character and started to make a new sketch of her face.

The way her hair fell and the shape of her face were established, but he'd been lazy with her eyes, and over pretty with her mouth. Lydia's lips came to the forefront of his mind as the pencil slowly, without being lifted from the paper, made a shape. It would not do. It was not a suitable mouth for this buttoned-up woman – but he could steal Lydia's nose. It had an extra, bony, middle-section, unusual for a tip-tilted nose. He practised it at the top of the sheet, not in a single, flowing line, but tentatively, touch by touch.

Soon, he had made three noses, and one was right. Then he found his fish references, and practised patterning a display that included saithe and snapper. At an unpremeditated point he was suddenly ready to go to the finished illustration – which he decided to begin again from scratch.

Like a percussionist who had stood to attention through a long performance, waiting for the moment when he adds his drumrolls to the final bars, the telephone began to trill just as Kenneth was taking a completing brushful of pale blue wash down the side of the fish-stall. The intrusion into his concentration, which had been so deep it was as though he had severed all links with everything except the components of the picture in front of him, made his hand slip slightly sideways. Defensively, he jerked the brush away from the paper, and a pale blue drop flew across to land on the woman's face. His heart pounding, he dropped the brush and reached for a strip of blotting paper to draw off the misplaced moisture.

As he picked up the telephone receiver, he squinted at the woman's face. The faint bluish blur that remained, lightly veiling one eye, one cheek and the nose, gave her the bewilderment that was in the text and which up till now had eluded him.

'Hullo.'

'Kenneth.'

'Pete. You've just invented a new art movement.'

'I have?'

'Telechance. The 'phone made me jump, and the ensuing blot has saved the picture.'

'Oh God, I'm – '

'No. It's true. If it had ruined it, I'd be shouting at you.'

'It doesn't sound your kind of art movement.'

'Perhaps I'm due for a change.' He looked at his watch. Still time to say he'd like to go to Frances and Jim's, to step back into the pattern as it had been.

'You too?' Pete spoke quietly. 'Look – Kenneth, I was 'phoning to see if you were free. If I could come and talk to you.'

'Now?'

'Could I?'

'Of course. My only commitment is a hospital visit some time this afternoon.'

He read *The World in the Evening* while he waited. Any scriptwriter who could turn this book into a credible film for the Eighties would be a prodigy.

'Did you find Rosewharf Close?' asked Pete, shortly after his arrival while he waited for Kenneth to make coffee. He had declined a drink, and seemed tense and on guard in a way that reminded Kenneth of when they first met. He'd fished out his battered tobacco tin as soon as he sat down, and had just rolled his first cigarette.

'Yes.'

'It's a nice building development.'

'Isn't it?' He spooned out the soluble coffee granules. 'I expect Jos told you I met a girl who lives there.'

'She did. She seemed to think you'd be glad it was a real address.'

'Mm.' He brought the coffee over and sat down.

Pete was looking at him with concern. 'Sorry. I didn't mean to pry.'

Kenneth had an eerie feeling that he must be very careful what he said because his words would somehow shape future events.

87

If he dismissed Lydia as unimportant, she would become unimportant; if he made claims for her, she would fulfil them. And, if he made a joke about picking up girls in galleries, she would be a pick-up for ever.

'You're not. There's no secret.' Which, he realized, implied that Ronnie knew. 'I met her in the British Museum. She seemed ... original.'

'Have you written the story?'

'Yes. I took it to her.' He was not going to say any more, then, about Lydia, and the ensuing silence emphasized the need for an explanation of Pete's visit. 'Is anything wrong?' he asked at last.

'Not ... really. Look, I feel bad about this, Kenneth. And if you think I'm asking you to betray your friendship with Jos, then just say. But, I'm faced with certain choices, and I don't want to make the wrong one. My main problem is that I don't really know what Jos wants. And I wondered if you could help me over that.'

'But I don't – '

'No, no. I know you can't divine Jos's thoughts. But, when she told me about the talk you had on Thursday, she said she'd mentioned her indecision over the cottage. And, as she so seldom talks to anyone other than me about domestic things, I just wondered ... Well, if she'd got more definite ambitions than she lets on.'

'Ambitions?' *Pete would be better off without me. If we separated.*

'Well, that's not the right word. Hopes – desires – dreams.'

'The change of direction in her painting is obviously important.'

'Oh?'

Kenneth frowned. It was as though he had mentioned something totally peripheral to Jos's life. Then he remembered Pete had said *her* indecision over the cottage.

'She said you made lists of pros and cons. Over the cottage.'

'Oh – yes. It was something she suggested ages ago. She trots the bloody list out every few months or so. I'd just like to tear it up.'

'You're not undecided?'

'I haven't got her impulse for an all-or-nothing decision. I'm quite happy to rub along with a run-down flat and a run-down cottage. They're both perfectly comfortable. I like an option between city and country. But she's been developing this urge for a bigger studio, and a modern kitchen – and we could only afford all that if we sold one of them.'

'Ah. I see.' He didn't really understand why Jos shouldn't have a bigger studio. If her paintings were changing, growing, perhaps it was time the easel moved from that particular roost after all.

'Did you get the impression she really wants to settle for the country?'

'No.'

'A bigger place in London?'

'It wasn't mentioned.'

Pete got up impatiently and went to look out into the road. 'Of course all this property talk is just a symptom. If we were more convinced of our worth, our work, we'd just be getting on with it.'

Kenneth momentarily distanced what had just been said by concentrating on the back of his friend's head as though he were about to commit it to paper. It was a long skull, with a slightly pointed top, and the thick, cropped hair had a burnish on it and was coloured straw and silver in equal proportions. 'I thought Jos seemed to be . . . ' His words trailed away. He remembered Jos had been stuck.

'She's been working on that car painting for months. Sometimes she just potters around all day avoiding it.'

He no longer prevaricated. 'You mean she's afraid to take the plunge into something new because her critical reputation isn't high enough to be assured of much notice being taken. And she might, by changing, cut herself off from her steady, if modest, commercial success, which no longer satisfies her.'

Pete turned and smiled. 'That's about it. You always did see things clearly.'

'But how about you? Your work plans?'

Pete turned his back again. 'There's a very disturbed-looking man over the road. He's staring at me.'

Kenneth went to stand beside him. He saw an unhealthily

89

pale boy, with neglected hair and clothes, clutching the lamp-post, who, on seeing him, lurched away. 'I'm afraid he looks like a drug addict.'

Very briefly, Pete put his hand on Kenneth's shoulder. Kenneth knew why. Drugs had taken their toll of people they'd known – friends, students, one friend's child.

'Sometimes,' muttered Pete, the level of his voice, which was always slightly uneven, wandering, 'I think: if Sky just comes through without being chained by dope, I'll concede everything else.'

'Yes.'

'But . . . if it were a blameless car accident? Or food poisoning? Perhaps that would be worse. The random negation. Drugs are . . . at least . . . oh – I don't know. Identifiable with today. That she lives today.'

'No.'

'No. I know.'

They went back to their seats and Pete, no less ill at ease, explained his dilemma. He wanted to leave the polytechnic, of that he was sure, and the lump sum of the redundancy money was tempting. He wanted to write his book, and for preference would do so in London with easier access to libraries. And he wanted Jos to be happier than she was, less lethargic. Kenneth asked if he intended to use the lump sum to buy time to write the book.

'I was thinking along those lines. But something else has come up.' The tobacco tin was brought out again. 'That Jos won't like.'

Kenneth raised an eyebrow.

'God, no. It's not a girl. There hasn't been a girl for . . . aeons. It's – something for the future.'

'Go on.'

'A special use for the cottage.'

'That's what Jos won't like?'

Pete nodded. 'It's the peace movement. You know I've been doing peace studies in the art department?'

'Yes. Jos said you wanted it to be an option for the whole Poly.'

'That's right. It became rather like trying to persuade them

90

to keep pig manure in the kitchens. Anyway, I invited Annie and Matthew Hobbold to give a lecture. You've heard of them?'

'Yes.'

'And we've kept in touch. They, plus others, a group, have this plan. This idea ... '

Kenneth listened. He could see that the plan was a beautiful one for Pete; the tenseness vanished from his face and he became eager again.

It involved the setting up of a handful of small, fairly secret centres – discussion cells, really – where people could meet undisturbed to develop peace projects. The project they wanted Pete to be involved in was a future television Peace Channel. And, after visiting him once at the cottage, the Hobbolds had jokingly said it would make an ideal centre. Pete had realised, after they had left, that he would like nothing more on earth than for that to happen.

'I went out for a walk. It was almost midnight, but it was June, and there was a sort of rim of daylight around the horizon.' He paused. 'Only five miles away there's an American camp. Normally you don't notice it except when the fighters rip open the sky. Of course it's a future missile base ... that's partly what attracted the Hobbolds. You know how we're circled by historical places like Little Gidding and Fotheringhay and Aldwincle. They think that visitors – particularly foreigners – would be struck by the juxtaposition.'

'What happened at Aldwincle?'

'Dryden's birthplace. Do you think I'm mad?'

'No. But you think Jos won't like it?'

'She's always set her heart on having the old barn converted into a studio. But the cottage just isn't big enough for a centre without the barn.'

'What would the set up be? I mean, to put it bluntly, would you be paid?'

Pete shrugged. 'It would depend how things went. I wouldn't be out of pocket. Expenses would be met.'

'Would you have to be there most of the time?'

'I think so. One of the things they want are people available who have time to talk on the telephone and write long letters. To make calls abroad and not be rushed by the commitments

91

of a busy office.'

'You'd be writing the scale book?'

'Oh, yes.'

'How do you see Jos fitting in?'

'I daren't really think.'

'Say what *you* would like.'

Pete began to fish for his tobacco tin. 'Well ... I suppose ... and I must emphasize I haven't really thought it out. . . .' He spread the meagre line of tobacco, and Kenneth remembered – sparked off, he supposed, by the pale boy they'd seen through the window – how it used to amuse him, when pot first became fashionable, to watch people rolling joints and to compare their clumsiness with Pete's deftness. 'I suppose I'd like to get dug in there. To get the centre established. Whatever that means exactly. . . . And my book started. And for Jos to come down, and for me to travel up – both regularly – and spend time together properly.'

'What do you think she'd object to most?'

'Losing jurisdiction over the cottage.'

'More than partly losing you, you mean?'

'Mm.'

'Would you like – ideally – her to share in the project? Work with you?'

'Like the Hobbolds? I don't know. I can't really answer that, because we don't. In a way, I'm a loner when I'm working. And her work is painting.' He dragged hard on the cigarette so the paper shrank back rapidly. 'I know one thing though. Sky will approve.'

It's just I have this idea that Pete might make more of a success of a work change if we changed too. My routines, my painting, are an insidious ball and chain. 'Why don't you put it to Jos? After all ... it isn't *too* radical. In terms of your life together, I mean. And if it's what you really want to do. . . .'

'I used to think teaching, education, was the be all and end all. But, well, it hasn't done much for Sky's generation.'

'Peace is no bad cause.' Jos would still be in London. She and Pete wouldn't have separated formally. It seemed quite positive after what Jos had said. Surely a barn was not much to lose?

'What other is there? But I don't feel too confident. And, for once, I want to see ahead clearly. Only I can't.'

You too? Kenneth thought.

He turned into the hospital, dodging a hideous, battered litter
bin that stood directly in his path, and crossed a strip of orna-
mental water in which a verdigrised Henry Moore lay like two
washed-up dinosaur's bones. The lager and pork pie that he
and Pete had shared in a pub had left him slightly drunk and
uncomfortably windy. He pushed through one of the stiff doors
into a large foyer. It reminded him of an airport lounge –
spacious, anonymous, serviced by lifts and escalators, and
peopled by a diverse cast who would rather be elsewhere.

As he went up in a lift, he realized he had no idea what to
expect.

'Mr Gray?' he asked the nurse in the office near the entrance
to the wing. 'May I see Mr Gray?'

She nodded, and when he hesitated said, 'Go right ahead.'

'I don't know where he is.'

'Oh.' She consulted a list. 'It's the single room on the east
side. Go out that door and round, and you'll see it on the right.'

'Thanks. Er ... how is he?'

'Very tired. Poorly. But doing fine.'

'Oh.'

She looked slightly concerned. 'You're related?'

'No. A friend.'

She relaxed. 'He's fine. Doing very well considering. And he's
got a wicked tongue.' She smiled into his eyes.

'Thank you.' His mouth felt dry.

He'd taken a few steps before she called out, 'Don't stay
longer than fifteen minutes.'

The spaces impressed him. The corridor outside the wards
was more like a hall than a passage. It had the air of public
money spent confidently in better times.

He glimpsed Bernard suddenly. It was the colour of the hair
of the patient lying in the bed beyond a half-open door that
alerted him. It was like London snow – snow stained by footsteps
and cars and dog pee. Only in Bernard's case it was mainly
nicotine. He appeared to be asleep.

Feeling absurdly shy, he went to the end of the bed and grasped the painted metal rail on either side of the temperature chart. Bernard's white face-flesh had collapsed; the familiar fatty shape had become lantern.

'Oh dear,' said Kenneth, without meaning to.

'Charming,' came a faint, salivary whisper.

Four seconds later, Kenneth found himself, for the first time, kissing Bernard – moving to the head of the bed, stooping over, and touching his ruckled forehead with his lips.

Bernard's eyes were barely visible behind and between the pleated skin of his lids, but they appeared to see very clearly.

'All this time,' he breathed, 'I've tried to invent a cast-iron seduction formula. Never realized it only needed a coronary.'

As Kenneth perched on the chair beside the bed, Bernard laboriously lifted a hand an inch above the covers and slowly moved it towards him. Kenneth took it in both his own.

'Dear boy,' Bernard whispered. 'I owe you an apology.'

'No.'

'Yes. I should have said ... should have *warned* ... about Fox ... not begun ...'

'Ssh. Don't think about it. *That* doesn't matter.'

Bernard's eyes were quite closed now. 'Live on air, can you? Like a bloody archangel?'

Despite everything, Kenneth found himself laughing, and felt a slight pressure from Bernard's fingers.

'Going to sleep now, dear boy.'

He seemed to be asleep within seconds. Kenneth went on holding his hand until his own began to get pins and needles, then he stood up and tried to arrange Bernard's arm so that he looked comfortable but not too formal. He was very conscious of all the cliché film scenes he had watched in which death was acknowledged by the folding of the new corpse's hands. Surreptitiously, he touched Bernard's wrist and found the pulse; it seemed to beat from very far away.

As soon as he got back, he telephoned William.

'Bernard seems so ... alone.'

'Yes.' There was a deliberate pause. Kenneth knew that

William was carefully selecting which information to pass on, and which not. He had a reputation for being discreet, but not too rigidly circumspect. 'I'm going to see him tomorrow, if he's well enough. To tidy up one or two things. And he asked me to contact his solicitor. Which I have.' Another, briefer, pause. 'I'm glad to say he seems a reasonable man, concerned. As much a friend as anything, I should think.'

'Good. I'll go back on Tuesday then, if you're seeing him tomorrow.'

'Have you made any decisions about going away?'

'No.'

'So you might be open to offers if anything comes up?'

'I suppose so. Yes.'

When he'd rung off, Kenneth reminded himself that William was not likely to have mentioned even the possibility of new work if he had not already something in the offing. Normally he would have felt intrigued, even a little excited. Now he just felt sad. Automatically, he dialled Ronnie's number.

There was no reply. He tried Frances, and a jovial, winey Jim told him Ronnie had left about an hour ago. 'Sorry not to see you, Kenneth. Not the same without you.'

'Thank you.' She should be back by now. He tried her number again, but there was still no answer.

After he had put the receiver back, he did not know what to do. He needed to talk to someone. About Bernard. About Pete and Jos. About what he should do next. Five years ago he would simply have waited for opening time and gone to one of several pubs, taking pot-luck for company. But now he was used to knowing when he would be seeing Ronnie, and to saving things up to tell her. He had come to rely on her.

He looked around the blue room, his self-created castle. And then at the telephone, the drawbridge between their domains whose efficacy he had completely taken for granted. But the illusion of mutual selective sharing was quite broken when Ronnie was missing.

The Fuseli catalogue was lying on top of his reference books, and he took it down. Perhaps he ought to consider him a bit more, Ronnie wouldn't have suggested him thoughtlessly. He picked at the text, allowing his own aversion to be shored up

95

by the histrionic language of one of Fuseli's friends who described him as 'everything in extremes – always an original; his look is lightning, his word a thunderstorm; his jest is death, his revenge, hell.' But finally he fell under the spell of the breadth and energy of Fuseli's own words. His knowledge and inventiveness were astounding. But the images still repelled him, making him want to turn the pages before he had properly investigated them. They were too uncomfortable to contemplate, and sometimes verged on the ludicrous. He had glanced at half the pictures when the muffled sound of the front door slamming made him get up quickly and cross the room. He stood by the door, breath held, listening.

He was sure that the footsteps he could hear going up the stairs were Ronnie's, yet they seemed so slow; normally she half-ran up the several flights and teased him because, at that speed, he got out of breath.

Why don't I just open the door and call her? he thought. Last Sunday, if I'd heard her come in and wanted to talk to her I would have done. But I'm not going to. I'm going to wait a few minutes and then telephone. See if the drawbridge is officially down.

When he dialled, there was still no reply. He felt a little spurt of anger tinged with concern. He was sure she was there. He broke the connection with his finger and immediately dialled again. This time it was picked up the other end after the fourth ring.

He waited for her to say something, but all he could hear was a faint choking sound.

'Ronnie? Ronnie! What's wrong?'

Still no words, just an escaped, hard sob.

'I'll come up. Darling – I'll be straight there.'

Her door was shut and, though he knocked, he also immediately pulled out his keys and found the one to her door.

She was still holding the telephone receiver, standing up, with her face broken by an almost-screaming mouth and two runnels of tears.

He'd separated her from the phone, led her to the sofa, and cradled her against him before he felt a wave of shock. He'd seen her cry before, but never be so devastated, beyond control.

He held her more tightly. 'What has happened, my darling?'

She seemed to make a great effort to suppress her sobs. At last she whispered, 'I've fallen in love.'

And he almost laughed.

'Oh, Kenneth. I'm so sorry.'

He took his arms from around her and stroked her hair back from her face. Her eyes were so swollen with weeping that he imagined her vision, without her glasses, must be very blurred. 'Is it something to be sorry for?'

'I feel so . . . *foolish*.'

'It *is* Alastair Faraday?'

She nodded.

Like a verbally incontinent child, he said, 'Have you been to bed with him?', furious with himself the second the words were out.

Briefly, they made Ronnie's chin come up defensively, and he had a glimpse of the girl he had fallen for.

'I'm sorry. I shouldn't have said that.'

'It is rather like being kicked when you're already down.'

You haven't answered my question, he thought; and couldn't think of anything to say which wasn't a form of reiteration.

'If you've got to know, I was with him until four o'clock this morning. We didn't go to bed. He was supposed to call me at Frances and Jim's. He didn't, and I called him. Someone else answered and said he was out.' The tears had begun again.

'Oh, Ronnie. What can I do?'

'Could you – just be patient?'

'I'll try.' He remembered he was seeing Lydia the next day.

'I think I'll go to bed now. I'm completely exhausted.'

'Would you like me to run you a bath?'

'Oh, Kenneth.' She laid her head on his arm. 'Thank you.'

She 'phoned in the morning, just after he had got up. 'Kenneth. Are you all right?' She sounded quite different. Her voice light and bright, as it was when she was excited or pleased.

'I suppose so.'

'You were so good to me yesterday.'

'Did you sleep?'

'Yes.'

'What are you doing today?' He meant, Are you well enough to go to work?, and realized, in their new situation, it sounded like, What can I expect today? Are you seeing him?

'I'm going to the gallery now. And ... Kenneth?'

'Yes?'

'I don't know if I can ask you this.'

'Try.'

'Could we spend tomorrow evening together?'

'Yes. I'm not doing anything.'

'Thank you. I'll make supper. And try to tell you. To talk about everything.'

'Okay.' He was about to tell her to drop in on her way down, perhaps stay for a coffee, when he understood the import of her words. She did not want to see him *until* tomorrow evening. That was to be their next appointment. It was like watching her turn and see Alastair Faraday in the restaurant. He was excluded.

He walked away from the telephone and stared at the high wall beyond the shrubs. Over the years, dead leaves and grit had silted up the angle between the bricks and the green-stained flagstones. For the first time, the wall made him think of a prison. He wondered what to do until it was time to wait for Lydia.

He forced himself to start to tidy his desk. Suddenly he seized one of the robot ink bottles and hurled it across the room. It broke against the sink unit so that spots of purple and fragments of glass rebounded onto the carpet. He stood there, ludicrously conscious that he was choosing whether to throw another bottle or to clear up the first one. Instead, he went out.

He walked very fast up to Kensington Gardens, but the cold damp day made the empty spaces between the trees seem so lonely he veered back towards the High Street. All the windows were decorated for Christmas, and he wondered whether he would be buying a Christmas present for Ronnie. Whether she would want one. For their first Christmas he had given her an amber haircomb, set with a mother-of-pearl rose. She used to wear it a lot. Before Ronnie, he had mocked the sentimentality of Christmas, of love expressed through gifts. But, with her, that had changed. She had taught him to see small, special gifts as precious between people. But if his whole presence, being, personality – sexuality – could become unnecessary, uncharged, after one dinner party with Alastair Faraday, what could a haircomb possibly represent? Better to give wine and roses, not an immortal object as a yearly gambling stake to mark out the diuturnity of love.

He passed the Underground and turned into a side street to make his way back home. When he came to a junk shop he paused out of habit to look at the 10p items displayed outside. There was a tipsy pile of unmatching small plates – dusty, some chipped – and the rim of one of the lower ones caught his eye: fluted, with an indigo pattern. The sort of china Ronnie sometimes liked. Gently he extracted it; it was pretty, and so was one other. He hesitated over a third, but it did not quite pass that indefinable test that suddenly makes a random object covetable.

'Not bad things.'

'No.'

'You get better things here, stronger, than the new ones they make.' Her voice was Irish.

'Yes.'

'Oh, my word!'

He saw she was looking down at an old milk churn, half-pushed under the table holding the boxes of cheap items.

'I used to scrub out ones twice that size. Every morning. They'd be filled for collection. Taken to the creamery.'

He looked at the tarnished churn, rather wishing it could summon up memories for him.

'But they weren't all good days,' she continued.

'No?'

'When they killed the pigs. Chasing them into the yard. I couldn't take that. Hanging them up to bleed. The blood. I used to take to the hills.'

'Yes.' He looked closely at her fleshy, almost merry, slightly mauve, face. 'It must have been horrible.'

'I can't stand cruelty to animals.'

'No.'

'Came here in 1935. He was a ship's cook. My husband. He was a brute.' She paused. 'A brute.' She lifted her right hand,

99

pantomiming drinking. 'But he loved me.' She sounded puzzled.

'I'm sure he did.' He surprised himself with the surety of his tone.

She smiled.

He tapped the plates he was holding. 'I'll go and settle up for these.'

She shuffled off. He was glad to lose her smell. Yet, in the old cliché, pleased to have met her.

7   He is found by Lydia and shelters Sky

He had forgotten about the ink bottle.

'Shit!'

He put the plates down on the draining board. The newspaper wrapped around them loosened, and he caught a glimpse of the indigo pattern, gleaming under its glaze. The ragged sun of purple ink shone where it had exploded against the sink unit. Shards of glass caught the light among the stained and trampled tufts of the carpet.

'Oh, shit!'

As he suctioned out the fragments with the vacuum cleaner, he remembered his illustration had to be packed and delivered. He ought to have done it first thing. Bugger Ronnie.

Carelessly, he unwrapped the plates. It seemed unlikely she would want them. Had he got to change his behaviour yet again? Revert to being unaccustomed to buying gifts?

He went to deal with the illustration. As he flattened it in a mount, he turned his hand and stroked his little finger softly down the outline of the woman's nose. Lydia's nose and Pete's blot. *There hasn't been a girl for . . . aeons.* He went to 'phone for a bike messenger to take the package away.

Lydia arrived at two exactly. She stopped at the threshold of his room so that he could not close the door, and stared inside. At first he took the opportunity just to watch her – he'd remembered the nose exactly right. When suddenly she turned, she looked afraid.

'Please come in.'

She stalked the perimeter of the room as though expecting to find hidden cameras or bugging devices. When she reached his workspace she did not look down at his things but through the window to the high wall. 'What's on the other side?'

'The road. The one that runs down the side of the house.'

'Can you go out there?'

'Only if I climb through the window. There's a door at the back of the house. But no one uses it now. That's why it's all so neglected.'

She came back to the middle of the room. 'Don't you mind that people can see in from the street?'

He remembered that the curtains in her room had been closed in the middle of the day.

'No. But I can shut them out. Look.' He pulled down the green blind and watched her smile.

'That's nice.'

They sat apart in the greenish light, she in a chair, he on the sofa.

'I'm sorry if I barged in on Saturday,' he said.

'It was a surprise.' Then she added, 'It was a lovely surprise.' She looked confused.

'Your father must think me a highly suspicious character.'

'No. Well . . .'

'It was such a coincidence that I should have bumped into him the day before.'

'Why were you there?'

'It's rather a long story.'

She nodded, as though assuming he would not tell it.

He felt challenged to try. 'Not such a long one in outline. Let's see . . . I'd been lunching with two people in Covent Garden and I left them very abruptly. I jumped on a bus in the Strand, and sat on it till I reached the Greyhound. Then I walked back and noticed Lysia Street and knew you were somewhere at the end of it.'

'You came to see me?'

'Your whereabouts. When I realised you were nearby.'

102

'You said on Saturday that you'd come to see if Rosewharf Close existed.'

'Well, I didn't find it on Friday. Didn't in fact look for it.'

'How did you know it was near Lysia Street? If it's not in the A to Z.'

'A friend had told me. He knows the new estate. You see, I thought you'd given me a false address. To give me the brush off.'

'You didn't!' She sounded shocked.

'It was a possibility.'

She shook her head. 'No.'

'Why?'

She would not look at him. 'I can't say.'

He moved along the sofa and leant forward to touch her hand. 'Why not?'

At the touch, her hand started to quiver.

'Why not, Lydia?'

'Don't make me say it.'

'All right, then.' He took his hand away.

Then she raised her head and looked directly into his eyes. 'Because when I saw you, the first time, I just thought you were beautiful.' She turned away, and he watched the blood slowly colour her neck.

He was stunned. His sharp feelings – those of anger and upset with Ronnie, his defiant quest towards Lydia – were obsolete. He had been suddenly placed on a strange pedestal, embarrassed and powerless.

She got up and jerked her donkey jacket off the back of the chair. 'I'll go. I should never have come.'

He stood up too, and put his hands on her shoulders. 'Lydia.'

'What?'

'Lydia.' His tongue seemed to curl around the name.

She bowed her head.

'What do you want me to do?'

He would not interrupt the long silence that followed before she whispered, 'Touch me.'

'I am touching you.'

'*Me*.' Her voice was suddenly loud. She lifted one of his hands off her shoulder and guided it to her waist, under the welt of her jumper. As his fingers touched her skin she gave a slight, involuntary, gasp.

He slid his other hand down her arm, took the jacket that dangled from her fingers and dropped it on the floor, then reached up under her jersey to run his palm slowly against her spine. He felt her sway against him, and saw that her eyes were closed. He kissed her, and her mouth opened, wide and moist. Her passion and stillness immobilized him.

She drew away just a second before he would have felt bound to develop the kiss, to probe and cling, to emulate the predator.

Her eyes were open now, alarmed. 'I . . .' She shook her head.

He waited for a few seconds, then smiled. 'What?'

When she still did not say anything, but stood stiffly, like a wax figure temporarily parked in the wrong setting, he went to the sofa, saying, 'Come and sit with me.'

At first he thought she was going to ignore his remark, but then she came and sat neither very close nor deliberately far away, drawing up her legs and twisting to face him.

'Aren't you going to say anything about my story?' he asked.

'I liked it.'

'Can't you tell me why?'

'Because it made me realise that things were just as complicated then. That it's not just people now. Creative people now. Their muddles.'

She was looking away. He wondered what particular muddles she was thinking about.

'When I'm in museums,' she went on, 'I forget that. With all the marble, and the gilt. Like altars.'

'I suppose altars imply sacrifices. Pain.'

'Yes.' She sighed.

'Thank you for reading it. Were you pleased I brought the son in?'

'He couldn't have been left out.'

'Well . . . I might not have chosen to decide so definitely that he actually existed. You influenced me there.'

'How?'

'I thought you might be cross if I left him out. So that made me imagine him – the circumstances.'

'And you wouldn't have done that without me?'

104

'No. I'm pretty sure I wouldn't.'

'What a strange way to make a child.'

'Yes.' He was disconcerted by this faint hint at his procreative capability.

'Though no weirder than some real ones, I suppose.'

'Is Arthur your only child?' He asked partly because with some women private life had to be explained before anything could begin, and partly because he was curious.

'Oh yes.'

'How old is he?'

'Twelve.'

'You must have been young.'

'Seventeen.'

He tried not to invent a scenario in the silence that followed. He almost leant to touch her again, but decided to talk instead. 'I thought I might –' He stopped. Why was he lying? There was no need. 'Someone suggested I should do more stories. About other painters.'

'Will you?'

'I might.'

'Did they read this one?'

'No. Not yet.'

'Did you tell ... them, how it came about?'

'Sort of.'

He thought she suddenly looked dejected. 'I said I'd met someone who didn't know about Wilson, and this was a way of telling.'

'You didn't say it was me.' It was a statement, not a question.

'No.'

'It was your woman.'

He choked back a defensive reply. The choice of the word 'woman' sounded crude in her light voice. 'Yes.'

'I knew you had to have one.'

'It may not be for much longer.' His reply surprised him. Then he understood from her quelled smile as she looked down into her lap that she thought he meant because of her; but as he made the statement, his mind had flashed up a glimpse of Alastair Faraday.

'Does she live here?' She glanced around the room.

'No.' He waited.

She gave a little sigh, and then just stared at him, the expression in her eyes making him certain that she wanted him with unshakeable intent. But not just for an afternoon, he thought. If he were to make love to her now, it would, as far as she was concerned, be like the preliminary casting-off before leaving harbour on a world voyage.

He moved close to her, held her against him, kissed her, ran his hand under her sweater to her small breasts, and stayed very still.

At first her body felt tense, as though she scarcely dared to breathe; then gradually she relaxed, and finally, after he had tried to imagine how he could possibly envisage a life with her, how he could even contemplate losing Ronnie, he thought she had fallen asleep. Her eyes were closed, and her fingers were no longer clenched.

'Are you asleep?' he whispered.

She shook her head faintly against his chest. 'No. But I don't want to wake up.'

He kissed her hair. 'What shall we do?'

'Whatever you want. But I must be home by five.'

'Supposing I want to ... oh, I don't know ... say, take you to *Gone With The Wind*?' The second part of her remark had relieved him. Her tone indicated that love affairs did not allow her to abdicate responsibility for everything else. In the past, he had met women who unquestioningly neglected jobs and children – and above all husbands – while they eagerly pursued a lover. The illogical nature of such affairs – total time and passion one week and complete rejection the next as they climbed back into the fold promising to observe the rules – irritated him.

'As long as there's time to see the bit where she tears down the velvet curtains and turns them into a dress, *I'll* be all right.'

'How about me? Suppose I can't bear to miss a word of the final credits?'

'Can't you?'

'It depends.'

'I walk out of movies I don't like. But Arthur won't. Even if he's bored stiff.'

He remembered being like that, particularly when he was in

the sixth form and they went to foreign films in which women walked endlessly along empty roads at dusk. 'You enjoy costume-making?'

'Yes.'

'Was that why you were in the British Museum?'

'Yes.'

'But you said you didn't design.'

'Well ... I adapt. And add bits.'

'Does the postcard you bought connect with something you're doing now?'

'I thought it might. But it didn't in the end.'

'But you put it in the middle of your board.'

'Yes.' She put her hand over his hand, and pressed it into her breast. For the first time he wanted unreservedly to make love to her. They both turned to kiss, gasping and probing.

She almost groaned when they separated for air.

'Lydia –' He plunged his tongue into her mouth, their teeth chipped sharply together, and he had the sensation of an unknown kind of desire smarting in his chest.

When the kiss ended, they drew right apart. He stood up, walking away from her to the sink. 'I'll make some coffee.'

The noises of spoons and water and heating kettle hung between them. He could not decide which mug to give her and allowed the choosing to fill his mind. He assumed he would have to find the words to break the silence.

'Which painter will you write about next?'

'I don't know. But I'd like to do Bonington some time.'

'Why?'

'Well, he died young for a start. I hadn't realised till I came to pursue Wilson through the decades what a bonus a short life can be. But mainly because of his visit to Venice.'

'What happened?'

'Nothing, really. He was there for about ten days, it rained nearly all the time, and he painted. Solidly.'

'I'd love to go to Venice.'

'Would you like to see some pictures?'

'Please.'

They sat side by side while he turned the pages of a large book of reproductions of paintings of Venice. He talked about the districts he loved best, trying to take Lydia beyond the famous façades to a few of the city's thousand secret pockets. 'I ate a pistachio icecream on those steps,' he said, pointing out the distant spot in a sun-drenched Guardi. 'It was May, and the wistaria was in bloom.'

At half past four she went away, and he watched her from the doorstep walking slowly along the pavement beside the cars that waited at the traffic lights, not at all like the time she had hurried away from the Bury Street gallery with her shoulders squared. She had not, he suddenly realised, returned his story.

The street lamps were lit, and when he got back indoors he released the blind and through a gap in the traffic, which was creeping forwards now, he caught a brief glimpse of the pale boy with neglected hair. Again, he seemed to be staring at his window, but as soon as the blind went up he turned away and was hidden by a bus slowing down at its stop.

Almost unconsciously, Kenneth began to prepare to go out. He washed up the mugs, washed his face, changed his shoes, and was pondering whether to put on a sweater under his jacket, when he checked himself. Why was he going out? Where was he going? Weren't there things he should be doing here? After all, he hadn't done any work that day. Unenthusiastically, he supplied answers to his questions. He was going out because he wasn't seeing Ronnie until tomorrow, and Lydia had unsettled him. Presumably he was going to a pub. And, since he hadn't done any work, there were certainly things he should be doing: a drawing for a Cotswolds hotel brochure, preliminary suggestions for a 1983 wild-life calendar, reading from a pile of art magazines and newspaper articles that he had kept for 'when he had time'. Then he noticed *The World in the Evening*. With a slight feeling of triumph and relief, he decided to return it to Pete. He didn't want to read any more of it, and since Pete had come to seek his advice perhaps he'd be glad to see him again – it might indicate that he was concerned. Which was deceitful, because it was his own need that was prompting him to go.

As he crossed Alderney Street, he saw that Jos and Pete's curtains were drawn back, and that they were standing facing one another on either side of the sofa. When he reached the pavement and peered down into the room, he heard Jos's raised voice, and could see from their faces that they were quarrelling.

For a few seconds he again felt the terror that Jos had aroused when she had mentioned separation to him. He gripped the railings with both hands and willed Jos and Pete to stop. The windows were shut, and the ticking engine of a waiting taxi prevented him from hearing their actual words. When he saw Jos jerk up her empty glass as though she were about to throw it, he bowed his head.

'Oh, for Christ's sake, not again.' The female voice, with a pronounced London accent, was resigned rather than irritated.

He turned to the girl who had arrived silently behind him, and found that he had to look up. What he mainly noticed was her thick hair, which lay in tawny skeins on the shoulders of her jeans jacket.

'Hullo, Kenneth,' she said.

'Why . . . Sky. I'm sorry. For a second I didn't –'

'It's all right. I've grown again. Three more inches this year.'

'Good heavens! But you've not changed otherwise.'

'I suppose not. How long have you been here?'

'Oh – only a few seconds. I . . .' He could not think how to continue.

'Are you expected?'

'No. I just came on the off-chance. To return a book.' He tapped the pocket containing it, feeling slightly foolish at this gesture which seemed to demonstrate a need to prove he was telling the truth.

'I'm supposed to have been coming round in time for supper. But I'm not going in if they're rowing.'

Kenneth glanced back into the room. Tears, smeared hastily away, made Jos's cheeks shine. Pete looked trapped and angry. 'But – if they're expecting you . . .' he said lamely.

'Would you want to eat with them in that state?'

'Not really.'

As they walked away, he supposed he ought to feel some responsibility for her. Difficult though he found it to believe as she strode beside him, she was surely vulnerable: sixteen years old and privy to her parents' dissension. 'Where are you staying?' he asked.

'I thought I'd be staying there. Till Friday. My boyfriend's mother's up.'

'Oh.'

'I hate the pretence. But it's just easier to clear out when she visits. She's so terrified I'll want to marry him, and just as terrified people will think he's immoral if he doesn't.'

'Surely ... these days?'

'I know. But she comes from the Rhondda. Still – look on the bright side. She'll clean the flat from top to bottom. And it's got really grotty.'

'What's your boyfriend's name?'

'Mal. Short for Malcolm. Put us together and we're Malsky. Like the head of the KGB or something.'

'A brand of vodka perhaps?'

'Oh, great. I like that. I'll tell Mal.'

'He's an economics student, isn't he?'

'Did Mum tell you about him?'

'Not really. Only that. Oh – and that he likes cathedrals.'

'Right. He's really good at the history bit. And I'm bad. So he teaches me.'

'How's the restoration work going?'

She jerked her hair back to look at him, as though trying to anticipate his reaction. 'It isn't. I walked out.'

'Ah. Do Jos and Pete know?'

'I was going to tell them tonight.'

Now he felt even more responsible. A pub ahead proffered respite. 'Why don't we go in there and have a drink? Perhaps we could go back to Alderney Street in a while.'

She slowed down and an obstinate expression settled on her face.

'Would you like a drink?' he asked.

'Yes. But I'm not going back home.'

'Okay.'

The pub was unashamedly cosy. They sat in a corner, under orange candle-lamps, away from the friendly banter between familiars at the bar. Sky took two large and noisy gulps from her lager and lime, reminding Kenneth of a time when she was

110

small and he had taken her to have a milk-shake. She'd had a
rim of foam on her upper lip then as well.

'What went wrong with the furniture restorer?'

'Oh – he said I'd been rude to his secretary.'

'Were you learning anything?'

'Yes. I've learned masses. That was the point. It's been going
really well. And he'd given me a proper job to do.'

'How do you mean?'

'Well, something a client had brought in. Rather than working
on stuff he'd picked up cheap.'

'What was it?'

'Oh – mending a broken stretcher on a Queen Anne chair.
And I told Fiona – that's his secretary – how much time I'd
taken. So she could calculate the bill. And we got talking. And
I found out she earns four times as much as me. *Four times*. So
I said typing couldn't possibly be four times as difficult as
carpentry. I mean, look at all the nitwits who type. Well, I didn't
say *that* to her.'

'So what happened?'

'Well, she didn't seem to mind. And I went back to the
workshop, and about two hours later he came through and said
I'd been rude and ought to apologise. That Fiona was fully
trained with two years' experience, and in the past workshop
assistants didn't get paid at all. I felt *exactly* like I used to feel
at school. So I walked out. I mean – what's the point?'

'Which point?'

'Well, if working, even if it's something you want to do, is
going to be just as rotten as school in the end, there must be
something wrong with it.'

He might have tried to talk about compromise, but he was
anxious not to antagonise her.

'Can I stay the night at your place?' she said.

'Of course not.' He watched her expression of stubbornness
intensify. 'I mean . . .'

'Mean what?'

'Well, I've only got one room. You remember that.'

'But it's *huge*. Oh – is Ronnie there?'

'No.' He felt cornered. 'Couldn't we both go and check out
Alderney Street again?'

111

'I'm not going to.'

He reminded himself that she must have other friends.

'I won't interrupt you or anything. If I can have the sofa, I'll read and sleep and be perfectly quiet.'

He felt awkward about mentioning the propriety of the arrangement, which was uppermost in his mind, and his next question was therefore unconsidered. 'How about supper?'

'Oh, we'll have a takeaway. I like Indian best. How about you?'

So half an hour later they both presented themselves at the Golden Lotus where Rafi, his expression bland, listened to the long list of things Sky liked best. Kenneth had assumed they would eat in the restaurant, but she insisted that taking things out was more fun because then it was like a picnic. Rafi, who only did this service for special customers, responded to her enthusiasm and they left with two carrier bags loaded with cartons and dishes and foil-wrapped chapatis.

Once indoors, Sky laid everything out, found the cutlery drawer, filled a jug with water and ice cubes, and turned on the little television set. 'We're just in time for *Coronation Street*,' she said contentedly.

It was the only occasion Kenneth had ever seen the programme. During the commercial break, Sky chattered about the characters as if they were her neighbours. 'I think Ken's much too wet for Deirdre. But perhaps she'll have another baby, and then decide to have a career, and he'll become a house husband. He's a druid, you know.'

'Who is?'

'Ken Barlow. In real life, I mean.'

'Ah.' He decided not to say 'Who's Ken Barlow?' because he sensed she had about fourteen years' experience to encapsulate into her answer. He didn't know whether to be irritated or impressed that she could recreate her preferred lifestyle in his home in about sixty seconds flat.

'That was really great,' she said, when she'd cleaned the last smear of gravy with the final piece of the last chapati. 'Mum and Dad never let me watch telly when we eat together. But you're like Mal and me. Have it all in the same place.'

He did not know what to say. It was absurdly comforting to

be included as an honorary member of the younger generation, even if it was under false pretences, but what the hell were they going to do for the rest of the evening? Surely he could ring Pete and Jos and get things back to normal?

'You've got a bathroom, haven't you?'

'Yes. Across the hall.'

'Would you mind if I have a bath? I'll clear this up first. Then you can work or whatever.'

'Okay.' Perhaps he could 'phone while she was out of the room.

He got as far as dialling their number, but then he quickly put the receiver down. It would be so awkward to explain, and Pete would be embarrassed, and insist on driving round to fetch Sky, and then she'd probably run off.

He went over to his work table and started the hotel sketch. He was doing it from photographs, a method he disapproved of, but neither he nor the hotel was predisposed to finance a conscience trip so that he could sit for a day drawing *en plein air*.

The problem was to make the mellow stone building look somehow more appealing than the thousands of other mellow stone buildings turned into hotels around the British Isles. One photograph showed a lilac bush in bloom. He decided to include that, repositioning it slightly, and giving it an unrealistic formality. It would, he thought, be the first lilac bush to have structure; normally they were like a shapeless woman wearing frowsty undergarments. Re-inventing lilac amused him, and so the drawing of the building was accomplished quickly. With surprise, he realized he had finished. He looked at his watch: nearly ten. That was an economical way to earn a hundred pounds. But what the hell had happened to Sky?

She came back ten minutes later, wearing her long shirt and pants and socks, but without her jeans. The ends of her hair were wet. 'Fabulous,' she said. 'You've got so many magazines in your bathroom, and the hot water just goes on and on. Have you been working?'

'Yes.'

'Good. What would you normally do now?'

'I'm not sure I have a normally.'

'If I wasn't here.'

'Mm – have a drink, read a bit perhaps, watch *Newsnight*, go to bed.'

'Fine. I won't have a drink, I've cleaned my teeth. You don't mind, do you? Since you've got *three* toothbrushes, I didn't think you'd mind sharing one. I rinsed it properly. And I never watch news programmes. So why don't you have the telly by your bed, and I'll kip down on the sofa. I'm pretty sleepy.'

'Okay.' His amenable tone quite surprised him.

'Have you got a blanket?'

'Yes.' He found the Mexican blanket he'd bought in America with Aline, and which they'd lain under on sand dunes beneath stars. He also searched for his only pair of pyjamas. They were split at one elbow, the white stripes were grey, and the blue ones dull; the cord was limp and unravelling. He went to the bathroom to wash and put them on. When he came out, he stood for a moment in the hall, his clothes over his arm, and looked up the stairwell. 'Oh, Ronnie,' he whispered, 'what on earth is happening?'

Sky was wrapped like a giant papoose in the blanket. Her eyes were already closed. 'Goodnight,' she said, her voice heavy with sleepiness.

'Goodnight.'

'You must watch the telly. It won't keep me awake.'

He did as he was bid.

8 | He is invaded

After Sky had left, intending to go to the L.S.E. and talk to Mal, Kenneth started to brood on his second story. When he had watched her go, he tried to guess what her life might become, and had found himself disapproving her behaviour to the furniture restorer. It made him feel middle-aged, no longer to be automatically on the side of the rebellious apprentice. And then the use of that old-fashioned word 'apprentice' in his thoughts reminded him of Tom Girtin: how he was put in Bridewell prison by the unstable painter Edward Dayes for refusing to complete his indentures.

He went to his books to see what other information he could turn up, and when he read the story of Girtin refusing to accompany Lord Elgin to Constantinople to paint Grecian remains after he discovered he would be paid less than the valet de chambre (and would be expected to assist Lady Elgin with her decorative firescreens and tabletops), he decided to write a Girtin story for Sky. He'd probably never show it to her but, as he tried to imagine Girtin's feelings during the hours spent waiting while negotiations took place to attempt to persuade Lord Elgin to increase his offer of thirty pounds a year, he remembered the blunt impatience in her voice when she'd said, 'I mean, look at all the nitwits who type.' The more he read, the happier he became. Girtin was generous, careless and beloved, and, like Bonington, died young. After his death, Dayes had tried to insinuate that he had destroyed his health through dissipation, and 'the fatal effects of allowing passion to over-power reason'. When Kenneth learned that Dayes had com-mitted suicide two years later, he was briefly amused.

He looked through his picture postcards to see if he had a Girtin, and found a cool painting of hills, the shadowed half prussian blue, and the sunlit half limey white. It was both gloomy and serene, a natural sepulchre. Turning it over and seeing the familiar British Museum imprint, he impulsively wrote a message to Lydia: 'He's pushed in front of Bonington. Died young too. No mystery about his son: became a surgeon and diligently collected his father's paintings. K.' He posted the card at midday, on his way to visit Bernard.

'I'm afraid he's not so good today,' said a different nurse. 'You'll probably find him sleeping. Don't expect too much if he does wake up.'

Nervously, Kenneth went to Bernard's bed. He was asleep, lying in a raised position against the broad hospital pillows. His breathing seemed very shallow, and the flesh on his face was folded like tripe. Kenneth felt as though Bernard himself, the Bernard he knew, was absent – back at his house perhaps, pottering in the kitchen where he let the washing-up accumulate until he'd run out of cups and teaspoons, and where a honey-suckle had tendrilled its way through the loose-fitting pantry window. This time he did not attempt to touch him. He stood for perhaps two minutes, deliberately did not whisper 'Good-bye', and went back to the nurse.

'Could you just let him know Kenneth called? You know – if he's well enough to be bothered with messages.'

'Of course I will.'

He telephoned William when he got home, needing to share his unease. 'Bernard was just sleeping. He seemed miles away.'

'He was very weak yesterday. Though we did have a talk.'

'It feels so odd. Having no experience of the borderland – between life and death. You don't know how far people have gone. Whether they partly choose, or if the whole process is involuntary.'

'Mm.'

116

'I'm so hopelessly ignorant about illness and death.'

'Bernard would be amused that you should start to practise with him.'

'Yes.' It was difficult for him to joke.

'Anyway – I'm glad you've rung. I wanted to speak to you.'

'Oh?'

'You know Ted Wing?'

'I know his work. Or the bits they've serialized in the Sundays.'

'His publishers are keen for him to do an illustrated book next. With original pictures. Some colour.'

'And?'

'He wasn't very thrilled to start with. He's planning to travel all around Indonesia for his next major book. But for various reasons he can't go for a couple of years.'

'Great life, being a successful travel writer. Nepal one year. Indonesia another.' He was beginning to feel excited, as he always did when William started to intimate the possibility of a commission.

'He doesn't like people to say that.'

'No. It won't all be roses. Well, then. Am I to deduce you're anxious to keep it in the agency stable and try putting my name forward?'

'Oh, I've already done that.'

Kenneth laughed. 'What's it to be then? London's river, or England's unknown villages?'

'Venice,' said William triumphantly.

Kenneth was silent. Then he said quietly, 'They'll never select me.'

'They already have. Ted Wing's daughter loves Fox.'

'Oh – God. What a mad world.'

'He's promised to do a text by Easter. Fairly short. And they'd like the pictures by the end of June if possible. The proposed terms are . . .'

From habit, Kenneth reached for a pencil and jotted down the details William gave him. But he didn't really take them in. Next year had suddenly acquired an outline, and the greatest challenge of his life shone at its centre.

That afternoon he selected another picture postcard for Lydia – the façade of the Ca d'Oro photographed from the

117

opposite side of the Grand Canal through one of the arches of the fish market. 'The gods were eavesdropping,' he wrote. 'I'm about to be commissioned to draw Venice in wistaria time. How about some Bonington research as well? K.' He looked at the last sentence. Did he really intend it as a veiled suggestion she might join him? The thought of Lydia in Venice was intriguing. He went out to the post-box singing.

His euphoria did not last. He began to wonder whether he should visit Bernard again next morning. All those hours alone must increase his capacity for sleep, and somehow it did not seem right to sleep away what might be his last days of life. Mainly, though, he realized how full of apprehension he was about the evening ahead with Ronnie. He didn't want to talk about her being in love with Alastair Faraday. But he wanted to tell her about Venice, and perhaps to share her bed. If only that could be simple. One of those nights when sex was so agreeable, so completely theirs; when it was mutually felt to have erased all the rough edges from their separate days.

Ronnie appeared quietly, at the door he had left ajar, at six. He felt almost shy as he went to greet her. Their kiss did not happen with complete simultaneity, and her now familiar new scent immediately darkened his dreads.

'Seven thirty be okay?' she said. 'I think I'll take a shower before I prepare supper.'

'Of course. Can I help?'

'No. But have you any black peppercorns? I only just remembered I'm almost out.'

She was talking with the brittle, slightly hepped-up voice she used to clients on the 'phone. 'Yes. I'm pretty sure I have.'

She walked into the room while he looked in a cupboard, and when he turned round she had the faded blue Isherwood novel in her hands.

'Why are you reading this?' she asked, her voice no longer light.

'Oh –' He felt caught out; foolish, and therefore angry. 'Idle curiosity. I saw it on Pete's shelves when I was round the other day.'

'I see.'

He gave her the peppercorns. 'It's not a crime, is it?'

118

She shook her head, put the book down, and left the room, saying, 'We'll talk,' as she closed the door.

He looked at the elderly book with distaste. If only Pete and Jos hadn't been quarrelling... As he went to pour himself a drink, he knew he should wait for a while: he could get through quite a lot in an hour and a half.

It was a matter of opinion whether the wine made him less sensitive to the fact that Ronnie's first remark of any substance after he arrived at her flat was obviously aimed to clear the air rather than to provoke.

'You've seen Jos and Pete since the night we had dinner at Rafi's?' She was speaking lightly again, but with gentleness.

He took too large a mouthful of the Beaujolais she had poured. He could tell her that Pete had been round ... that he'd watched both of them through their basement window ... that Sky ... He didn't want to begin to explain. 'Not round at their place,' he said, shaking his head.

'Oh – sorry. I thought ... The book.'

'Ah. Well, if it's important, I borrowed that the day I had lunch with Jos. That I told you about.'

She frowned slightly. 'Oh ... I ... Before we went to Joe Allen's?'

'Of course.'

'How strange.'

'I don't see why.'

'Well ... we hadn't said anything. About Alastair.'

He longed to lie, as a child longs to lie; to say, 'It's got nothing to do with Alastair Faraday. I just borrowed something to read.' Instead, he said, 'One's allowed to be curious. When famous faces stalk the stairs.'

'Yes.'

It was worse than he'd imagined it would be. They were on the verge of a quarrel before they'd started to talk at all. 'I hope you're not doing anything elaborate. I'm not very hungry.'

'A simple risotto and salad. You can eat as little as you like.' She sat very upright. 'Kenneth. Please try to help me straighten things out.'

He filled his glass. 'All right.'

'I want to be honest. Obviously being attracted to Alastair

like this has confused me. But you and I did have that talk. About going to the States. And I felt we weren't really getting anywhere. Then . . . you told me about Bernard. How is he?'

'Extremely ill.'

'I'm sorry. I really am. And – what difference does this make to your work schedule?'

'Every difference. He's not started the next Fox.'

'Is it too soon to know if he'll be able to work again?'

'He doesn't look as if he will.' He realized he wasn't going to tell her about Venice right away. Yet, when he'd been drinking on his own downstairs, he had planned to tell her with pride. To show her it didn't matter giving up being a critic. That better things turned up.

'I've been talking to Frances about everything. I must let you know that.'

He gave an impatient sigh, hating the thought of all those words, partially concerning him, being bandied back and forth.

'She won't discuss it with anyone else. And I've also been talking to Serena about prospects in the States. She's very shrewd. And supportive too.'

Not of anything involving me, he thought. 'So what have you decided?'

'I haven't made a decision. I need to talk to you.'

'Well – what do *you* want to do?'

'I'd like to talk about the plan I outlined the other night. About going over for two months. Only with a bolder plan in mind.'

'What's that?'

'To explore the idea of opening a gallery on the West Coast.'

'You mean you're going back.'

'Oh, Kenneth – please. You haven't begun to hear anything yet.'

'You can hardly run a gallery in L.A. from South Kensington or Covent Garden.'

'Were you drinking before you came up?'

'What on earth does that mean?'

'That I need to know if you can't talk yet because you're too angry or alienated, or because alcohol has brought your feelings briefly to a head.'

120

He burst out laughing. 'So my whole life's suddenly reduced to whether I've got a short-fuse alcoholic boil, or chronic jealousy.' He waited for her to say something, but she sat looking down at her lap. 'What does Alastair Faraday have to say about the matter?'

'I haven't discussed my plans with him at all.'

'But you've seen him again?'

'Yes. I have.'

He suddenly felt quite sober and rather desperate. 'Tell me what you wanted to say.'

'Please listen.'

'Yes.'

'The two months is a test. To find out how I feel about working and competing in the States. It's a challenge to me. I don't feel I've pulled up my professional roots there completely. I love working in London, but it isn't everything. We'd keep the gallery here, and Frances would be in charge. But the two galleries would be in partnership and would complement one another. There'd be a lot of interchange and I would visit London regularly. I would have to have another partner helping me in the States, and Frances would need some advisory back-up here. We both thought of you.'

He managed not to say, 'What, me watch over Frances, whose judgement you've never quite trusted, while you sip vodka sodas with Alastair Faraday in L.A.?' He said, 'And?'

'So – and this is only a suggestion, one idea – it might make sense for both of us to go for these two months, get the lie of the land, and then at the end we could make up our minds, individually, whether we thought the two gallery idea was on, and, if so, what involvement, if any, you could consider.'

'Have you spoken to your father?'

'I made a 'phone call. Yes.'

How different life was, he thought, when you had access to real money.

'But you're avoiding the central issue,' he said.

'What's that?'

'Oh, come on, Ronnie. Stop playing games.'

'I am *not* playing games.'

'Charades, perhaps. We have a private relationship, in case

121

you'd forgotten. Get asked out as a couple. Share our nights.'

'Kenneth, I don't need to be told that.'

'Well, are you trying to tell me that Alastair Faraday is over? That we forget it's ever happened, and go to the States?'

'No.'

'It isn't over?'

'No.'

'So what are you telling me? That I can fit in when Faraday's not around?'

She stood up. 'I've never hinted at anything like that. I've been closer to you than I've ever been to anyone. I didn't ask for Alastair to come along. But I won't lie. Won't deny.'

'So on what terms am I expected to come to the States?'

'Closest friend. Partner.'

'But you still see Faraday?'

'I . . . think so.'

'And am I expected to be your lover under these circumstances?'

She turned away. 'I've never slept with two men at the same time. Never wanted . . .'

'And you slept with him yesterday.' It was a statement rather than a question, and she gave no reply. He drained his glass. 'So that's it, is it? For me?' He could see she was starting to cry. 'Oh, for God's sake, Ronnie. You can't be opening a chain of galleries one second and bursting into tears the next.'

'Why can't you help me?' she whispered, getting up and walking away to the kitchen.

He followed her shortly. 'There's not much point in cooking, is there?'

She was just standing by the sink, weeping. 'No.'

'Come on. Come and sit down.' He took her to the sofa and held her. 'You've fallen in love. You're not mine any more. Not tuned to the same pitch. I can't trail around America after you just to make you feel safe professionally – and socially when Faraday's not around.' He realised that she would go and, when she'd gone, everything would lose value.

He sat at his work table, rigid with temper, a bottle of wine in front of him. Upstairs Ronnie would be putting the uneaten meal away, and somewhere Alastair Faraday would no doubt be having an evening out, completely unaware of the unhappiness he was causing. To him, Ronnie would be just an interlude while he waited for Hollywood's mills to grind.

It was a brave idea, the new gallery; why hadn't she had it before, when things had been going along as usual, and their days and weeks had a consistent shape and feel? Before Faraday, and while he was still writing about paintings rather than painters. He pulled out her Fuseli catalogue, and looked again at the histrionic pictures. Perhaps if he were to do a story after all, for Ronnie, things would come right. A present that was really from him, rather than second-hand plates off a pavement stand. Lydia need go no further.

If Ronnie carried out her plan without him entirely, what would happen to him? The glee over Venice had ebbed. He had imagined Lydia there; but he had not thought of the upstairs flat without Ronnie. Though he *had* emptied his mind of her for a brief while – almost as if he'd been practising?

Girtin made him feel puny and pusillanimous. Going to Paris for his health when his wife was eight months pregnant, and spending six cold months drawing inside closed carriages. Five months after his return he was dead of either asthma or consumption. Twenty-seven years old. It seemed appallingly young. Before Paris, he'd exhausted himself painting a circular panorama of London, nine feet high and two hundred feet around. Standing on a rooftop in Southwark, next to the Albion flour mills, he had caparisoned the sky and tall buildings with the veils and trails of smoke that gave London its atmosphere and subtle colour, and which so damaged his own chance to live. Kenneth tried to imagine executing a work on such a scale, and failed. Vertiginously high, with pinnacles and tiled slopes massed below, and the slow grey Thames cluttered with ships dividing man's shelters and shrines, where would one begin? Across the river, the comfortable majesty of St Paul's coloured peony and silver by the September sunset – would you leave it until last, or devour it first with your brush, our greatest, favourite house of praise? Girtin must have had such discipline of eye, intensity of will, and stamina of limb. A marathon painter standing in wind

123

and stillness, smoke and sunlight, rain and dust, and called by Turner 'honest Tom'.

No one would ever give *him* the epitaph 'honest'. Yet any deviousness he had was unspectacular: narrow, spidery cracks, like the ones in the paint on his ceiling.

The doorbell, a ratchety buzz in the box above his door, sounded briefly. 'Lydia' was the name that came to his mind, and he went enthusiastically to the hall. When he pulled back the heavy front door, the tall mass was obviously not Lydia.

'Kenneth?'

'Sky?'

'Can I stay?'

'Oh, no,' he thought. It had never occurred to him that she would seek his help again. 'I don't think so. But – come in, if you'd like to tell me what's been happening.'

'You've got someone with you?'

'No.' As he said it, he realized she would have swerved off if he'd said 'Yes', and mainly wished that he had.

'That's okay then.' She moved forward to come in.

This time she did not look at ease in his room. She perched on the edge of the settee and did not take off her jacket. He guessed she knew she was pushing her luck.

'I've had a row with Mal.'

'I see. I'm sorry. Would you like some coffee? And tell me about it?'

She heaved a sigh and hunched further back into the seat. 'I'll do the same for you one day. I *promise*.'

In the end they didn't talk about Mal much. That part was fairly straightforward. He'd told Sky, when they met at the L.S.E., that he'd forewarn his mother she would be there for the night, but he'd chickened out and had failed to do so. Sky had arrived at the flat to be given a Rhondda-style Methodist lecture and had stormed out. She'd gone straight to Alderney Street, to find Jos on her own, weeping in her studio.

'Was she worried about you not turning up last night?'

'No. She never mentioned it. It's Dad. He wants to use the cottage for a Peace Studies retreat, and she's freaking out.'

'What did she say?'

'Oh, she wouldn't really say anything to me. Tried to pretend everything was perfectly all right. But then he came back and they started up again.'

'Did you stay long?'

'Long enough.' Her voice became angry. 'I can't stand it.'

Kenneth realized that, if he tried to diffuse the anger, she'd probably cry. 'Is that what it seems to be about? The use of the cottage?'

'I think so. But it would have to be more than that, wouldn't it?'

'Yes, I'd say so.'

'Do you have any ideas?'

'Vaguely. Failure of nerve. Failure of confidence.'

'What about?'

'Work mainly.'

She sighed again. 'They're always going on at me about how I must find something I really want to do, and look where it's got them.'

'Where has it got them?'

'Mum has to screw herself up even to work at all and drinks too much. And Dad isn't appreciated by anyone at the Poly and can't really run the courses he believes in.'

'And I suppose they've both seized on the cottage as an image for a second chance.'

'Explain please.'

'Jos by imagining the work she could do if only the barn were converted, and Pete by anticipating the stimulus he'd get if he could help the Peace Movement he so believes in.'

'When they were rowing just now, they talked of splitting up.'

'Mm.'

'Do you think they really want to?'

'If they *really* wanted to, then there wouldn't be much to row about. But . . .' He stopped; he must be careful.

'But what?'

'In middle age, if you're unhappy in one area, you start thinking of options. And separation, solitude, independence, must be one of the areas at least to think about.'

'Why don't you live with Ronnie?'

'I don't think she ever wanted me to.'

'How about you?'

'To start with, I think I was secretly delighted at keeping my separate den. Though once or twice I made a bit of a fuss.'

'And now?'

Now? Well, if they'd married, as some people had hinted they really should since they seemed so suited, wouldn't she still have become besotted by Alastair Faraday? But then they might have been living differently altogether: with a child. He couldn't imagine it. 'The delight's clouded over. But I think it's going to prove to be for the best.'

She gave a huge yawn. 'I'm terribly sorry. I'm suddenly so tired.'

He guessed that talking about her parents had performed a simple catharsis. She looked calmer, younger, and very drowsy. He sent her to wash, brought out the Mexican blanket, and within a quarter of an hour she was asleep.

Just past midnight, he finished the Girtin story. He stood up and stretched, facing the black window, and then walked over to look at Sky's smooth swathe of hair which completely hid her face. He did not think she had moved at all. Girtin had been much more supple to deal with than Wilson, and he'd even continued unexpectedly into a final paragraph that took place fifteen years after his death. It told how Girtin's brother, John, struggled to carry his invalid wife from the flames and smoke of their burning house. Inside the house were most of the contents of Girtin's studio – claimed by John in compensation for money lent. The paintings were destroyed, and the sick wife was found to be dead. Kenneth was surprised to find how satisfying it was to write about such things. The poetic paragraph he had attempted earlier, describing the Russian nobleman who had bought Girtin's London panorama as he supervised its erection in a circular chamber in St Petersburg – a soft, smoky indoor city to contrast with the brilliant snow and frozen river outside – had not worked at all. And he'd rejected as vulgar and somehow irrelevant an ending that referred to Edward Dayes's suicide.

He woke, in deep night, and began to reconstruct the sound that had wrenched him back to consciousness. A slow crash, a dragging thump, something heavy thrown over –

Then a shrill, keening groan scraped his nerves. All his teeth seemed to ache.

126

He swivelled his legs from under the duvet, switched on the lamp, and stood up. Then he remembered Sky.

When he lookd down at her from the back of the sofa and saw she was still fast asleep, he felt profound relief. He hadn't begun to imagine that anything had happened to her, yet was so glad to see she was safe.

He walked to the green blind and raised it halfway. There had been car accidents out there before. But he could see or hear nothing. Trying to control his breathing so his heart didn't thump, he waited. A car obligingly came into earshot, cruised to the lights, paused, then revved off down the empty road. Minutes later, when two more cars had passed and he was starting to shiver, he got back into bed. He was still half-waiting for another groan, but the duvet swaddled him against the outside world and he stopped straining his ears.

He was drifting into a waking dream, when there was a very loud knock on his door.

When he opened it, the thick plaid dressing-gown that ballooned out from the shiny cord around the waist of the man who lived upstairs made Kenneth defensively aware of his threadbare pyjamas. For a fraction of a second he was angry. The man had no right to assume he was responsible for that dreadful noise. His reputation could not still rest on one all-night party held two Christmasses ago.

'Mr Worrell,' he said.

The eyes behind Mr Worrell's heavy black-rimmed spectacles glanced from Kenneth's face to his bare feet and then over his left shoulder into the room. Kenneth tried to believe that he was blocking any view of Sky.

'Did you hear it?' Mr Worrell's rasping voice had more fear in it than accusation.

'I heard something. Yes.'

'It's out there.' He was now looking over Kenneth's right shoulder towards the back window.

'It couldn't be.' Even as he spoke, the words became meaningless, like small wads of cotton wool proffered to stem a punctured artery. He realized that that was exactly where the sound had come from.

'It is. My wife can definitely see it.' He tapped the thick lenses of his glasses to indicate his own disadvantage.

'You want me to look?'

Mr Worrell took a step back and folded his arms. Kenneth slowly turned. The reflection of his room in the black glass seemed a very long way away – another world. There, the lamp shone on the bright cobalt stripes of the duvet, and the carpet merged softly with the surrounding shadows. There was no sign of Sky or Mr Worrell in that reflection.

When he reached the window, he cupped his hands around his face and stared intently through the glass. His nose, flattened and cold, exhaled steamy breath. He rubbed the pane clear again with his fist. It was not completely dark outside, but one of those ashen nights with surprisingly clear outlines. Even before he wiped the window, his eyes had recognized that the awkward horizontal shape on the disused steps was a person. But he was experiencing difficulty in getting that message through to his mind. He held his breath and stared for as long as he needed.

The body was utterly still. Its arms were flung out towards the house. There was a bend, an angle, about the torso that sickened him. He tilted his forehead onto the cold glass and briefly closed his eyes.

'Can you see it?' Mr Worrell's loud voice across the room startled him.

'Yes.'

'My wife says it's a ... man ... a body.'

'Yes.'

'If you climbed out of the window ...'

'It's screwed up.'

'Like the back door?'

'Yes.'

'Is it someone you recognize?'

'No.' Kenneth felt himself begin to panic. 'I can't see that clearly,' he said slowly, frying to sound calm.

'You must call the police.'

Why can't *he* call the police? But surely he means an ambulance?

'I'll wait, if you like. While you do it.'

In other words, see that I do it. 'You think the police? Not an ambulance?'

'Over that wall?' exclaimed Mr Worrell. 'That's a job for the police.'

As Kenneth was explaining to the desk sergeant as clearly as he could the reason for his call, Sky sat up and said loudly, 'What the hell's happening?'

Kenneth continued to talk into the telephone – '... Don't know, but we both heard the noise. I can discern what looks like a b–, a man. And my neighbour's wife upstairs can see it. No ... Short sight, I think ... Because the access to the garden is nailed up ... Yes ... Yes ...' – but at the same time listened to Mr Worrell's reply to Sky: 'There's been an accident.'

'Who? Where?'

'Out the back.'

'What's hapened?'

'We don't know.'

'Who is it?'

'A man it would seem.'

'But what's *happened*?'

'We don't know. There's a man ... lying in the back area.'

'Then why aren't you both getting out there?'

'Dangerous. Anyway – it's nailed up.'

'For Christ's sake!' Sky flung back the blanket and strode over to the window. Kenneth watched her reach up and struggle to try to open it. Her shirt lifted, showing red knickers; the socks around her ankles were red too. The desk sergeant was repeating the address and telephone number. 'Yes, that's right. ... Thank you.' He put the receiver down.

'Sky. Please.'

'Ken. I can *see* someone out there.'

'Yes, I –'

'For God's sake open this *window*.'

He went over and mutely pointed to the screws through the frame.

'Then get a *screwdriver*.' She turned and shouted to Mr Worrell. 'You. You get a screwdriver.'

But Mr Worrell had gone.

'Where d'you keep your screwdrivers?'

Kenneth's glance flickered to a rack of tools and Sky rushed across the room. She came back with a screwdriver that was too big for the screws. He laid a restraining hand on her arm.

She sent his hand flying up into his face and stamped her foot. 'Get the right screwdriver. *Get* it.' Then she cupped her hands around her eyes and pressed her nose to the glass, just as he had done. 'Ohhh . . .'

'I'm going to get Ronnie.' He was speaking to himself.

Ronnie answered at the first ring. As he begged her to come down, he knew she had desperately hoped it would be Faraday.

She appeared down the stairs just as the police rang his bell and banged hard on the door. Alarmed by the noise, she stopped. He had to climb up to her to deliver his message. 'Please. Sky is in there. Please watch her for me. She's trying to undo the window. Someone's fallen over the wall at the back. I think she may get hysterical. And the police have come. I must let them –' The bell and the knocking were repeated, longer and louder. Mr Worrell came running down the flight of stairs above Ronnie.

'Why doesn't someone –'

Kenneth was at the door. Two policemen strode past him and a third started to ask questions just as the crash of breaking glass began.

He knew that Sky was fighting her way to the body in the garden.

9 | He takes Ronnie to Rosewharf Close

The doctor had left, and so had the police photographer. Sky stayed with the policeman who stood by the body – the pale head and thin clothes now covered with the Mexican blanket. Kenneth could hear them through the broken window exchanging occasional remarks. He and Ronnie sat tensely either end of the sofa. The second policeman stood by the street window, and the third was at the front door. They were all waiting for the ambulance. A passage had been cleared through the room for the stretcher-bearers.

The young man who lay dead had no means of identification. Kenneth's reason for calling Ronnie had been futile. Sky had been desperate, but not remotely hysterical. She did not need care. The policemen obviously admired her. When one of them had suggested she put on her jeans he did so because the night was cold, not out of prurience. And now Kenneth was trapped in the unreality of being concerned more to explain away Sky's presence to Ronnie than with discovering the reason for the young man's death. This ethical imbalance had even prompted him to lie to the police.

Everyone in the house had been asked whether they recognized the dead man. For a time Kenneth's room had been full of bustle and commands, and when the question was put to him, 'Have you ever seen this man before?' he'd said 'No', because he'd felt that if he'd mentioned he had twice seen the boy staring at his front window from across the street, Ronnie might have found the circumstances that suddenly seemed to surround him even more suspicious.

'Have you spoken to Jos?' she asked suddenly.

'How do you mean?'

'About Sky staying here.'

'I couldn't. Not in front of her.'

'But won't she and Pete be out of their mind with worry?'

'No reason. She usually stays with her boyfriend.'

Ronnie said nothing.

'She had a row with him ... She tried to go home, but Jos and Pete were rowing too. That's why she came to me.'

'Why?'

'Because I know about Jos and Pete. She knows I do. Their rows.'

Ronnie shook her head hopelessly. A siren crescendoed until its bray filled the house.

The ambulancemen and policemen, a dark-blue unit with a tacit chain of command, accomplished the removal of the body. Kenneth stood with his head bowed as the stretcher was carried past. A red blanket had replaced the Mexican one; on it, carefully placed in a dent caused by one of the corpse's arms, was a sprig of laurustinus. He looked up to find Sky staring at the stretcher, tears streaming from her wide eyes.

After the ambulance had driven away, one of the policemen set about organizing Sky's removal. No, the policeman realized that she had been staying the night, that she would be looked after, that Kenneth would accompany her home in the morning, or indeed accompany her in the police car now, but he was going to call a female colleague and together they would take her. Gradually it dawned on Kenneth that this way they could check immediately on Sky's explanation of her presence in his flat. It therefore came as no surprise when the other two policemen hung around his room with vague pretexts, depriving him of an opportunity to phone Jos and Pete and warn them.

He started to make some coffee. He knew Ronnie desperately wanted to go, to withdraw, but he needed her to stay until the police had gone. Busy at the sink, with his back to her, he could avoid her signals.

A bus lumbered up to the lights in the road ouside; lorries were beginning to grind past the window at regular intervals. He looked at his watch. It was nearly six o'clock.

One of the policeman's walkie-talkies sputtered to life. The words it emitted were incomprehensible to Kenneth. They reminded him of watching cartoons when he was small and being frustrated because he could not fathom the distorted American dialogue. He put the policeman's coffee down beside him and handed a mug to the other. Ronnie refused hers. He stood close to her and murmured, 'Please hang on. They won't be long now.' She stared down, running her forefinger over the smooth silk of the magenta and purple chrysanthemums embroidered onto her kimono.

The policemen moved to the doorway and whispered to one another.

'Mr Flete?' one of them said suddenly, loudly.

Kenneth looked up. For the first time he saw them as individuals and not just uniforms. The younger one speaking was anxious, sweaty; his flesh had an oily sheen.

'Yes?'

'Does the name Drew Forsyth mean anything to you?'

He was looking into the expressionless blue eyes of the older policeman when he felt his shoulder give an involuntary jerk. 'No,' he said quickly, as though trying to cover the jerk with the word.

'Is that the dead man?' Ronnie asked. 'Drew Forsyth?' She inflected the second syllable of 'Forsyth' upwards so the name became soft and soaring.

'Yes.'

'How did they identify him?' She stood up and walked over to the policeman.

Kenneth listened.

'They recognized him at the hospital. He'd been a patient there.'

'Oh. He was ill?'

'It seems he had a drug problem.'

'Do you think . . . Might he have needed money? Been attempting a burglary?

'We can't rule that out. But at least we have a lead now.'

'Yes. So what will happen next?'

'They've sent someone over to his wife.'

'Poor woman.'

'Well – apparently they were living apart. But she might know something.'

'She lives in the area?'

'In the North Fulham Estate. With their son.'

Into the silence that followed, Kenneth forced his question. His throat contracted around each word, as though trying to strangle it. 'What's . . . Do you know her name?'

'Mrs . . . er . . .' The anxious policeman consulted his notebook. 'Mrs Lydia Forsyth.'

'No!' His eyes gave three uncontrollable blinks, the lids clenching so tightly they made faint, moist creaks. 'She lives in Rosewharf Close.'

'You know *her*?' The blue eyes were no longer expressionless. The random tragic incident had acquired a rationale. 'Why didn't you say so?' The policeman moved nearer to him.

'I didn't know of his existence.'

'You didn't know she was married?'

'No. I hardly know her.'

The policeman stood right in front of him.

As the questions started, the last ten days, which had been spiralled privately in his memory, the conflicting aspects of his behaviour tightly concealed from view, were brutally unravelled, disconnected chunks of information elicited which he felt must make Ronnie see him as a contemptible hypocrite. 'No,' he heard himself say, 'it was Monday. Not yesterday. I made a mistake. I'd forgotten we were into a new day.'

'Monday that Mrs Forsyth was here?'

'Yes.'

'What time of day?'

'Afternoon.'

'For how long?'

'From two until half past four.'

'You are very precise.'

'That's how it was.'

'And you say she,' the blue eyes expressed curt disbelief, 'came to talk about a . . . story.'

'Yes.'

'Nothing else?'

'We looked at some pictures of Venice.'

'You were planning to go there together?'

He felt himself flush. 'Good heavens no.' *The gods were eavesdropping.*

And afterwards the boy had been staring across from the pavement opposite the window. The same boy who had made that shrill, keening groan in the godforsaken time between the slow crash and his death. Lydia's husband.

The questioning continued, and then the younger policeman came to say that the car had been intercepted on its way to the North Fulham Estate and had been redirected to Rosewharf Close.

Kenneth imagined the loud knocks on the shiny red front door. 'I must go there,' he said.

'To her?' The blue eyes narrowed.

His mind pulled back from his fear for Lydia, his memory of her face, to see the thin, muddy boy with the giant cabbage and the angry man in the donkey jacket. 'To all of them. She lives with her father as well as her son.' In the slight pause that followed, he had an intimation that his answer had subtly altered the policeman's attitude. Building on this, he leaned over to Ronnie and touched her. 'Come with me. Please?'

He felt her stiffen with resentment then, as he kept his fingers on her arm, she looked at him furiously. Whatever she read in his face did not lessen her anger, but it made her lift her chin and say, 'If you need me.'

'I do.'

'Will that be all right, Inspector Crowther?' she asked. 'May I go and dress?'

'Er . . . yes, Miss Max. I don't see why not.'

Kenneth was alarmed that they had remembered one another's names, that out of the maelstrom they had retained such specific information and, thus armed, could proceed with a semblance of conventionality.

'I'll call a cab,' he said when Ronnie had left, moving towards the telephone.

135

'No need for that.' Inspector Crowther's voice was firm. 'I'll get that car contacted again. It can pick us up first. We'll go together.'

Kenneth covered his eyes with his hand. He needed to be alone with Ronnie. He could hear the crackle of the walkie-talkie and knew that he should concentrate, be alert to what was happening. But instead he went over to the broken window and gulped in deep breaths of air. He wanted to shout at the police to get out, to get off his territory. He wanted to tell that boy, that ravaged dead boy, that his troubles were nothing to do with him. But the message came thundering into his mind, repeating until everything else was obliterated: 'He was Lydia's husband, Lydia's husband. An addict. A drug addict. And he was watching me.'

When Ronnie came back she was cocooned in her white winter coat and carrying a bulging tote bag. Kenneth's throat contracted again: evidently she had planned her day beyond this ordeal. Away from him she could enter normality – the world of decisions, appointments, dictation, couriers. Framed in the doorway, she was like an eighteenth-century portrait, larded with the symbols of her nature and success: the swanky calf boots, the alpaca coat, the mussed hair, the bag woven in Greece and stuffed with executive and cultural phenomena; the pearl bracelet, glimpsed beneath her left cuff, which her father had given her when she was ten: the slightly pointed, milky teeth, glimpsed below her top lip, with which she liked to caress men's flesh.

Kenneth blinked harshly. This time he was in control of the fierce squeezing of his eyes. He had been stark, staring mad. Mad to have jeopardized everything by refusing to ride out her infatuation. Mad to have dallied with a strange girl in a manner that could ignite an infatuation. Mad to go on behaving like a twenty-three-year-old in cerulean shoes.

Then Ronnie sneezed, drew out her handkerchief, and the perfume thus released crossed the cold room, crumbled his control, and made him hate Faraday more fiercely than ever.

In the police car he was straitjacketed between Ronnie and Inspector Crowther, staring at the two back-of-necks in front of him. This time he'd memorized their names. Varley was the one whose dark hairs bristled from deeply embedded follicles, and Macpherson had bright pink ears.

He concentrated on not allowing his thigh to touch Crowther's. Suddenly he found himself releasing a compressed sigh, and realized he'd been holding his breath.

'Is there anything you want me to do?' Ronnie spoke very quietly.

'No. I'm all right.'

'When we get there, I mean.'

'Oh – no. Just... I can't imagine what will happen. How they'll take it.'

Ronnie glanced across him at Inspector Crowther. Kenneth felt that their eyes had met.

'You really had no idea,' she said, 'about her husband?'

'I told you.' The question made him angry.

When the car was parked, and the five of them walked towards the river where the gulls were swooping above the flotsam and jetsam of a low tide, he wanted to cut and run. A cat with a feathery tail appeared round the corner ahead, followed by the straight-backed woman and the slow black dog. She stared hard at him and half-raised an eyebrow. Embarrassed by the police escort, wanting everything to seem normal, he gave her a stretched smile and she nodded in return.

'An acquaintance?' asked Crowther when they were out of the woman's hearing.

'She directed me when I first came here,' he said.

Approaching the red door, Crowther guided him and Ronnie to the forefront, leaving Macpherson and Varley by the gate. Just before he pressed the bell he said to Kenneth, 'What's Mrs Drew's father's name?'

It felt as though the path swayed like a deck under his feet. 'I...' – don't know? am not sure? can't remember?

'Don't you know?'

He shook his head. Any credit he'd felt he'd gained through expressed concern for Lydia's family was cancelled.

The silence inside the house seemed interminable. Then, just as Crowther pushed the bell again, harder, there were soft clicks and the door opened.

Lydia's father had grey eyes, dark like wet slate. In one

137

resigned second they had taken in what he assumed to be the situation. 'So you're a copper,' he said to Kenneth.

Kenneth was so shocked he could not immediately reply.

'No,' said Crowther, watchful. 'Mr – er – '

Lydia's father made no attempt to help him out. He just stood, arms barring the doorway. Kenneth could see his mesh vest under a white nylon shirt.

'This is where Mrs Forsyth lives?' Crowther asked at last.

Lydia's father now glared at Kenneth. 'You know that.'

'Yes . . .' He fumbled for words. 'You see . . . something awful . . . there's been an accident. A dreadful accident.' Kenneth thought he detected a positive flicker of interest, of relief almost, on the man's face. 'I wanted to come with the police. To tell you.'

'What is it then?'

'Well . . .' Kenneth looked helplessly at the Inspector.

'Please.' Ronnie's soft voice was firm. 'May we come in? I'm sorry – I don't know your name. Mine is Ronnie Max. I am a friend and neighbour of Kenneth's. The accident took place outside our flats.'

'Is it Drew?'

'Yes,' said Ronnie.

'Dead, is he?'

'Yes.'

No one spoke. Kenneth could hear someone in high heels walking quickly behind them past the house.

Then, 'Well . . . fuck me,' Lydia's father whispered, and he smiled. 'What happened?'

'May we come in?' asked Inspector Crowther.

He looked at his watch. 'The boy'll be down any minute.'

'How about Mrs Forsyth?'

'She'll sleep till I wake her.'

'Well, shall we come in, and you go and see the boy? Ask him not to come down for a few minutes.'

'If you like.'

Crowther nodded to Macpherson to stay outside, and then led Kenneth and Ronnie and Varley into the small house. Lydia's father seemed not to know what to do. He stood in the middle of the room while the others hovered awkwardly around the

138

sides nearest the door.

A lavatory flushed upstairs. Kenneth looked at the open stair-case, expecting Arthur to appear. He thought of the effect of the sight of the two policemen.

'Please,' he said. 'How will ... how do you think Arthur will take it?'

'He'll be all right. As long as his mother is.' He made no move to go upstairs.

'I think I'd better take down a few particulars, then,' said Crowther. 'How about if we all sit down?' He walked over to a round pine table with matching chairs. 'May I?' he asked, before pulling out a chair.

Lydia's father watched him, and then sat down himself on the opposite side of the table.

'Your name, please,' said Crowther.

'Harrow. Jack Harrow.'

Kenneth, more conscious than ever of sounds from above, whispered to Ronnie: 'Shall we go and sit on the stairs? In case Arthur comes down?'

'I shall leave soon, Kenneth. There's no point in my being here. I have an early appointment.'

'But ...'

'All this has nothing to do with me.' She turned to Varley. 'Excuse me. Do you have the right time?'

Kenneth crossed the room on his own. Before sitting down, he looked up to the bend in the stairwell. He had the feeling someone was up there, listening. Inspector Crowther's voice was not loud, but it was clear.

'Drew Forsyth was your son-in-law?'

'He was.'

'But he had not been living with your daughter?'

'No.'

'You knew he had a drug problem?'

'Among others.'

'Did he have any family? Parents?'

'He's got a father. In Wales. His mother's dead.'

'His father's name?'

'Rhys Forsyth.'

'R ... E ...?'

139

'R – H – Y – S.'

Kenneth saw the man, wild-haired and voluble, lecturing . . . where was it? Somewhere like the ICA, in the Sixties. Lecturing on esoteric aspects of the counter-culture. Words pouring out of him like Celtic champagne. 'The writer?' he asked.

'He's written books,' said Jack Harrow.

'You know him,' stated Crowther.

'Of him. Not personally.' Kenneth had retained an impression of the man's vitality, the implied virility, which he now juxtaposed to the dead boy's slack pallor.

Crowther now returned to Harrow. 'Have you any reason to suppose that Mr Flete here may have known Drew Forsyth?'

'I wouldn't know about that.'

'I've said I didn't,' Kenneth said exasperatedly.

'Are you going to tell me what happened then?' Harrow turned from the table to look at Kenneth.

He strained to hear any definite sound from above. Then, lowering his voice, he said quickly: 'Someone climbed over the wall, the very high wall, at the back of our flats. In the middle of the night. Last night. He fell. The police were called. He was dead. The hospital identified him.'

'That was Drew?'

'Yes.' He looked towards Ronnie for reassurance, but she wouldn't catch his eye.

'It seems a big coincidence,' said Inspector Crowther. 'Him entering your property.'

'He would have killed you.' The child's gruff voice from the top of the stairs made them all start, except Jack.

'Arthur,' he said, 'have you been listening?'

Kenneth still could not see the boy.

'Come down,' said Jack. 'You might as well.'

Kenneth heard the soft thud of bare feet on wood, and stood up to make way as Arthur, in washed-up brown pyjamas, confronted them all.

'Where's Mum?' His gruff voice pitched upwards with anxiety.

'Asleep,' said Jack. 'Where d'you think?'

'Hello, Arthur,' Crowther's tone was gentle. 'I'm sorry, this must have given you a bad shock.'

140

Kenneth detected, with surprise, that Crowther found it easy to speak to children.

'Not really.' Arthur walked across to the table and stood behind a vacant chair, holding the back tightly. His grandfather gave him a close, once-over look, but said nothing.

'You knew your Dad lived in some danger?' asked Crowther.

Arthur nodded, staring at Crowther. 'You're an inspector?'

'Yes, I am. And over there is Sergeant Varley.'

The boy looked cursorily at the sergeant, and then at Ronnie. 'Is she a policeman?'

This time Kenneth did catch Ronnie's eye. It gave him no solace. She looked appalled and impatient.

'No,' said Crowther, watching Kenneth.

'She's my friend,' he said. 'Her name is Ronnie.'

'That's a man's name,' said Arthur noncommittally.

There was a short silence.

'Can I ask you a serious question?' Crowther leaned slightly into the table.

Arthur hesitated. It was, Kenneth thought, as though he were sizing up the possible risk involved. 'All right,' he said cautiously, concentrating hard on what was to follow.

'Why did you say your father would have killed Mr Flete?'

Kenneth froze.

Arthur's reply was confident. 'Well, he would have. Any man who saw my Mum he'd want to do in.'

'Do you think he knew that Mr Flete had seen her?'

'Dunno.' Suddenly his concentration had gone. He looked lost, vague.

'Thank you,' said Crowther.

'He knew,' said Jack Harrow dully.

'Did he? How's that?'

'That woman warned me.'

'Warned? What woman?'

'There's this woman. Don't know her name. She's always along by the river. Walking her dog and cat. Never seen a cat like that before. Goes everywhere with her. Well, she told me, after he'd been here that time, that Drew had been hanging about. Staring at our house. He must have ducked out of sight when Arthur and me came home.'

Arthur suddenly lurched away from the table and opened a door into the kitchen.

It's his father we're talking about, Kenneth thought. He's just been told his father's dead. He heard the sound of a kettle being filled and then a refrigerator door was opened and shut.

'I'd better go to him,' Jack said.

'Of course,' said Crowther. 'Just one thing.' He was talking quickly, quietly. 'Was that the only time Drew came here? As far as you know?'

'No. No. He found out we'd moved within a week. I tried to keep it from her, 'cos that's mainly why we moved from the Estate. To get away. His scenes. Harassment it was. But he soon traced us. I found myself telling that woman all about it . . . one day . . . down by the river. She's sympathetic like. So she used to report to me . . . when she saw him. That's how I know he saw him.' Again he looked at Kenneth.

'So he could have followed Mr Flete to his home?'

'Wouldn't surprise me.'

'Thank you. Now . . . please see if Arthur's all right.'

Jack went to the kitchen, and Crowther looked down at his notes. Ronnie walked across to Kenneth.

'It seems you've had a lucky escape, Mr Flete,' Crowther said.

Kenneth felt numb. Ronnie took his hand and led him back to the stairs where she sat down next to him.

'I can't . . . ' he said, then faltered.

'Ssh,' she said.

Crowther went over to Varley and they talked in undertones. Kenneth heard Rhy Forsyth's name mentioned.

'Mr Flete,' said Crowther finally, 'since there were no means of identification actually on the body, we're going to ask Mr Harrow if he'll be good enough to come and give a formal identification. Just to make everything ship-shape. So we'd better get down to the business of informing Mrs Forsyth. All right?' Then he went into the kitchen.

'Am I . . . ' Kenneth fumbled. 'Am I supposed . . . ?'

'Just wait,' said Ronnie.

They were no longer holding hands, but Kenneth felt as long as he remained close to her he was safe, linked to his real world, the world-before-Drew.

Across the neat, new room Sergeant Varley looked bored and slightly embarrassed. Would he, Kenneth wondered, have been spared the boredom if a murder had occurred?

The frivolity of his own thought processes horrified him. This was not his place, this claustrophobic crisis gathering. He must leave, go back with Ronnie now. Technically there was nothing to keep him.

Jack came out of the kitchen carrying a cup of tea. As he advanced to the stairs, Kenneth and Ronnie stood up and stepped aside. On the third stair he turned, and said to Kenneth, 'You'd better come, then.'

Kenneth felt a surging flush of embarrassment, as basic as that of a child who's wet his pants. To leave Ronnie and go up to Lydia's bedroom, escorted by her father, seemed perfidious.

'I'm here if you need me,' said Ronnie gravely.

10 He is grounded

Jack Harrow did not knock on his daughter's door. He twisted the knob, pushed with his foot, and felt around the jamb for the light-switch in an apparently familiar series of movements, the cup of tea steady in his left hand.

The first thing Kenneth noticed was that the emerald and indigo satin dresses had gone, leaving bare wire hangers dangling on rows of hooks. Below the drawn red curtains the chaise was hummocked with a pale yellow duvet. Jack walked over, put the cup on the floor and lifted the edge of the cover.

'Lyddy. Lyddy. It's Dad. Wake up.'

Kenneth stood behind the sewing table, staring across the room at what he thought was Lydia's hair, its colour merging with the quilt. He both dreaded and longed to be seen by her.

'Wake up, Lyddy. Someone else is here. There is something to tell you.'

With a speed that made Kenneth's stomach clench, she jerked upright, her bare arms pressed rigidly down, her skin almost as pale as her white cotton nightdress. When she saw him, the terror in her eyes was replaced with disbelief.

'Why are you here?' Her voice was thin and croaky.

'I'm sorry. I'm ... I've got ...'

Jack stood at the head of the chaise and waited. Kenneth realized that he was not going to share the breaking of the news,

144

yet his presence prevented him moving closer to Lydia so that he could be in a position to comfort.

'Lydia.' He rested his knuckles on the edge of the crowded table and leaned forward. 'It's something dreadful. Your husband. Drew. Somehow – in the middle of the night – he scaled the wall at the back of my flat. You know, beyond the big window. And he fell. And I'm afraid ... when they came ... well – before that ... straight away really ... he was dead.'

The words abruptly stopped dropping from his mind to his tongue. He swallowed dryness.

Lydia's shining eyes seemed to be trying to pierce his dumbness. He fumbled for something more. 'It was ...' The keening groan sawed through his memory; he couldn't say 'instant'.

'It all happened so quickly. I ... we ... the police who came ... we didn't know who it was. They recognized him at the hospital.'

'You're –' her voice cracked. She tried again. 'You're absolutely certain that he's dead?'

Kenneth nodded, incredulous. It was almost as though he were an assassin being scrutinized by an anxious accomplice.

'He's been in comas before,' Jack announced.

Lydia put her arms round her knees and rested her forehead. Kenneth could see the knobbles of her backbone through her nightdress.

'I'm going to the hospital now,' said Jack. 'They want me to do the identification. Official like. The police are here.'

'I'm sorry, Dad,' she mumbled, not sitting up.

'That's all right. Get it over.' He leaned forward and touched her shoulder, then left the room without looking at Kenneth.

Once the door was shut, she straightened up. 'What have I done to you?' she said.

'You ...?'

'Letting you into all this.'

'But you didn't know.'

'I know Drew. Knew ... God, can it really be true?' She reached out towards the curtains and jerked one back a little way. As the daylight harshened her face she began to cry.

He held her, gently, perched awkwardly on the edge of the

145

chaise, most of his weight on one foot.

Soon she said, 'I'm all right,' and he released her and gave her a handkerchief.

'What's the time?'

'Nearly eight.'

'Arthur!' She quickly swung her legs around him and out of the duvet.

'It's all right. Well ... I think so. The policeman has been talking to him, and your father of course. And my friend is down there.'

'What friend?'

'Ronnie. Her flat's in the same house.'

'Why is she here?'

'To help – if needed. We all had to talk to the police...'

'Is she just a friend?'

He remembered how she had used the phrase 'your woman', and was appalled that in this situation she should, of all things, manage to make him feel resentful.

'Ask her to go. Please.'

'Shall I go too?'

It was as though he had snapped a trap, cornering her, she looked so desperate.

'She has to go to work,' he said. 'Of course I'll stay if you want me to.'

She was pulling on a housecoat, her head turned away from him.

'Shall I ask Arthur to come up to you?' he asked.

'Yes.... We'll come down. When...'

'I'll let you know when she's gone.'

Inspector Crowther and Arthur were sitting at the table, their heads bowed over a seed catalogue. Otherwise the room was empty.

'That's the one,' Crowther was saying, 'Red Knight. It's a grand bean. Juicy and doesn't need stringing.' He pushed the catalogue directly in front of Arthur, who studied it closely. 'Mrs Forsyth all right?'

'I think so. She'd like to see Arthur.'

'Fine.' He let Arthur finish reading the description of Red Knight. 'Now, why don't you go up to your Mum, we'll be here, and I'll see if I can find that cabbage. Show it to you when you come down.'

'Not a savoy. Mum don't like those.'

'No. It's not a savoy.' He watched Arthur walk slowly across the room and disappear up the stairs. 'He knows a lot about gardening. Seems he helps with his grandfather's allotment.'

'Have the others gone?'

'Yes. Sergeant Varley's taken Mr Harrow to the hospital.' He paused.

'Ronnie went with them?'

'A last-minute decision. They'll drop her off.' Again he paused. 'The postman came.' He looked at Kenneth, who waited for him to say something more. 'Miss Max picked the post up from the mat,' he said at last.

'Oh.' Kenneth couldn't understand why Crowther seemed to be making meaningless conversation. He'd heard the door of Lydia's bedroom shut so Arthur would not be hearing what they said. 'Did she leave a message for me?'

'No.' He went on staring at Kenneth. 'Arthur took his seed catalogue to open. And Miss Max put Mrs Forsyth's post on the table in front of me. I have placed it on that shelf. Perhaps you'd better look at it.'

As he turned to find the shelf, to seek the spot with a letter upon it, Kenneth remembered. By the time his eyes had focused on the small reproduction of the sunlit façade of the Ca' d'Oro, blood was rushing up his neck into his cheeks. He couldn't pass it off. He had to go and pick up the cards and see exactly what he had written.

He read the bottom one first.

He's pushed in front of Bonington. Died young too.
No mystery about his son: became a surgeon &
diligently collected his father's paintings. K.

Then he turned over the inaccurate aquamarine of the Grand Canal.

147

The gods were eavesdropping. I'm about to be
commissioned to draw Venice in wistaria time.
How about some Bonington research as well? K.

He thought of Ronnie sitting in the police car with the
knowledge that he had withheld William's news from her. That,
more than anything else, would seem a betrayal.

He wanted to leave this compressed modern cottage, this
threatened space, and find once again the territory that Ronnie
had helped him develop and defend. How could he have treated
the Venice commission so cavalierly, a counter in a game of
flirtation?

'Well,' said Inspector Crowther, 'I will leave you now. There'll
have to be an inquest of course, but I don't anticipate any
problems.'

Kenneth blinked hard.

'I had taken the liberty of authorizing a search of your room.
After we left. Can't be too careful where drugs are concerned.
The all clear came through while you were upstairs.'

'You've ransacked my room? Without a warrant?'

'In the circumstances my procedure was justifiable. And ransacked would not be my choice of word. If I had not informed
you, I doubt you would have noticed. But I prefer to be above
board whenever possible.'

Kenneth held the postcards gingerly between his left thumb
and forefinger, like infected dressings. 'You thought...' He
faltered. It was futile to challenge, to bluster. A drug addict
desperate enough to risk life and limb to raid a dealer's flat –
why not? It sounded more likely than the real scenario.

'It's my business to think of all possibilities, Mr Flete. I get
into trouble if I don't. Now, before I go, may I just show you
the cabbage I have marked for Arthur? He'll need practical
things to concentrate on for a while.' He was standing up with
his hand pressed down on the catalogue to keep it open. Kenneth
went over to him. 'That's the one. Jupiter. Tell him that, if his
Mum likes salads, it's good for those as well.'

Kenneth looked at the postage-stamp illustration of an
emerald football of a cabbage. 'All right.'

Crowther prepared to leave. 'They'll bring Mr Harrow back

soon. If they ask, tell them I decided to take a walk back to the station.'

'I will.'

'And remember, should you ever have cause for our help again, the strict truth always speeds things up. It looks to me – if you'll pardon the pun – that a trip to Venice *is* on the cards.'

Kenneth watched him through the window with helpless loathing as he disappeared down Rosewharf Close. What had happened when Ronnie read the cards? Had she said anything? Or was her decision to leave the only statement she had made? He put the cards in his pocket. He would destroy them later.

Alone in the room for the first time, he looked around. Beside one of the three lightweight armchairs stood a mahogany what-not holding a *Reader's Digest* gardening encyclopaedia, some football coupons, a *Fulham Chronicle* and a dog-eared Zane Grey paperback. *His* father had read Zane Grey. In his bedside cabinet, with the Indian brass ashtray and the ivory shoehorn, there would be books by Zane Grey and John Buchan, collected by Mrs Pennington from the Boots lending library. Kenneth used to steal in and examine them when he was small, feeling that some mysterious power lay in their pages since his father read them only in the secrecy of his bedroom – a room which Kenneth was forbidden to enter.

'Mr Flete?'

He had not heard Arthur come down the stairs.

'Oh – hullo.'

'Have you seen Mum's post?'

'Post?'

'I said I'd take it up to her. She's going to get dressed and come down. It was on that shelf.'

He could deny all knowledge. Inspector Crowther could have taken them.

'She said I could look at the pictures. They're postcards.'

'Oh ... of course.' His hand went to his pocket. 'Here they are.' Arthur's expression was one of deep suspicion. 'I was going to take them up to her.' He held them out.

'Where's Inspector Crowther?'

'He had to go.' This time there was such a look of disappointment on the boy's face that Kenneth felt compelled to try to alleviate it. 'He's marked that cabbage for you... Shall I show it to you, when you come down?'

'All right.' Arthur disappeared up the stairs, the cards pressed against his chest.

Kenneth sat at the table and closed his eyes. Lying to Arthur tasted almost nastier than being found out lying to Ronnie.

When Lydia came downstairs, he thought that she seemed to have shrunk. Dressed in jeans and white sweater she appeared more orphan than widow.

She sat down at the table. 'If only it had been just the gods that were eavesdropping.'

'Drew, you mean?'

'He must have been watching me.'

He was, he thought.

'I don't know what to say, Kenneth.'

'Nor do I. You must be so ... shocked.'

'No. I mean about Drew coming to you. I shouldn't have let myself come to your flat. It was too much of a risk.'

'Has it ... have things been like this for long?'

She pulled her fingers through her hair so the centre stood up in a jagged coxcomb. 'It seems like forever.'

'When did you separate?'

'When Arthur was nine. About three years ago.'

'Is he all right?'

'I think so. He's getting dressed. It takes him ages.'

'You must have been very young when you married.'

'Seventeen ...'

'Was it mainly drugs?'

She shook her head vehemently. 'No. No. He was just ... dangerous. A little mad – a lot mad, I don't know. Like his father.'

'Didn't his father try to help?'

'He thinks he did. But he's worse than Drew.'

'I saw him lecture once. He seemed very ... forceful.'

'He mesmerizes people. Drew couldn't quite do that. He used to have the looks... And the charm. Buckets of charm. But he couldn't hold anything together. Not like his father. Rhys can make you think he's got the whole world in his head.'

'Yes. I sort of remember that.'

150

'I used to think I just wasn't clever enough for them. Well . . .
I wasn't. I'm not. You know that . . . And Drew needed a mother.
That was something else I couldn't do.'

'Of course you couldn't. You have your own son.'

'Yes.'

'Did . . Was Drew involved with Arthur . . . earlier?'

She sighed. 'When I was pregnant, and when Arthur was a
baby, there were moments . . . moments when I thought we were
perfect. It was like a sort of dream. Rhys had given us some
money. We lived in a flat full of dried flowers and wind chimes.
And Drew was writing songs.'

He nodded. 'The Sixties . . .'

'Yes. But it was the end of the Sixties. 1970 to be precise.'

'How did you meet Drew?'

'At an Arthur Brown concert.'

'The Crazy World of Arthur Brown . . . I'd forgotten about
them.'

'That's why Arthur's called Arthur. That and King Arthur.
Drew saw us as some kind of psychedelic Camelot . . . God, it
sounds so pathetic and stupid.'

'He looked so young.' The remark slipped out; quickly, he
continued. 'To have been a father for twelve years.'

'Did he? He's thirty-two . . . Was.'

She started to cry and he reached across and took her hands
and kissed the knuckles.

Staring into his face she controlled her tears and said: 'It was
like chasing after a stray animal. Trying to understand Drew. I
kept going after him into territory I didn't know, couldn't
understand. Like when you're a child, and you let a bird out of
its cage – you've been warned not to, but you're sorry for it.
And it escapes. And you go after it, follow it. At first you know
where you are, and then suddenly you don't. You land up
somewhere completely strange. And you're frightened because
you don't know how to get back . . . And of course you've lost
the bird.'

The metal tips on Arthur's boots clattered on the stairs.

'Arthur, please . . .' said Lydia. 'It hurts the wood. I've asked
you not to wear them indoors.'

'I'm going now. I'm late.'

151

'You're not going to school today.'

'No one told me.'

'But . . . Do you want to go?'

Instinctively Kenneth intervened; it was no time to be offering choices. 'They'll not expect you,' he said. 'We'll ring them and explain.'

'We haven't a 'phone,' said Arthur. 'We used to. At the last place. But Dad kept ringing up all the time. So now we don't . . . and the one on the corner's wrecked.'

'I'll 'phone them later. When I go home.' He realized that both Arthur and Lydia were looking at him, adjusting to his unexpectedly taking charge.

'I could go,' said Arthur. 'I don't mind.'

Kenneth knew that he was saying he didn't mind that his father was dead in order to see how his mother reacted.

'I'd like you to be home,' said Lydia.

Kenneth reached for the seed catalogue. 'Do you want to see that cabbage?'

'All right.'

When Jack Harrow came back, Lydia had made coffee and Arthur was telling Kenneth exactly what they grew on every square inch of their allotment. He did not break off when his grandfather sat down next to him, but persisted with the list and its ramifications as though challenging Kenneth to admit that his interest was contrived. At last he hesitated, and Jack gently supplemented his inventory.

'Shallots,' he said. 'That's what we had before we set the late cabbage. Shallots. It was straightforward,' he used exactly the same tone of voice, but turned slightly towards Lydia. 'Knew him at once.'

'Yes,' she said.

'There are arrangements.'

'Shall I . . .' Kenneth didn't know quite what to say.

'I'll tell you what, mate,' said Jack, completely surprising him by his friendly tone, 'If you could let Arthur show you the shop, get a bit of bacon and a loaf, then we'll all have a sandwich. And get things settled.'

'Dad –' Lydia began, protesting.

'Of course I will,' said Kenneth, feeling that his involvement was being extended in a way that was outside his control.

'Shall I take this?' Arthur asked as they were ready to leave, picking up a battered brown purse from the mantelpiece.

'Yes,' said Lydia.

Outside, Arthur's boots rapped on the paving tiles like castanets. Kenneth was pretty certain he banged his feet down hard on purpose.

'Do the metal tips save wear on your soles?'

'Dunno. Mum hates them. Robert's Mum won't let him have them.'

'Why do you like them?'

'Well, you've gotta have them, haven't you? For fighting. When we have gangs at school, and we do kicking contests against the second year, you've gotta have tips, haven't you?'

'Have you?'

'Course.'

In the corner shop, when the bacon and bread were wrapped, Kenneth started to pay.

'This is the housekeeping,' said Arthur, producing the purse.

'Well ... let me.' He was conscious that the man behind the counter, who had pleasantly offered choices of green or smoked, wholemeal or white, was taking everything in.

As they walked back towards the river, he said: 'Do you like living here?'

Arthur slowed down, concentrated. 'It's not that I don't. But I'm not sure that I do.'

'He paid for it,' Arthur remarked as he deposited the purse back on the mantelpiece.

Lydia and her father were still sitting at the table.

'He does have a name,' said Jack. 'There was no need for that,' he added to Kenneth.

'Well, I hope perhaps I can have a sandwich too.'

'You most certainly can.' He took the food and went towards the kitchen with alacrity. 'I'll call you down when they're ready,' he said to Lydia.

'Oh – all right.'

Kenneth hovered.

'Do you mind coming up?' She looked embarrassed.

'Can I have the telly on?' Arthur already had his finger on the button.

'If you must.'

As they reached the stairs, Kenneth heard a pair of safe, well-scrubbed young voices begin to explain how to make a paper duck. He turned to watch Arthur's reaction. Skewed sideways in a chair, with his legs swung over one arm so that Kenneth had a full view of the ferocious boots, Arthur was totally absorbed and half-smiling.

The curtains in Lydia's room were drawn right back. It had lost all the mystery of his first visit. The bedding had been put away and he went over to sit on the chaise. Lydia stayed by her work table, nervously picking things up and putting them down again.

'What's happened?' he asked.

'My father's done something he shouldn't have.'

'What sort of thing?' He could imagine Jack behaving only cautiously at the morgue and with the police.

'It's about Rhys,' she said.

He waited, replaying the image of the copious lecturer in his mind.

'The police said they would inform him. Because he lives alone, and we're not in touch with him, they thought it better for someone to call. Rather than just ring up. So they'll ask the local station to send someone round.' She stopped.

'Seems a sensible idea.'

'But they wanted a 'phone number. In case Rhys wants to talk to anybody.' Again she stopped.

He saw what she was going to say. 'So your father agreed they could give mine. Since you've not got one.'

She gave a slight nod and looked down at the floor.

'Well, that's all right, isn't it?'

Her head came up as though she'd been given a reprieve. 'Is it? Is it really?'

'Of course. As long as you tell me what to say ... about any arrangements.'

'We don't know about the funeral yet. Because of the inquest.'

'Quite.'

'And ... you see ... they'll want you at the inquest.'

154

'I realize that.'

'It just seems...'

'Lydia, stop. I don't mind talking to Rhys Forsyth. If it'll help. I imagine he'll be very upset.'

Lydia didn't look as though she'd considered that possibility. 'I told Dad he shouldn't have said it.'

'I'll put his mind at rest.'

The smell of bacon was beginning to sidle into the room. He couldn't get over how ordinary everything seemed. Only four days ago each object in this room had appeared curious, slightly exotic, and Lydia had been unexplained. Now he could see, in the broadest of outlines, how the pieces fitted together.

The first thing he noticed when he opened his front door an hour later was Ronnie's *Guardian*. It lay on the dingy black-and-white tiled floor, pushed aside by one of the tenants. He realized he had been hoping that she would be upstairs after all, but this confirmed that she had not returned. He was very cold and beginning to feel lightheaded.

As soon as he opened the door of his room, he saw something was terribly wrong. The Inspector had lied. It *had* been ransacked. Letters and sketches were flung across the floor. And the air was icy. The only warm thing he could feel was a pocket of bile rising to his throat.

Then, as he pushed the door open wider, a draught lifted some of the papers so that they eddied back towards his worktable. Beyond, the smashed window lay open to the November morning. It was the gusting wind that had scattered his papers. The rest of the room seemed undisturbed.

Without removing his jacket he searched out a sheet of plastic that would cover the broken pane. The broad adhesive tape he used made a rending sound that set his teeth on edge as he ripped it off the roll. Then he picked up the dispersed papers, sorting and smoothing them, and put them back into piles. Their glimpsed contents seemed quite foreign, fragments from another country.

He was just filling the kettle when the telephone rang.

'Excuse me, but am I speaking to Mr Kenneth Flete?'

'Yes.' Forewarned, he recognized the lilting voice.

155

'Thank you. My name is Forsyth. Rhys Forsyth. I break into your world on an unhappy morning.'

'Yes, Mr Forsyth. I am so extremely sorry.'

'No. No. That is not for you. You were but a bystander. It has been explained. I am afraid the world, the world in all its psychic, natural and practical aspects, was too much for my son. He seemed to need less. A simpler place.'

It was just as it had been at the lecture. Words seemed to propel Rhys Forsyth.

'You never knew him of course. He had the cast of an early Christian. But the knowledge and leanings of a modern existentialist. He could not embrace what was happening around him. Being young is a burden that we shed only slowly. Yeats put it better.' The intonation briefly changed from Welsh to Irish. ' "It is so many years before one can believe enough in what one feels even to know what the feeling is." Dear Drew never reached that stage. He did not find his journey. Now, I must not keep you. I have a young policeman here with me. But I thought I should contact you straight away.'

'Thank you.' Silence hung between them. 'Shall I ... shall I telephone you? After ... well, after the inquest?'

'Of course. Of course. You must telephone me whenever you wish. I am always here.'

'Will you ... Do you ...' He swallowed. The room was beginning to swim.

'You want to ask me something now?'

'The funeral.' He forced the words out. 'I don't know yet. Arrangements. Who ...'

'Someone will take care of all that. His wife probably will. Unfortunate girl. Don't you fret about that.'

'No – I mean, do you ... will you want to come? Be informed?'

'I never attend funerals, Mr Flete.'

The line went dead. Kenneth felt very sick.

He slowly took off his shoes and jacket and lay down under the duvet, his teeth chattering, his neck clammy with sweat. Gradually the nausea faded, his body warmed, and he allowed his mind to shrink towards a narrow aperture through which it seemed it might squeeze into sleep. When he was almost there, he remembered his promise to ring Arthur's school.

He felt in his trouser pocket for the slip of paper and pulled the telephone towards him. He waited so long for someone to answer that he thought he must have the wrong number.

'Stevenage School.' It was a man's voice, young and impatient.

'Good morning. I'm ringing to report why Arthur Forsyth is absent.'

'I'm afraid the secretary isn't here. Could you ring back later?'

He thought what that would have meant to Lydia if she had had to go in search of an unvandalized public telephone.

'No. I'm afraid I can't.'

'She'll be back any minute.'

'Please will you give her a message for me.'

'Well —'

'As I said. It's about Arthur Forsyth. His father died this morning. So he won't be coming to school.'

'Oh . . . oh dear.'

'Please see the right people get the message. Thank you.' He waited a second in case the man spoke, then put the receiver down. Now he was wide awake. He got out of bed and went to put on the kettle.

While he waited for the water to boil, he forced himself to go and stare through the back window. The area looked, as usual, neglected. The body might never have hurtled onto the dank steps, its arm outflung, one leg curiously bent. Yet in his mind he could *see* the body, but as though he were looking from behind, and instead of the feet being covered with plimsolls, the legs with jeans, and the back with a grey shirt, they were naked, and a red loincloth was stretched across the buttocks. And the body was alive, its muscles still desperately taut.

He shook his head and covered his eyes with his hand. Red darkness formed into rocks and mountains, a torrent gushed down, and the body became diminutive in scale, struggling on the overhanging edge of a precipice. Slowly he realized where it was.

He left the window and opened the file drawer where the Southampton Art Gallery's catalogue still lay on top. Quickly turning the pages, past the smooth surface of Wilson's Lake Nemi, he came to John Martin's nightmare landscape of volcanoes, furnaces, incarnadine clouds and powerful cataracts

157

where, right at the bottom of the picture, a figure clung to a lip of rock that jutted above an abyss, its right arm straining forward and its right knee bent to get a purchase. It was called 'Sadak in Search of the Waters of Oblivion'. Kenneth did not know the story behind it.

He covered the image of the figure gently with his forefinger, looked up towards the window where the laurustinus pressed against the glass, and prayed. It was not a prayer with words directed to a god, but a concentration of his mind on Drew, reaching towards him wherever he might be, even though he knew he was dead and wasn't anywhere. The pity which Sky had felt naturally when she placed her sprig of blossom on the unknown corpse had been induced in him by Rhys's rhetoric.

Then he removed his finger and closed the catalogue.

After he had drunk a mug of tea, he decided he must telephone to check if Sky was all right. As he dialled the familiar number he felt a slight return to normality. He would be able to tell Jos and Pete all about it. He would have someone to talk to. The tension in his muscles began to relax.

'Hullo,' It was Jos's voice, very flat, unwelcoming.

'Jos. Hullo. It's me. How is everything? Is Sky all right? It's been such a dreadful –'

She cut straight across him. 'I don't want to speak to you.' And she put the 'phone down.

Once again he was left holding a dead receiver. He felt bereft. Surely she couldn't ... she *couldn't* think he was somehow responsible for what Sky had witnessed? He fell back on the bed. Whatever had Sky said?

Then a very unpleasant light began to dawn. Might Jos not believe Sky? Might she think that he'd encouraged her to spend the night with him; that he'd ... Christ! Surely not? He started to reach for the telephone, but stopped when he heard voices in the hall.

He held his breath, willing his ears to confirm what he had instinctively guessed – that one of the voices was Ronnie's. But there were only footsteps now, and he leapt off the bed towards the door. He opened it just in time to see Frances at the foot of the stairs and Ronnie reaching the top of the first flight. They had both turned when they heard him.

'I thought it must be –' he began.

But Ronnie whisked away and vanished round the bend in the stairs. He and Frances were left looking uncomfortably at one another.

'Oh dear,' she said. 'I think I'd better go straight up.'

'Frances ... please. I don't know what Ronnie's told you.'

'Well ... it's been awful, I know – last night, I mean, dreadful, for you ... But ...'

'But Ronnie thinks I've been two-timing her.'

Frances's kindly, open face could not conceal that this was the case. 'She is ... she is very upset. *Very*,' she added emphatically, with what sounded like an attempt at reprimand.

'I know. And I know why. Look – I've got to talk to her. Will you tell her? It needn't be now. She's probably tired. I know I am. But later. We must get things sorted out. There's such a lot to talk about.'

Frances took a deep breath. 'Kenneth, I'll have to tell you. Since you're here like this. Ronnie's been talking to me for the last two hours. She's going now. She's going to New York. I'm going to drive her to Heathrow. She's just come back to pack.'

'Going?'

'Yes. She feels she's tried to talk. To you. Done her best. But it didn't do any good. And the chance came ...'

'What chance?'

Frances looked embarrassed. 'Of a ticket.'

'What do you mean?'

'Well ... Serena was due to fly back today. But I knew she didn't particularly want to. So –'

His mind crashed. 'So Ronnie's flying off with Alastair Faraday.'

She shrank back. 'Ronnie feels that she's been honest with you. And that you've not been honest with her.' She held his gaze with her troubled, wifely eyes.

'Tell Ronnie ... tell ...' He tried to think what, out of all the turmoil, he could tell Ronnie.

'I'll go up then, Kenneth.'

'Yes. Go on.' He waited until she had disappeared, and went back into his room.

He wanted to lie down, but he couldn't. Even to sit seemed

159

difficult. He had to keep on the move. Although he was too exhausted to think, his limbs seemed to jerk and flex with a life of their own as he paced round the room. And they ached, as did his throat – as though he were going to cry.

He remembered the panacea. He looked at his watch – five to eleven. He felt as though he'd been through two whole days already.

The brandy bottle still had a wineglass of liquor in it. He drank it straight back and waited for something to happen. When nothing did, he put on his jacket.

As he slammed the front door shut, his telephone began to ring. He listened to its muted summons for a while, his head bowed. He wanted to answer it, yet was too weary to make the effort. It seemed easier to set off down the road. Even to wait for a bus was complicated. He started to walk the mile and a half to Lydia's home.

11   He sleeps in Jack Harrow's bed

He was drunk when he arrived. He had passed a pub just as the
barman was unbolting its doors and had veered in; two double
whiskies had melted down all the discipline in his body. But he
did not know he was drunk. He would have said it took very,
very much more than that.

Jack Harrow knew. He pushed the door half-shut in Kenneth's
face and called to Lydia. 'Lyddy. *Lyddy*. It's him. He's been
drinking.'

Kenneth, amazed, swivelled and leaned against the porch. The
red paintwork on the neat houses opposite jazzed up and down.
He felt in need of dark glasses, though the sun was trillions and
trillions of miles away behind a fathomless bed of cloud.

'Dad. What are you do –'

'– it's no good, Lyddy. I won't let it happen again.'

Kenneth heard the catch snick, and waited. The heat that had
built up in his body started to evaporate. As the red paintwork
gradually stilled, he had to clutch his arms together to stop
himself shivering. He thought perhaps he would sit down, but
the front door suddenly opened.

Jack Harrow came out, followed by Arthur. They both had
their outdoor clothes on, and Arthur seemed mutinous and
frightened.

Jack did not look Kenneth in the eye. 'We will be back in one

161

hour,' he said. 'One hour exactly.' As he reached the gate Kenneth heard him blurt out in icy anger, 'That should be in time to repair any damage.'

Arthur's boots stomped leadenly away, and Kenneth looked in through the half-open door. Lydia was standing by the shelves, staring into the middle of the room, her eyes, cheeks and even her chin wet with tears.

'Lydia? ... Lydia?'

She didn't move, and slowly he walked in, closing the door behind him very quietly.

'Lydia?' He watched a tear drip off the edge of her jaw onto her sweater. His senses were beginning to tack back fast from the drunken shore to the sober one.

'I don't know what to do.' Her words were slurred and soft.

'Your father thinks I'm pissed?'

'He . . . he said he could smell whisky.'

'He could. I called in at a pub.'

'He . . .' She shook her head.

'He thinks, if I drink scotch the minute the pubs open, there's not much to choose between me and Drew.'

'How do you know?'

'I'm not stupid, Lydia.'

'He shouldn't behave like this.'

'He's frightened. Frightened for you.'

Now she looked at him, and he remembered how she had kissed him unreservedly. He understood why Jack was afraid. 'What do you want to do?' he said.

In reply she lurched towards him, her arms held at her sides, and butted her head into his chest. For a moment they remained like that, his arms hanging loose, hers stiff, while he leaned awkwardly forward to take her weight. Then, slowly, he embraced her, and a clear image of Ronnie walking across tarmac to an aeroplane flashed through his mind.

At his request, she made him some coffee. While she was in the kitchen he sat at the table, unable to control a series of compulsive yawns.

'You need sleep,' she said, bringing in the mugs.

'I hope this will get me going again. What does your father want you to settle – before he comes back?' The coffee was

162

really too hot to drink, but its scalding passage down his throat revived him. He watched her walk away to the window. 'Well?'

'I feel too embarrassed to tell you.'

'He wants me out of the house?'

'Only ... only if you drink. You know ... as a ... a lot. Or ... anything else.'

It was, he saw, a chance to leave. Had that been Ronnie on the telephone as he left the house?

But he realized that he didn't want Jack Harrow to think he was a drunk.

'He wondered if ... if you and ... Ronnie ... were married, too. I said you weren't.'

He could feel her excruciating tenseness as she waited for his reply. 'You know we're not.' He felt angry at her absurd jealousy. 'She's left, in fact. Flown off to the States.'

She turned towards him, incredulous. 'But she was here.'

'She took advantage of a friend's unwanted ticket.'

'Why?'

Nearest to the truth would have been 'Because she's in love with Alastair Faraday'. 'A mixture of things. Partly business. Partly to see her family. Partly the rather unsettling events.'

'Drew, you mean?'

'Yes. The implications.'

'Me ...?'

'Well.' He wasn't going to be too specific. He'd co-operate with Jack Harrow's ultimatum, but he wasn't going to be wholly circumscribed. 'I'll have a chat with your father when he gets back. Then I'll go home and rest.'

She was staring at him and he knew she was thinking, 'And then – shall I ever see you again?' He said: 'Perhaps you'd come round in the morning? Just for an hour or so. Have some coffee, and a break.'

Briefly her eyes enlarged into perfect, frightened circles before she turned away.

'What's the matter?' When she didn't reply, he realized: she was afraid to come to his flat now. But wouldn't it be better if she faced up to everything? He thought of the broken window; the cold, neglected steps outside; the wall. If, as Ronnie'd always wanted him to, he'd had a curtain, a nice lined thick curtain to

163

blot everything out, then he could have persuaded her to come. But Drew's death would still have been out there.

'I don't think I could face it,' she said, speaking with a great effort at control. 'I want to come and see you. More than anything. But ...' Her voice was wavering towards tears, desperation.

'I understand. I should have thought.'

'No – I'm being stupid. After all, if he'd died outside here I couldn't have run away. It's just ...'

He knew she was thinking of the wall. 'I know. Don't worry.'

'It's the final bruise.'

'The –? Sorry?'

'Final bruise. He used to bruise himself so he didn't have to think. Bruised his brains with drink and drugs, and his feelings with violence, so he was suffering too much to work his way out through it at all.'

'His father phoned.'

'Oh?'

'He didn't seem to want anything. Information, I mean. About the funeral.'

'Good. I hate him. He fucked Drew up.' She paused. 'But he could have fought back. Grown through it. He just didn't try.' She began to cry. 'I tried to help him. I did try.'

He went and held her, stroking her hair, murmuring things as they came to him. They were sitting, subdued, with some more coffee when Jack and Arthur returned.

Kenneth waited as Jack looked him up and down and then took off his jacket and hung it on a row of hooks inside the kitchen door. He noticed that Lydia's jacket, which hung next to it, was exactly like her father's – navy duffle with plastic binding round the cuffs. Arthur hovered, his anorak firmly zipped up and his attention on the blank television screen.

'I'll get some more coffee,' said Lydia. 'Would you like a drink, Arthur?'

'No.'

'There's some Coke.'

'I know.'

'It's all right,' said Kenneth, 'I don't usually start drinking first thing in the morning.'

'When, then?' Arthur didn't look at him as he asked the question.

He didn't reply immediately. Then he decided to tell the truth to Arthur. 'Usually not till after I've finished working. In the evening. And not *every* evening. Occasionally I meet up with a friend and have a drink at lunchtime. But I try not to do that very often now. In the past I sometimes used to do it too much, and it meant the afternoon got wasted because I was too dozy to work.' Halfway through this reply he realized he was making things too complicated. Arthur was looking anxiously at his grandfather for a reaction. All he'd wanted, Kenneth guessed, was a brief answer that would have settled once and for all whether Kenneth was welcome in his grandfather's home. Which way the decision fell probably did not matter so much as that it should be made and be clear-cut.

'What do you do – if you don't mind my asking?' Jack faced him squarely, ignoring his daughter's embarrassment.

'I'm an illustrator. I draw illustrations for articles and stories in magazines – and books.'

'An artist?' Jack handled the word with deep caution.

'Well ...' For once in his life he reached gladly for the word he had so hated his own father to use. 'A commercial artist. I do what people ask, rather than make up my own pictures.' He sensed that Lydia was about to round on Jack and tried to lighten the atmosphere. Turning to Arthur he said, 'I think the Fox books by Bernard Gray are probably too young for you, but you may have seen them. I did the pictures for those.'

'I've seen them,' said Arthur.

'What are those, son?' Jack asked.

'Books in the school library. One of them's got a fox on the front.' He screwed up his eyes tightly in concentration. 'It's standing in front of a big clump of rosebay ... and some brambles.'

'That's the one,' said Kenneth, amazed at the boy's memory. 'Well, I did that drawing – picture. On the front of the book.'

Arthur's face broke into a smile. 'You didn't?' The smile faded. 'Pity it wasn't the BMX books though.'

Kenneth began to laugh. He could feel the laughter taking hold of him, pushing into the stage when it became automatic, pumping out in gushes like a spring. He closed his eyes for a few seconds to calm himself. But white rocks seemed to soar through blood-red space on the inside of his lids. When he opened them again, everyone was looking at him.

'You've not had much sleep,' said Jack. 'And it's been a bloody shock. Would you like a lie-down?'

'More than anything in the world.'

'Come on then.'

He followed Jack up the stairs and into the room at the end of the landing. It was small and neat, dominated by a large mahogany wardrobe.

'Get under that cover.' Jack drew back the brown candlewick bedspread and bent to check that the pillowcase looked clean. 'Slip your shoes off.'

Kenneth was about to push each shoe off at the heel with the toe of the opposite foot as he usually did, but in case that seemed slovenly he bent down and untied the laces and pulled the shoes off with his hands. Then he hesitated, waiting for Jack to leave the room before he collapsed onto the bed. He saw Jack was staring at a framed photograph on the bedside table. In it, a cheerful girl with curly hair and print frock held a baby in a shawl and squinted against the sun.

'That's her mother,' said Jack. 'Ten years before she died. She'd never known illness till then. It was the Festival of Britain when that photo was taken. Lyddy was born about the time it opened. They were fighting against all that mud and bad weather to get it open. There was a lot of art pictures there. In a big pavilion.'

'The Lion and Unicorn Pavilion,' said Kenneth.

Jack frowned. 'You're right. But *you* don't remember that.'

'I remember the fuss about the opening. My father used to say it served them right and they shouldn't have wasted their money in the first place. He was like that. I was – nine. I only read up about the Lion and Unicorn Pavilion later. When I was a student. One of my tutors had been involved in it.'

'Just think of that. Lyddy's mother ... Sadie ...' He whispered the name, as though it hardly ever touched the surface of speech any more. 'She really enjoyed it.'

166

He dreamed he was in the life studio at Steayne with an unknown man who deliberately burned his bare back by sitting too close to the model's electric fire. The man screamed and screamed and clung tightly to Kenneth's shoulders. It was only when a woman came in with a syringe and gave him an injection that the grip of his fingers loosened.

It was with such relief that he woke to discover he hadn't got to cope with the man's wounds. Then he saw a string vest hanging over the back of a chair, and felt an unfamiliar, tufty cover soft against his chin, and wondered where on earth he was. Focussing nearer, he saw the photograph, and remembered. He looked at his watch: he had been asleep for four hours. From downstairs, he could just hear the sound of television.

He wanted to get up and go to the lavatory and have a drink of water, but lay still for several minutes trying to work out what he should do next. The idea of going back to his flat depressed him, rather as if he had been infected by Lydia's dread. Yet he didn't want to sit downstairs with the three of them, waiting for the end of this extraordinary day to be mulled by Coronation Street. And that reminded him of Sky, and Jos and Pete, who normally would have been his refuge at a time like this. Except there had never been a time like this.

After going to the bathroom, he went down with the intention of asking Lydia if she felt like walking along by the river with him, just for half an hour.

To his surprise, she was alone. The television had been switched off, and she was standing in the middle of the room. He smiled. 'Hullo. I'm afraid I flaked out completely.'

'Hullo.' She sounded very nervous.

'Where are the others?'

'At the allotment.' She lookd across at the window. 'They'll be home soon. It's beginning to get dark.'

'Arthur all right?'

'Yes.'

'And you?'

She gave a little shrug.

He was so aware she loved him. He could have pressed her to him, imprinted his body on hers, obliterating the rest of the world. Something made him be careful.

167

With conscious control he went and stood beside her, his arm briefly round her shoulder, a short kiss implanted in her hair, and said: 'It will be better when today is over.' Then he walked to the window. 'I suppose I should be getting back.'

'Now?'

'Well . . . Could I have some coffee first?'

She blushed. 'Oh . . . You must be so hungry. We had some pies. There's one for you. Would you like it?'

'Please.'

It was a chicken and mushroom pie, neat in its foil case and still warm. He devoured it, the slightly glutinous filling and moist pastry unexpectedly satisfying.

'Shall I . . .' Her voice faded away.

'What?'

'No.'

'Come on. Tell me.'

'I was going to say . . . Shall I 'phone you . . . because of us not having one?' She could not look at him.

So far, the next day had no shape. It would mean fixing a time; no point in her going out to telephone him if he wasn't in. 'Yes. Do. Could you make it . . . before ten?' That left most of the day open.

Her whole being seemed to relax.

Then Jack and Arthur were at the front door. Kenneth stayed just long enough to take a winter lettuce from the trug basket of vegetables which Arthur offered him for selection.

'It's a Valdor,' Arthur said. ''Orrible. But Mum likes them.'

'Oh.' Kenneth saw that it was the only one. 'Perhaps I shouldn't take it.'

'Yes,' said Lydia. 'Yes. You must.' She fetched a plastic bag and he walked away down Rosewharf Close carrying an advertisement for Sogans, School Outfitters, Greyhound Road.

He decided not to go straight to the Fulham Palace Road, but turned into a short road of small terrace houses adorned in a ragbag of colours ranging from old tenant cream-and-green, through ex-hippy purple and gleaming Trinidadian sky-blue and scarlet to Sloane mushroom with matching burglar alarm. Three of the dustbins kept behind walls of varying heights in the narrow front yards were adorned with cats. One, a shaggy black

168

and white monster with RAF whiskers, stood up and arched its back and miaowed. Tentatively, Kenneth put out his hand and felt the cat's spine curve and push against his palm.

When he turned the next corner, he found himself suddenly sole deep in pellets of glass. Just ahead, the door of a shattered telephone kiosk was wrenched awry, and inside its fittings and instrument had been ripped away. At the edge of the smithereens, a fresh, beehive-shaped dog turd steamed. A few doors down, a newsagent's and general store had a blue-lettered fascia which advertised a brand of cigarettes over the shop's proud name: PARADISE.

Kenneth walked down to the main road. He was about to turn to the bus stop, thinking he would take a cab if one came along first, when he remembered he was only five minutes walk away from the hospital. The dusk was deepening to darkness, and the lights from cars, traffic signals, streetlamps, shops and garage, swerved and blinked and glared. Perhaps Bernard, hoisted high on the eleventh floor with views across south-west London down to Surrey, wasn't there any more to see the lights. It seemed so very much longer than just a day since he'd seen him lying asleep. He couldn't return home now, but had to go along to the hospital to find out.

'I'm having a *rally*, dear boy,' said Bernard, backed by a cliff of pillows and flushed like the underneath of a flamingo's wing. 'It won't last, but it's interesting while it does. Now ... I don't want to talk about my illness. I want to talk about you. What have *you* been doing?'

Kenneth found himself relaying exactly what he had been doing – or, rather, what had been done to him – over the past eighteen hours. Halfway through the story he was overcome with guilt, and tried to stop. 'I'm sorry. I should never have begun all this. I'm most terribly sorry.'

'It's the most interesting story I've heard in years. Go on – for heaven's sake. What happens next? Does our young heroine break the window? Is the intruder dead or merely shamming?' Bernard's eyes had lost their veil of sickness and were gleaming in pursuit of scandal.

To fuel that pleasure seemed the least Kenneth could do. Thus, for an interlude, the messy, sad events were reassembled into a tragi-comedy, confined, like an entertainment, to the duration of its performance. The end, Bernard seemed to decide by giving three weak handclaps, was the dog turd.

'And your carrier bag,' he said, his faulty breathing exacerbated by excitement, 'Where does that fit in? *Sogans* hardly sounds like Daniel Neal.'

'Lydia gave it to me. It's got a Valdor lettuce inside. From her father's allotment.'

'An unlikely name for a lettuce. I thought Valdor was a paraffin heater . . . And what are you going to do with your new-found family?'

'*Bernard.*' He felt, and sounded, indignant.

'You can't be angry with me. I'm dying.'

'I've lost Ronnie. I don't *want* a family.'

'Why not? You're thirty-nine years old, and you've never had one yet.'

12   He and William exchange confidences

There were three envelopes addressed to him waiting in the hall. One contained a note from Ronnie.

> Dear Kenneth,
>   Frances will call by & collect my post until I return. And she has a key to my flat. To go away seems the only thing I can do – everything has become so confused. I feel sure that you need space to think things through.
>
>   R.

He put the note, with the two unopened letters, on the arm of the sofa. Space. What space? The space between here and the broken window? The space that now inhabited her flat upstairs? The space that made up the next twelve hours? Presumably Alastair Faraday had no need of space; and what space would she have, trailing him?

He slumped down, legs stuck out in front of him, gazing at the floor. Particles of fluff and bits of extraneous matter were clinging all over the lank blue flock of the carpet. The slightly greasy London dust which gathered on the shelves and work surfaces had reached the stage where he could write his name in it. When he first lived here, when the carpet was new, he'd hoovered and wiped regularly.

171

He tore open the other two envelopes. One contained a printed letter and form inviting him to submit an entry for a biographical dictionary of illustrators with the option of later purchasing the dictionary at a concessionary £12.50 (or £30 leatherbound), the other a private view card for an exhibition of small paintings 'as Christmas approaches' in a gallery in Turnham Green. He pushed them to the other end of the sofa. Was it conceivable that any illustrator would pay £30 to see his name and abbreviated life between leather covers? The picture on the private view card still caught the corner of his eye. Footsteps imprinted across a foreground of snow led to a brick house with an open door. It was titled, *Coming Home*. He thought of Jos's painting: the car, the disunited family, the suppressed Sunday struggle.

When he went to make coffee, he found he'd used up all the milk. The mugs from the morning, the policemen's, and Ronnie's untouched one, remained around the room. He collected them but didn't wash up. There were three bottles of wine in the rack under the sink. He drew down the blind. Now he was completely alone.

He made himself turn and face the room, outstare the far, black, cracked window. Nothing happened. He didn't feel anything. Drew certainly wasn't present.

With a small sigh, he decided to go and have a bath.

In the womb of steam that drifted into all the corners of the bathroom, veiling the crude plumbing and the pink tiles that always reminded him of his father's boxes of Passing Cloud cigarettes, he was surprised by an overwhelming and urgent need to masturbate, an act accomplished, uniquely for him, in a blank tunnel of desire unaided by any images, thoughts or mumbled words.

By two in the morning, he knew he'd never get to sleep. His afternoon crash-out was too recent for him to be really tired and the events of the previous day were going round and round in his mind. He could not lose himself in anything. The wine remained unopened; books and magazines were discarded; an all-night chat programme had been turned on and off, the callers' problems seeming trite and insignificant. It was as though the power to divert had been leached out of everything.

He considered going out and walking the streets to make

himself tired, but that seemed rather pointless. If only he had someone to talk to. Tomorrow he'd walk round to Pete's, find out what had happened. Though he couldn't set out until after Lydia had called. Eight more hours. A whole working day.

He got out of bed and put a bottle of wine and two glasses on his work table. Then he settled down, with a sketch pad on his knees, and drew them. He drew some window panes too, but not the broken one, as background. It was a cosy drawing, intimate and menu-ish. He removed one of the glasses from the table and started again. This time he included the broken pane. Beyond it, where his pencil made shadows, he left some white space. Its shape was crudely and unintentionally reminiscent of John Martin's figure of Sadak. He was about to alter it, remove the reference with a few soft lines, but could not bring himself to do so.

At four o'clock, he picked up the book of Venice paintings. He'd never gone there with Ronnie. He'd thought of it once or twice, but held off from making the suggestion. They'd been to Paris and Amsterdam together and, briefly, Berlin. She'd gone to Rome to stay with friends. One summer they'd been to Portugal. He'd always had it at the back of his mind that she might not like Venice, an idea that he couldn't substantiate, but he wasn't going to risk finding out.

He had loved the city with a calm, unqualified passion ever since he'd first tumbled down the steps from the station into the light and stared across the Grand Canal at the green copper dome and milk-white marble portico of San Simeone Piccolo. That was twenty years ago, when he'd been with a group of students travelling to Greece by the cheapest route. Their boat was waiting at the Zattere, and they'd had seven hours' grace before it embarked. He could still account for those hours. It was as though they were held in his memory in featherweight glass spheres tinted in shades of silver, blue, topaz, garnet, mauve, oyster and stone. When Lydia had said, 'I'd love to go to Venice,' he had immediately seen her, walking across the *campo* where the children played on the back of the jolly winged lion at the foot of Daniele Manin's statue, and he'd had no doubt whatsoever that she would be happy there.

At eight o'clock he fell asleep, leaning sideways on the arm of the sofa where he'd sat to read Ronnie's *Guardian* which he'd heard drop through the letterflap. It was after nine when he woke, cold in his bones, and half-guilty that he just might have slept through Lydia's call. But the telephone always did wake him, and Lydia was obviously not a particularly early riser. He made black coffee, did some perfunctory tidying, and waited.

At exactly ten o'clock he sat down by the telephone, anticipating its trill at any second. Then he remembered the smashed kiosk. How long would he have to wait until she found another one?

He went back to the sofa and picked up the *Guardian* again. The main photograph on the front page was of Lord Scarman holding up his report on the Brixton riots. Kenneth remembered watching part of the riots on television. He'd had the impression of an inferno as silhouetted figures ran through blood-red air in front of blazing cars. The following week a friend who lived very near the area said she hadn't been too bothered, but had added she was mightily relieved not to have a teenage son since it would have been difficult to keep him away from the action. Kenneth had dismissed the remark as characteristic of what he thought was her rather over-developed need to empathise with people's problems: surely any mother would be able to stop her child joining a dangerous riot? But what was it Arthur had said about the metal tips on his boots? 'Mum hates them. Robert's Mum won't let him have them.' So why did he have them? 'You've gotta have them haven't you? For fighting.' And he was a boy who could talk civilly to a policeman, enjoyed gardening with his grandfather, and lived in a prime new council house.

The fights at his own school had been with fists. Urgent, very sporadic outbreaks, when one boy antagonised another into the realm of blind anger. The aftermath of those uncontrolled feelings had a curiously restraining effect on everyone else's behaviour. The fights were barely discussed publicly, though friends would privately refer to them, making rudimentary but earnest attempts to analyse their cause. A smashed telephone booth would have... Would have what? He looked at the window. Have been as unlikely in the environs of his school as a dead intruder in his garden was today? Or more unlikely? He tried to read Lord Scarman's measured, humane, recommendations.

When, by eleven, the telephone still hadn't rung, he felt trapped. He longed to leave the room, walk out, but it would have seemed like betraying Lydia. Today she would probably be feeling at her worst, any vacuum in her mind caused by shock readily filled with remorse or unhappiness. He would have to go down to Rosewharf Close.

As soon as he had made the decision, the telephone did ring.

'Hullo.'

'Kenneth, hullo.'

'William.'

'You've heard then?'

'Heard?'

'About Bernard.'

'No ... why? What?'

'Oh, I thought you must have done. You sounded shocked. Well, he's dead, I'm afraid. Last night.'

'He...' He was about to say, 'He can't be.' 'But I saw him yesterday evening. He seemed so much better.'

'Did you? You must have been his last visitor.'

'Oh. Oh dear.'

'Was it a difficult visit?'

'No, not at all. It was just ... William, look, something very strange has happened. And I told Bernard about it. He encouraged me to. And seemed ... well, rather to enjoy it. But it wasn't the sort of thing to tell a dying man.'

'Whatever was it?'

'Someone died in the back garden here. In the middle of the night before last. Fell over the wall.'

'What?'

'The thing is ... He was connected with someone I've recently met.'

'Kenneth, what are you saying?'

'Well ... he was her husband. But they've been separated for a long time. He was on drugs.' His voice tailed away.

'Kenneth, are you all right? Is someone taking care of everything?'

'All the official things are being dealt with. There'll be an

175

inquest . . .' There was a pause. 'He was Rhys Forsyth's son.'

William reacted very quickly. 'Do the papers know?'

'I don't see why they should.'

'Well, they'll probably find out. You know what they're like . . . Can you go away for a bit?'

'Why ever should I? Anyway, I'll have to go to the inquest.'

'Yes. But do be warned. They're awful when they latch on to something.'

Kenneth waited. He could tell William was thinking, choosing carefully what to say next.

'Ronnie's there, isn't she?' William's voice sounded deliberately casual.

'No, as a matter of fact. She's gone to the States. Why?'

Again William did not reply immediately.

Kenneth, who wanted just to have a pause, on his own, to think about Bernard, became defensive. 'I haven't got Lydia – Rhys Forsyth's son's wife – here, if that's what you're getting at.'

'No – no, of course I'm not. Look, Kenneth, I'm terribly sorry. The last thing I want to do is make things worse. It's just the press – well . . .'

'They won't be interested in me. And I wouldn't have thought Forsyth was *that* public a figure any more.'

'No . . . Er . . . Look, it's awfully complicated to talk on the 'phone. And there's something else I have to discuss with you. Could . :. no . . .'

'Could what?'

'I was just wondering if you could come over. But that's too much to ask. I'd come to you. But I've got someone coming here at noon I can't really put off. Perhaps . . .'

'Will you be free after that? No . . .' It was an old joke between them that William was never in the office in the afternoon until four because of long lunches. What was the 'something else'? 'Has the Venice job fallen through?'

'Most certainly not. Look – could we have a drink and a sandwich? I've got to be –' A careful pause. Then, deliberately, 'I've got to be at Bernard's solicitor's office at 2.30. Could you possibly get here by 12.45?'

'Yes.'

'Good.'

Kenneth was about to ring off, when William suddenly said: 'Is Ronnie going to be away for long?'

'I don't know.'

Kenneth hailed a taxi outside the front door to take him to Lydia's. While they were waiting at the traffic lights to cross the North End Road, the driver made his only remark: 'He needs to come and live on our estate for a bit. Then he'd know where to put his community ideas. Community! Piss on the stairs and drums at midnight.' Kenneth, who had been thinking about Bernard, took a few moments to realize that it was Lord Scarman who was under attack.

The driver of the taxi he picked up to take him to William's office in Spitalfields was a different kettle of fish.

He'd just dropped a really nice lady off at her house in Lysia Street. Brought her from Hammersmith Hospital where she'd been getting her kidneys checked. Not a bit sorry for herself though she looked really groggy. Worn out like. There were only two things she couldn't stand in the world, she'd said, and they were people who were cruel to animals, and hooligans who tore up plants and young trees. Didn't concern herself with the rest. Had thirteen cats of her own. All strays. A baker's dozen. She'd called the thirteenth Baker. You could tell how old the first must be. It's name was Donovan. Did he remember Donovan? They call me mellow yellow?

Yes.

His monosyllabic answer silenced the man. He could have given a much longer reply. He could have told him about the gold October afternoon at Steayne when some of the students were outside drawing Tansy, the beauty from the pottery depart ment. She sat crosslegged in front of a tangle of seeding grasses and michaelmas daisies, listening to Donovan singing 'Sunshine came in through my window today' out of the transistor at her side. When he reached 'Now I've made my mind up, you're going to be mine', she had raised her honey-coloured eyes and stared straight at Kenneth.

She was the most beautiful girl he had ever slept with. Jos

had once heard a rumour that she had married a Brazilian millionaire.

He hadn't seen Lydia. As soon as he'd paid off the first taxi, he'd noticed the woman with the dog and cat coming towards him. Again, he was struck by her proud way of walking. She lifted her hand in greeting.

When they were level, she said, 'I think I am on my way to telephone you. You are Mr Flete? Mr Kenneth Flete?'

'Yes.'

'Jack – Mr Harrow – asked me to do it. The local box is smashed. And there's been a reporter hanging round their house. So when he disappeared – I suppose even muckrakers have to answer the call of nature – they came round to me. And I'm very glad they did. Because Mr News-of-the-Gutter's returned. I've just walked by there.'

'That's dreadful.'

'They wanted me to let you know what's happened. That Lydia hadn't forgotten to ring.'

'Thank you.'

'I'm glad to help. It's been a dreadful business ... I'm having a 'phone put in myself later this month. It would have been handy for them today.'

'I did wonder what was happening. That's why I've come down.'

'I expect you'd like to see her?'

'Well ...'

'And you're welcome to come back with me. But the fact is, she's just got off to sleep. She had a bad night. So I put her to bed.'

'In that case ...'

'She'll probably not sleep very long.'

He looked at his watch. 'I've got to be the other side of London in an hour. I was just calling by on my way.'

'Shall I give her a message?'

'Please. Could you ... could you say ...'

'Don't rush yourself. Why don't you write it down?'

So he had fished out his pocket book, pencilled 'Dear Lydia, Hope you wake up feeling better. You seem to be in good hands. Perhaps call me, or send a message, before 11 tomorrow? Try

178

not to worry, K.', tore out the page and handed it over.

'By the way,' said the woman as they parted, 'my name is Mrs Thorndike. Maggie Thorndike.'

He had been relieved to find another taxi so quickly. Because of William's warning, he'd wanted to quit the area as soon as he'd heard about the reporter.

He still wasn't used to William's office being in Spitalfields. He knew he ought to have enjoyed the old silk weaver's house which the agency now rented, and have taken time to get to know the area with its market and Hawksmoor church, but the fact was the plain modern office just off Piccadilly whose lease price had shot through the roof had been much more convenient. The journey went on for ever, and the meter ticked towards a sum that once would have taken him to France.

He asked to be dropped in Bishopsgate, then crossed the wide, hectic road and walked past a new office block towards the turning that led to the cobbled streets where, despite the racket of traffic and building construction all around, the small houses seemed to draw together and turn their backs on the intervening centuries. Kenneth found the lurch from one scale to another, both in time and building dimensions, unsettling.

But, once he was inside the agency's house, its proportions and atmosphere began to soothe him. A short wooden staircase carpeted in brown led up to a landing where visitors could wait on an old oak settle. Photographs of clients hung on the walls, the illustriousness of some giving Kenneth a combined feeling of inferiority and pride. He went into the front office where William was saying goodbye to a woman. William winked at him over her shoulder.

'Do you know Philippa, Kenneth? Philippa Allan?'

Kenneth and the pale-eyed, expensive young woman exchanged cautious glances and shook their heads.

'Ah! Philippa, this is Kenneth Flete. Kenneth, Philippa is preparing a book on royal babies.'

Kenneth wondered if this was a joke. She didn't look the sort of person who would be interested in babies, royal or otherwise, and William was a republican.

'Mustn't get left at the starting gate,' she said. 'Now we know Di's definitely preggers.'

'Philippa,' said William with what Kenneth could tell was false interest, 'has just bought a word processor.'

'Only way to store the info. Now they're all at it like rabbits. Do you use one?'

'I'm an illustrator.'

'Oh – well. Same thing really. Computer graphics and all that.'

William told Kenneth to go up to his office while he saw Philippa out.

Waiting in one of the two comfortable chairs in front of the crowded yet orderly desk, Kenneth felt as though he had been given a reprieve from the inescapable circumstances of the past few days. Never had the lingering remnants of literary London seemed more agreeable: the wall of books dating back to the thirties when the agency had been founded; the gilt-edged invitation cards to launches and celebrations. Kenneth knew that William attended most of them, yet still remained as lean and energetic as when they first met. But take him north of Watford, it was said, or even as far as the Green Belt, and he would languish.

'What a perfectly frightful woman!' William had run up the stairs and walked quickly behind his desk. Then he changed his mind and came to sit beside Kenneth. 'I'm so sorry.'

'Don't be. Are you really handling a book on royal babies?'

'With a barge pole. With a barge pole. Can't afford not to.'

Kenneth imagined that both their attentions strayed to the older books on the shelves, many written before they were born, with their imprints of real people: Jonathan Cape, Hamish Hamilton, Victor Gollancz.

'It's very good of you to come over.'

'I'm glad to be here. It's a relief to get away for a few hours.'

'It all sounds ghastly. And with Bernard on top of everything else ...'

'Yes.'

'Do you want to tell me about it? Or rather not?'

'Well ... I certainly don't *mind* telling you.'

'Tell you what. We'll talk in the pub. I'll just explain here why I needed to see you.'

'Okay.'

'Oh, and by the way, Venice is absolutely definite. Haven't quite got the details settled. But I'll be able to come back to you in a day or two and then we can draw up a contract.'

'Wonderful. I'm ... Well, more glad than I can say.'

'Yes, with no more Fox it's come at a good time. Though – Well, this is what I've got to talk to you about.'

He told Kenneth that, while Bernard was in hospital, he had remade his will. His old one had left everything to his lover, Colin, who had died twenty years before, and he had asked William and his solicitor to come to supervise the new one.

'Apart from anything else, he suddenly realized Colin's mother – you know, that awful ninety-year-old gaiety girl who's always on chat shows – would be deemed next of kin.'

Kenneth thought of the Angus McBean photograph of Colin that hung in Bernard's crepuscular drawing room. A haughty yet vulnerable profile, the sharp chin stretching out from a paisley cravat.

'So,' William was saying, 'as far as the literary estate goes, which is really only Fox, he wants me to go on acting for him, and you to have all the royalties.'

'Royalties?'

'Yes. He always hated the fact you got a flat fee and no royalty.'

'Really?'

'There didn't seem much point in mentioning it. I knew the publisher wouldn't budge. And you get pretty well their top whack. Bernard obviously never said anything?'

'No.' He couldn't help wondering how far off their top whack he got.

'Embarrassed, probably. He was a caring man in many ways. Great sense of fairness despite that scabrous tongue.'

'It wasn't unfair. I never feel the illustrations add very much.'

'Well ... The books wouldn't have been published without them. Children aren't allowed neat texts. Might get addicted.'

'What's going to happen? About the funeral?'

'Oh – James Nall, his solicitor, is seeing to it. I'll let you know, of course. End of next week I suppose.'

Kenneth tried to think that far ahead but couldn't. He was aware that William was looking at him rather strangely.

181

'I may be able to ring you about it this afternoon,' William said. 'After I've seen James. Will you be in?'

Kenneth found he couldn't even think that far ahead. 'I'm not sure. But I'll definitely be in tomorrow morning. Until eleven. Well – and tonight.'

'I might try you latish.'

Kenneth realized he hadn't responded at all gratefully to Bernard's legacy. 'It was terribly good of him to think of me.'

'He enjoyed working with you. Of course, the will has to go to probate. But I'm sure there won't be any problems.'

'I suppose they'll remain in print for a bit?'

William laughed. 'A *bit*! I've already informally set up a new deal.'

'What do you mean?'

'Well, when I heard the news this morning, I knew I had to tell Suzanne, and after I'd spoken to you –'

'You don't mean you did a deal this morning?'

William bridled. 'I certainly did. Suzanne's dead keen to keep Fox at Maybooks. And now we know there definitely won't be any more... Anyway, she wants to bring out a special boxed set for next Christmas. She'll be able to tell me yea or nay on Monday, after their weekly meeting. And she's pretty sure they'll want a new drawing. An elaborate one for a special poster. For which they'll have to pay very handsomely.'

Kenneth felt rather sick. He knew this was being needlessly respectful. Bernard wouldn't have cared less that William was wheeler-dealing before he was stiff. Indeed, he would have been delighted. But he still felt sick. He admitted to himself for the first time that he didn't like Suzanne. She was always so serious about the periodically re-improvised credo of Maybooks, and wore such stern navy blue skirts. He'd worked out once that she'd been only ten when *Who's Vineyard?* was published. When he told her about his book over a routine drink, it had been rather like mentioning venison to a vegetarian.

He managed to smile at William. 'Thanks.'

When they walked out to the pub, striding fast round the builders' skips and scaffolding, William spoke only of generalities. Kenneth wondered whether to mention the Wilson and Girtin stories, but decided not. They would scarcely excite

182

William, and it seemed unfair to force him to put on his delerately noncommittal expression as they dodged the tra... around Spital Square.

The pub was crowded enough to blur concentration and hearing, but very well-staffed so that orders were quickly met. The ideal lunchtime pub, Kenneth thought, as they talked about the SDP's chances in the by-election in Crosby, so long as you weren't bent on real communication. He envied, as he had had occasion to do before, William's enthusiasms for the ups-and-downs of politics.

Once Shirley Williams's prospects of winning the by-election had finally been laid to conversational rest – Kenneth was amazed how much William seemed to know about her – he said, thinking he'd better get it over, 'You were right about the press. When I went down to Lydia Forsyth's home this morning, a neighbour warned me off.'

'Oh?'

'A reporter had been hanging around.'

'He – or perhaps it was a she – didn't speak to you?'

'I never saw him. The neighbour had taken Lydia into her house when he disappeared for a while, and since she was resting I came away.'

'It all sounds a dreadful business.'

Kenneth knew that William was pausing tactfully in case he was willing to expand. 'Yes.' He filled his mouth to the roof with beer and swallowed. It was good beer.

He looked between the drinkers standing near them, urgently talking, across to the bar where a boy in a white shirt and red bow-tie was pulling a pint to join the row frothing gently on the counter in front of him. A man in a dark blue suit waited – not impatiently, the boy was quick without being over-hasty – stroking a folded ten pound note with his thumb.

Kenneth drank another mouthful. Despite everything, it was going to be possible for the womb-effect to happen. This pub could, for a while, shelter him from the consequences of the last two days. 'I met Lydia last week. Last ... Monday. We had lunch once. I visited her home once. She came to Old Brompton road once. I didn't even know she was married. She lives with her father and her son. And then, the night before last, a man

183

fell into the back garden – the wall is very high – and was ...
found to be dead. And the hospital identified him as Drew
Forsyth.'

'Was,' William blinked hard, 'was he trying to get to you?'

Kenneth shook his head. '*I* don't know. It would seem so.'

'You said he was on drugs?'

'Yes.' He drained his glass.

'Let me get you another.'

'No, it's my –'

'Stay there.' William took his glass and went to the bar.

Kenneth leaned hard against the iron pillar by him. The voices
around seemed to crescendo. He'd definitely go and see Pete
next.

William soon returned, empty-handed. 'I've ordered us a spot
of lunch. Seafood salad. Is that all right?'

'Er ... yes.' He was uncertain if he was hungry.

'We'll go through there to the tables. They'll bring the drinks.'

The plates of salad were generous. Prawns, squid and crab-
meat were housed thickly among rice and mushrooms, endive
and orange, and sliced tinned artichoke hearts. A basket in the
centre of the table was piled with triangles of buttered brown
bread, and a blue china Japanese dish with matching spoon
contained fresh mayonnaise.

'I seem to remember you mentioned a sandwich on the
'phone,' said Kenneth.

'Actually their sandwiches *are* pretty good. But I thought we'd
have this so we could sit down.'

Gingerly, Kenneth spiked a prawn with his fork. 'I'm starving.
I hadn't realised.'

William looked relieved. They ate without talking for a while.

'Is there anything I can do?' William asked carefully. 'You
mentioned an inquest. Do you know when it is?'

'Not yet. But I suppose I'll hear soon.'

'Will Rhys Forsyth be involved?'

Kenneth laughed harshly. 'He will not. I had to speak to him
on the 'phone. It was awful.'

'What happened?'

'I tried to indicate that I could let him know when the funeral
was arranged. He virtually slammed the 'phone down on me.

Saying he never went to funerals.'

'Christ.'

'Well . . . I think it will make things easier for Lydia.'

'Her son is Rhys Forsyth's grandson?'

'Oh yes.'

'And you say she lives with her father?'

'Mm.' Kenneth dug into the diminishing rice. Covertly he was looking at William. 'On a new council estate. Right on the river in Fulham.' He watched his friend's suppressed surprise.

'Really?'

'I'll be glad when the newshound goes. For obvious reasons Lydia can't face coming to my flat at the moment. And they're not on the 'phone.'

'If it would help, I could lend you a key to a small flat in Stockwell.'

Kenneth stopped chewing. The remark amazed him. William lived, with his philosopher wife Jill, in a house in Notting Hill which had belonged to his grandparents. He'd lived there all the years Kenneth had known him. He'd seen their daughter, Sophie, grow from a good and precocious baby into a good and benevolent woman, and over the years three or four Siamese kittens had arrived to replace three or four deceased Siamese cats. Jill, who was now beautiful where once she had been pretty, lectured at the London School of Economics.

'I haven't told anyone else. Apart from Jill, of course. But I've been in love with an Australian opera singer for two years. When she's in London, we stay at Stockwell.'

Kenneth tried to conceal his surprise. 'You are a dark horse.' The phrase sounded ludicrous.

'I suppose I am.' William seemed quite pleased by it. 'Anyway – the flat is there if you need it. We shan't be using it until early spring.'

'That's very generous.'

'I know Marie won't mind. Given the circumstances.'

Kenneth tried to think. He saw Jill, wearing one of her long, faintly oriental dresses, standing by a new gas log fire in their comfortable living room last winter, saying, 'I do *so* enjoy breaking the rules of taste in such an outrageous way.'

'I've got a spare key in the office. So I could give you the one

185

off my ring. And if you need ... well, any support over the inquest or anything...'

'Thanks.'

'You did say Ronnie was away?'

'Yes.' The penultimate prawn did not seem to have so much flavour.

'I saw her briefly last week. We were having lunch in the same place. Friday, I think.'

'Joe Allen's.'

'That's right. I had a very late appointment, and she was just leaving. With a most striking American painter she introduced me to. She'd stopped by Alastair Faraday's table. She must know him?'

'She's gone to the States with him,' Kenneth blurted out, and immediately wished he hadn't.

13 He hears no sound but his own

As Kenneth sat in the empty carriage rattling gently round the Inner Circle from Liverpool Street to Victoria, it occurred to him that there had been something odd about William asking him to come over to his office. He had said there was a complicated matter he wanted to discuss. But all he'd done was report Bernard's legacy, which was important but not complicated. Surely that could have been mentioned on the telephone? Perhaps he had just been reacting to Kenneth's news – wanted to make sure he was all right. The more he thought about it, the more unlikely that seemed.

He came out of the underground on to the main line station, and walked towards the side exit to Wilton Road. He looked up at the indicator as he passed, and saw that an Orpington train was about to leave. Two women, laden with plastic carriers, were hurrying to catch it. A month till Christmas.

The continental booking office near the side exit was empty. He was tempted to go and study the timetables displayed on its walls. There was some money in his wallet, and a credit card... But he no longer carried, as he used to do, his passport – just in case. Like the time he and Pete and Jos had dashed to Paris for seventy-two hours when Jos's father had offered out of the blue to have Sky to stay. Mrs Shepheard had been most disapproving when the four-year-old was handed over with the news that her

187

parents were rushing off to catch the evening train to France. Mr Shepheard had died, quite unexpectedly, two months later. Jos had said he must have had a premonition, must have felt compelled to spend some time with his granddaughter. Usually such visits were planned weeks ahead by her mother.

There was a florist's stall on the corner of Warwick Way. He'd occasionally bought flowers there for Jos, knowing she sometimes liked to draw them. Mixed bunches of chrysanthemums would not appeal, he thought, nor pots of polyanthus; but then he noticed some bunches of anemones. Their stems were tightly confined by rubber bands, and their petals were scrunched together above their crushed green ruffs. They looked nothing, lying like that on the raffia grass matting. But he knew that in a day or two they would open, one by one, at different intervals; satiny, black-eyed creatures, changing shape from cup to saucer on stiff, angled stems, their petals like stained glass with the sun shining through.

He bought two bunches and hurried towards Alderney Street with a blank mind, not allowing himself to think of Jos's behaviour on the telephone, or what was happening between her and Pete, but ready to unburden everything as soon as he reached them, like a wave that has gathered its water and runs smoothly before it rears and crashes onto the shore.

As he ran down the basement steps, he saw Jos through the window walking towards the sitting room door. She must have seen him. He waited for her to come up the passage.

After a couple of minutes he decided she couldn't have seen him, and pressed the bell. Again nothing happened so he pressed it harder. He thought he heard a door shut, and then there were footsteps: precise, firm heels, muffled by the cork tiles.

He knew the woman with make-up and mauve cardigan who opened the door was Jos's mother – they had met two or three times in the late sixties – but she gave no sign of recognizing him.

'Hullo,' he said. 'May I see Jos?'

'They are both out.' Her face was stony.

'But –' He stopped. He couldn't humiliate himself by saying, But I *saw* her. Not if she was going to refuse to see him. Pete. Where was Pete? He looked at his watch. Half-past three. 'Do you know if Pete is at the Polytechnic this afternoon?' He could ring him, arrange to meet.

'I don't know Peter's plans.' She was beginning to close the door.

Stinging anger made him clench his hands, and he felt the stalks of the anemones crush underneath their paper. Dropping them on the ground, he turned, stumbled quickly up the steps, and half-ran along the pavement. At the corner he stopped and tried to compose himself.

He must find out what had happened. What on earth had Sky said? Surely she hadn't lied? She wouldn't pretend there had been something between them...? No. But why? And why was Mrs Shepheard there? He started to walk towards Lupus Street. He must find Pete.

The telephones outside the post-office were crammed with kids just released from Pimlico School. There were two or three in each booth, and others milled around outside, jeering and jostling and banging on the glass of the kiosks. He stood for a moment, watching them helplessly. Then two boys who towered over him stepped aggressively near and asked for a light.

'Sorry, I don't smoke.'

They veered away, one of them imitating his accent in a mocking falsetto, 'Sorry, sorree, sorreee.'

He set out for the underground, but what seemed like hundreds more kids, their school uniforms worn with more distortions than would have been thought possible – ties round bare necks, sawn-off grey trousers, navy sweaters over frilled dresses, a tight blazer over a black singlet – were thronging the entries.

It was beginning to get dark, and the late-afternoon traffic was building up to saturation point around Bessborough Gardens. The cars inched forward, some in aggressive jerks ejecting blasts of exhaust fumes, and Kenneth realised that to go home by bus or taxi would be painstakingly slow.

Without consciously making any real decision, he started to walk to the Tate Gallery. Once there, he could telephone. It began to rain just as he reached the wide steps leading up to the entrance. He ran up them, two at a time, and hurried across the foyer to the stairs down to the basement.

As soon as he started to dial the number, the reasons why he avoided trying to contact Pete at work came flooding back. If the switchboard answered, they would probably cut him off before putting him through to the department. Or they would put him through to the wrong department. Or there wouldn't be any reply from the department, right or wrong. Or, if there was, the person who answered wouldn't have any idea where to find Pete. Or mightn't even know who Pete was.

This time he did get through, and a laconic male voice told him that Pete hadn't been in all day.

He immediately dialled Alderney Street, but Mrs Shepheard answered and he put the receiver straight down.

He moved away from the telephone. The coffee shop looked quite full. A warm, slightly menstrual smell emanated from the passage outside the ladies.

A fat man was looking at the Beatrix Potter drawings hanging by the main restaurant. Flopsy, Mopsy, Cottontail and Peter, his mind recited from nowhere.

Flopsy, Mopsy ... Mrs Pennington reading Beatrix Potter to him as they waited for his father to come home. The moquette sofa that prickled the backs of his knees and had a lozenge-shaped stain on one arm. Autumn ... damp. The year he began to go to infant school. Peter Rabbit, jaunty Peter Rabbit in his blue jacket defying Mr Macgregor. Already he could make out most of the words himself, but it was perfect if, uninterrupted, Mrs Pennington would read it right through from beginning to end. She put little expression into the story, but the words flowed fluently, and in her rather soft voice she spun a web that held him in a state of happiness, just outside the real world.

He walked slowly back to the foyer. The people straggling in through the revolving doors were shaking rain out of their hair, throwing back wet anorak hoods, or holding out dripping umbrellas. He looked around for somewhere to sit, but others were waiting for the weather to improve and the only space was alongside a girl with pale red hair and a roving eye. As he studiously avoided catching that eye and walked into the echoing sculpture hall, he felt a surge of defiance.

So that was what Jos was saying. That he'd been picking up girls on and off ever since she'd known him, so why should she believe he'd be different with Sky? Why *should* he be different with Sky? If that's what they'd both wanted. Though he couldn't imagine it. But if they had? That red-head was only about nineteen. He could go back to her, and after a chat whisk her out of the gallery, the two of them pressed into one section of the revolving door. They'd run down the steps, pause to sniff the river, perhaps comment on the lights reflected in the water, then wander along the wet pavement, waiting for the pubs to open.

And, until Lydia, that had never changed the course of history.

He stood still. He was, after all, free. No one had tabs on him. He could easily turn back.

Rodin's *The Kiss* reclined in the distance, deceptively safe and familiar. How white hot it had seemed when Mr Cremorne brought them on a school trip in his third year. Kenneth had waited until the other boys walked away, their titters of embarrassment ill-concealed, and had furtively dropped a florin in the box for donations towards buying the work. He wanted to be able to see it whenever he returned.

Everything was so messy compared to marble.

He walked towards the door leading to the new extension. After wandering through three galleries, ignoring the paintings, he discovered that the seat in the centre of the Rothko gallery was empty.

At first he felt very self-conscious, sitting in what he imagined the ever-present attendant must think was an attitude of respect or reverie. No one else was there to appraise the eight canvases. The attendant stared at the floor. Kenneth stared at the ceiling.

It was a false ceiling, diffusing the greyish light through an opaque skin that looked as though it had been stitched over the space, like a huge graft over old, unhealed flesh.

The paintings, dark rectangular islands inhabited by hazy layers of plum, maroon, black, red and grey, emanated depression.

Kenneth tried to forget the image he had seen in the viewer on Ronnie's coffee table of the man on the stool, his bleeding arms facing the spectator.

He remembered that Rothko had believed in large paintings because he thought they were inhabited by the artist. Small paintings, he'd said, happened when the artist looked at the world through a reducing glass. Large paintings were therefore more intimate, more human.

Serena Stein was certainly an adept with the reducing glass.

He concentrated on the biggest canvas in the room, an enormous black rectangle hovering over maroon. Could Rothko demonstrate a truth, a truth that he needed to learn? Had he been avoiding the spirit of his own age?

He stared at the centre of the black. It was the dull black of an empty blackboard. Tabula rasa. His vision began to swim.

He was aware of someone coming quickly into the gallery, their footsteps loud. Gradually they slowed down, and he felt them walk stealthily behind him, as though anxious not to disturb. They did not stop in front of any of the paintings, and seemed to speed up with relief once they reached the exit.

He blinked slowly. For a second, the black rectangle was replaced by a pale one.

The attendant gave a sudden cough. Kenneth had his back to him, and the man's presence, or rather his sense of his presence, seemed to swell, occupying the space behind him like an inflating barrage balloon.

Kenneth flicked his attention to the pair of paintings on his right. Black on plum, red on plum.

How many hours did the attendant have to spend here? How many days? Did he know about the slit veins?

Perhaps, unlike himself, he understood.

The attendant coughed again, the barrage balloon deflated, and Kenneth found himself standing up. He swivelled to look at a painting of deep red on grey on plum: three in one and one in three. He'd never grasped the implications of the Trinity.

He turned towards the attendant, smiled without seeing him, and left the way he had come.

As he dashed across the sculpture hall to the Turner rooms, the girl with red hair was standing by *The Kiss* talking to a skinny boy in black. Kenneth felt a slight flicker of pique.

The taxi that took him home half an hour later crawled through the rain past the tall houses of Cheyne Walk. Turner died here, he thought, before those houses were built and Chelsea was still half-country. Died with the winter morning sun streaming through the bedroom window of his cottage. In the Tate, he had just looked at Turner's evening suns, suns that soaked the world in gold and seeped into his own heart with consolation.

He opened a bottle of wine as soon as he got indoors, and pulled out his three books on Turner. He was about to take them to the sofa so he could sit with his back to the broken window, but stopped himself. He never worked there.

He went to the swivel chair, put the books on the work table and sat looking at the reproduction of Turner's self-portrait on the jacket of Jack Lindsay's biography. It was a beautiful young face: oval, sensuous and strong. One word dominated Kenneth's mind: integrity. Other artists had depicted the older Turner as stout, hook nosed and coarse, but at twenty-three, with his nose fore-shortened, he had portrayed himself as a romantic prepared to look the world squarely between its eyes of good and evil.

Kenneth made himself stare at his own reflection in the dark window. People had always said he looked young. Now he looked tired and apprehensive, and he realized boyish faces do not grow old with dignity.

He began to dip into the biography, switching forwards and backwards between decades, humbled by Turner's energy and discipline and genius. He was searching for a strand of his life that he could isolate and try to write about. When the strand began to emerge, he felt almost blasphemous. Turner had never been known to mention his mad mother after her death. What right had he to try to disinter her?

Much later, when he was hungry and a little drunk, he went to look in the refrigerator. At first he could not think what the plastic carrier bag contained. Then he remembered the winter lettuce. He decided to go to the late-night delicatessan up the road to buy some bread and cheese to go with it.

When he returned, a brown envelope with his name on it had been pushed through the letterbox. The note inside was written in an old-fashioned, flowing hand:

The police tried to contact you this afternoon. The inquest is on Tuesday, 3 o'clock. It seemed I'd better try and tell you. You know they need you to be there.

Jack Harrow

193

He deliberately continued to set out the food as he had intended: two thick slices of granary bread, several deep green lettuce leaves, their stalks broad and white, and a generous slice of dolcelatte. He carried the plate to his work table and took a few mouthfuls of bread and lettuce; then he broke off a piece of cheese and wrapped it in a leaf, biting into the crisp parcel with its creamy centre with relish.

Mary Turner's madness had been of the fierce, raging kind.

He tried to imagine a childhood spent with a mother who flew into uncontrollable bouts of anger. He tried to imagine the effect of the death of Turner's sister, when she was eight and he eleven. But he could only feel his own childhood: the empty rooms and Mrs Pennington in the kitchen.

Mary Turner had been put in Bethlehem Hospital for the Insane when she was sixty-one. She died there four years later. Did Turner and his loquacious, jockey-like father visit her, he wondered?

He tilted the desk lamp to shine more closely on Lindsay's text. He discovered that Edward Dayes had committed suicide the month after Mary Turner died. Turner had learned a lot from looking at Dayes's work, and his death would have touched him. And reminded him of his friend, 'honest' Tom Girtin.

He raised his head, seeking a rest from facts.

The repositioning of the lamp meant that the four punched holes at the back of its metal shade now threw four coins of light onto the plastic sheet stretched over the broken window.

It was only forty-eight hours ago.

His mind clawed out to Turner, whose mother 'stood erect and looked masculine' and died one hundred and seventy-seven years ago.

He hadn't even asked about Drew's mother.

The only things he knew about the future were that Lydia might contact him in the morning, and he had to attend Drew's inquest on Tuesday.

William would say that he also knew about the Venice commission, but one of his Turner books contained a colour sketch of Santa Maria della Salute in a lemon dawn light, and he no longer knew about Venice at all. What on earth was the point of making more images of exactly the same buildings since he could never remotely match Turner's perseverance and courage, and totally lacked his genius?

Those early years at the end of the eighteenth century, when Turner had travelled all over Britain making thousands of topographical drawings with increasing brilliance, were like the million wooden piles sunk underneath the Salute. Just as the beautiful baroque church appeared anchored on water rather than shored up by a felled forest, so Turner's painted image of it was delicate yet true, free from pencil outlines or marks of measurement.

When critics had written that Turner must be mad because his pictures were so tumultuous and indistinct, he had read their words with tears in his eyes and said he felt ready to hang himself.

He couldn't have told them, Kenneth imagined, how he knew better than anybody that the state of mind needed for the creation of his most ambitious, stormy paintings was as far away from madness as it is possible to be. In order to analyse and portray a tempest, he had to enter the eye of the real storm and keep his wits sharp and his hand steady. Afterwards, in his studio, he might force, cajole, nurse the paint in an unconventional manner, but that was not madness. That was trying to express experience and feelings with an open mind. His mother had been flying in the face of experience with the doors of her mind tightly shut.

Kenneth turned the page with the Salute on it and was faced with the Campanile and the Doges' Palace. Just a trace of pencil here, particularly around the top of the Campanile, but otherwise summery washes of blue and yellow, with not a trace of meretriciousness. There probably hadn't been a trace of meretriciousness in the whole of Turner's career. None of the slickness or shallowness that Kenneth privately dubbed 'margarine'. When he was working, sometimes the only way he had of avoiding it was to be over careful. Faced with the Campanile, he'd probably end up drawing every brick.

He remembered something. Around the turn of the century the Campanile had fallen down. It had just toppled and subsided, like a giant fainting in the heat. Of course it had been rebuilt, faithfully, brick by brick. But it wasn't *quite* the same Campanile that Turner had painted.

195

He'd use that as a talisman. His Venice was slightly different from Turner's – and Canaletto's and Carpaccio's and Bonington's and Wilson's.

Suddenly he felt impatient to be going there, and began to think of the materials he would need to pack. He even started to make a list.

Ten minutes later he stared at the little clumps of words on the sheet of paper in front of him. Clumps of pencils and pens, of colours, of brushes, of papers, of books. His mind had been circling eagerly around the respective merits of all the items at his disposal like a fly let loose in a pantry of uncovered foods.

But, before the day came when he could leave his meticulously packed cases with the airline baggage control, walk through the chrome and imitation leather departure lounge and onto the plane, there were all these unplanned responsibilities: an inquest; a girl who loved him whom he did not know; parents of another girl, who were also his best friends, to placate. And in the flat at the top of the house above him there was a void which he did not understand.

He got up to go and open another bottle of wine.

He had the corkscrew firmly through the cork and was about to pull it, but stopped.

He left the impaled bottle and went back to the work table. He found the Girtin story, read it through and made a minor correction, wrote a short note to Pete saying he'd written the story for Sky, put them both in an envelope which he addressed and stamped and placed ready to post in the morning.

Then he took a deep breath and walked round the side of the table to the window. The broken pane was level with his face, and he gently fingered the jagged edge through the plastic. He pressed a little harder and thought of Drew. If he'd never met Lydia and Arthur, but had still known Drew as a stranger dying out there, would he have felt, as he did now, that he ought to find out more? He was pretty sure he would have put it behind him, out of his mind, as quickly as possible. The first step would have been to get the window mended.

Well, he could organise that. In the morning.

His eye strayed to the bottle on the draining board. Lydia could never be the girl in the British Museum postcard shop again; the alert, shy girl who might or might not be Scandinavian. His senses quickened at the memory. His mind isolated the scene and made it special. He walked over to the draining board.

14   He goes to the country with Pete

Shrieking brakes woke him.

He kept his eyes shut, waiting to hear if something serious had happened. Then an engine revved, a car roared off, followed by the tentative, muted acceleration of another car whose driver had probably been badly shaken.

Relieved, he opened his eyes and saw the bottle on the draining board. It was still impaled by the corkscrew. He had decided not to open it after glancing across the road to the spot under the lamp where Drew had stood.

He stretched both legs and wriggled his toes. He felt – not exactly better, more normal. Eight hours' sleep had righted him. He would post that story to Pete and then settle down to work at something until Lydia 'phoned. Not Turner, but one of those fiddly jobs he kept putting off, like the hand-drawn letterhead for an acquaintance which he hadn't wanted to do but found no way of refusing, or the cover drawing for a construction company's brochure which he also hadn't wanted to do so had suggested a, to him, ludicrous fee which had been agreed without a murmur.

On his way back from the postbox he picked up Ronnie's *Guardian* and learned that Shirley Williams had won the Crosby by-election. The news did nothing for him, and for the first time in his life he felt a twinge of guilt about his apathetic attitude

198

to politics. He'd always voted Labour, but sometimes with no knowledge of the candidate by whose name he placed a cross. He'd done so because he vaguely believed in material equality and was willing to pay all his liable income tax to prove it. That had always seemed sufficient personal commitment since everyone else he knew – be they Tory, Labour, Liberal, Marxist or Anarchist – grumbled about their taxes and avoided paying whatever they could.

He went to start on the brochure drawing. It would earn about a hundred pounds for the government. He'd never approached a job with that thought in mind before. A hundred quids' worth of teachers' time – or CS gas? His first attempt to plan the drawing went avoidably wrong. That'll teach you to extend your concentration to things outside your control, he thought.

For the next hour nothing else existed other than the factory units built by the construction company, and their placement in a drawn setting which included trees, a distant cathedral city, several parked cars, and possibly two or three people – the latter being optional in the agreed brief.

When Lydia rang, he was just getting up to make some coffee.

As soon as he heard her voice – quiet, slightly husky, accentless – he was back in the new world she had made for him.

After finding out that the reporter had disappeared and she had slept a long time, and confirming that, yes, he had got her father's note, he asked her to tell Arthur how good the lettuce was. That made her draw her breath, almost laugh, and say, 'Oh, he'll really like that. He takes the allotment so seriously.'

'I know he does,' said Kenneth. She was in a 'phone booth in Bishops Park Road, he discovered, near some tennis courts. He didn't know the road so visualised her by some grass tennis courts he'd sometimes played on just before he left school. In his mind, she was wearing the pink jersey with the flower.

Without forcing anything to be spelled out, he ascertained that she still couldn't face coming to his flat and that they'd both like to meet away from Jack and Arthur. They settled to go to the Crabtree pub, a few minutes walk from Rosewharf Close, at six.

'Shall I pick you up?'

She hesitated.

199

'Not if you don't want me to.'

'I . . . '

'What?'

'. . . I'm not used to it. Being collected and things.'

'We'll meet there.'

'I'd love to be collected. But . . . '

'But what?'

'It's too good. We'll meet there. And . . . '

This time he didn't help her out. The silence stretched.

'Sorry. What I want to say is . . . that you'll turn up. I got used to that not happening.'

'I'll be there.'

She was there first. He wasn't late, but when he walked into the long bar she was already sitting at a table with an almost empty glass of orange juice in front of her. She was wearing the pink jumper.

'Hullo,' he said.

'Hullo.'

'Shall I get you another of those, or something else?'

'Could I have half of lager?'

When he brought the drinks back to the table she said, 'I'm not always early for things.'

'No?'

'Arthur and Dad were watching the telly. I thought I'd rather come out and watch the people.'

He looked around at the groups of men – some clearly builders, others probably from offices – and two girls who were standing awkwardly, drinks in their hands, watching the door.

'I decided one of those girls has made a date she's not sure of,' said Lydia, 'so she's brought her friend along in case.'

'Won't he be annoyed?'

'If he turns up . . . Though he might do the same – bring a friend.'

'They're probably just waiting for the third girl who works in the hairdresser's to join them.'

'On Friday? They should be working late.'

He smiled, and they fell silent. Then, gently, he said: 'How are things?'

'Arthur's been to school today. He seems all right. I think

200

Dad's rather het up about the inquest. He was bothered by the police not being able to contact you.'

'I was out virtually all yesterday. I had to see my agent. Then I went to the Tate.'

'You will be able to go with Dad?'

'Yes. In fact a policeman called this afternoon to check.' He didn't add that the sight of the constable's uniform, even though the young man inside it was perfectly pleasant, had made the blood drain from his face. For some reason his first irrational thought had been that he was going to be taken to the mortuary to look at Drew.

'I'm sorry.'

'Why? He was only doing his job.'

'I know. But it must all be interrupting your work.'

'Well ... Something else has happened. Since ... Drew.' He tried to martial his thoughts.

'You mean her,' whispered Lydia. 'Going to America.'

He almost laughed, but checked himself. That kind of jealousy could not be teased. 'Well ... there is that.' He wasn't going to deny Ronnie. 'But it's nothing to do with Ronnie.' He could tell that just to hear her name hurt Lydia. 'It's Bernard Gray. Do you remember me telling Arthur about Bernard Gray's Fox books?'

'Of course I do.'

'Well, it's about Bernard.' He noticed the two girls who had been watching the door were leaving, unaccompanied.

He started to describe Bernard to her. How unsure he'd felt when they first met in William's office; unsure because he hadn't decided if he wanted to illustrate a children's book, and Bernard's reputation as a daring, if marginal, writer in the Thirties made him feel slightly in awe. But, within ten minutes, Bernard had made him laugh so much, he would have agreed to illustrate anything he wrote.

'I knew you'd get on,' William had said afterwards, looking smug. 'That there'd be no problem once you met.'

He told her about his first visit to Bernard's house, when they drank pink gins in the overgrown garden and Bernard deflected all his practical questions about the illustrations with wicked anecdotes. Another time, when he'd taken over some finished drawings, Bernard had decided to make him some soup. 'It was very cold, and the house is a long way from the bus stop. Somehow he'd acquired one of those packet soups, and the idea of adding a pint of water to a tablespoon of unidentifiable powder did not appeal. So he made it with a mixture of sherry and cream!'

'What was it like?'

'Indescribable.'

'Go on. Tell me more. Bernard sounds lovely.'

He remembered Ronnie calling him a spoiled old queen. 'He was in a way.'

'Was?'

'He died the night before last. I went to see him after I left you. He'd had a bad heart attack. He was in the hospital down the road. And William 'phoned me in the morning to say he'd died in the night.'

The telling made him sad, brought tears to just behind his eyes, but it also made him feel better. The here-and-now, the situation between him and Lydia, became more normal. He had told her something important about himself. He put his hands round his tankard and stared down into his remaining beer. It occurred to him that maybe Bernard had not behaved well on the few occasions he'd met Ronnie because he hadn't liked her. When he looked up, Lydia was fiercely wiping away a tear from each eye with her thumb.

'Why . . .?'

'Sorry. You'd just made him seem so real.'

They finished their drinks slowly. Neither really wanted another, but there was nowhere to go. Lydia had eaten tea at home and didn't need a meal, and it was too raw and damp to walk by the river in the dark.

'I think I'll go back,' she said.

He knew she didn't want to leave him but that she felt she must so as not to be a nuisance. It was only seven o'clock. If he went straight home too, he could get that drawing done.

'All right. I'll do the same. I've got a job I'd like to finish.'

They left the pub and walked along the road. He wondered whether he could leave her at the corner and walk directly to the bus stop.

She was the first to slow down and halt. 'It's such a long time till Tuesday.'

He realised she meant that Tuesday, the day of the inquest, was the first when she might expect to see him.

'What will you do over the weekend?' he asked.

'I've got a new batch of sewing. Twenty skirts to make over. And I must see Arthur's kept occupied. He feels much better when he's being useful. But it's difficult to think of things he'll agree to do. If I suggest something he doesn't like the sound of, well, that scuppers it. He won't listen to any more suggestions that day. Insists he's got plenty to do when really he's bored stiff.'

He was impressed by her fortitude and spontaneously leaned forward to kiss her goodbye. 'If you want me to join you and Arthur on Sunday afternoon – perhaps go to a park or something – ring me around noon.'

He woke gradually in the morning, feeling sleepy, sexy and complaisant. The drawing was finished, and he'd vowed as he went to bed that he would clean his room and 'phone a glazier. He was completely free for the day. Any regret he might have felt at missing Saturday breakfast with Ronnie was compensated by the fact he didn't have to face an argument with her because he wouldn't contact his insurance company to claim for the cost of the window. He could get it done as soon and as expensively as he liked. Ronnie was fierce about claiming all dues.

He rolled over. It was absurd to feel contented over such trivial things.

Last night, sitting on the bus coming back, he had wondered fleetingly if he could use the key William had given him and take Lydia to Stockwell. But it wasn't on. An empty flat, someone else's love nest, was out of the question.

Restlessly he rolled over again. At this moment he would dearly like to take her in Stockwell, Fulham or Timbuctoo.

Half the pile on the carpet was standing up like blue stubble as he dimly heard knocking on the front door through the noise of the vacuum cleaner. Cursing, he switched it off and went to see who was there.

'I thought you'd never hear me,' said Pete. 'I jumped up and down on the pavement in front of the window, but you never took your eyes off the bloody hoover.'

'God, it's good to see you.' He stood aside to let Pete in.

'I did try to 'phone you. Thursday it must have been. Then I got your story this morning. Just as I was leaving. And I had to come and see you.'

They went into the room.

Without looking at Pete, and feeling deeply embarrassed, Kenneth said very quickly, 'I've got to say this. Put it on the line. I didn't invite Sky back here. Didn't – didn't get involved with her. Other than . . . as your daughter. A friend. Who seemed to need a bit of help. That was all. And then that dreadful thing happened. With the boy.' No, he mustn't pretend he was an anonymous boy. But all that still had to be explained.

Pete replied slowly. 'I know. I've talked with Sky. Though . . . it wouldn't be too much of a crime in my book . . . if you had.'

At first the remark made Kenneth feel awkward, naked almost. Then he saw it as a compliment and blushed. 'You're an unconventional father.'

'I hope so . . . from what I know of a lot of conventional ones.'

'You've certainly taken a load off my mind. But . . . Jos?'

'She's in a bit of a fix at the moment.'

'I called on Thursday. Her mother answered the door. Said Jos was out.' He hesitated. 'But I don't think she was.'

'No.' Kenneth thought how careworn he suddenly looked. 'She wasn't.'

'How about some coffee?'

'Well . . .' He looked around the room. 'You're busy.'

'Busy but not working.' He went to put the kettle on.

Pete walked to the other end of the room. 'This is the window? Where it happened?'

'Yes. Pete? Sky is all right?'

'She seems to be. She's with Mal. I saw them yesterday.'

'Thank God.'

'Listen. Are you doing anything today?'

'Not really.'

'I'm on my way to the cottage. Will you come with me?'

Oh yes, he thought, yes. He visualised the straight, narrow road that ran between open fields and dwindled to a cart track just outside the cottage and its dilapidated barn. He'd once said it was like arriving at England's secret navel.

Then he remembered that he'd invited Lydia to 'phone him. He sighed.

'No?' asked Pete.

'I've promised to be here at noon tomorrow.'

'We could be back by then.'

He tried not to look too pleased. 'That's not fair on you.'

'I'd planned to be back by early evening. So it won't make much difference.' He looked at his watch. 'If we leave now, we'll be there just after eleven.'

'Done.'

'Don't bother with coffee. Get your things.'

He switched off the kettle, changed his shoes, put on his jacket, and stuffed some spare socks and a toothbrush into a canvas bag that already contained sketching materials.

Once outside, they both sprang down the three steps from the front door and almost ran to the battered red Fiat parked round the corner.

Pete drove across London by a route which an experienced taxi-driver would have acknowledged as masterly. Kenneth had not been to the cottage for three years and had forgotten quite how finely honed the journey there had become. As they skipped over an amber traffic light at Finchley past an unlovely line of Thirties-Tudor houses, a continuous Vivaldi climax burst from the radio into the confines of the car like a troupe of acrobats erupting into a parlour. He looked through the windscreen and saw that the cloud cover had broken; a widening arc of Canaletto-blue sky was forming ahead.

Pete turned the radio off once they were on the A1. 'Do you want to talk first,' he asked, 'or shall I?'

'Yes. You.'

'Okay.' He lit one of the two rolled cigarettes lying ready on the ledge above the dashboard.

'Late last Tuesday, Jos had a 'phone call from her brother. He and his wife are splitting up. And, as you know, Jos's mother lives with them.'

'When I saw Jos last week, she'd just had a letter from her. All about setting out a buffet supper to celebrate – is it Jonathan or Tom's? – 'O' levels.'

'Tom's. Quite. So it was a surprise. Well, a shock. Though Jos won't admit that.'

'How do you mean?'

'That she's shocked at her brother's behaviour. Just like her mother is.'

'What's he done?'

'Fallen in love.'

'Irrevocably?'

'Apparently. Mrs Shepheard refused to stay in the house. Inevitably Theo and Elizabeth are rowing. So Theo rang to say she was coming to us the following day.' His voice was flat, weary.

'The day the police brought Sky home in the early hours?'

'That's right. We'd been up talking till four. We've been at loggerheads. Sky told you that.'

'Yes.'

'Jos was furious with her family. And scared. She can only cope with visits from her mother on a strictly controlled basis. Anyway ... We'd only been asleep a couple of hours when the police arrived with Sky. I answered the door. Jos didn't see them. But she picked up that Sky had been with you, and just launched in once they'd gone. It was because of Theo of course. Because his sexuality has upset her life. So any hint that anyone else close to her might have been up to anything just toppled her.'

'But did she realise what had happened? Why the police were there?'

'She didn't properly take that in until later. Sky stood it for about two minutes, and then just turned and left.' He dragged on his cigarette, and Kenneth watched the burn mark creep up the paper. 'I ran to the top of the basement steps to stop her. And Jos started to scream. She was almost hysterical. I just stood there, watching Sky disappear down the street. She was walking very ... resolutely. And I thought, "That's my daughter." Do you know, it was the first time I'd ever seen her

like that. As my daughter. She's always been Sky. Herself. Then
I looked down the steps at Jos, and I couldn't see her as my
wife. It occurred to me then, daughters are real. Because they're
not arbitrary. Your daughter *is* your daughter. But anyone could
be your wife.'

'Except, once you've got the daughter, only she can be her
mother.'

'That's what I realised by the time I'd got to the bottom of
the steps. But I resented very much, I still do resent, that moment
of being forced to choose between them.'

'Sky went back to Mal?'

'Yes. Fortunately.'

'They'd been rowing over *his* mother.'

'So I gathered. She decided to go back to Wales a day early
after Sky turned up. Back to the right-minded Rhondda.'

Kenneth took a surreptitious glance sideways at Pete, who
turned and caught his eye. Kenneth watched as his mouth gave
a little twitch, and his expression lightened. They both burst out
laughing together.

'It's a bloody great farce,' said Pete. 'Mothers taking trains
all over the country to escape their children's sex lives. And
nobody getting any work done . . . except you, of course. Diligent
Kenneth. Just like you were at the College.'

'I wasn't.'

'Compared to ninety per cent of the others you were.'

Even at this distance in time he felt pleased.

'Linking Sky to Girtin like that,' Pete continued, 'it's an
ingenious way to tell her something. I've posted it on to her, by
the way. I thought of delivering it. But it had already been
decided I should remove myself to the cottage for a night, and
Tooting Bec is a bit of a detour.'

'Is Jos coping?'

'Well, she's decided she wants a day alone with her mother,
to thrash things out. If I'm there, then Mrs Shepheard can
exercise avoiding tactics. Worry about what time I'll be in for
meals, and whether Jos has got enough food in. That kind of
thing.'

'I get the picture.'

'But the accident. Sky said no one knew who the man was.'

Kenneth wanted to tell Pete that he had seen Drew. He wanted to acknowledge that moment when they had both looked across at the man who was staring at them from the pavement opposite. But it would mean explaining that he'd lied in front of Sky and he didn't want to do that. 'We do now. He was Lydia's husband. The girl I met in the British Museum.'

'Good God!'

'They'd been separated a long time. He was on drugs. He used to keep watch on Lydia. He must have seen her the time she visited me.'

'Was he that boy across the road? The one we saw?'

Kenneth swallowed. He was about to say 'No'. 'Yes.'

'But Sky said you didn't recognize him.'

'I know.'

'Is there something else?'

'No. It's difficult to explain. Ronnie. Like Jos, her antennae went up when she realised Sky had been staying over. And I just felt that, if I told the police I recognised him, she'd ... oh, I don't know. Read more into it. And, at that stage, that was all it was. A complete stranger whom I'd seen on two occasions staring at the window.'

'So when did you find out? And what was he doing? Trying to get at you? Have you seen Lydia?'

Kenneth started to try to unravel the events of the last three days. It took quite a long time, and he found himself telling Pete about Alastair Faraday and Serena Stein, and Bernard and William, as well as Drew and Lydia and Arthur. Right at the end, as they were turning off the A1 and heading between fields green with winter wheat and seedling rape, and saw a Northamptonshire church spire with its three tiers of open lights appear behind bare trees ahead of them, he remembered to mention the sprig of laurustinus that Sky had laid on the blanket.

Pete blinked. 'Rhys Forsyth used to be rather a hero of mine,' he said.

The cottage was cold inside when they arrived. The long hearth in the living room, into which the front door opened, contained charred logs that had failed to burn, and the air smelled musty and damp.

Kenneth had never visited without Jos before, and he recollected that she had a swift arrival routine which involved firelighters and kindling, hot water bottles for the beds, and coffee. Pete, however, was eager to plunge him straight into ideas for the proposed peace cell, followed by a visit to the pub in a neighbouring village.

They went into the barn, which was cobwebbed and huge, its vast timbers under threat from leaks in the dilapidated collyweston roof. Around the walls and on the floor were vestiges of another era: a horse collar and several black, cracked pieces of harness; a dented feed scoop, an iron bucket, two curved hayracks, and an assortment of rusted implements. Pete was talking about building a mezzanine or gallery, developing his vision of a sanctuary that would have a medieval banqueting table for conferences and shared meals, and a sophisticated computer system that would store information on peace studies around the world.

'We'd site the computer and radio receiving equipment through there,' he explained, pointing towards the wooden wall that partitioned off one end of the barn. 'It would become the technical heart of the place.'

Kenneth went towards the doorway in the wall to take a look. As he stepped over the threshold he could tell the floor had been swept: his feet didn't sink into a felted mixture of antique straw, peat and dust. And it was much lighter in this section, due to high horizontal windows on two sides.

There was a brightness in the corner immediately to his left, and he turned to see a half-finished painting, about five feet by eight, raised on a makeshift platform of planks and bricks, and leaning against the wall. It had a naked figure in the middle distance which he could see was Pete, and the foreground had overlapping forms, reminiscent of flowers. On the left-hand side of the canvas they were carefully, delicately painted in minute, hard-edged bands of colour; then gradually, as the eye moved towards the centre, the segments softened and curled, until on the right they were knotted and whorled like varicose veins or wormcasts. He felt an involuntary rush of excitement and was about to walk up close to the painting when he heard Pete behind him.

'So she came in here after all.' He sounded angry.

Kenneth's pleasure at discovering what he thought was the best painting of Jos's he had ever seen, was halted.

'I didn't know Jos used the barn.' He wished Pete would look at the painting properly and share his excitement.

'She didn't. She's always said it was too cold and dirty. This must have been set up last month when she was down here on her own. During that warm spell.' He went up to examine the brick and plank platform. 'Cock-eyed arrangement.'

Kenneth drew nearer. He wondered how she planned to fill the incomplete spaces. He wondered what story the picture told. Pete's figure, tawny and beige, was in the act of turning away from the viewer; he looked sad and private beyond the screen of tender colours. Kenneth's eye concentrated on a small strip of green. It was the kind of soprano green that leaves have when they are young and the sun shines through them. Very briefly, it blotted out all the speculation from his mind.

'It's almost as though she knew what I've been planning,' said Pete.

He could not imagine Jos being calculatedly vindictive. 'Was she here when the Hobbolds came?'

'No. They called for a few hours when I was on my own. After a demonstration outside the American camp.'

'I'm sure she doesn't know. There was no hint of it when we talked last week.' Though there was no hint of *that* either, he thought, looking at the painting.

They left the barn and walked up the narrow meadow path at the end of the track to the top of the gradual slope. From there Kenneth swivelled to take in the all-round view of uninterrupted square miles of fields and spinneys and villages and spires.

'You can't see the American base in daylight,' said Pete. 'But, at night, the lights are over there.' He pointed to the horizon at a point where a line of trees dipped snugly into a bluish smudge of land. 'They don't usually fly at the weekend. But on weekdays the F11's rip John Clare's universe right open. It would take them just ten seconds to destroy it.'

Kenneth felt a fist of fear at the back of his skull.

'Now,' Pete's tone lightened, 'do you remember the pubs? Any one you particularly liked?'

'I liked them all.' It was true. The pubs, like the villages, had

210

adapted to consumer expectations unselfconsciously. Scampi and campari had arrived without fuss.

'How about one with very reasonable beer and the biggest ploughman's in England for one pound twenty-five?'

'Done.'

'You didn't exaggerate,' said Kenneth, when they were sitting in a beamed bar by an open fire, and were brought platters of rolls, cheeses, pickles, salad and a mound of fried onion rings. 'I shall never eat all this.'

But he almost did. Towards the end, when he had already had quite enough, he was picking at the remaining bits on his plate and eating them slowly in order to disguise the fact that he was not bowled over with enthusiasm by Pete's plans to collaborate with the Hobbolds. It wasn't that he disagreed with the theory; he was, and always had been, a unilaterist. But in his bones he felt sure the venture wouldn't really come to anything. There would be discussions and letters and meetings and telephone calls; perhaps some work would be done on the barn, and perhaps Pete would be involved in organising peace programmes and publications. But he couldn't see it the way that Pete idealised it, with the barn a crucible that would go down in the annals of peace.

Then, as they finally left the pub, over-full and slightly drunk, and took a leisurely walk around the village, which had a brook running down the centre of its main street crossed by white foot-bridges, he felt guilty. Part of his negative reaction was caused by self-interest. He didn't *want* to find Pete's schemes compulsive because then he would feel compelled to take part, or else suffer a perpetual bad conscience. It was much more inviting for him to praise the actual painting in the barn and dismiss the hypothetical computer. That way his established patterns of behaviour would not be disturbed.

They paused on one of the bridges to look up and down the stream just as a bevy of small children came running out of one of the stone-and-thatch cottages and assembled on the bank to play what was obviously a well-established game with garden canes and floating plastic lids. 'What it amounts to,' Kenneth thought dismally, 'is that I am not prepared to fight for those children. The men who were pacifists in 1914 and 1939 were

211

honourable. They could not bear to kill human beings. I am the lowest of the low because I will not give up time to join a struggle which I believe in and which may one day save those kids' lives.'

Pete was smiling. 'Isn't it great,' he said. 'They can run about with no supervision, and have a small universe of water, grass and trees completely at their disposal. I was driving over Spaghetti Junction past those tower blocks last month. I'll swear life on Mars is more hospitable than that.'

On the drive back to the cottage, Kenneth made a promise to himself that if anything did come of Pete's scheme he would try to help in a limited but regular way. It didn't have to be all or nothing. A day a month for those kids by the stream was better than nothing at all.

By ten o'clock in the evening, when the cottage was at last beginning to feel warmed through, Pete said, 'Do you want to walk up and see the lights around the base?'

Kenneth, who was stretched out on an old rexine chaise, almost acquiesced. Then he spoke the truth. 'No. I won't forget they're there. But I don't want to go and see them.' He looked around at the blazing logs, the bottle of wine in the hearth, and the piles of books on the straw matting either side of Pete's chair. 'When I went out into the garden just now, I was looking at the stars. They made my head feel clear. And there was no noise. No noise at all.'

'Apologies. I was forgetting you've had enough for one week.'

'What do you think's going to happen over Jos's mother?'

'I just don't know. In principle, I feel sorry for her. Her world's blown apart just as much as Elizabeth's has.'

'Does she have enough money to set up on her own?'

'Just about. But she's never been by herself. And she finds it so difficult to debate anything. Everything has to be clear cut, black or white. I always find she has no grasp of the continuous, linear, way life goes on. No acceptance of the fact that its troughs and peaks are all interconnected. She only recognises the peaks. She likes to freeze the past into a series of happy tableaux, and to think about the future simply in terms of possible additions to those tableaux. Jonathan's 'O' levels. Theo and Elizabeth's silver wedding.'

'I remember the first time she visited you in Steayne. You and

Jos snuck out to the pub at lunchtime, and Jos was convinced she would cut your hair off while you were asleep, she was so appalled by it.'

'You know the first thing she said to me when she arrived on Wednesday? "Peter! You look terrible. Just like a convict!"'

Kenneth ran his fingers through his own hair. 'Do you know who I bumped into the other day? Rosemary Nene.'

That led them back to the Royal College and reminiscences of people they'd not thought about for years. Another bottle was opened. They discussed the validity of art education in times of unemployment, and marvelled that a decade they had lived through should now be regarded as legendary.

'To think I once gatecrashed a dance at Chelsea Art School when the Stones were playing,' said Pete.

'What were they like?' Kenneth knew, he'd heard the anecdote before, but it was comforting to hear it again.

'Tremendous. Camp and raw at the same time. It seemed a great sound. And the girls couldn't keep their eyes off Jagger and Jones. They didn't half dance in those days when they were excited. Disco! You can keep it . . . Jesus! I am sounding old.'

They fell silent. Kenneth tried to remember something else from those times, but his mind would not linger. It raced forward, rushing by an imagined image of the Forsyth flat with its windchimes and dried flowers, to the sight of Sky at the window and the sound of breaking glass. He didn't want to break the thread of self-indulgent memory, but a different kind of self indulgence, guilt, made him say: 'And it all led to Drew.'

Pete had an immediate response. 'Are you going to stick with Lydia?'

Be stuck with, do you mean? Kenneth wondered. 'Early days,' he replied.

15   He is given a piece of advice by Jim Sheran

It was still dark indoors when Kenneth went down the steep wooden stairs and opened the latched door into the kitchen. He made a mug of coffee and carried it outside.

Along the eastern horizon the sky was pale opal and gold, and the two old apple trees behind the garden shed stood out in tangled silhouette.

He took deep breaths of sharp air, and walked around in the half-light looking at the packed clumps of dormant plants in the border, the bushes to which a few cold, unopened roses still clung. A wooden fence separated the garden from the fields, and he put down his empty mug and climbed over.

All the farther fields were ploughed, sown with rape and winter wheat, their seedling green just beginning to catch the light, but this was an old grass meadow, soft as moss. He found himself running, leaping over molehills, stamping on the springy surface.

When he reached the end of the field, he turned to face the cottage and barn. The rest of the hamlet was several hundred yards away, and the two buildings formed the centre of a perfect pastoral composition. No wonder Pete wanted to spread its influence around the world. And small blame if Jos wanted to keep it to herself for ever.

He walked slowly back, climbed the fence, and went into the

barn. There was not enough light for the painting to reveal itself fully, but the forms were clear. Pete's figure in particular seemed to have a strength he had not fully appreciated the first time.

Behind an area of bare canvas at the top left-hand corner of the painting there was a shadow, and when he went to investigate he discovered a small piece of paper, covered with Jos's hand-writing, tucked into the stretcher. Guiltily, he took it out.

Her firm, black script was easy to read. At the top of the paper, ringed around, she had written: 'Sartre's death, April 1980.' The words underneath were in disconnected note form:

Daffodils, grape hyacinths, lenten roses, chalky albia
Patches of sunlight
Pete through the kitchen window, crying
The light on his cheek where the skin glistens
Male tears – shock
Nature emulsified, melting, whirling to some kind of chemical drain

He put the piece of paper back and looked at the picture again. The wet shine on the cheek was a jagged rhomboid.

A buried, nagging guilt began to stir in his mind. A promise made to Pete on a dark spring afternoon in the corridor by the tea trolley at the College. They had been debating whether to continue working on a lithograph Pete was helping him with, and Pete had said, 'The trouble with three o'clock in the afternoon is that it's always too late or too early for anything you want to do.' The observation had struck him as maddeningly accurate. Pete explained it wasn't his but came from one of Sartre's novels, and this had led to a discussion on existentialism and a promise from him to read *The Age of Reason*. Only he never had; and Pete had never mentioned it again.

Now, he would have made an effort to follow through such a promise. Then, enthusiasms were thick on his ground, and he'd probably felt he'd 'done' existentialism at school by reading *The Outsider*. The only novels he'd been reading during that period were American.

Later, as he helped Pete mend a broken gutter and they made fried-egg sandwiches before setting off for London, he wished he could mention the painting. Pete was talking about the barn

215

most of the time, spelling out the stages in a possible conversion; and he never once mentioned Jos.

When they were speeding along the country roads towards the A1, the key to the cottage front door returned to its usual place under a stone, Kenneth said, hesitantly, 'What's your next step, do you think? Vis à vis the Poly? And your book – and the barn?'

Pete took a long time to reply. 'All I know is, Sartre was absolutely right when he said, "When one does nothing, one believes oneself responsible for everything."'

At first Kenneth thought he meant that he had recognised the incident in Jos's painting. Later, as they talked, he was not so sure.

Pete dropped him at his flat at ten minutes to twelve, and sharp at noon the telephone rang.

Lydia's voice sounded strangulated. 'We're going to be out this afternoon. Maggie Thorndike's asked us to lunch. And the others want to stay and watch the western.'

He felt unreasonably disappointed. 'Oh. Well . . .' He realised she probably didn't want to watch the western. But that wasn't what he'd proposed – seeing her. He'd made a tentative stab at a family occasion.

'I think I'll have to stay too.'

He knew she was giving him a let out. That she could easily be persuaded to meet him, but he mustn't feel he had to make the suggestion.

'Never mind,' he said. 'Another time. Is Arthur still all right?'

'Oh yes.'

'And you?'

'Yes.'

'Well . . . I –'

'I'll see you Tuesday,' she interrupted. 'After the inquest.'

The line went dead.

He felt relief, even though he knew she was probably near to tears. The rest of the day was his own.

He went out to buy some food and newspapers. A telephone call in the evening was his only interruption.

'I've been trying to get you for two days,' William said.

216

'I've been to Pete Brown's cottage with him for twenty-four hours.'

'Ah. How's Jos?'

'Family problems.'

'Oh. Well, don't tell me about them. Unless you want to, of course.'

'No.'

'I've had enough of problems. Every single author seems to write about nothing else. They're all commissions of course. So blame the publishers. "Find me someone who'll do a *really* exciting book on post-honeymoon depression, or mortality, or erosion of the ozone, or mislocation of the erogenous zones," they bleat. And the trouble is I do. People seem to be falling over to write them. Then I have to spend my weekends reading the buggers.'

'What's the subject this weekend?'

'Oh – senility. Actually it's awfully well written. Andrea Box. You know how good she is. Such a stylish writer.'

'Mm. Ronnie's very keen on her.'

'Don't suppose you've heard from her?'

'No.'

'What I rang about is Bernard's funeral. I thought it was bound to be this week. But James Nall rang me late Friday and said it's booked for the 7th, a week tomorrow. One-thirty. Damned uncivilized time.'

'Whereabouts?'

'Oh, one of those ghastly megalithic cemeteries up in Finchley or thereabouts. I'll give you the exact details. The only way to get there is by cab. And make sure you have a driver who knows which one he's going to. I missed Fergus Linton's funeral completely. The driver practically took me to Scotland.'

'Wasn't that the funeral when a posse of poets tried to peer through the hole where the coffin glides away to make sure it wasn't recycled?'

'It was. And insisted on reading their own frightful verses after the hymns the poor family had chosen. By the time I got there, they were collapsed with a bottle of vodka under a flowering cherry planted in memory of someone's sainted mother.'

217

'Will there be many people at Bernard's?'

'Hard to say. He always said that all his friends were either dead or should be. But I shouldn't be surprised if quite a few people turn up.'

'Yes, I remember him saying that.'

'Have you got the date of that inquest yet?'

'Tuesday.'

'The newshounds might sniff around again.'

'Yes.'

'Let me know if I can be of any help. And don't hesitate to vanish to Stockwell. If it suits.'

'Thanks.' He paused. 'Thank you, William – very much.'

He stood awkwardly in the doorway between the living-room and the kitchen while Lydia made some tea. At the last minute he had panicked and put on his only suit, a grey one, for the inquest, and now that it was all over he felt cold – he had no respectable overcoat – and uncomfortable. He had left Jack behind at the undertakers near the coroner's court to arrange the funeral. Arthur was due back from school any minute.

'I didn't tell Arthur about this afternoon,' Lydia said.

'Okay. Thanks for warning me.'

'You're sure it was all right?'

'Yes. Accidental death.' It had all seemed to happen so quickly, in a curious mixture of officialdom and informality, that even he hadn't felt quite convinced it was over as he and Jack walked down the side alley back into the Fulham Palace Road. But Jack had been almost cocky, insisting that Kenneth went straight back to reassure Lydia, and quite happy to visit the 'death hunters', as he called them, on his own. 'I'll tell you one thing, mate, they won't talk me into having no solid oak nor brass handles. And don't look behind you now, that reporter chap who was hanging round our house is following.'

She leaned onto her hands against the kitchen unit, her back to him. Her head was bent and she was breathing slowly and very deeply.

'Are you all right?'

She nodded her head.

He took the three steps across the kitchen, and she turned, was pressed against his cold grey suit. She thrust both her hands inside his jacket, reached round under his armpits and pulled him as tightly as she could so that he felt strapped, bound. During the split second before he bent to kiss her in a hellbent need to extinguish Drew's bleak, lingering aura, he saw inside his closed eyes the blurred image of a man tied to a mast.

They broke apart within moments, and she made the tea, and they were sitting drinking it when Jack came in, closely followed by Arthur. Jack had brought a bag of doughnuts with him, sugary and greasy. Kenneth bit indiscriminately so that unnaturally scarlet jam spurted onto his lapel and they all laughed. There was a sense of relief. He accepted a second doughnut.

Arthur was sent upstairs to do his homework as soon as he had finished his tea.

'Do I have to?'

'Yes,' said Lydia. 'I've put the fire on. You can't waste that heat.'

'I've only got maths to do.'

'Fine. Then you'll soon be down again.'

'Can't I watch the cartoons first? Then do it?'

'No.'

'Oh, please. I'll do it at news time. I hate the news.'

Kenneth watched Lydia hesitate.

Arthur was quick to take advantage. 'It's always about boring wars and people dying.'

'Go upstairs, son,' said Jack. 'No one's ever forced you to watch the news yet.'

Arthur went, and Kenneth felt Lydia's relief.

Once they had heard his door shut upstairs, Jack said, 'The funeral's fixed for Monday. Not too much damage, considering.'

'How much?' asked Lydia.

'Never mind. It's all in hand.'

Kenneth wondered if he should offer to help.

'Have you made up your mind about it yet?' Jack said to Lydia.

'I don't want to go, Dad.'

Kenneth thought Jack looked concerned.

'All right, love.'

219

'No,' she said. 'It's not all right.'

Jack said nothing.

'Do you want me to come with you?' Kenneth asked.

Jack considered, glancing at Lydia and then giving Kenneth a half-smile which seemed to admit appreciation. 'Will you?'

'Yes.' Then he remembered that Monday was the 7th. 'What time is it?'

'Noon.'

'Whereabouts?'

'Golders Green. I'll get Alf to fetch us there.'

'Alf?'

'His friend,' said Lydia. 'He's a cab driver.'

When he left the house half an hour later he hadn't told them about Bernard's funeral. He thought they might feel obliged to refuse his offer over Drew's and just hoped Alf knew his way round all the megalithic cemeteries. Arthur had come downstairs by then, high-spirited now that he had completed his task. 'Do you know what happened to Robert?' he had said to Lydia. 'He lost his dinner money playing pontoon, and he was so starving he nicked some rockcakes Fiona Sands made in domestic science. And she told Mr Vinson. And Robert had to stay in after school.' Having told the tale he'd sought no reaction, but settled down with a contented sigh in front of the television news.

At the doorstep Kenneth had stretched out his fingers and lightly touched Lydia's wrist. ''Phone me?'

'When?'

'Whenever you like.'

He chose to walk home, collar turned up and hands in pockets, hunching his jacket round him. The east wind made his eyes water and, as the daylight faded and the blurred streetlamps brightened against the black clouds tearing melodramatically across the sky, he realised why he had thought of the man at the mast. Just before he'd fallen asleep the night before, he'd been reading Turner's gruff remarks about sailing on the Harwich steamboat in a January storm. The sailors had lashed him to the mast for four hours so he could watch the sea. 'I did not expect to escape, but I felt bound to record it if I did.'

The painting he had made afterwards was one that helped people label him as mad. It looked like soapsuds and whitewash, one critic had said. Yet nowadays Tate visitors stood before it and were instantly convinced by Turner's portrayal of the overwhelming experience of storm. Not that he would have particularly welcomed their empathy. He'd been rude to a friend whose mother had been very taken by the picture, saying it reminded her of a storm she had once endured. 'Is your mother a painter?' he'd asked. And on hearing she was not, had growled, 'Then she ought to have been thinking of something else.' He wanted other artists to look at the work and understand what he'd achieved with paint. Amateur anecdotal praise did not interest him.

None of this added up to anything, he thought. He might feel in unknown waters with Lydia when she held on to him so tightly, but he had never been brave. He'd never fought for anything – Aline, for example – or gone out on a limb to explore new territory in his work. He'd just let things happen.

He walked faster, leaning into the wind. Had Turner been rude to his friend just because he was not interested in the reactions of non-painters? Or had there been a moment of subconscious jealousy because the man had a companionable mother he could take round galleries and talk to? Turner presumably had never received his own mother's praise.

Kenneth snorted with laughter, and the wind snatched the sound away. This kind of Freudianising was Ronnie's territory. She'd be highly amused to know he'd caught the habit. Or would she? Locked in Alastair Faraday's spell, she'd no doubt find the information exceedingly tedious.

When he got home he took the Turner books to his work space. There was comfort in wandering among the facts and narratives of the painter's life. He was no longer looking for a story he could tell to others, but discovering one he could tell himself. A story whose hero he was beginning to love and did not want to share. Like a child with a father.

William telephoned at nine o'clock the next morning.

'How was the inquest?'

'All right. Accidental death.'

'No problems?'

'Only that the funeral's been arranged for the same day as Bernard's.'

221

'Oh God. Do you have to go?'

'I said I would. Otherwise Lydia's father will be the only person there. It's well before Bernard's. I'll manage both.'

He could sense that William would have been angry if it were otherwise.

'What I'm mainly ringing about is the Venice book. Is it all right to talk?'

'Rather.'

William reported that Ted Wing had just gone out to Venice on his very first visit, and would return in a few days with a list of places that would almost certainly feature in his text. Kenneth needn't keep to them absolutely rigidly, but they would provide a framework. 'Ted asked me to tell you that he doesn't wish to seem rude – not getting in touch with you himself. But he realises you know Venice well and he wanted to go with as few preconceived ideas as possible. I said I thought the right time to meet up would be when he's nearly finished and you've completed some of the pictures and got a pretty firm schedule for the rest. What do you think?'

'Absolutely fine.' Kenneth knew that would be the plan that suited Ted Wing.

'When will you be able to go for a preliminary assault?'

'Mm . . . I'll have to think about it.' He felt a rising surge of excitement and energy. 'Pretty soon.'

'Good. I'll get the contract off to you today. And try to extract the first payment before Christmas.'

'That would help.'

'Let me know if you have any queries on it.'

'I will.'

They rang off. Kenneth sat for a moment enjoying an uncomplicated sense of purposefulness and well-being.

In the afternoon Lydia telephoned to ask if he would have lunch with her at home the next day. 'Dad's going to be out, and I could make lasagne. I'm quite good at that.' She sounded very nervous, but euphoric too.

He accepted, wondering what would happen.

Everything seemed slightly different when he arrived. The television had been pushed back; there was an aroma of garlic and herbs, and a vase filled with grey silk roses on the table.

222

He commented on the appetising smell.

'I'm going to sound awful,' she said. 'But, now I'm not scared Drew's suddenly going to appear, I'm beginning to feel restricted. I didn't want to do things my way when I was frightened. But now I'm starting to mind because Dad hates foreign food. I could kick myself. He's been so good to me.'

'Well ...' He wasn't sure what to say.

'Ideas keep opening up in my mind that I didn't even know I had. I mean we've only just moved in here, and I was really pleased about it. But this morning, when I was tidying away my bedclothes and checking over the work I did last night, I just thought, Hell, what I need is space. Space for a workroom. Space to sleep. Space for Arthur to play. Space for Dad to get away from the smells ... Sorry, I seem to keep talking. And I haven't even given you a drink yet.' She pushed her fingers through her hair.

'Stop worrying.'

'You will have a drink? I've got a bottle of wine.'

'I certainly will. Would you like me to open it?' He'd almost brought one with him, but didn't in case Lydia had not provided drink and felt awkward.

'I've done that. It's warming near the stove.'

He followed her into the kitchen and watched her fill two glasses. It was so different from the last time. She seemed to be creating a cordon sanitaire of busyness that she did not want him to cross. When, after her telephone call, he had wondered what would happen, he had really only wondered what would happen between them physically. Now it seemed obvious the answer would be 'nothing'. He felt let down that any element of spontaneous choice had been removed. Though he knew he ought to have felt relieved.

And he knew he should have been pleased that the Cabernet Sauvignon wasn't cold and raw, and that – later – the lasagne was creamy and tasty. But he found it rather disappointing that Lydia provided a lunch that he might have had with Ronnie or Jos. Only the flowers were different.

'Did you make these?'

'Yes. I hope you don't hate artificial ones?'

'No. For years, when I first came to London, I had a red

223

plastic rose that came free with a packet of Daz.' He didn't add that he had finally given it to a girl from Newquay who had red pubic hair.

She sighed and smiled. 'That's just what I wanted.'

'A plastic rose?'

'Things to be ordinary. Like they were when we first had lunch. Well – not ordinary. It's not a bit ordinary talking to you. Normal, perhaps I mean. Talking about normal things. Like the plastic rose.'

'Or Richard Wilson.'

'Yes.'

He felt guilty about his earlier sense of let-down and set out to entertain her.

When he returned to his flat, Frances was in the hallway collecting Ronnie's post. She accepted his offer of a cup of tea.

'Have you heard from Ronnie?' he asked when they were sitting down.

'Only a message on the answering machine at work. About shipping Serena's paintings.'

'Well – obviously she got there safely.'

'Yes.'

'And everything's all right at the gallery?'

'Oh yes. We've sold quite a few of the smaller things from the Christmas show. And one of the provincial galleries is interested in Penelope Wragg's *The Supermarket Till*.'

'Good.'

'Kenneth, I was sorry to read about Bernard Gray.'

'Yes. No more Fox I'm afraid. But do you know what he's done?' He told her about the royalties and enjoyed receiving her genuinely pleased response.

'And ... the other – thing.' She spoke diffidently. 'The accident?'

'That's more or less over.' He was being less than honest here.

'I'm glad. Look ... we're having some people round on Sunday. You know, the usual thing. We didn't manage to have half the people we wanted a fortnight ago. Will you come? You needn't make your mind up here and now.'

'I'd like to. Thanks very much.' He realized he wouldn't have been invited if she knew he'd just had lunch with Lydia.

'Well – let me know.'

'No. I'll definitely come.'

He woke up on the morning of the lunch party with a vivid image of his father's house in his mind. He'd been dreaming about breakfast time there, breakfast time on a Sunday when the *Sunday Express* and the *Sunday Dispatch* were shared between them – later he was jibed at for introducing the *Sunday Times*. They'd been eating mussels of all things, smothered in sugar and milk and still in their shells. He was about to dismiss the dream when a detail from it, the coloured glass in the top three panes of the dining-room windows, pulled him back. Violet, yellow and green lozenges; he'd loved them when he was small, and grown to loathe them as an adolescent, just as he'd grown to loathe the house as a whole. Perhaps he should go back, find out what had happened. Perhaps there was a way it could easily be made his again if Mrs Pennington was still there. Then he could sell it, and buy a proper studio ... That thought was even more stupid than the dream.

Ronnie'd implied he'd never faced up to giving the house away. Did the dream signify now was the time to try? Violet, yellow, green. He quite liked that sequence of colours now. But he'd rather keep just them, and bury everything else. As he'd declared to himself the other day, he wasn't brave, wasn't a fighter. He didn't want to work at understanding his childhood to make things easier for the Ronnies of this world; nor could he ever take the train to Orpington and work on Mrs Pennington – if she still existed – for his own gain. He was glad to be going to the Sherans; a bit of uncomplicated company was what he needed.

He arrived fairly early and spent the first half-hour talking to a couple he knew he'd met there before, who remembered his name, his occupation, and where he lived, and about whom he could recall nothing whatsoever. He was too embarrassed to ask any leading questions, and allowed Jim to fill his glass as often as he passed. When Frances, preceded by the dog dangerously waving its silver palm-frond tail, wheeled in a huge platter of hot food to join the salads already laid out, he made his excuses and went to the table. Jim was encouraging everyone to heap their plates, and he said to Kenneth, rather awkwardly, 'Haven't really seen you for ages. Why don't we take a bottle with our food and sit down?'

'Good idea.' It was very unlike Jim to abandon his overview host role. 'Lovely grub.'

'You know Frances. There'll be enough to feed us until Wednesday.'

They perched in the window seat overlooking the garden. Like the house, it was charming. 'Only Frances could have so many things that look alive in the winter. What's that little tree with the pink flowers?'

'Haven't a clue. I'll tell you when the daffodils come out, but that's about my limit.' Jim's usual hearty tone softened. 'I do like it though. She makes everywhere pretty.' He drained his glass. 'Nice people the Tomlinsons, aren't they?' He was looking at the couple Kenneth had just been talking to.

'Mm,' he muttered through a mouthful of halibut and mushroom pie.

'It's such good news about his new appointment.'

Tomlinson . . .

'I thought that was quite a sympathetic piece about him in the paper last Sunday. Did you see it?'

He shook his head. 'Away.' Tomlinson . . .

'Frances is doing her stuff. Hopes he'll buy one of the Stein woman's pictures.'

Kenneth suspected he did not care for Serena Stein. Tomlinson . . . Ronnie always said he was hopeless about remembering what people did and making the right noises.

'Ronnie,' said Jim, and then seemed to get into difficulties.

Kenneth took another bite of pie and tried to look encouraging.

'Dreadful business at your flat. But Frances tells me things have straightened out. And Bernard Gray too . . . dreadful.'

'Yes.' He waited a few seconds before crunching into some celery filled with Roquefort.

'Ronnie,' said Jim again. Then, in a rush, 'Take a bit of advice, if you will. I'd wait and see what happens, if I were you. Wait a week or two. She may be back sooner than you think, and then . . . well.'

Kenneth felt surprised and was sure that he looked it.

226

'Oh, it isn't that we know anything,' Jim went on. 'We're not privy to anything. But – well – I talked it over with Frances. Just briefly, you know. Because I like you both, the pair of you. And these things happen. And I think it's worth waiting – see if they get ironed out. We've had a bit of experience, Frances and me. Not always a completely smooth run, you know.'

He was very touched. Wanted to say something, but didn't know what.

'Hope you don't mind me bringing the matter up?'

'No. No, of course not.'

'I just felt I'd like to say. She's a fantastic girl, Ronnie.'

'Yes. Yes, she is.' Lydia, he thought for no special reason. Lydia.

The Tomlinsons came towards them with full plates. 'May we join you?'

'Of course, of course. Sit down.' Jim got up. 'It's time I was doing my bottle round. Just saying to Kenneth how glad we were you could come.'

'Oh, Kenneth and I agreed just now, one can't be writing and thinking about art all the time. It's good to have a break.'

'What's that tree?' asked Mrs Tomlinson as Jim wandered off.

'A slintomon,' Kenneth said, reverting to a childhood anagram habit.

'What a strange name. I must write it down. It's such a pretty tree.'

British Council? Arts Council? Sheridan Foundation? Tate Gallery?

If he 'phoned for a minicab now, it might be here by four.

16   He hears something to his advantage

Kenneth stood in the middle of his room in his underpants and socks, shivering. Outside, there were a good four inches of snow and he did not know what clothes to put on for the funerals. He'd planned the grey suit, but not for this weather. He'd have to wear his fleece-lined leather jacket – it was the only warm and weatherproof garment he possessed. And his black boots. That would have to do. One day, when he was fifty perhaps, he'd get an overcoat.

Jack had 'phoned to say that he and Alf would pick him up. 'It's a good job it's a cremation, mate. They'd never get a spade into the ground this weather.'

When he'd first woken, he'd know by the sepulchral light that there was snow, and drinking his coffee at his work place he had been glad. The untouched white overlay that softened the angles of the wall and rested in the concave evergreen leaves, helped to bury the bleakness out there. But, listening later on to the traffic news and the forecasts of more snow, he realized how cursedly inconvenient it was going to be.

Alf turned out to be a joker. He addressed a slipstream of remarks to the back of the cab, where Kenneth and Jack were sitting straight-backed and awkward, as he set off towards Kensington Gardens. 'Looks like a bloody Russian steppe, don't it? What a day to bury the dead. Real Captain Oates stuff. Mind you, once you get to them cemeteries up there, the Antarctic would seem like Butlin's. I keep thinking they must have filled them up by now. But no, there's always another bugger to be seen off. I'm certain positive I'm not going to lay there. Not even in an ashtray.'

Jack, who was clearly used to letting most of Alf's remarks pass him by, intervened. 'No? Where are you putting yourself then?'

'Not there, mate, I can tell you.'

Kenneth thought that Jack was satisfied to prove his friend had made no firm plan for his body, despite the boast. He decided he'd better voice his problem.

'Er . . . I'm in a bit of a quandary.'

'Oh,' said Jack, 'how's that?'

He explained about Bernard's funeral, and how he wasn't sure of its exact location in relation to Drew's.

'No problem,' said Alf, 'I'll get you there. Chap you worked with, you say? Pity that.'

Jack was shaking with laughter. 'Blimey, Kenneth,' he said, 'You don't half fall in it. I've never known anyone go to *two* funerals the same day before.'

Kenneth began to laugh too. And Alf, relieved that news of the second funeral didn't mean he'd got to sober up, caught Kenneth's eye in the driving mirror and winked. For the rest of the drive they swapped bad weather stories. Alf remembered getting lost in fog and snow on the Yorkshire moors while he was doing his national service: 'Like being swaddled from head to toe in wet washing three hundred miles from home.' Jack recalled the eighty-three stairs up which water had to be carried from a stand-pipe in the street during the 1947 freeze-up. Kenneth told them about nine hours in a stranded train after visiting Wales in 1963: 'Difficult to know what was worst – the cold, the uncertainty, or the state of the lavatories.' United by past discomforts, they drove companionably towards the cemeteries.

More snow began to fall as Alf slowed down to turn into the gates of the crematorium. Fat flakes filled the air in a restless grey swarm and splodged onto the windscreen.

'Christ,' said Jack. 'I hope they've got the coffin here all right.'

229

'We'll soon find out.' Alf leaned over to the platform by the driving seat and pulled a bridal bunch of white flowers out of a black plastic rubbish bag.

'What ever you got those for?' Jack asked.

'To make me feel comfortable. I hate a funeral without flowers. And I know how you feel about the boy. But he's dead now. And a coffin looks better with a bunch of flowers on it.'

'I thought Lyddy might want to send something. But it seemed she didn't really want to know about today.'

'That's all right,' said Alf. 'As long as we all do as we please.'

They hunched their shoulders against the snow and made their way towards the chapel. The undertakers were already there, and visibly relieved to see them. As Jack, looking pinched and uncomfortable, confirmed arrangements with the priest, Alf walked over to the pale coffin and placed his flowers on top.

They were motioned to take their places in a pew, some piped music filled the empty spaces with ersatz solemnity, and the priest, who wore horn-rimmed spectacles, gave them a diminished, practised, smile of comfort before walking to face them from the centre of the chapel. The music faded, and as the minimal service was spoken into the cold air, and the three makeshift mourners bent their heads, Kenneth felt immensely grateful to Alf. If it weren't for the flowers, a generous bouquet of incurving chrysanthemums and perfect greenhouse roses, he would probably have cried, the coffin would have seemed so abandoned.

He watched it slide away through a blue curtain and the realization of the enormity of what had happened flooded through him, making him dizzy. Drew had died in desperation because he, Kenneth, had been able to attract his wife. Lydia had fled Drew, tried to escape his pleadings for months – years. And he had lingered over a postcard of Richard Wilson's Italian wine flask and been desired. That was all.

Suddenly, fiercely, Kenneth clenched his eyes and thought of his own father. Like Drew, he had slipped beyond a curtain without the accompaniment of his son's prayers or grief.

Oh God, he said inside his head, rather ashamed, please give sanctuary to them both.

Afterwards, as they made their way back to the taxi through

230

deepening snow, a hooded figure came towards them from the direction of the gate. Jack muttered something that Kenneth did not catch and went round to get in the other side of the cab. Alf was climbing into the driving seat, and Kenneth was left waiting to see what the stumbling, anxious-looking man wanted.

'Is Drew Forsyth's funeral over?' he asked.

'Yes.'

The man seemed nonplussed.

'Did you ... are you a friend?'

As Kenneth waited for a reply to his question, the door beside him opened.

'Get in, for God's sake,' said Jack.

Kenneth frowned at him.

'Get *in*,' Jack repeated.

He started to move, and the hooded man lurched nearer. 'What do you want?' asked Kenneth, holding the side of the door.

'Where's Rhys Forsyth?'

'Rhys Forsyth?'

'Yes. Where is he?'

'I've no idea.'

'But he must be here.'

'Why?'

'I spoke to him.'

'What about?'

'For God's sake!' hissed Jack. 'Get *in*.'

Kenneth did so. But he was concerned about the man. 'Rhys Forsyth doesn't go to funerals,' he said to him just before slamming the door as Alf drove off.

'Didn't you recognize him?' Jack was tight-lipped.

'No.'

'It was that journalist. The one that was hanging around.'

'Oh ...' Of course, the black anorak, this time with the hood up. 'Sorry. I thought he might be ... well, a friend or something.'

'I don't think Drew had many of those. The way he was. Anyway – what did he want?'

'He seemed to expect Rhys Forsyth to be here. Said he'd spoken to him.'

'Thank God he wasn't. A madman if you ask me. Just like

his son.' Jack settled back in his seat. 'That's what he was on about before, Maggie said. When he was outside our house. Wanted information about the old man.'

Kenneth decided not to say any more. With any luck, the man's pursuit would be over now.

Visibility ahead was very poor, and for a while it seemed they were the only vehicle on the road. Alf went slowly but steadily, and the windscreen wipers just managed to clear the snow jerkily first to one side then the other.

Jack let out a long sigh. 'I can't tell you how glad I am that's over.'

Kenneth nodded. 'Yes.'

They all remained silent until Alf drew into the kerb saying, 'I think this is it,' and Kenneth could see the headlights of a line of vehicles crawling along, their indicators flashing as one by one they turned into some tall black gates.

'Seems a bit of a turn-out,' said Jack.

'At least we're not the only loonies out in this weather.' Alf swivelled round to look at Kenneth. 'Now. What would you like us to do? Go and park in there and wait till it's over and drive you home?'

'Good heavens no. I couldn't ask you to do that.'

'You can. I'll keep the engine running – keep us warm.'

'You did me a favour,' said Jack. 'It looked better, like. Having the three of us.'

'I'm glad I came.' It was sort of true. 'And I'll be fine now. There's bound to be someone'll give me a lift back.'

'All right. But I'll take you to the door.' Alf edged into the queue of vehicles.

They waited as two other taxis dropped their muffled passengers at the entrance to the chapel, while others ploughed across the courtyard from parked cars. It contrasted so starkly with Drew's funeral.

'Must have been a popular man,' said Jack.

'Yes.' Kenneth prepared to get out. 'Will you let me buy you a drink some time?' he said to Alf.

'Of course. But there's no need.'

He watched the cab drive away towards the gate, the snow quickly blurring everything but its red rear lights. He wished he was still inside. He felt quite unprepared for the occasion that lay ahead.

Many middle-aged and elderly people, clad in fur and Burberry and tweed, were nodding and exchanging muted greetings before sitting down in the pews. The coffin was heaped with flowers, and he felt ashamed that he had sent none – that he didn't know how to behave. Then William came towards him with a man carrying a black homburg, whom he introduced as James Nall. Kenneth thought that Nall gave him a rather searching look before he said, in a precise Scots voice, 'May we have a wee word after? You're not in any rush?'

'No.'

'Good,' said William. 'We'll see you then.'

Kenneth realised they were going to sit in the front, in appointed seats. He looked for somewhere near the back, and was just making for a vacant seat next to a man with a pink shiny pate, when he realized that he was a very famous actor. Worried lest it appeared he was going next to him on purpose, he veered towards another chair, only to realize that he was sitting down by a rather distinguished author. He concentrated on looking at the order of service laid out on the chair. It hadn't occurred to him that the people Bernard told wickedly funny stories about, whose characteristics he had freely borrowed for Fox's milieu, would be here to mourn him.

The service was not so anonymous as Drew's. The priest gave colloquial but respectful thanks for the life of the man he had never met and which he recounted in scant outline, and the mourners sang 'The day thou gavest, Lord, has ended' quite lustily. Kenneth started to imagine what Bernard would have made of it all, but stopped. It was too bizarre. Despite the priest's address and the gathering of friends, this ceremony somehow seemed less to do with the Bernard he had known than Drew's funeral had been to do with the boy they'd carried into his room and covered with a blanket.

For the second time that day he was bidden to say the Lord's Prayer. He had closed his eyes the first time. Now he held his head up, kept his eyes open, and said 'Thy will be done, in earth as it is in heaven' towards the clear glass window at the end of the chapel and wondered what exactly that would mean were it to come true.

It had stopped snowing when the chapel doors were opened, and some of the mourners walked along a covered way to the terrace where flowers that had shrouded the coffin were now arranged in a tasteful row. Kenneth followed them since William had indicated Nall would not be ready straight away, and watched a few august personages tilt forward in their thick clothes to try to read the messages on the wreaths without their spectacles.

The cemetery that stretched out into the distance on either side was like a sea of icing sugar filled with wrecks, the encrusted tops of stone crosses and marble angels poking out as far as the eye could see. Kenneth stood looking at it for a while, the cold seeping up through his already chilled feet and down through his slightly aching ears. He could understand why stranded people had the urge to lie down in the snow to keep warm. It had the deceit of comfort about it.

Someone came to stand next to him, and he realised it was the very famous actor, his head now covered with an astrakhan hat.

'I know it is impious,' the actor said, his fine diction making the words seem as if they had undergone expensive vocal topiary, 'but the only lines that keep going through my head are Cleopatra's "The stroke of death is as a lover's pinch, Which hurts, and is desired".'

'Bernard would have liked that.'

'People always say at funerals that the deceased would like whatever it is that has just been done or said. But for once I think you may be right.' He gave Kenneth a small smile and walked away.

Kenneth thought of Fox's Vixen, who owed her meticulous housekeeping and penchant for home-truths to the actor.

'I didn't realize you were acquainted.' William was at Kenneth's elbow, his eyes on the disappearing actor.

'We aren't. He just spoke to me.'

'Lucky you. I saw his Hamlet four times when I was sixteen.'

Kenneth gave an uncontrollable shiver.

'You look frozen. Yet it didn't seem too cold in the chapel.'

'I think it's all beginning to get to me.'

William looked concerned, then disconcerted. 'Oh God, I'm sorry. I'd quite forgotten. You've already been through this once. Was it awful?'

'Not really.' He looked once more over the white acres of graves. 'It all seems rather unreal.'

'Come to the car. James is warming it up. And something very real awaits you there.'

Kenneth followed him. During the service he had not tried to anticipate why Nall should wish to see him. Now, as the moment approached, he began to imagine it would be something to do with the legal formalities in connection with the royalties; or perhaps a suggestion that some of the money – or even all the money – should be spent on a gift to charity as a memorial to Bernard. It seemed like a good idea.

William took him to a Volvo estate, and Nall leaned over from the driving seat to open the passenger door for Kenneth as William got into the back. The car was already quite snug. Kenneth wriggled his toes inside his boots and rubbed his fingers together. Nall produced a metal thermos flask and poured three small cups of black coffee.

'Hardly the baked meats,' he said. 'But it will warm you through.'

The coffee was generously laced with whisky. Kenneth felt it rush down the centre of his body and inch out into the extremities.

'Great foresight, James,' exclaimed William cheerfully, draining his cup.

'I did not like the sound of the weather forecast,' Nall replied. 'Now, I must first apologise for not inviting you to my office, Mr Flete. But, since William here has an important meeting at three, I thought it best for us to have a brief session at once, so I could formally inform you both of Mr Gray's will.' He pulled some papers from a folder at his side. 'As I think you know, Mr Flete . . .' He paused, and ran his finger down a page.

'Please call me Kenneth.'

'Thank you. And you will call me James. Now . . . Kenneth . . . Bernard Gray made a will in which he left the royalties from his two books to your goodself. I think William has already told

235

you that. And William is to administer his literary estate for which he is to receive the usual percentage of any monies, plus receiving a personal benefice of some shares and other holdings. It is a little difficult yet to estimate what these will amount to, but I should guess roughly in the region of ten thousand pounds.'

Kenneth turned to grin at William. 'Isn't that great?'

'It certainly is. And quite undeserved.'

'Any other outstanding monies,' James continued, 'which won't, I think, amount to a very great amount, but a nice legacy nonetheless, are to go to the London Library. Which leaves Bernard's main asset.' He paused, a little theatrically.

Kenneth thought it unlikely that Bernard had a Cézanne or Van Dyck stashed away. Family porcelain, perhaps.

'You have been to his home?' asked James.

'Oh – yes.' His memory returned to the cluttered living room and could find only a Minton Mediterranean landscape among the bric-à-brac. It was a nice Minton, but hardly worth a fortune.

'Well, after probate, and I foresee no problems, it is yours.'

Kenneth's first flicker of a reaction was that he did not desperately want the Minton.

Then it dawned: Bernard had left him his house.

17   He receives a note from Lydia

A note awaited him in the hall from Mr Worrell. 'It is only fair that we should all take a share of clearing the snow.'

As far as Kenneth could see, a small path, less than six inches wide, had been made down the middle of the doorsteps at some point in the day, but it was now almost filled with fresh snow which had fallen later. He smiled. Normally Mr Worrell's communications irritated him intensely and drove him to inaction. Now he got out a broom and hand shovel and went briskly to work.

The street lamps were on, and the noise of the diminished traffic was muffled by the flattened snow on the road. Kenneth attacked the steps, brushing and scraping, the shovel rasping against the concrete, until there were thick banks of snow on either side; then he set about the pavement and cleared a pathway ten yards long.

He was sweating when he went indoors, though his boots and trouser ends were soaked and his fingers so stiff they could hardly hold a pen to write shakily: '4.45 p.m. Have just cleared snow from steps *and* pavement.' Mr Worrell would probably think he was drunk.

He certainly felt drunk. He'd ridden to Gloucester Road on the Underground in a complete daze. James and William had dropped him at Edgware Road, and the only other time he could remember feeling quite so light-headed was when he'd walked across the tarmac at Gatwick to board the plane for the States in '63. On both occasions it had been like floating on an invisible cloud of freedom.

'Bernard knew how difficult it was for people to start buying property these days,' William had said. 'And he wanted to make it easy for someone.'

'But why on earth me?'

'He said you'd seemed to like the house. Most people didn't. And that you never made difficulties over things. And most people did.'

'There is, of course, no obligation on you to keep it, once probate is through,' James had explained. 'It has an approximate market value – approximate, mind you – of £75,000.'

It appeared, Kenneth thought, as he peeled off his clothes and prepared a hot bath, that being a man of property made him more generous towards the Mr Worrells of this world. He'd clear the steps again tomorrow, if need be.

'Wheee!' he suddenly shrilled into the steam. 'Bernard ... thank you!'

When he was stretched out in the water, he counselled himself not to make up his mind about anything quickly. Not even perhaps to talk about it to anyone. This was nothing to do with William saying cautiously, 'I was a bit worried what people might say. If they got to hear about it. But then I thought you probably wouldn't mind anyway', it was to give himself time to think, to examine what had been done to him. And how did he feel about William's worry? The idea that someone might assume he'd been Bernard's boyfriend rather intrigued him.

When he pulled aside the green blind at six o'clock the next morning, the street lamps shone on new snow. One set of footprints marched along his channel on the pavement, indicating there were three or four inches to be swept away. He contemplated doing it there and then, he felt so wide awake, but all the time a more urgent motivation was propelling him to dress and go out.

His boots were still wet, and he rummaged in the cupboard for an old pair of desert shoes that would leak but also accommodate two pairs of socks. It was a deep cupboard, and he

238

realized he could no longer remember all the things it contained. Once, that would have been unthinkable, he had had so few possessions. Then he had despised the growing habit among his contempories to stockpile old clothes and display odds and ends, mementoes from the branch lines of their lives. Now, as in so many other things, he did not really know what he thought about possessions or the aesthetics of domesticity.

When he was ready to go out he turned the heating up so that the room would be really warm when he returned. Whatever else happened, he must do some work today. He must return to a semblance of normality after he had completed this secret, self-indulgent mission.

He had to wait fifteen minutes for a bus, stamping his feet and exchanging mumbled greetings with the few passers-by who in ordinary weather would not have uttered. The bus conductor was the cheery sort, determined to make his very meagre load of passengers rise to a level of good humour and not wallow in winter depression. Kenneth rather admired him.

At Putney Bridge he changed buses, waiting this time twenty minutes before a 220 appeared in a line of gingerly approaching traffic. Being a one-man operated bus, the atmosphere on board could not be manipulated by a conductor, but was governed by the mood of the passengers. Kenneth went upstairs and sat with several silent, smoking workmen. They looked at their tabloids and he looked out of the brightly-lit bus to the strip of park that loomed white in the fading dark.

Soon the bus had moved cautiously round the traffic system that made this part of Wandsworth impenetrable to strangers and was picking up a few passengers along the mile drive to Cranstead. Kenneth alighted by the station where early commuters were on their way to the West End and the City. A news vendor huddled behind a display of papers whose front-page pictures were all of expanses of snow which had brought cars, trains or livestock to a standstill. Kenneth turned the corner into Cranstead Rise and set off up the hill. The daylight was beginning to strengthen, and the allotments on his left looked like a scene in an American rural painting, with portions of rudimentary sheds − corrugated iron, old painted doors, rusty panels of steel − showing starkly against the virgin snow. On his right, a continuous row of three-storey, semi-detached houses was showing varying signs of life. Three people were clearing snow off cars, and two were shovelling their front paths. A lanky paper-boy in tight jeans and plimsolls waded up an untouched garden.

At the top of the hill, just before the allotments ended and a second row of smaller houses began, Kenneth stopped. Now he was here, he felt conspicuous. He took out his handkerchief and blew his nose. While doing so he looked surreptitiously at the house immediately opposite. Because it must be cold inside, its roof was thickly covered with snow, which also clung to the sills, window frames and weatherboarding, concealing the peeling green paintwork. The front gate had clearly not been opened since the snow started, and the laburnum and lilac looked almost picturesque, each branch and twig rimmed with white.

The front door of the neighbouring but not adjoining house suddenly opened, and with reflex embarrassment Kenneth bent to pretend to tie a shoelace buried in snow.

'Doris, Doris,' called a scolding, anxious female voice.

He peered up and saw a tall, grey-haired woman in a blue dressing-gown calling towards Bernard's house. There was a movement at the side, and a cat emerged from somewhere, balancing on the thin crust on top of the snow, then sinking in as it jumped from the low fence between the houses to go to the woman. Kenneth watched her try to entice the cat indoors, but it stayed in the porch, tail erect, looking up at her. Finally she gave up, and brought out two bowls. The cat settled to eat and drink and the woman went inside.

He had completely forgotten about Doris, the plain black cat that mistrusted Bernard's friends. He looked again at the house, which for some reason seemed bigger and emptier now that he knew the orphaned cat was refusing to abandon it. He tried to imagine the house being his, and did not succeed. The invisible cloud of freedom was not there that morning; just the feeling that something was finished, and an intimation that the map of the future had been changed.

At first, when he got back home, he thought that despite the warm room he was not going to be able to settle to work. He almost took the shovel out to the steps, but checked himself.

That hand-drawn letterhead shouldn't take more than a couple of hours.

He was interrupted by the telephone. Sky wanted to know why there was such a horrible piece about Drew Forsyth in one of the daily papers. Kenneth ascertained that it was a gossip column paragraph about Rhys Forsyth not going to his wastrel son's funeral. He made Sky read it out and uppermost felt relief first that he wasn't mentioned, and secondly neither was Lydia.

'Pete's obviously explained to you that the boy was Drew Forsyth,' he said carefully.

'Yes, he did. And that he used to admire Rhys. And felt awful when you told him about his 'phone call. But *why* do they write things like this? *Wastrel*. That's a horrible thing to say. He was such a gentle-looking person.'

'Mm.' That bloody journalist. All that hanging around and effort just to earn a few quid selling a bit of information. 'Wastrel' had probably been supplied by the columnist himself. The kind of emotive word that ensured his readership. Drew's only printed epitaph.

'Kenneth? Can I come over? Just for a bit. I won't stay or anything.'

He looked at the unfinished letterhead. A poncey bit of work. 'All right.'

The first thing Sky said when he let her into the room was, 'You've mended the window.'

'Yes. I got someone to come and do it last Monday.'

She walked over to it and rubbed at the smears of fresh putty along one side. 'I'm glad there's snow out there.'

'I felt that too.'

'Pete said it was probably drugs.'

'Yes.'

'And that you were friendly with his wife.'

'I'd met her a couple of times. I didn't know about Drew. They'd been divorced a long time.'

'He must have loved her a lot.'

Kenneth didn't respond. He decided to put the kettle on. While he was spooning out coffee, Sky suddenly declared, 'I don't love Mal at all.'

'Oh?'

241

'No. I realised I didn't when he started telling me how much he loved me. So I'm going to go and live at home for a bit. Only I haven't told him yet.'

Kenneth checked himself from saying, 'And have you told your parents?' Presumably Jos's mother was sleeping in Sky's bedroom. Instead he asked, 'When are you going to tell him?'

'Tonight, I think. It's a horrible thing to do. But it's only fair.'

'Perhaps you'll be able to find a way to remain friends.'

'I want to. I suppose Drew and your friend, his wife, didn't manage to.'

'I think it was all rather complicated, Sky. Very long drawn out. And Drew had been pretty sick, ill, for some time.'

'Yes ... Mal's very healthy. Except for a bunion. He must be the only twenty-year-old with a bunion.'

Kenneth decided to change track. 'Presumably Jos's mother is still staying at Alderney Street?'

'Oh yes. Pete says it's driving them potty. But at least it means they can't spend their time having rows. Actually,' she looked at Kenneth to watch his reaction, '*I* think Jos is secretly pleased her sainted brother's done something wrong at last.'

'I hadn't thought of that.'

'I feel jolly sorry for Tom and Jonathan. Having a keep-fit instructor as a prospective step-mother.'

'She's not!'

'She is. Gran calls her "that common gym mistress".'

'Oh dear.'

'It's all such a *muddle*. That's why I'm going to tell Mal. *I* don't want to start getting into a muddle I'll have to dig myself out of ten years and six children later. Though I really do like him.'

'Very commendable.' Honest Sky. 'What did you think of my story, by the way? About Tom Girtin.'

She blushed. 'I didn't *really* understand it. I mean ... well, Pete said it had something to do with me. But all that bit about Lord and Lady Somebody going to Constantinople, I didn't really get it.'

He was ashamed because he felt briefly hurt. He hoped she didn't realise. 'Don't worry.'

'But I liked that bit about him painting up on the roof. That's

242

a lovely description.'

'Thanks.' Now he was a little ashamed that her praise gave him such pleasure.

Something made him glance towards the window overlooking the road, and Lydia's askance grey eyes met his.

He knew from her expression that she had already seen Sky, who was standing by the bed holding her coffee mug. Lydia's impression would have been of a tall young girl with lots of hair, wearing a red sweater.

He feared she was about to turn and go.

'Wait!' He half-shouted, though she wouldn't have been able to hear.

'What?' asked Sky.

He was on his way to the front door.

She hadn't gone, but was still standing below the window, looking down at the pavement.

'Lydia,' he called softly. 'Lydia. Come in.'

She started to walk towards him, and stopped again at the bottom of the steps. She was wearing a white knitted hat and scarf and the navy duffle coat. Her jeans were stuffed into wellingtons. She looked barely older than Sky. How he wished that Sky were not there.

He went down two steps and held out his hand. 'Careful,' he said, 'they're rather slippery.' He thought she wasn't going to take it, but in the end she drew a cold, bare hand out of her pocket and placed it in his. He didn't say any more until the front door was safely shut behind them.

'I've got Sky Brown with me,' he said brightly. 'My friends' daughter.'

The ignominy of the situation was extreme. He had never told Lydia that Sky had been present at Drew's death. Her reaction to Ronnie had prevented any likelihood of him reporting the whole sequence of events. In any case she had not asked him to. And though Sky's name had been mentioned at the inquest, along with Ronnie's and Mr and Mrs Warren's, nothing had been made of her presence on that night. Jack never referred to it.

'Sky,' he said, releasing Lydia's hand, 'this is Lydia. Lydia Forsyth.'

243

The two seconds in which Sky's expression changed from wary to shocked to concerned seemed interminable. Then she took a step forward and said, 'Hullo. You look frozen.'

Lydia made no response.

Kenneth did not know what to do. He felt the three of them were fixed there, in a kind of ghastly tableau vivant, and that whatever words he spoke would set the action going again in an unbearable direction.

'Shall I . . .' Sky began.

He knew that she was about to offer to make Lydia a cup of coffee, and dreaded the appearance of familiarity with him and his room that this would create. But something made her stop, and the two words hung in the air.

'I think,' she went on finally, 'I'd better go now. Uninvited guest and all that.' She put down her mug and went to get her coat.

Lydia remained rigid in the middle of the room.

Kenneth watched Sky, and when she was ready walked with her to the door of his room.

'No need to see me out.'

'All right. I hope things go okay with Mal. And please give Jos my love. And Pete, of course.'

'Mum made a bit of a balls-up about my early morning entry with the police, didn't she?'

'It's all over now. Pete explained.'

'Oh.' Rather embarrassedly she fished into her pocket and took out a torn piece of newspaper. Whispering, she explained, 'I brought this in case you wanted to see it.'

He took it, registering the paragraph heading, 'Guru cold-shoulders son's funeral'. 'Thanks, Sky. Thanks.'

'I'll go,' said Lydia dully after he had closed the door.

'Lydia.' He went up to her and put one hand on her shoulder, while shoving the piece of newspaper into his pocket with the other. 'You've only just this moment arrived.'

'Uninvited guest.'

'What?'

'She said I was.'

'She was talking about herself.'

'No.'

244

'Lydia, she *was*. For goodness sake. Sky's young and a bit headstrong. But she's not deliberately rude.' He watched her eyes begin to water. 'Lydia. Sit down. Please. Sit down, and I'll make you some coffee.'

He waited until she at last began to move towards the settee.

While the kettle was coming to the boil, he looked out into the road. It was barely more than a fortnight since he and Pete had noticed Drew standing over there.

'Has something happened?' he asked. 'I know how apprehensive you felt about coming back here.'

The tears were pouring down her face. It was hopeless. He knew it was because of Sky. Not because of visiting the scene of Drew's death.

'What is it, Lydia? Why are you crying?'

But she just shook her head, gulped, and went on weeping.

He made the coffee and set it down beside her. He didn't join her on the settee, but went to a chair and waited. Patience was not normally one of his virtues, but the anger and bewilderment that her behaviour had begun to rouse dwindled, neutralized by an almost euphoric feeling that he had all the time in the world to sort things out. He had never taken a tranquillizer, but he imagined this might be how it would feel. As he watched her cry, there was, at the back of his mind, the knowledge of the snowy hill, the allotments, the unopened gate, the house. He was not trapped. He had – he smiled – a foxhole.

After several minutes, Lydia quietened. Her now red face, still framed in the white scarf and hat, took on an expression of fear rather than misery. He could see it was still possible she might suddenly run away.

He shifted in his chair, and felt the piece of paper in his pocket crackle. Without calculating, he took it out and said, 'Sky brought this for me to see. Have you seen it?' He held the paper up so that she would recognize it if she'd read it earlier.

She nodded. 'Maggie brought it round.'

'That damn journalist ought to have better things to do.'

'I suppose all your friends know about it anyway.'

'Why?'

'If their children are bringing round bits from the newspaper.'

The naked jealousy, that would leap at anything, destroy

245

anything, like a fire spreading through a well-loved room, absorbed him.

'You had better know,' he said, 'that I'm not going to conceal innocuous information from you just because you get upset.'

She no longer looked afraid. There was a sense of challenge in the way she removed her hat, loosened her scarf and stared across at him. He glimpsed the person he had met before Drew and Arthur and Jack were known to exist.

'Sky was here when Drew died. That is why she brought me the cutting. She was with me because she'd had a row with her boyfriend and, when she went home to get away from him, she found her parents were rowing. She came to me because they are my friends. Jos and Pete have been part of my life for a long time.'

Lydia sighed.

'The only other person I've told about Drew is William Hurley who is my agent. Oh, and Bernard – who is dead.'

'Ronnie,' she said flatly.

'I didn't have to *tell* Ronnie.' He was getting annoyed now. 'Her flat is in this house. You know that.'

'I just meant that she knew about it.' Her voice sounded almost spiteful.

'Lydia!' The hardness, loudness, of his voice took him by surprise. 'What are you trying to do to me?'

She got up immediately and made for the door. He held back, didn't try to stop her. She left it open, and he watched her cross the hall, tussle with the unfamiliar fastening on the front door, and disappear, slamming it behind her.

He went straight to his work table and finished the letterhead. Then he sat for a long time, head propped by his hands, watching more snow fall on Drew's death bed.

When the telephone rang, he was sure it would be Lydia.

'How dare you! How dare you!'

Even in anger, the lilting voice was unmistakable.

'How *dare* you misrepresent me, misrepresent my grief. To the press. The *gutter* press.'

Kenneth held the receiver away from his ear and went on looking out of the window.

'Are you there? Are you there? Flete, is that you?'

246

'Yes.' If there had been deep snow on that night, would he still have died?

'You see! Lurking! Afraid to speak. I shall sue. My lawyer will be approaching you. What do you have to say? Now, what do you have to say?'

'Nothing,' said Kenneth, and put the receiver down.

He swiftly dressed to go out, and walked through the snow up to South Kensington where he went into the pub he used to frequent as a student. He seldom used it now. The present generation of art students – pale punky boys and bizarrely painted girls – made him feel old. But today he barely noticed them. He ordered a pint of beer and – his reason for coming – shepherd's pie, and went to sit by a radiator in the corner. The shepherd's pie had remained constant over twenty years. Finely minced meat, always a fair proportion of it lamb, moist with good onion gravy, and the tops of the forked ridges in the buttery mashed potato on top well crisped.

He looked around. The girls didn't seem so fierce today, wrapped in shawls and scarves and knee-length woollens, standing under the criss-crossing tinsel garlands and paper chains. One of them went to activate the juke-box, and the high tones of the old Sam Cooke number *Havin' a Party* cut clearly through the voices and clatter. He watched the girl dance a few steps, make jivey signals to her friends. There would be parties galore for them these next few weeks. And it would still be possible – just – for him to slip back into it all. Some of his contemporaries who were teaching would know where the parties were, would tell him if they met him in the Fulham or King's Road pubs on a Friday or Saturday night and take him along. He had no responsibilities . . .

Last Christmas, he and Ronnie had been invited out to small, private parties on Christmas Eve and Boxing Day. Each occasion had been perfectly pleasant. Boccherini in the background at the first, old Beatles albums at the second. A good deal of dry sparkling wine and avocado dip; a small amount of smoked salmon. On Christmas Day Ronnie had invited an American couple, friends of hers on holiday in London, to dinner. The couple had been concerned about the best place to buy silver; they were going to take small silver items home as presents.

247

Kenneth was sure they hadn't believed him when he said he hadn't the faintest idea where they should go. That they'd thought he had a secret, cheap source which he wouldn't reveal. The man knew a great deal about Henry James, which he'd found interesting. Perhaps Jim was right: he ought to mark time till Ronnie returned.

After a second pint he left the pub. He'd call in at the bookshop to see what some of his rivals had been up to for the Christmas trade. Perhaps get one of Ted Wing's books in paperback.

But his eye was taken by a large-format gardening book with an extremely good watercolour of cabbages and onions on the front. He guessed, correctly, who the artist was, and while checking her credit on the inside cover wondered if this was something Arthur would like. There were many more coloured drawings inside, and he decided to make a test: if Valdor lettuces were mentioned, he'd buy it; if not, not.

They were, and he went out into the street carrying a Christmas present for Lydia's son.

There was a pencilled note from Lydia written on a paper bag and enclosed in a used envelope waiting for him on the hall floor.

Kenneth, I can't help it. I won't come any more. I have loved you ever since I first saw you. I'm sorry I came this morning. My father thought you should know about the bit in the paper. And I so wanted to see you, I didn't 'phone. I just came. I shouldn't have done that. But I wanted to get over everything that had happened – to get it behind me. To show I can visit you ordinarily. But I can't. I mind about everything. I can't stop it. I love you.
All my love for ever, L.

He put it down face upwards on the bed. When he'd taken off his jacket, he read it again. He looked at the used envelope which was originally addressed to someone in Bina Gardens. She must have got it from a nearby litter-bin. The paper bag had a faint grease stain on it.

When the 'phone rang, he had no intimation who it would be.

'Ted Wing's back,' said William. 'I've got his list for you. Shall I put it in the post?'

'Please.'

'I've never heard of half the places. Do you know the church of the Gesuiti?'

'Yes.'

'He seems to have fallen for that.'

'Good.'

'And he even mentions a particular waiter in All'Angelo. Seems a bit strange. Unlike Ted. Of course I know the restaurant.'

'The waiter who looks like Harry Belafonte?'

'Good heavens. Have you two been colluding?'

'No.'

'Oh well, I suppose that means the omens are good. Made up your mind when you can go?'

'I will very soon.'

'Presumably you've got somewhere in mind to stay?'

'Mm ... I think so.' Would she feel comfortable in the rather spartan hotel he always used?

'Well ... let me know.'

'Of course.'

Was he mad? Was Venice really the place to begin?

18 He touches the marble damask with his finger

'Won't – *mightn't* she be in the way? Given you're going to be working?' Jos asked.

Kenneth noticed the tactful correction.

They were sitting by the fire at Alderney Street, drinking their first glass of wine and waiting for Pete and Sky to arrive back from the cinema. The flat was filled with the smell of *peperonata*.

'I hope not. She knows I'll be walking a lot and looking a lot and that the Giorgione isn't the Ritz.'

'And you've completely broken with Ronnie?'

It was a statement more than a question and its baldness almost affronted him. 'I haven't heard from her since she left.'

'But presumably she'll be coming back?'

'Presumably.' She was looking at him, trying to understand exactly what was being said. 'Jim Sheran said I should wait till she returned. In case the Faraday thing has blown over.'

'Do you think it will?'

'I've no idea.'

'Common sense dictates it's almost bound to.' She gave a broad smile. 'Bugger common sense. Love's much more interesting. Who – *whom* – do you love?'

'Oh, Jos. What a question ... Lydia loves me.'

'Poor Lydia. She must feel dreadful guilt.'

He remembered the sheer stillness of her joy when he had asked her to come to Venice. And the conspiratorial afternoon they had spent talking about it. 'Shall I tell you what finally made me decide to ask her?'

'Mm.'

'It was last Sunday. When there was that blizzard in the early morning. I listened to the lunchtime news, about the army taking over in Poland. During the afternoon the snow changed to drizzle and everywhere began to look stained and pock-marked. I was reading about Turner. He would never have dreamt of cluttering up a working tour with a female companion. And – I just decided to ask her.' He drank some wine. 'That doesn't make any sense, does it?'

'Turner makes us all feel inadequate.' There was zest not envy in her tone.

'Oh – Jos. I meant to say, as soon as I saw you, how very much I liked your painting in the barn. I saw it when I went down with Pete.'

'Really liked it?'

'Really.' He knew there was no need to say more.

'That's my first and best Christmas present.' She stretched her arms wide, the full sleeves of her black velveteen blouse hanging down like soft, swollen wings. 'It might even encourage me to get back to that beastly car painting. I haven't been able to face it since Mother took one look and said, "I *never* liked that car. I couldn't understand what made your father buy it."'

'What's happened with your mother? You just said on the 'phone that she'd gone back.'

'She has. Elizabeth is absolutely insisting that Theo must spend the three main days of Christmas at home with the boys. So mother has offered to go back until the holiday is over. To help with the cooking and things like she's always done. Elizabeth seems genuinely relieved ... I had a brief private talk to her on the 'phone, and it sounds as if she'd much rather Mother stayed there whatever happens. With or without Theo.'

'Would she do that?'

'Let's put it this way. She certainly won't admit anything of the kind at the moment, but she's so damned uncomfortable

251

here I think she's bound to.'

'How's Theo?'

'I haven't talked to him.'

'Might *that* blow over?'

'I don't think so. But I'm sure Mother's gone back determined to see that it does.' She stared into the fire. 'Poor Theo. I can feel some sympathy for him now. But there was a really dreadful few days when I hated him. I thought we were going to have to sell the cottage, leave here, and buy a tidy semi somewhere.'

'You couldn't do that.'

'No, but I *should*.'

'I don't see why.'

'It's all right for you. You haven't got a family.'

As she finished speaking, Pete and Sky could be heard at the top of the area steps. They were talking, and sounded light-hearted. Kenneth watched Jos's face as she waited for them to come in. She looked so happy.

He peered through the blur of spray on the window of the *motoscafo*. Across the choppy lagoon, the indistinct rim of buildings that was Venice gradually took shape. He hesitated to point it out to Lydia – she could only be disappointed: just a meagre filling of dark grey between the medium grey of the water and the pale grey of the sky.

The boat bumped its way between the poles that marked out the sailing channels. The other passengers, three Italian men who looked like brothers, talked seldom. Kenneth imagined from their serious expressions that they had been summoned to a family crisis. Or perhaps they always came home to Venice on the day after Christmas and were merely stealing themselves for Mama's feast.

Now they were actually here, actually at the point where individual buildings were beginning to emerge on the skyline and he was trying to see the salt-bleached statues poised in perpetual readiness to fly off the top of the façade of the Gesuiti, he felt very strange. He could not quite envisage the scene, only half an hour ahead, when he would lead the way up the steep marble stairs of the Giorgione to the room which they would share for four nights. And as his uncertainty about the nature of the immediate future grew, so did his profound consciousness that he must concentrate on the specifics of the visual present. Venice was no longer the city of permanent consolation: Ted Wing had turned it into a terrifying challenge.

He watched the poles fly by the watery window. His left side, which faced the draughty door onto the deck, was quite cold, but his right was warmed by contact with Lydia's coat. When he had called to pick her up early that morning, she had been standing outside the red front door, a neat red nylon bag beside her, wearing a long grey hooded coat and red boots. She looked exactly right for Venice in the winter. It was his first intimation of how meticulously she could plan. If he'd thought at all, he'd have expected the duffle coat and a bag bulging with sweaters. But in the twelve days since the trip had been agreed, during which he'd seen her only three times, she had made the coat, completed a theatre consignment, and tried to orchestrate Christmas so that neither Arthur nor Jack would feel let down when she left them on Boxing Day. As they talked in the taxi on the way to Heathrow, he'd gradually realized that, once she had known she was going to Venice, her energy had been formidable.

When the buildings were so close they had blotted out the sky, and it was only a matter of seconds before the boat would decrease its speed and go smoothly under a bridge in the Fondamenta Nuove into a canal, like a creature returning to a fabulous womb with many entrances, he took Lydia's hand.

The old walls reared up on either side. The rubbed brick, pitted stone, and crude patches of concrete were all thick with green weed to the high-water line. He felt her fingers squeeze tightly. He did not know whether she was overcome with a claustrophobic sense of decay, or thrilled by the intimacy of centuries.

They passed a boatyard where an ornate funeral gondola was hoisted up for repair.

'Look,' she whispered. 'A gondola.'

He did not tell her its purpose, or that ordinary gondolas were not encrusted with old gold. He did not want to say anything that might disappoint her.

They passed a barge loaded with bulging black plastic rubbish sacks.

'Where will they put it?' she asked.

He shook his head. He thought they took it to one of the deserted islands out in the lagoon, but he was not sure. Would she think it was dropped into the water? That the canals did therefore smell just as people who had never been here always said?

The canal narrowed, and they slowed down to give two oncoming motorboats easy clearance. He could hear the slap of water now, the incessant slap against the fabric of the city.

He dared to turn and scrutinise the expression on her face. But he realised he did not know her well enough to interpret with confidence the wide eyes, the slightly parted lips. Enchantment or appalled disbelief?

Shortly after they gathered speed again, the three men stood up. One of them went to stand over the driver as he steered into a little quay cut with narrow steps. Kenneth watched them spring easily, one by one, from the side of the boat onto the slippery stone, and felt Lydia's grip tighten. This time he knew her expression was one of apprehension.

'What's the matter?'

'I'll be scared to do that.'

'It's all right. He'll see there isn't a gap for us. And I'll hold your arm.'

'I think this is only the third time I've been in a boat.'

'How does it feel?'

'I just can't believe it's true. Any of it.'

They had reached the end of the canal and the boat took a sweeping leftward curve into a wide stretch of water. Kenneth said: 'This is the Grand Canal and that's the Rialto Bridge straight ahead.'

And there's the central post-office, he thought, which centuries ago was the headquarters of the German mechants. And there's the fish market and the fruit market and all those masked, semi-inhabited palazzi whose ground floors look permanently flooded and fast collapsing, but into which you can look at night from a *vaporetto* and see their first or second floors lit up like a series of stages: old Venetian, bohemian atelier, steel and glass and

254

greenery like East Manhattan.

They passed under the bridge with its arcade of shops, and saw the blue-and-yellow striped mooring posts in front of the Riva del Ferro gleaming against the grey water.

'Oh,' said Lydia. 'I hadn't realized it would be like *this*.'

He relaxed. In a minute they would be turning into the Rio di San Lucca between a grand high Renaissance palace and a prettily-ornamented Gothic one. Filling the upper part of the cabin window now was a plainer building.

'That orange house, there, with the red mooring posts, was where Turner stayed. The first time he came here.'

'How long ago?'

'Oh . . . about 160 years.'

'Richard Wilson came too, didn't he?'

'Yes. Over 200 years ago.'

'And now we're here.' She gave a deep, satisfied, sigh.

The boat had turned, and soon he could see the bridge by the Campo Manin where they would disembark.

The driver brought them gently to rest, and when Kenneth had stepped ashore put a steadying palm to Lydia's back as she sprang towards his outstretched hands.

'*Grazie*,' said Kenneth, taking their bags.

'*Prego*. You know quite sure the way?'

'Yes, thank you. Along the Calle Mandola, and then left.'

'*Si, si.* Have a good time.'

'*Grazie*.'

Lydia was looking across at a group of small boys who were racing round Manin's statue, leaping up the steps to touch the head of the winged lion each time they passed.

That day when he had imagined her walking across the *campo* she'd been in the distance, walking into a summer sun. Now, in winter, she was close and everything was real.

'I can't believe that this time yesterday Dad and I were watching Arthur unwrap his presents.'

He didn't want every Venetian schoolboy to remind her of Arthur.

'What were you doing?' she asked.

'Oh . . .' He looked at his watch. 'Arriving at William and Jill's, and being mildly appalled that there was a couple already

255

there called Tomlinson whom I didn't know they knew, and whose names and occupations I can never remember.'

'We mustn't waste time talking about London,' Lydia said, and picked up her bag.

He thought she had felt his censorship of Arthur, and put his arm around her shoulders as he guided her across the bridge into the network of shop-lined *calli* that felt to him like home.

They turned a corner by a *pasticciera*, closed, like the rest of the shops, for the holiday. Ahead, a vertical illuminated sign read GIORGIONE in plain black letters. The hotel had a narrow, unprepossessing frontage, and the doorway was modern – a functional conversion imposed on an old building that rambled backwards beside a narrow canal. The owner was at the reception desk and recognized Kenneth despite the lapse of five years. On discovering it was Lydia's first visit, he made a little speech of welcome and Kenneth felt glad that he hadn't elected to stay anywhere grander. He handed over their passports, assured Signor Boschini that they did not need help with their bags, and agreed that he remembered the way.

Climbing the stairs, he felt pretty sure he'd slept in Room 102 before. What he couldn't remember was whether he'd been alone, or if it had been the time he'd met a Swedish girl on the train and had shared some of his stay with her. How encyclopaedic was the memory of Signor Boschini? Did he remember details that he himself had forgotten?

He unlocked the door and saw one of the familiar heavy white cotton bedspreads with the big cursive 'G' woven at the centre. The shutters on the tall window were half-closed and he walked over to push them back and check that the room overlooked the canal and an apartment building on the other side. Yes, in the deep crevasse between the two walls a channel of dark water supported a moored dinghy, and he remembered how, in the early mornings, the metal churns of milk were unloaded with a fearful clank and scrape onto the stone steps. In summer, the little iron balconies outside each window of the apartment building were crammed with flowers and caged songbirds, and now looked rather forlorn. He turned to glance through the open door into the bathroom, and recognized the Giorgione's faded mauve towels and distressingly bright turquoise fitments. The hotel was blessedly warm. He took his leather jacket off.

Lydia was standing just two steps into the room. When he had draped his jacket on one of the basket chairs and lifted his bag onto the bed to start to unpack, she unbuttoned her coat. He saw that her fingers were shaking. The bed seemed to yawn between them.

'Do you want to unpack now?' he said. 'Then we'll go and find somewhere to eat.'

'All right.'

'Come and look at the view first.'

She left her coat on the bed and walked round to the window. He stood behind her, not quite touching.

'If you're woken in the morning by a loud crash, it'll be the milk being delivered.'

'I don't wake up very easily.'

He knew that, but said nothing. He wanted to try to keep that morning when he'd seen her under the pale yellow duvet out of these four days. Taking her hand, he said, 'There's the bathroom. I'll have a wash before we go out. Do you want to use it first?'

'No.'

He took his sponge-bag and was careful not to spread his things right across the shelf over the washbasin. His toothbrush looked tacky. Peeing into the turquoise bowl, he wished there were more hours of daylight left. It was not an easy city to sketch, or to show to someone, after dark. He would have to plan the time very carefully.

She was still standing by the window, her bag untouched.

'All yours,' he said.

'I've got to say something.'

His stomach turned slightly. He didn't want anything to spoil the next few hours. The process of reunion was too precious to be marred.

'What, Lydia?'

'I've never had anyone but Drew. I'm not sure how to behave.'

His first feeling was one of relief. He gave her a quick hug and said, 'I don't want you to behave in any way. I want you to enjoy Venice.' But, even as he was speaking the words, he was thinking: 'That means there's no turning back – or else one day

257

I'm going to have to behave like a complete shit.'

They had lunch at a small restaurant near the hotel, sharing a dish of rigatoni smothered in aubergine sauce and pouring their wine from a jug shaped like a cockerel.

'This is an improvement on the last Italian meal we had in a restaurant,' he said.

'I felt so stupid. Cutting up my spaghetti.'

'I admired you for being sensible.'

'You'll tell me when you want to be on your own, won't you?'

'Yes. If I do. When you've got your bearings.' Just to know she wouldn't mind, wasn't totally dependent, encouraged him.

Afterwards, they walked slowly through the Campo Sant' Angelo and the Campo Morosini to the Accademia Bridge. Kenneth stopped to make some notes, and Lydia watched two old ladies feeding the cats that were crouching among the bushes. He wondered whether to make a quick drawing of the scene, but decided it verged on cliché.

They crossed over the Grand Canal and wandered through the quiet *calli* towards Santa Maria della Salute. Kenneth took her up to the high gates, crafted from tangled black wire and coloured stones, that sealed off Peggy Guggenheim's museum.

'I wish we could go inside,' she said. 'I love these gates.'

Kenneth, who thought they were hideous, replied, 'I'm afraid it's closed in winter.'

'I love all this corner. It's so private and secret. Oh – I just can't believe I'm here.' She turned and butted her face into his jacket. 'Thank you.'

He could feel the two muffled words resonate quietly against his chest. His blood stirred. He bent his face into her hair. It smelled of rosemary.

When he looked up, a boat piled with a set of new dining chairs had appeared behind them on the Rio Pietre Bianche and he watched as it chugged slowly out of view.

Within three minutes they had stepped out of the seclusion of high walls and narrow bridges and were standing at the mouth of the Grand Canal on the steps of the Salute. Lydia gazed up at the gigantic baroque scrolls that buttressed its huge dome.

'They look like slices of fruit stuck round the most enormous cocktail in the world,' she said.

He laughed, abandoning the slight duty he had felt to explain the history of the church.

'And I love those statues on top of them ... I don't know, perhaps they look more like unicycles. Statues on unicycles.'

'They're the twelve apostles.'

She giggled. 'Matthew, Mark, Luke and John, Bless the bed that I lie on.' Then she blushed.

He took her hand. 'They will.'

Her image of unicycles had unlocked a piece of information gleaned long ago and since forgotten. When Baldassare Longhena had submitted his design for the Salute, he had indicated that its airy rotundity referred to the towering, circular floats, like giant merry-go-rounds, the Venetians made for regattas.

'I'm just going to walk to the end. You've given me an idea.' He could see how much that pleased her.

'Is it all right if I go inside?'

'Of course.'

He spent ten minutes standing under the customs house at the tip of the quay, his eyes watering in the wind as he stared across to the island church of San Giorgio Maggiore. Even on this grey day Palladio's white marble façade shone, and the tall golden angel on top of the campanile looked newly burnished.

He mustn't be overpowered. Mustn't dwell on the fact that thousands of artists had taken out their sketchbooks at this very spot. Or that Turner had painted Venice after dark just as beautifully as in the light of dawn.

He must hang on to that image of the floating merry-go-round.

When he turned, he could see a *vaporetto* veering into the Salute stop and he broke into a run.

Lydia was sitting in a niche on one side of the main door of the church underneath a statue of a saint. She looked, he thought, rather like a saint herself, with her hood framing her face and the folds of her coat hiding her red boots.

'Come on,' he called, pointing at the boat.

She sprang up, hurried down the steps, and they reached the floating station platform just as the *vaporetto* was being winched into its side.

'Are you cold?'

She shook her head.

'We'll stay up on deck then. We're not going far.'

As the boat drew away, its prow facing towards the San Marco stop on the opposite shore, Kenneth was about to point out the Ducal Palace and the Campanile when she said: 'It's quite different inside.'

'What is?'

She pronounced the unfamiliar Italian words hesitantly. 'Santa Maria della Salute.'

'Did you like it?'

'Oh ...' She tried to find what to say. 'I stood in the middle of that spiral pattern ... on the floor. And ... and asked to be made – oh, I don't know – I didn't use words ... *better*.'

'Better?'

'It's so light in there. Spacious. Airy. I felt like a snake shedding a skin. They must feel better when they do that. Better in spirit as well as body.'

'You chose the right place.'

'Why?'

'It was built to commemorate the end of a dreadful plague epidemic. *Salute* means both health and salvation. There's a special feast day every November when they build a bridge of boats across here and half Venice walks over to the church. It's the only time when the main doors are opened.'

'I'd love to see that.'

'So would I.'

He decided not to say anything about where they were going next. The Piazza – which they would enter from the dark passage between the heavy columns of the Ala Napoleonica – would be a surprise as it suddenly stretched before her, tilting ever so slightly downwards towards the jewelled Basilica.

'I feel as though I've been here at least two days.' Lydia took off her coat and boots and sat in one of the basket chairs with her legs stuck out in front of her.

'Is that good or bad?' He opened the bottle of wine they had bought on their way back to the hotel.

'Good. We've seen such a lot. And we've only been here seven hours.'

'Remember you promised to tell me when you feel tired.'

'I don't get tired walking.'

That, he realized, was one of the reasons he'd never asked Ronnie to come to Venice. She didn't walk. He collected the tooth glasses from the bathroom and poured the wine.

'I could never have imagined quite how wonderful it is not to have traffic. It's like having a severe mental or physical handicap completely removed. The one city where people are completely normal.'

He sat down in the other chair. 'Do you write?'

'What do you mean?'

'Poems, stories?'

'Why?'

'You talk in images.'

'I read a lot of plays ... I don't always understand them.'

'I don't understand a lot of the paintings I see.'

'Don't you?' She sounded surprised. 'Are you still writing about Turner?'

'... I'm not sure. I think he's too big for me.'

'Did *he* have a son?'

'Two daughters.' He hesitated. There was mention of a son, but as with Wilson it was a shadowy area and this time he didn't want Lydia trying to illuminate it.

'What happened to them?'

'Oh – one of them married a diplomat. Lived in Africa.' He sought a neat gloss on their life. 'Their mother was the widow of a musician. She and Turner never married. But their relationship lasted over twenty years.'

'Did they come to Venice together?'

'No.' It was absurd, but he felt slightly guilty about suppressing Turner's hypothetical son. 'We must find something special to take home for Arthur.' He could see from her smile that he had made up for his reaction in the Campo Manin. He leaned over and stroked her hand.

The milk churns did wake him, and for a split second their

noise made him afraid. Then he remembered where he was and breathed in the comforting smells of sex and rosemary and real linen. Lydia's buttocks were curved against his body. He felt whole.

A church bell began to clang, and then another. It was an old, medieval sound which reminded him of carnival as much as prayer.

When the light started seeping between the shutters, he realised it was going to be a clear day and swivelled quickly out of bed. He stood at the window, naked, watching the darkness drain away above the tiled roofs to leave an empty sky of faintest blue. He must go out.

Lydia did not stir as he washed and dressed. He wondered whether to leave her sleeping. But if he left her, he would have to come back soon and he wanted to be free to go as far as he pleased.

'Lydia. Lydia? *Lydia*.' He sat on the bed and took her hand. It was mysterious to him that someone could sleep so deeply; that last night his touch on any part of her body had affected her so profoundly, and now he might just as well be touching a dummy. He pinched the tip of her forefinger quite hard, but nothing happened. Then he pulled back the covers and softly touched her nipple. It stiffened, and she opened her eyes.

'*Now* I know how to wake you.'

She did not answer. But she got up, slowly, as soon as she realized he was dressed and ready to go out.

He could see what an effort it was as she almost sleepwalked to the bathroom. Tonight, he thought, we must come to some arrangement about the morning so she can sleep in.

The little *caffé* beyond the Campo Manin was just as he remembered it. People came and stood at the counter, eating their brioches wrapped in a napkin and drinking small green cups of espresso. Occasionally a man would have a glass of red wine as well. He and Lydia sat at one of the four tables and he watched her slowly revive as she drank two big cups of *cappucino*, its froth sprinkled with flakes of chocolate. For the first time since they had been alone together he felt that she was not susceptible to any slight remark he might make; that this early morning deadness gave her a respite before the events of the day

262

began to bombard her.

Finally he asked, 'Are you up to a walk?' and she nodded emphatically.

When he took out his battered street map, she said, 'I thought you knew Venice backwards.'

'The day one thinks that is the day one gets lost. I don't want us to walk for half an hour and then find we're further away from our objective than when we began.'

'What is our objective?'

'Ah!'

They walked away from the shops and restaurants into the Cannaregio. The low winter sun struck through the gaps between buildings, flashing off dark water and lighting up corners where ancient brick and stone seemed to be held in place by time and custom as much as by mortar or beam.

After a quarter of an hour they crossed a bridge into a dingy *campo*, bordered on one side by a run-down block of flats and on the other by a low, peeling building whose top heavy Venetian chimneys, flanked by spinneys of television aerials, looked distinctly precarious. Apart from a few pigeons, everywhere seemed deserted.

'Once upon a time,' said Kenneth, 'this was a hive of industry. Tailors and silk-weavers and gold-lace-makers worked here. When Venice was thriving.'

'I might have worked here.'

He remembered the emerald and indigo satin dresses. 'Perhaps.'

'But ...' She was looking past the flats to a giant marble façade, alive with angels, that jutted out into the *campo* and up into the sky.

'Wait till you see inside.'

It was dustier than he remembered. And colder. And darker. And the altar seemed, if possible, even more bizarre, with its candy-twist columns and white marble statues of God the Father and Christ – the latter clutching a full-length cross – perched sideways on a globe, rather like circus people trying out an improbable act on the slippery rump of a robust grey mare.

But Lydia's attention had not got as far as the altar. She was facing the pulpit on the left-hand side of the nave, staring up at

263

it with her mouth open.

'What happens there?' she whispered.

'The priest pronounces his sermons.'

'What do you mean?'

'It's the pulpit.'

'It *can't* be.'

'It is.'

'What are those curtains for? It looks like a royal box in a theatre. All those tassels and fringes. I thought it must be where very important people sat. So they could be hidden.'

'Look around you. Carefully.' He put his hands on her shoulders and swivelled her gently.

'Everything's covered in the same pattern,' she said. 'The same pattern as the curtains. They've covered the columns and the walls with it.'

'It isn't a covering. It's all inlaid marble. Every little bit of it. Including the curtains.'

'They can't be. They're all bunched up and draped.'

'Go and look.' He knew that, as she drew nearer, the curtains would suddenly petrify: change from draped ancient damask into carved surreal stone.

He watched her walk right around the church, stopping to stroke the huge oriental patterns inlaid on its pillars, and to finger the little balusters, each with its intricate inlay, that supported the altar rail.

He went up to her. 'Come round behind the altar.'

The light was slightly brighter there, revealing screws of discarded paper on the uneven floor and a large puddle.

'Whatever . . .?' she asked dubiously.

'It's flood water. The water rises under here.'

'It's coming in now?'

'Only a bit.'

She shuddered. 'It's unbelievable. That the water's so close.'

They returned to the nave, and while she looked again at the pulpit he went to the chapel by the entrance and found the switch to the light which visitors could use in order to see Titian's *Martyrdom of St Lawrence* properly.

But, as soon as he caught sight of Lawrence's arm reaching desperately towards the beam from heaven that pierced the night

264

sky, he thought of Drew. For the first time he reacted to the picture in terms of its story: a man being burnt to death on a gridiron. Before, he'd been anxious to admire Titian's skill in painting the glowing coals, the flaring torches, and the light reflected on the temple, because he'd read that this was one of the very first *nocturnes* in the history of art. Now he could only see the saint's torture and remember Drew's outflung arms.

He heard Lydia's footsteps and guiltily extinguished the light. 'How about some coffee to warm us up?'

She nodded.

She walked very slowly out of the church of the Gesuiti, turning to look back several times. 'This is the most fantastic place I have ever seen in the whole of my life.'

She faced the last column and flattened both her palms against it. He touched the marble between each of her splayed fingers with the little finger of his left hand. Then they turned and held both hands tightly, like children playing ring-a-roses.

Without the extra light, the lineaments of St Lawrence were barely visible.

19 He makes a shaky start to 1982

Kenneth tried to liven up the sitting-room fire while Pete was in the kitchen making coffee. The Alderney Street flat felt cold, and rain dripped from the railings into the area outside. Jos was away at the cottage. Sky was staying with Mal, even though they had officially parted. It was New Year's Day. He pushed a piece of kindling between two lumps of coal and a weak blue flame flickered.

'I've just been listening to the news,' said Pete as he came in with a tray. 'It's been the worst December since 1878 and the cold has caused 12,600 deaths.'

Kenneth didn't reply.

'You don't want to know that, do you?'

'I always loathe New Year. And it's worse now it runs into Christmas and everywhere is shut.'

'Some of the shops are open round here.'

'I don't mean shops. I mean offices. You can't ring anyone up.' He'd wanted to talk to William, to ask some questions, to seek some guidance. He could ring him at home, but he didn't like to. 'Anyway, how do they know the difference between dying of cold and just dying when you happen to be cold?' He watched Pete's attempt to conceal his detestation of that remark.

'All I know is, it's a bloody disgrace. Taxing people via the energy bills. Where's our cheap North Sea Gas, cheap atomic electricity? Did you see Thatcher on television last night?'

'No.' He'd taken Lydia out for a meal, returning to Rosewharf in time to toast the New Year in with Jack and Maggie Thorndike. It had been a subdued evening, overshadowed by memories of Venice.

'We've nearly three million out of work and she has the gall to say "I think we are over the worst. I believe we passed the depth some time during this year."'

'You weren't out celebrating, obviously.'

'I'm supposed to be working. Jos wanted to get on with that painting in the barn. Whatever it was you said to her seems to have given her encouragement. So we agreed to have a week working on our own.' He started to roll a cigarette.

He's missing Jos, Kenneth thought; and my praise of the painting discomforts him. 'How's your book going?'

'Oh. Much the same.'

'You're sure I'm not interrupting?'

'Completely sure.'

'I ought to be working too.'

They sat, staring at the fire which had begun to blaze.

'Why,' asked Kenneth after a while, 'do we spend so much time avoiding what we ought to be doing?'

'Who gives you your "ought"? I'm pretty sure if I finish my book, when I finish my book, I'll have to hassle to get anyone to take it. There's no one out there saying I *ought* to be doing it.'

'But you think you ought. You think the book is needed.'

He noticed that Pete did not respond to that, but just reiterated, 'Who gives you your "ought"?'

'Myself, I suppose.' He'd probably have included Ronnie six weeks ago.

'Anyway, our circumstances are different. Unless I take redundancy, there's no absolute financial need for me to do anything other than teach.'

'I don't think there's quite the same financial need for me now.'

'Oh? Is the Venice commission that good?'

'Not really. I ...' He felt ridiculously diffident.

'What?'

267

'I've been left a house.'

'You've what?'

'Bernard's left me his house.'

As he explained, emphasising his utter astonishment at Bernard's action, he could see that Pete was having a bitter struggle to suppress his envy.

Kenneth watched Jack turn his key in the heavy padlock on the high iron gates into the allotments. A group of men were standing just inside, talking, smoke rising from their cigarettes into the damp January air. They nodded to Jack and smiled at Arthur who was carrying a brand-new fork.

'Taking over from your grandad?' asked one.

'No,' said Arthur. 'But I'm big enough for a full-size one of me own now.'

The man winked. 'You'll have to look out, Jack.'

None of them really looked at Kenneth, but he knew they'd all given him a covert inspection as he followed Jack in.

'Excuse me! Excuse me!' The voice was female, impeccably vowelled.

A young woman in jeans, guernsey and wellingtons, dragging two toddlers similarly clad, came running up to the gate.

'I'm most frightfully sorry. But I've forgotten my key. Could you possibly let me in?'

For a second, Jack hesitated.

'I am a member. I promise.'

He went to unlock the gate.

'It's terribly kind of you. So silly of me to forget. But, if I don't pay the rent today, my husband will never forgive me.' With a fulsome smile, she started off down the path ahead.

'Miss!' One of the men called out. 'Miss!'

She slowed, and half-turned.

'If you've just come to pay the rent, the hut's that way.' He pointed to some sheds.

'Oh! Thank you!' She plunged at right angles down one of the grass strips that intersected the allotments. One of the toddlers started to cry.

'There's a lot of new people here now,' said the man to

268

Kenneth. 'But most of 'em don't last long.'

Jack and Arthur set off down the path. Kenneth followed them, marvelling at the number of plots – hundreds – and the variety of modes of care. Some were bare, waiting to be dug to a fine tilth all over; others had several rows of crops; a few were overgrown with weeds, the black, limp remains of last year's bean plants still clinging around the poles.

Jack's plot had a tool store, frames and a compost heap, and several even rows of vegetables. There were boards around the edge to stop the couch grass spreading from the paths. Two bushes at one far corner, lavender and sage, were neatly clipped. Beyond the plot, a very high wire fence separated the allotments from an adventure playground.

'Tell you what,' said Jack. 'I'll go and get the rent paid. You stay here with Arthur. He can show you what we've got.'

'Okay,' Kenneth replied.

Arthur immediately went to pull up a cabbage, using his new fork to loosen the earth with relish. He brought it to Kenneth, and whipped out a knife from his pocket to trim the stem and outer leaves. The soil on its roots, still saturated after the rains, smelled good. Kenneth began to feel glad that he had come.

Suddenly a group of boys erupted into the playground on the other side of the fence, shouting and swearing. They were all carrying thick sticks and proceeded to hit the metal scaffolding that provided a climbing frame up into the trees. The noise was deafening.

Kenneth watched Arthur stop what he was doing. He seemed to freeze like an animal that has been startled. Only his right thumb moved, slightly stroking the blade of the knife.

'There's fuckin' Forsythia,' one of the boys suddenly shouted. 'Look! Fuckin' Forsythia in his garden.'

The others took up the chant. 'Forsythia! Forsythia! Fuck-in' Forsythia!'

Then, just as suddenly as they had come, they ran off, screaming more obscenities.

Kenneth did not know what to say. He felt acutely embarrassed for Arthur.

The boy finished trimming the cabbage.

Finally Kenneth said: 'Do you just have to pay rent once a year?'

'Yeah. First Sunday in January.'

'What are those greens over there?'

'Sproutin' broccoli.'

'And those are the Valdor lettuces?'

'Yeah. The wet's rotted them a bit. I'll go and pull the mushy leaves off.' He seemed glad of an opportunity to move away.

Kenneth watched him as he worked slowly along the few lettuces that remained in the row. Last night, while Lydia was on the telephone inviting him to lunch – Jack and Arthur were going to Maggie's – Arthur had suddenly instructed her to ask him to come early so he could be taken to the allotment first. She'd been reluctant to pass the request on, and Kenneth had been reluctant to accept, but he'd felt he must. Now he wished that he hadn't.

When Jack returned, he wondered if he should say anything about the boys. But Arthur quickly abandoned the lettuces and came to stand near them, and Kenneth sensed he was willing him not to mention the incident. On the walk home, as he asked questions about the rules the allotment tenants had to follow, Jack said: 'There's only one drawback, and that's the savages that use that adventure playground. He says he wants to play there sometimes,' he looked at Arthur whose head was turned away, 'but I tell Lyddy not to let him.'

Two hours later, when he and Lydia were sitting at the table talking about set design, the remnants of the meal around them, Arthur came bursting in.

'Grandad says I can go if you say I can.' He wrinkled his nose. 'Yuck. I can smell garlic.'

'You haven't been asked to eat it,' said Lydia. 'Go where?'

'Out with Robert.'

'I thought Robert was never allowed out on Sundays.'

Arthur said nothing.

'Where are you going to go?'

'Dunno. Park I s'pose.'

Kenneth noticed his hand was in his pocket, and he thought he could see the outline of the folded knife.

'When did you fix this?'

'S'morning. I saw Robert on the way up there.'

Kenneth frowned. He didn't remember Arthur speaking to anyone.

'So I can go?'

'Oh – all right. But you must be back by dark.'

'Arthur?' said Kenneth.

'What?'

'You're not going to the adventure playground, are you?'

'Why should he?' asked Lydia quickly.

'There were some boys being rude. I thought he might be going to get his own back.'

'Robert won't be allowed there,' she said.

'You're sure you're meeting Robert?' Kenneth asked.

'He's said he is.' Lydia's tone was icy. 'Go on, Arthur. You haven't much time.'

He vanished immediately.

Lydia got up and went into the kichen.

He followed her. She was standing with her back to him by the sink.

'Lydia?'

He went and touched her back, but she flinched away.

'Don't you see how awful it is?'

'What?' he asked.

'Accusing him. Just because he is a child. You wouldn't speak like that to an adult.'

'I only asked him because I'm worried. It was very unpleasant at the playground.'

'Why?'

He explained as best he could, and to his utter consternation she started to cry, sobs welling up as she leant over the sink, almost as though she were vomiting.

The tiles around the stove and on the work surfaces had sprigs of blue flowers at their centres, faint echoes of centuries of calm Dutch domesticity. The noise that emanated from Lydia killed all calm.

'Lydia – please.' He did not dare touch her again.

'Please *what*? *What*?' The words were spat out.

'Please talk to me.'

'What about? You've let it all happen. Accused him of lying.

271

Not told me about anything. The boys. The knife. *You* think he's gone off to be violent. *You* think he's a delinquent. And you should have *told* me what they said to him. What they called him. Oh . . .' She cried more loudly.

'I didn't know what to do. I wanted to tell Jack. But I could see Arthur didn't want me to. We never even mentioned it between us. I felt very embarrassed.'

She swirled round, her face red all over, saliva at the corner of her mouth. 'Embarrassed! Embarrassed! *You* felt *embarrassed*?'

'What's wrong with that? I knew how he must be feeling.'

'You knew how he must be feeling? Hoh, that's really funny. You, from your background, knew how Arthur was feeling.'

'I have been a boy, you know.'

'You're telling me that boys swore at you? Called you fucking Fleabite or something?'

'No – of course not. Just that –'

'Of *course not*. You don't know what it's like to be Arthur. What he's had to cope with. How he feels. And you're *never* to accuse him of lying *ever* again.' Her voice broke on the last words, ending in a croak, and she turned and buried her face in her arms on the draining board.

He went into the living-room, returning automatically to his chair at the table. He picked up an orange and stabbed a knife into its side. God, he thought, what am I doing? Carefully, he pulled the knife out and proceeded to quarter the skin meticulously, not letting the blade penetrate the flesh beneath the pith.

Lydia was suddenly there, watching him.

Deliberately he continued to peel off the skin and pull the orange apart into sections. Its sharp scent made his nose prickle. He laid the segments out on his plate and looked up at her.

'And that's all you can do,' she said. 'Eat an orange.'

He wasn't going to eat it.

She went away, and came back dressed for going out.

'Where are you going'

'To look for Arthur, of course.'

'Wait –' he stood up.

But she had slammed the door behind her.

The frenzy of her behaviour appalled him. He sat down and tried to think what to do. Run after her? But by which route, there was such a dense network of roads between here and the playground. Go to Jack and Maggie? Go home ... why the hell didn't he go home?

He stalled. He cleared the table and washed up the dishes, waiting for someone to return of their own accord. But no one did, and when it was dark he left the house that seemed to have invisible veins of violence running through its anatomy.

By the time he arrived at his own front door, guilt at not having gone to look for Lydia was uppermost in his mind. It was closely followed by chagrin at his complete failure to deal with the incident at the allotments. He thought of turning back, going to Maggie Thorndike's to tell Jack what had happened. Then he remembered Maggie had told him she was getting a 'phone and he decided to ring directory enquiries to find out if she was listed.

She was, and she picked up her receiver just as he was beginning to think there would be no answer. He began, very awkwardly, to explain, but did not get very far before she interrupted.

'Don't worry. They're here. Turned up about an hour ago. All's well.'

'Oh ... thanks. You're sure?'

'Sure enough for the moment. Best not to talk much. Walls and ears and all that.'

'Of course.'

'See you soon, I expect. Goodbye for now.'

'Goodbye.'

He put the receiver down. He was surprised at the intensity of the relief that suffused his body.

A quiet knock at the door instilled no anticipation or foreboding, and he strode across the room to see who it was.

'Kenneth. I'm so glad you're in.'

Ronnie stood there, her case and flight bag on the floor, giving him an uncharacteristically nervous smile.

His first emotion was annoyance. Ronnie never just turned up. She always 'phoned to say when she was arriving and where. 9.30 at Heathrow, 20.10 at Kings Cross. She liked to be met.

Then he sensed the energy that her presence always seemed to generate. 'Ronnie!'

'How are you?'

'Oh ... fine. You?'

She made a little expression with her mouth that he knew so well, pursing her lips in a kind of labial shrug. He had forgotten how attractive she was.

'Do you want me to carry your case up?'

'I hoped you'd give me some coffee.'

'Of course. Come in.' As he turned back into the room, the image of the Salute, which was pinned up on the wall, and which he had exuberantly and rapidly drawn on a double elephant sheet of paper, reproached him.

'So you've been to Venice?'

'Yes.'

'With her?'

'Yes.'

'I often wondered why you never took me there.'

'You never said you wanted to go.'

'Kenneth, you can't invite yourself to people's very special places. You have to wait to be asked.'

He went to make the coffee.

'Did you have a good time?' He could not hear any hostility in her voice.

'I'm doing the illustrations for a book by Ted Wing on Venice.' He knew she'd be impressed.

'Gosh ... though I'm surprised you wanted anyone along if you were working ... it *must* be serious.'

He was about to say that since it was only a preliminary visit he hadn't been doing any substantial drawing, but decided not to.

'Is it serious?'

'Ronnie ...'

She did not speak again until he took the coffee and sat beside her on the sofa.

'Well?' she said.

'It can hardly be exactly light-hearted, after what happened.' He remembered their last lunch in Venice, sitting in the San Stefano restaurant with its crushed raspberry tablecloths and napkins, both of them in fits of giggles over nothing. Then he thought of Lydia sobbing over the sink.

274

'No ... I've missed you, Kenneth.'

'I've missed you.' There's no one for me to talk to properly, he could have added, when I need them.

He asked about her family, and whether she'd thought any more about opening a gallery in America.

'Aren't you going to ask me about Alastair?' she said at last.

'Do you want to tell me about him?'

'Not now.'

A few minutes later he carried her case upstairs, then waited while she let herself in. 'By the way, I cancelled your *Guardian*, a few days after you left.'

'Okay.'

Before, he would have offered to go to the newsagents and reorder it for her. Now, he just said, 'Let me know if there's anything you need.'

Her return unsettled him. Whereas earlier he'd been worried about Lydia, now he was worried about himself. He hadn't thought about Ronnie very much recently, and the impact of her presence, bringing with it an intense reminder of their shared past, like overhearing a once-celebrated symphony, confused him.

Without thinking, he picked up a Turner book, opening it at random to find a passage that would distract him. He came upon a description which Francis Hawksworth Fawkes had given to Thornbury, Turner's first biographer. Fawkes was the son of one of Turner's very few close friends, and when he was fifteen he had been invited to watch the normally extremely secretive painter at work while he was staying at Farnley Hall, their home in Yorkshire.

... he began by pouring wet paint onto the paper till it was saturated, he tore, he scratched, he scrubbed at it in a kind of frenzy and the whole thing was chaos – but gradually and as if by magic the lovely ship, with all its exquisite minutiae came into being and by luncheon time the drawing was taken down in triumph.

Kenneth sighed. Imagine ... imagine if something like that had happened to him. Turner – anyone magnificent – in his father's house. It was unthinkable. Anyway, it would probably have put him off trying to paint for ever. One of the many good things about learning from Mr Cremorne had been that there were moments when he had glimpsed it might be possible to outstrip him.

Was Turner thinking of his own shadowy son when he opened up to young Fawkes? Or subconsciously missing him perhaps. If he knew of his existence. If he existed ... Now that he had seen the vehemence of Lydia's feelings about Arthur, he had a better sense of why she had wanted Wilson's son in the story.

And what was going to happen to Arthur? With those cruel, taunting boys at large, and a knife in his pocket, and no Turner coming to stay to shape lovely ships before luncheon, as if by magic.

What should he have said to those boys? Shouted, rather. What could he have said that wouldn't have made it worse for Arthur?

What would Turner have shouted?

While he was speculating like this, at the back of his mind the idea was forming that he would ring Ronnie and ask if she'd like to go out to dinner later on.

'I mus' go.' The tall man with lank silver hair pressed his knuckles against the surface of the table and pushed himself up onto his feet.

'Have another,' said Kenneth.

He shook his head wearily. 'She'll put me on the street. Las' chance. Nice seeing you.'

Kenneth watched him stumble out of the pub. It must be ten years since they'd last met. He was still waiting for the sculpture commission that would establish him and still being threatened with the push by yet another patient, hapless girl.

He felt awful. He couldn't drink beer as he used to. He'd have a scotch and leave.

At the counter, Tom, the landlord, came to serve him.

'It's been a long time.'

'I know, Tom.'

'Work going well?'

'Yes – yes, it is.'

'I saw Bernard Gray died. You signed a book for my daughter. Remember?

'Of course.' Barely.

'Your American friend all right?'

'I hope so. She got back from New York today. Haven't really talked to her yet.' When he'd called up to ask her out she'd already arranged to have dinner with Frances.

'Seen Pete Brown recently?'

'Day before yesterday.' He relayed what little news there was, at bar level, about Pete.

Tom bought him a drink, then went off to serve a crowd of new customers. When he returned several minutes later, Kenneth bought them another.

'Remember Nellida?' asked Tom

'Could I ever forget?'

'Don't look round, but she's just come in.'

'She's not barred then?'

'She's much quieter these days. Harry's death knocked the stuffing out of her. You knew he died?'

Kenneth nodded. He could tell from the impassive expression on Tom's face that Nellida was approaching.

'I know that head.'

She still has the same voice, he thought; that extravagant, husky croak.

'It's Kenneth Flete.'

She was at his side. 'Hello, Nellida. What will you have?'

Tom pulled down a glass. 'My round,' he said.

Kenneth knew he was enjoying seeing old customers reunited. That however much the pub prospered with the changing fortunes of the area, Tom had a soft spot for the alchie-arty types who'd opened his eyes when he arrived as junior barman in the Sixties. Probably only he remembered which ones Nellida had been home with – he was pretty sure she didn't. Though Harry had always tried to guess, stomping around the Fulham Road at midnight, knocking on the doors of houses where regulars had their studios and bed-sits and shouting: 'Throw out your whores. Throw out your whores. Throw out my *wife*, God damn you!'

'You're getting older,' said Nellida. 'You're looking strained. Was it that boy?'

He knew she meant Drew. 'You heard about that?'

'Someone said it happened at your house.'

'What's that?' asked Tom.

'Rhys Forsyth's son,' she said. 'Didn't you read about it?'

'I don't think so.'

'Fell off a high wall and died. Wall behind Flete's house.'

'That so?' asked Tom with interest.

'Yes,' he said, reminding himself he must never bring Lydia into the Seymour Tavern.

'What happened?'

Kenneth gave the short version and bought another round.

Nellida had not changed very much. She was a bit quieter, didn't use that raucous laugh quite so much, but her thick, short hair was still dyed exactly the same shade of red, and the kohl and lipstick were still skilfully applied. It had been rumoured fifteen yars ago that she was fifty.

'Have you ditched that American then?'

'I think she may have ditched me.'

She looked him directly in the eye. 'It takes two to cease to tango ... unless one of them drops down dead.'

Tom moved down the bar to a customer pushing forward a clutch of empty glasses.

Kenneth said he was sorry about Harry. That he hadn't seen her since. He thought her mask slipped for a moment and that he glimpsed someone pretty old and very tired trying not to get out.

'I could have murdered him,' she said. 'The night after he went, I found the bloody bottle of antibiotics. He hadn't even bothered to take them. Pleurisy he had.'

Perhaps *you* were supposed to administer them, he thought. 'It'd have been worse for him. If you'd gone first.'

'Don't be slushy.'

'Sorry.'

'You never did take me back to your place.'

'No.'

'You said you hadn't got anywhere private.'

It had been a lie. He'd been drunk enough to take her. But not too drunk to fear the effect of her laugh and language on the stairs on his landlady. That'd been when he had a room in Cathcart Road. He'd always been a cowardly bohemian he decided.

'What've you got now?'

'Now?' he procrastinated.

'Yes.'

'Well ... I've got a room – and a bathroom – in the same house as Ronnie. My American friend.'

'Is that all? I thought you'd've done better for yourself.'

The drink, he thought, seemed to harden and enlarge the mystery, the buried life, behind her appearance. The myth had always been that she'd once been a dancer and that her Russian father had killed her Irish mother.

'So you've got nowhere to take me? Only a room in your Jewish American's house?'

'It's not her house.'

Tom took their glasses and refilled them.

Kenneth raised and drained his. 'Actually,' he said with difficulty, 'I will shortly have a whole house of my own in Wandsworth. And I've got the keys to a flat in Stockwell.'

He was rewarded with the full force of Nellida's laugh, jeering up from her belly as of old.

'Oh, Flete,' she gasped. 'Wandsworth and Stockwell. We have risen!' Raising her glass to Tom, she croaked, 'Cheers. To Chelsea!'

Kenneth realized, from the careful, soft look on his face, that once, way back in his junior barman days, Tom had agreed to take Nellida back.

He wished he didn't feel left out.

20   He witnesses an engagement

He had forced himself to his work table at eight. His head felt awful and the coffee was making him queasy. But he was damned if he would draw a bloody bottle. He was trying to discover how to tackle the Gesuiti.

At nine, James Nall telephoned. 'I hope I'm not disturbing you. Either from work or rest.'

'The work's pretty sticky today.'

'Then you might be interested in my proposition. I have to go over to Bernard's house just now, to find some papers, and it occurred to me you might like the opportunity for a look around. Five or ten minutes on your own.'

'Why – thank you.'

'Shall I pick you up in twenty minutes?' He checked the address.

'I'll be waiting on the front steps.'

'There's always more to these decisions than people imagine,' said James as they drove in five-yard spurts down a jammed Lillie Road. 'Even if you decide in principle to sell everything, there'll probably be the odd thing you'll like to keep.' He braked, gently, yet again. 'Are you working on anything in particular at the moment?'

He told him about Venice, thinking, as he spoke, that he wasn't ready to make any decisions about sellings and keepings.

'I've never ventured there. I'm nervous of being disappointed.'

280

Kenneth approached the house warily. James had gone to warn the neighbour, Mrs Williams, that they were visiting, and had given him the key. He told himself that it was more or less his key, his house; that he shouldn't feel like a trespasser.

It was as he remembered – cluttered, draped, dark, with a great deal of deep red – but cleaner. Someone, Mrs Williams perhaps, had given everywhere a good polish. The air smelled fresher.

He went straight through to the kitchen and unbolted the back door, not liking the idea of going immediately into one of the living rooms to inspect its contents. The garden was an over-grown dead mess of dun grasses and rusty weeds, and he pushed his way through to the bottom where he could stand and gaze at Fox territory.

The first line of the first book came to him. 'Fox knew the facts of life.' He smiled and felt better. Then he turned to take stock of the back of the shabby house, and discovered he had tears in his eyes and the green drainpipes were blurred against the red brickwork. He could just hear James still talking to Mrs Williams at her front door, and decided to go indoors and explore the top of the house. He had never been up to the second floor.

It turned out to be one large room with wide windows at either end. There was a faded Chinese carpet on the floor and all the other furnishings were vaguely oriental. A plain divan was covered with a fringed flowered shawl, and when he walked round the open door he found himself face-to-face with a black lacquered chiffonier. It was not quite as formidable as the one he had coveted in the Pimlico Road, but almost. He held his breath as he approached it.

The pleated silk behind the lattice work on the doors had a pattern of peonies, and the fronts of the drawers were inlaid with scenes of lakes and storks and snow-covered mountains. He took one of the pendulant brass handles and gently pulled it. The drawer ran smoothly, revealing a French edition of Genet's *Our Lady of the Flowers* with 'Colin Teller' written in pencil on the front cover. So this must be Colin's room. He felt as though he'd walked in and broken a spell.

Sounds from downstairs indicated that James had come in,

281

and he went off quickly to find him.

He was standing in the hall at the foot of the stairs looking very ill at ease.

'Is something wrong?'

'Are you able to cope with cats?'

'How do you mean?'

'They are my Achilles heel. And that woman – I should say that nice Mrs Williams, for so she is – wants me to deal with the despatch of Bernard's cat. She tried to show it to me.'

'It's sick?'

'Dying, it seems. She expects me to take it to the vet. I could more easily take myself.'

'I'll take it if you like.'

He managed a faint smile. 'I do apologize.'

'No need.'

After James had found the papers he wanted, and Kenneth had taken a cursory look round the rest of the house, his mind unfocused, they locked up and went back to Mrs Williams.

She was flustered by James's earlier reaction, but when he explained that Kenneth was a good friend of Bernard and would, unlike him, be able to help her, she became effusively grateful.

'You see,' she said, 'I've never had animals. I did try to do my best for her. But she wouldn't come in when there was that snow. And she can barely stand. Poor Doris. I know it's the end. And,' she glanced nervously at Kenneth, 'I'm frightened for her to die here.'

'Don't worry. I'll take her to the vet.'

'It seems too silly. I wasn't frightened when my husband died. Very sad, of course. But not frightened. The vet isn't far. Just at the top of the road.'

'Fine.' He turned to James. 'You go back now. I'll catch the bus when I've dealt with the cat.'

'I ought to drive you to the vet.'

'I wouldn't feel safe! Go on.'

'Well . . . if you're sure.'

'Thanks for bringing me over.'

Mrs Williams took him down into her kitchen where Doris was lying on a mat in front of the Aga. Her eyes were open and she looked very, very weary.

282

'She's gone down-hill so quickly. She was as right as rain before Christmas. But now, as I said, she can hardly stand. She just hangs her head over a bowl of milk giving funny little sneezes. Sometimes she sticks her tongue into it, but she doesn't seem able to lap.'

'Poor old Doris.' He crouched down and very gently touched her head with his finger. To his surprise, she began to purr.

'Listen to that,' said Mrs Williams.

'She must be pretty old?'

'Do you know, I worked out she was well over twenty. They had her together, you know. As a kitten. Brought her home together. Mr Gray and Mr Teller.'

'Good heavens.'

'Of course, it was dreadful when *he* died. Tragic.'

'Yes. Now – have you some old thing I could wrap her in? To carry her. I don't think I'll need a box. She seems too weak to struggle.'

'Plenty of things. I know just the one.' She went off to an outer scullery and came back with an old blue bath towel. 'Will this do?'

'Admirably.'

'I don't need it back. Though ... if you'd like to come? For a cup of tea when it's over?'

'Perhaps not this time. I'd better get back.'

'But I'll see you again. When it's all finalised.'

She didn't seem to expect a reply, and he wondered whether James had dropped a hint or if Mrs Williams was simply intuitive.

He lifted Doris onto the towel and could feel her fragile, knobbly bones through her dull fur. She remained quite impassive when he took her up into his arms and didn't move during their walk to the vet's house. The woman who answered the bell barely needed to listen to his explanation after she had taken a quick look at her.

'I'm afraid you'll have a bit of a wait, but Miss Thorogood will see you as quickly as she can.'

He took a seat in the pleasant waiting room among the owners of various dogs – a friendly randy mongrel, a nervous alsatian bitch, a pair of elderly fat dachshunds – and Doris settled herself

283

within her towel on his knee and purred. He felt very calm, holding the dying cat and thinking about the house down the road.

When it was his turn, Miss Thorogood looked at him over her half-moon spectacles and said in a brisk, kindly voice, 'Now. This is Mr Gray's old cat, isn't it?'

'That's right.'

'Put her down on the table, please.'

A girl in a white overall had just finished laying out a clean paper towel.

Miss Thorogood felt Doris's legs. 'Yes. The end's not far off. Do you want just to leave it to me? Leave her here?'

'Will you do it straight away?'

'Oh yes.'

'I'd like to stay.' He thought she gave him a faint smile of approval.

'Caroline, you hold the cat. And, please, Mr – er ... do talk to her or touch her, if you wish.'

He stroked Doris's head while Miss Thorogood clipped a patch of fur away on her upper foreleg. When she dabbed it with sharp-smelling alcohol Doris miaouwed surprisingly loudly, but had relaxed and begun to purr again by the time the syringe was produced. She collapsed and was dead virtually before all the shot had gone into her.

Kenneth removed his hand. It was a sad little body to leave behind.

I tried to get you before I left – could we spend some time together this evening? Please call me at the gallery – R.

He had found the note slipped under his door and telephoned immediately, glad to have something fixed for later. It gave him an excuse for not doing anything about Lydia.

The first thing Ronnie said after she had poured him a drink and put out some olives – the room had, he noticed, been quickly spruced, and there were five stems of freesia buds in a glass on the table – was, 'I am really sorry about Bernard, Kenneth. Frances told me. You must have been very upset.'

284

'Well . . . it's all been rather strange.'

'What happened?'

'Oh – he died just after you left. I'd seen him the evening before. I think they expected it. No – it was afterwards.'

'How do you mean?'

He took a sip of wine and ate an olive, savouring having Ronnie there to listen. 'For one thing he was buried on the same day as Drew Forsyth, and I had to go to both funerals. And, before that, William had told me he'd left all the Fox royalties to me. They're going to reprint.'

Ronnie sought elaboration, and when he had finished said, 'So Lydia didn't go to her husband's funeral?'

'No.' He wanted to say something in her defence, but couldn't think of anything quickly.

'And her son. How is he taking it?'

He hedged. 'All right, I think.'

'Do you see much of him?'

'I went up to their allotment on Sunday. He wanted to show it off to me.' What on earth had made him tell her that?

'So you're getting close?'

'Not really. He's pretty abrupt.'

She sighed. 'Do you know? I can't imagine you with them. For any length of time. It's as though you must be another person. Tell me, unless you don't want to, was Venice really successful?'

'Yes.'

'So what's going to happen?'

'What's going to happen with you?'

She turned away, giving a slight shrug.

'How was your trip generally?'

'Confused. I wasn't with Alastair all the time. He can be amazing company. But he has problems. He's a complex person.'

A two-timer, he thought. 'Did you see your parents?'

'Yes. I thought I'd go home for a few days and recuperate – meditate. It was nice. Apart from my mother asking too many questions.'

'How's your father?'

'He wants me to go back. I told him my idea for a West Coast gallery. He'd like to help with that.'

He was about to have his 'It's easy for some' reaction when he remembered the house.

'Kenneth, I want to ask if you'll do me a favour.'

'I'll try.'

'I've got some salad and smoked fish. How would it be if I tell you the favour, and then make us some supper while you think about it?'

'All right.'

'It's Serena's show. Would you write a piece for the catalogue? About a thousand words. Frances and I talked about it today, and we both feel you're the right person.'

She'd never asked him to write for the gallery before. Once, when she'd shown an artist he'd particularly liked and someone had written a rather vapid piece, he'd hinted he could have done better, but she'd said very firmly that the essays must be written by women. Women on women.

'Isn't that rather a turn-around in policy?'

'Not really. We've always been open to change when we felt it was right.'

'Why a change this time?'

'Well ...' Ronnie wiped a wet ring from the table with a tissue. 'You responded so positively to her work. And you understand the background of the subject matter.'

Frances has approached one or two women, he thought, and they don't like Serena's paintings. 'But she loathes me.'

'Don't be so hyper-sensitive. She knows more about you now. She'd like you to do it.'

Bet you had to twist her arm. 'If you really want me to.'

'Oh, Kenneth, thank you.' She got up, gave his hair a quick touch, and disappeared into the kitchen. Within a few seconds she reappeared. 'We'll pay you, of course.'

'It's all right.'

'Don't be silly. It's on a professional basis.' Then, rather tartly, she added, 'Venice can't be making you that rich.'

He had to tell her. 'Bernard's left me his house. As well as the royalties.'

'What!'

Like Pete, she did not look instantly pleased. Later, when they had talked about it, he realised she suspected there must have been something between him and Bernard. He'd been prepared, after William's warning, for outsiders to think whatever they pleased. but not Ronnie.

After they'd eaten, he helped her wash the dishes.

'What does Lydia think about the house?'

'She doesn't know about it.'

She jerked her hands out of the bowl, suds dripping off her red rubber gloves, and faced him angrily. 'For God's sake, Kenneth. Aren't you ever going to grow up? Life isn't built on one long series of secrets.'

'I need time to think about it.'

'Like your father's house, I suppose.'

'I wasn't able to think about that enough.'

'At least you admit that now.' She returned to the bowl.

'You're not really suspecting Bernard and I had an affair, are you?'

'I don't know what to think. These days.'

So it was as much to do with Alastair as him. 'That's one secret I didn't have.'

'I wish I understood where I go wrong. I trust people, and then everything seems to fall apart.'

'But –' He was going to say he didn't think he had ever betrayed her trust, then thought better of it. He didn't want to be drawn into dissecting the sequence of events concerning Lydia. 'Has something happened? That you want to talk about?'

'I don't think there's much point.'

When they returned to the living room, Ronnie opened the Courvoisier she had bought in the duty-free and told him about the exhibitions she had seen in New York. Then she said, 'So have you put a timetable on your plans?'

'Plans?'

'For moving. When you've got the house settled.'

'I haven't made any plans to move into it.'

'It's probably too far out. But when you've sold it. You could get a really nice flat. One with a studio perhaps.'

'I haven't made any plans to sell it.'

'Oh, Kenneth! It can't just sit there. By now most people would be talking to estate agents, seeing what's on offer. Finding out roughly how much you can expect to get for it.'

287

He was about to say 'Around £75,000 according to James Nall' but didn't. He didn't want her to explain what he would be able to do with that.

To change the subject, he began to tell her about taking Doris to the vet, forgetting that Ronnie was uninterested in animals. Halfway through the story he could tell that she would shortly say she felt tired, and he would thank her for supper, kiss her cheek, and leave.

He was back in his room fifteen minutes later. Ronnie was right, he realised. He would want to move. He no longer felt secure at the centre of his small universe. Rather, he felt squeezed. The boundaries had contracted severely after Drew.

Could he ever colonise Bernard's house? He didn't know where to begin. Yet selling it, stripping out rooms that had not been disturbed for decades, Colin's room, would be a brutal task. Wouldn't he like to buy a flat with a studio, though?'

The idea didn't stir his imagination, not in the way taking over this room had. He could still remember the day the carpet was laid, the fresh smell of wool and the way its colour affected the light on the wall and ceiling.

There were all those cupboards he'd built, cavities now crammed with stuff. Surely a lot of it could be thrown out? What was in the one at the top?

Standing on a chair he discovered two cardboard boxes with 'School' written on them. So he'd still not jettisoned his sixth form work and good reports. Underneath were bundles of magazines from the days when he had subscribed for a year first to *Encounter* and then to the *New Left Review*. Further along he found a pair of boots, absurdly heeled, that he'd worn when it had been fashionable to elevate himself to average height. And beside the boots was a single shoe. He fumbled in the space behind to find the other, but there was nothing there.

He took the shoe out. The blue paint had cracked along the creases at the front, revealing the dull black leather underneath. The laces, which he remembered dipping into the paint, were stiff. He stepped off the chair and put the shoe down on the carpet: cracked blue on grubby blue. Where had he abandoned the other one? In his prevous flat in the Finborough Road, or the room in Cathcart Road, or under the bed among the rolls of dust and blanket fluff in the little room in Bramerton Street where he'd written *Who's Vineyard?*

He picked the shoe up and was about to throw it away, but hesitated. Perhaps he'd hang on to it. He ran his finger over the cracked paint. *Tangled up in blue.* Dylan's phrase. Tangled up in sex and music and bright images. Walking out on early summer evenings in his blue shoes and watching girls' thighs through the fringes of their skirts. Dancing to The Chiffons singing 'He's So Fine' while Marie Baynard mouthed the words at him.

Suddenly he dropped the shoe. Dumped it in the bin on top of coffee grounds, teabags and balls of screwed-up lay-out paper. He hadn't behaved very well to Marie Baynard.

But it *had* all been fine. Tangled up in blue. So fine.

It was dark, steep, windy. Big black gothic buildings. One tall church steeple with no clock face at its base. An infinite night sky. Out of which hung a gigantic iron pocket watch, tall as a town-hall, which swung wildly on its thick chain. The chain was fixed to a hook in the bed of the sky. Lydia clutched his arm as they walked against the wind. 'Oh, look,' she said. 'Isn't it marvellous?'

'An incredible optical illusion.'

'It's not an illusion.'

'It must be.'

'No. It's my sky watch. It just swings in the wind and tells the time.'

'No mystery behind it all?'

'None ... well, just the problem of how the hook it hangs from is welded to the sky.'

He woke up.

It was the first time he had dreamed of Lydia. The dream left him feeling optimistic, as though something good if inexplicable had occurred. He did not try to work out its meaning, he had no experience of that sort.

It was six, so he decided to get up and start work. Yesterday he had not wanted to include Lydia in the Gesuiti composition, it had seemed a dangerous idea. Today he did not see how he could possibly leave her out.

As he worked throughout the first half of the morning, he knew he must contact her today. The problem was whether to pretend to ignore what had happened, or take the bull by the horns and try to find out how she thought he ought to behave with Arthur.

When the 'phone rang, he did not think it would be her.

'Hullo.' She sounded very hesitant.

'Lydia. Hullo. I was going to get in touch with you today.'

'Oh. Why?' Now she seemed suspicious.

'Just to see you. See how you are. Is Arthur all right?'

'Yes. Well . . . I think so.'

'I'm sorry about Sunday.'

'It's my fault. I —'

'No. I should have done something.'

'I don't see why.'

'You did then.'

'I've said I'm sorry.'

'Yes. But . . . well, perhaps we can talk about it sometime. Generally, I mean. So that at least if I'm not a help I needn't be a hindrance.'

She didn't reply immediately. Then she said, 'Kenneth?'

'Yes?'

'Maggie and Dad have asked me to ring.'

'Oh?'

'They . . . they're having a bit of a celebration this evening. Just a drink. At about six. They asked me to see if you could come. But I said you'd probably be busy.'

'A celebration?'

'Oh – they've decided to get married.'

He thought from her tone that she was upset.

Later, as he made his way to Rosewharf Close, he tried to imagine what it must be like to have your middle-aged parent embarking on marriage. He had to admit that his first reaction to the news had been amusement. But that had been very shortly followed by a feeling of approval. Jack and Maggie in partnership seemed a nice idea. However it would not be so simple for Lydia.

Expecting awkwardness, or false jollity, he was quite unprepared for the wholehearted sense of celebration that greeted him. Arthur opened the door and immediately asked what he would like to drink, reciting solemnly the choice available. Jack and Maggie, dressed up a little, were laughing with Alf, and Lydia was setting out sausages and vol-au-vents on the table. Two cheerful women, one wearing bright blue, the other bright red, were talking animatedly at the foot of the stairs. Kenneth soon learned that the blue one was Alf's wife, and the red one Maggie's sister, for as soon as Jack saw him he came over and made introductions.

'Well, what do you think then?' said Jack, when he and Kenneth and Lydia were gathered in the kitchen while Arthur opened some wine for Kenneth. 'An old lag like myself?'

'It's wonderful news.'

'I hope so. For Maggie, I mean.'

'She looks very happy.'

'She's got a couple of gins inside her!'

'When did you know about it?' Kenneth asked Lydia.

'Last night. Dad came home and told me.'

'And she's mighty pleased to get rid of me.'

Kenneth looked from one to the other, anxious not to put a foot wrong.

'I only said it'll be great to have a separate work room.'

'See,' said Jack. 'She's thrown me bed out the door before we've had time to publish the banns.'

'You're not getting married in church, Dad.'

'Same difference.'

'So you're going to move into Maggie's house?' Kenneth asked.

'Rather. We don't want to lose one of them. And it'd be a tight squeeze in here. Especially with that dog and barmy cat.' Lydia had gone to help Arthur, and Jack dropped his voice. 'I'll help her out, mind. With the bills like. While she needs it.'

Arthur came with a brimming glass of wine which Kenneth raised, saying, 'Let me say good luck to you three. Before the proper toast.'

291

'What proper toast?' Arthur's voice was slightly truculent.

'Well, the toast to your grandad and Mrs Thorndike. I suppose you'd call it an engagement toast.' He hoped Jack wouldn't mind his jokey inflection on what had always seemed to him an uncomfortable word for an uncomfortable state.

'Blimey,' said Jack, 'makes us sound like a public toilet.'

'You mean with a ring?' asked Arthur.

'Well . . .' said Kenneth.

'Grandad, have you got Maggie a ring?' He turned to Kenneth. 'I don't call her Mrs Thorndike. She says I must call her Maggie.'

'No, son, I haven't.'

'I'll go and ask her if she wants one.' Arthur beetled out of the kitchen.

'I'm beginning to wish we hadn't asked you,' said Jack, 'if you're going to run me up a Bravington bill. I'd better go and check the damage.' He followed Arthur, and Lydia reached for a glass and poured herself some wine.

'I went up to the school,' she said. 'After I'd had a talk with Arthur. About those boys.'

'Good. Did you get anywhere?'

'They already know that two of them have been bullying younger kids. And they've promised to keep an eye out.'

'Thanks for telling me.'

'Maggie's been a help. I can talk to her.'

'She seems a sensible person.'

'It's going to be nice. Having them near. But with more space here.' She looked around.

'Yes.' He remembered Ronnie's anger. 'There's two things I should tell you.'

'What?'

'Ronnie's come back.' He watched the shadow of distress alter her face. 'It doesn't make any difference. But I thought I should tell you.'

'Yes.' She made an undisguised effort. 'She had to come back some time.'

He nodded. 'Now . . . the other thing.'

She looked very apprehensive, as though it could only be worse.

292

'Perhaps I should have told you this before. But I needed time to take it in.'

She still didn't speak.

'I learned just after Bernard's funeral. His solicitor told me. He's left his house to me.'

The shadow fled. 'But that's wonderful!'

'Yes . . .'

'Oh, Kenneth, it's marvellous.'

'Yes, but –'

'But what?'

'I don't know.' Her spontaneous pleasure had come as an unexpected relief.

'I wish I'd met him.'

'I don't know what I'm going to do about it. The house.'

'You mean whether you'll live there?'

'Mm.'

'Whatever happens, I hope you'll visit me here. When I'm straight.' She looked away. 'Stay with me sometimes,' she added quietly.

'How about Arthur?'

'I don't hide things from him. He understands about Venice.'

He was surprised to find that rather shocked him. The idea of Arthur knowing.

They went back into the living room. Alf opened a bottle of champagne and proposed the toast. 'To Jack and Maggie. Maggie and Jack. May they have all the happiness they deserve.'

'Hear, hear. To Jack and Maggie. Maggie – Jack,' Kenneth joined in with the blue and red ladies. 'To Dad and Maggie,' said Lydia. 'To Maggie and Grandad,' announced Arthur, and drained his champagne like lemonade.

Kenneth watched the new couple turn to each other and kiss, and realised there was as much life in Jack's kisses as there was in his own. He thought of the photograph of the cheerful girl with curly hair upstairs, with her baby in a shawl. Lydia was standing near him and, when Jack raised his glass to her in a private salute, she lifted hers with a heartfelt smile. Arthur, having ascertained that there wasn't any more champagne, was eyeing the sausages. Kenneth went over to join him.

21 He sees a crimson petal fall

A shaft of fitful afternoon April sun suddenly pierced the glass door of the gallery and made a rectangle on the pale parquet floor next to where Kenneth was standing. He side-stepped into it, and attempted the opening line of 'Come to the Cabaret', but his voice cracked.

'Don't call us, we'll call you,' said Frances, who was starting to Letraset numbers on the wall by Serena Stein's paintings.

Ronnie came through from the back office, crying, 'It's all right, folks. The catalogues will be here first thing in the morning.'

'Was there a problem?' he asked.

'I just thought I'd double-check.'

He thought she seemed unusually elated. 'You were right about changing those two paintings around. They do look better.'

Ronnie swivelled to look. Her gathered dress was cinched tightly at the waist with a red belt that matched her new glasses. 'They're a knock-out. I know Serena's going to be thrilled.'

Kenneth, who realised he was already a little bored by the pictures after being in their company for only an hour, noticed the frailty of her shoulders and thought she had lost too much weight. When she whirled back into the office he walked over to Frances and said, quietly, 'Ronnie seems to be getting awfully thin.'

She straightened up and stood away from the wall. 'She doesn't eat. I have tried.'

'She never has, very much.'

'She usually used to have a salad with me at lunchtime. If she hadn't anything else on. But now she always makes an excuse. We've asked her over quite a few times while you've been in Venice, but she just pushes the food around her plate. It drives Jim mad.'

'I know how he feels. You don't think she's ill?'

She shook her head. 'Disorientated. Unhappy.'

'I haven't asked her directly. But I assume Alastair Faraday didn't come over during March? She'd mentioned he might.'

'No. Well – not unless she kept it a secret.'

'You'd have known.'

'I think so. In fact...' She stopped, apparently changing her mind about something.

'Just now?' he ventured.

'Yes. Something's happened. I spoke to the printer only yesterday afternoon. There's never been any question that the catalogues wouldn't be on time.'

Somebody tapped on the door behind them. They turned to see Richard Mafeking peering in, the sun making a halo of his frizzy fair hair.

'Oh, lord,' said Kenneth.

'He'll have to wait till the press view,' said Frances firmly, smiling her conciliatory public smile as she went to unlock the door.

'I'm so sorry to interrupt, Frances. But seeing you there, Kenneth, it seemed *such* a coincidence, I thought I just *must* have a word with you.'

'Hullo Richard. What coincidence is that?'

'The Richard Wilson exhibition.'

'Richard Wilson exhibition?'

'You mean you haven't heard?'

Kenneth didn't say anything since the answer seemed obvious.

'There's going to be a major exhibition at the Tate. In November.'

295

No one interrupted his stumping, rocking progress back from the tavern.

'Really?'

'I'm surprised you didn't know. Of *course* I hope you will write about it for us.'

Other midnight pedestrians, drunk and sober, stepped out of the path of such a bulky man.

Richard Mafeking's eyes were darting greedily around the gallery, sharply assessing the canvasses. 'I've asked Patrick Mendip to write about Stein.'

'She'll be at the private view,' said Frances. 'She's arriving from New York in the morning. And we'll have photographs of all the paintings at the press view earlier. If you want to use one.'

Mafeking took a sly glance at the painting of Robert Rauschenberg and Jasper Johns busy in a studio in the nude. 'Possibly,' he said.

'Yes,' said Kenneth. 'I will.'

'Who's Patrick Mendip?' Frances asked as soon as Mafeking had left.

'Haven't a clue.'

'That's nice about Richard Wilson.'

'Yes.' He was longing to tell Lydia.

'When are you back to Venice?'

'Next Monday.'

'Have you still got much to do?'

'Yes and no. Nothing major. But some loose ends to tie up. And three extras to do. Small ones.'

'Ronnie said they're lovely drawings.'

'Did she?' He felt the old pleasure at her praise. He'd rather thought she found them trivial.

'Yes. She said they were luminous. I think ... well ... she finds it a bit painful she hasn't been part of it.'

He thought of the Gesuiti drawing. Lydia's enwrapped face in the foreground.

'She wouldn't have come back to me.'

'Well ... it wasn't on, was it?'

He looked across at the dying Rothko. 'I suppose not.'

'By the way,' Frances changed the subject, 'I had a patrol

296

down Cork Street yesterday. Jos Shepheard's got a stunning painting in Humphrey Lamborn's mixed show. Have you seen it?'

'Yes. I went to the gallery with Sky last week. It does look good.'

'I didn't get the title. *Sartre's Death*.'

He explained.

'How is Sky?'

'Top of the world. She's just left for Venice, oddly enough. She's joined a scheme that's training volunteers to clean and restore old wood and stonework. It's in a disused monastery on one of the islands in the lagoon.'

'Sounds good.'

'It'll be good for her, I think. I'm going to meet her on Monday. See how she's getting on.' He looked at his watch. 'I'd better be off. I'll say goodbye to Ronnie.'

'Thanks for coming in. It's been a help.'

'I've enjoyed it.' He gave a rueful smile. 'Bit like old times.'

'Just a bit.'

Ronnie was on the telephone when he put his head round the door. They raised hands cheerily to one another.

Before he went down into the Underground, he gave Lydia a call. He stood for a few seconds in the 'phone booth, receiver in hand, trying to remember her number. He'd always prided himself on being good at telephone numbers, but this new one kept eluding him. 385 ... was it 7 or 9 first? He put the receiver back and got out his diary.

'Hullo.'

'Lydia. It's me.'

'Hullo, me.'

'I thought I'd just let you know I'm on my way.'

'Has it gone all right?'

'I think so. Ronnie and Frances seem pleased.'

'Good.'

'See you in about forty minutes.'

'Great.'

He went towards the escalator with a light heart. The plan was working. Every time he thought she might be jealous about his involvements elsewhere, he reported back as soon as possible.

Arthur let him in, clutching a half-eaten beefburger roll. A Roadrunner cartoon was in full spate on the television.

'Mum's upstairs.'

'Thanks. You okay?'

'I got 19 out of 20 for the maths test.'

'Well done.'

Arthur returned eagerly to the screen, his social duties fulfilled.

She was at her sewing machine, as immersed in her work as Arthur was in the cartoon. They looked, he thought, much more alike when they were preoccupied.

The room had been rearranged now that she no longer slept in it. There were light curtains at the window and a table of plants. The theatre costumes were hung on a free-standing clothes rail. A photograph of him, taken in their room at the Giorgione, was pinned up alongside the British Museum post-card.

She did not hear him until she took her foot off the electric switch, and then she pushed back her chair and rushed into his arms. They kissed for a long time.

'Thanks for ringing.'

'Guess what.'

'What?'

'There's going to be a big Richard Wilson exhibition at the Tate in November.'

'Will your postcard drawing be in it?'

'I hope so.'

She hugged him tightly. 'Can I come and see it with you?'

'Of course.' He realised he'd committed himself to her far ahead without hesitation.

'I'll get some tea.'

'You finish what you're doing. I'll get it.'

He liked being by himself in the kitchen. Now that Lydia and Arthur were on their own, it had become more idiosyncratic. There were Arthur's growing things – jars of sprouting alfalfa and mung beans for Lydia, boxes of cress for Maggie, orange pips and avocado stones – and Lydia's display of dry foods on open wire shelves because, she said, she forgot what she had when everything was shut away in the cupboard. And she'd made a big blue sunflower to match the tiles.

'Would you like some tea?' he called to Arthur.

'Wouldn't mind another Coke.'

He suspected he'd already had his ration, but got one out of the fridge.

'*Thanks.*'

He took the tray upstairs.

'I saw Maggie this afternoon,' said Lydia. 'She and Dad would like to come to the house again on Saturday.'

'It's very good of them. They were there for hours last weekend.'

'She knows how much Dad enjoyed it. He hasn't had a proper challenge like that since the factory closed.'

'Well, if we *could* draw up a list of things to be done before I leave on Monday . . .'

Kenneth had learned, gradually, that Jack's work life was not the well-ordered affair it had at first seemed. He'd imagined him happily retired from the local factory where he'd worked for twenty years, and willingly available for the odd jobs he was frequently asked to do. In fact, he'd been made redundant with a meagre pension when he was only fifty-three, and did not like being in a position where he felt he must accept people's offers of £10 for jobs that saved them spending £50. The allotment helped to fill in time and provided vegetables, but it was only Arthur's involvement that gave him a degree of real enthusiasm for it.

When Kenneth had returned from his six-week stint in Venice, he'd been unprepared for the news that Bernard's house was now legally his: all his concentration had been channelled into the drawings. He went over to Cranstead thinking he might spend a couple of hours there and come to a decision, but in the end had spent most of the time talking to Mrs Williams about damp walls and wobbly fence posts while being plied with her home-made fruit cake. The following morning he'd asked Lydia to go over with him. That had been better, for she was able to see the house clearly and almost convinced him that Colin's room would make a perfect studio. The front room, she pointed out, could easily be let to help with running costs. That afternoon, without telling her, he went to an estate agent and asked if they had any studio flats near the Fulham Road. The first one he saw, its small pristine spaces tastefully and econ-omically fitted with all the up-to-date domestic essentials, put him off so much that without really making a decision he realised he was going to keep the house. Then, during supper, Lydia had tentatively suggested that Jack might help him with clearing out and repairs. So, at the weekend, Jack and Maggie had come over and between them had helped him see the decisions he needed to make if he was going to live there. It was Jack telling him that the damp walls were simply caused by blocked gutters that clinched it. 'If we could agree a schedule of things that need to be done immediately, would you undertake it for me? At proper rates?' They were standing alone in Colin's room while Maggie was downstairs discovering what did and didn't work in the kitchen. Jack had glanced first out of one window, then the other. 'With these salubrious views, old son, I think I will.'

Lydia laughed. 'You'll be in the dog house if you *don't* get that list made. He's itching to get started.'

Half an hour later, Kenneth almost changed his mind about going back to the flat. He'd planned to work late into the night, but he didn't want to leave Lydia. It was she who said reluctantly, 'You'd better go, if you're going to get that drawing finished,' when he reached out and started to stroke her cheek.

Towards midnight, the bulb in the lamp on his work table flickered and died. He looked for a replacement, but the only one he had was too powerful. Cursing his bad housekeeping, he tried to manage with the general lighting, but it was no good. Ronnie might be asleep, so he wouldn't ring her, but he could go upstairs and see if her light still showed under the door.

It did, and he tapped gently, using the special knock that she would recognise. At first nothing happened. Then he heard movements, and finally her voice, rather frightened, saying, 'Is that you, Kenneth?'

'Yes. It's me.'

She opened the door.

'I'm so sorry to disturb you, Ronnie, but –' He broke off as soon as he saw her properly. She was deathly pale and had obviously been crying. 'Ronnie?'

'Has Frances been on to you?'

'No. I . . .'

'What?'

'I was working. My light bulb went.'

'You want a light bulb?'

'Well ... only if ...'

'Come in.' Her voice was dull.

'I've only got a 150 watt. I need a 60 – or a 40 would do.'

'I'll go and look.'

He stood in the living-room while she went into the kitchen, and noticed that the shelves at the far end had been emptied. Their contents – books, plants, ornaments – were in neat piles on the carpet. There was a sheaf of lists on the coffee table.

'Here you are.' She gave him a 60 watt bulb in a yellow carton.

'Thanks. Ronnie...?' He looked towards the piles. 'You're not spring-cleaning at this time?'

'I'm packing.'

'*Packing?*'

'Kenneth, I don't want to talk about it. I'm going home. Back to the States.'

'But –'

'Please, Kenneth.' She looked him in the eye for the first time. 'I mean it. I don't want to talk about it.'

'Can't I –'

'No.'

She preceded him to the door.

'Ronnie...' There was such steel in her sad eyes. 'Thank you.' He held up the bulb.

'You're welcome.' She closed the door.

He thought at first he wouldn't be able to work. He almost telephoned Frances, but it was so late. So he fitted the bulb and after a few minutes was back within the compass of the drawing.

In the morning, after four hours' sleep, when he felt low and deeply uneasy, he did ring the Sherans.

Jim answered. 'Oh. It's you, Kenneth.'

'Sorry to disturb you so early. But I'm worried about Ronnie. I wondered if Frances...'

'I'll put her on to you.'

Even Jim sounded weary, he thought.

'Hullo, Kenneth. Have you seen Ronnie?'

He told her exactly what happened.

'I wanted to contact you. But I swore to her I wouldn't.'

'What is it?'

'It's that bloody, *bloody* man.'

He had never heard her so angry. 'Alastair Faraday?'

'Of course.'

'What's he done?'

'Do you remember we thought something had happened? Ronnie seemed so high?'

'Yes.'

'It was him. He'd 'phoned to say he was at Heathrow and was planning to call at the gallery at six.'

'And . . . ?'

'He omitted to say he was with Serena.'

'"With" in the full sense?'

'Yes.'

'Oh – Christ . . . thank goodness you were there.'

'I suppose so.'

'What happened?'

'Oh, they both raved over the show for about five minutes like a couple of imbeciles, and then left to go to some drinks party.'

'That's all?'

'Apart from the tears and the recriminations and the soul-baring afterwards – yes.'

'Will she definitely go, do you think?'

'I'm afraid so. She 'phoned her father.'

'So you're left holding the baby again.'

'Jim would like me just to drop it.'

'Perhaps you could find another partner.'

'Perhaps. But I shall miss Ronnie most dreadfully. She's completely changed my life.'

He walked in the early evening sunshine down the Piazza past Florian's just as their band struck into a selection from *The Gondoliers*. Among the scatters of tourists ahead, and the well-dressed Venetians walking purposefully home after work, he could already see Sky. And he could also see that she had a boy in tow. He tried not to feel annoyed, but he really didn't want to have to take a stranger out to dinner.

'Isn't it dreadful?' were Sky's opening words.

Oh lord, he thought, she's not turned into one of those people who's decided that Venice is ruined because of the tourists. He'd arrived only a few hours before, and had spent the afternoon walking happily around the Giudecca, stopping to draw one of the many walls fly-posted with red-and-white Primo Maggio notices for the workers' parades and communist speeches that had taken place on Saturday.

'What, Sky?' He made brief eye contact with the boy, who was tall and watchful.

'The Falklands, of course.'

'Oh ... yes.'

'You know she's torpedoed an Argentine cruiser, don't you?'

'I read about it on the plane.'

'Aren't you absolutely *boiling*? I half-expected you wouldn't come.'

'It does seem to be getting rather serious,' said the boy.

'Yes,' said Kenneth lamely, realising that all his attention until late last night had been on organising things at the house.

Then, since Sky didn't seem to be about to introduce her friend, he said, 'I'm Kenneth Flete,' and held out his hand.

The boy's grasp was strong. 'Hullo. Darce Nene.'

'Oh – sorry,' said Sky. 'I should have done that.'

'Rosemary Nene's son?'

'Why – yes!' His smile made him look younger.

'I bumped into her for the first time in years about six months ago. She told me you were at Cambridge. Studying ... physics?'

'That's right.' He looked pleased.

'We overlapped at the Royal College for a year... Are you on this restoration scheme too?'

'Not really. But I came to see a friend who is. Just for a week. He said I could share his cell if I rubbed down a few angels or something.'

'Well ... why don't we have a drink at Florian's? Celebrate meeting like this?'

'It's far too expensive,' said Sky.

'I'll take you both to dinner somewhere extremely cheap afterwards to compensate.'

303

When they were settled at a table inside, and had been made to feel like nineteenth century gentlefolk despite their jeans, Darce said: 'Didn't Proust translate Ruskin here?'

'He did.' He sipped his campari soda and looked around the walls decorated with females who were so delightfully vapid they didn't seem to have any bones at all.

'I wish they wouldn't play such awful music,' said Sky, then blushed. 'Sorry, Ken. It's lovely otherwise.' She drank her fresh lemonade.

Darce smiled at Kenneth. 'I had a feeling Gilbert and Sullivan wouldn't be Sky's cup of tea.'

'You mean they're yours?' she asked.

'Not exactly. But it sounds just right here.'

There was no escaping the Falklands over dinner. Kenneth would have liked to learn all about the activities at the monastery, but both Sky's and Darce's energies were focused on the *General Belgrano* and Mrs Thatcher. Sky was returning to England with him on Friday. To work for peace.

She's fallen in love, Kenneth thought. Though she doesn't realise it yet.

The boat which took them back to their island left at nine. Kenneth walked down to the Riva to see them off.

'Henry James stayed there,' he said to Darce, pointing to a door near the Victor Emmanuel statue.

'God,' said Sky. 'I tried to read him once. All those *words*!'

Darce took her hand. 'When I was at school, my mother bet me five pounds I'd never get through *The Golden Bowl*. It's amazing what one can read for money. But of course I got hooked.'

After their boat had drawn away, they stood at the rail waving to Kenneth for as long as he could see them.

I hope it lasts, he thought, starting to walk towards the Molo. Before he turned into the Piazzetta, he took a final look out into the lagoon, where the greys and golds of sunset converged on the dark smudge of the boat.

Then he remembered that Darce's father didn't know of his existence. The father's deprivation seemed much sadder than the son's.

At six the next morning, when the air was sharp, he set off

for his private heart to Venice – the Campiello del Remner. A little courtyard overlooking the Grand Canal just above the Rialto, it cradled him against all alarms. The modest *palazzo* that faced the courtyard should have been destroyed four centuries ago after its owner committed treason, but legal minutiae had prevented that. Now its open marble staircase, decorated with hunched Venetian lions, had just been restored, and its façade, embedded with the remains of Byzantine capitals and arches, calmly carried the record of more centuries than Kenneth's imagination had access to.

The veiled sun glistened off the water, making him screw up his eyes as he looked down towards the bridge, hung with a broad blue banner advertising an exhibition, and across to the markets on the other side. Long delivery barges zig-zagged slowly to and fro, and a man passing in a motor boat raised his hand. Kenneth responded. He thought he had been mistaken for a Venetian.

When the boat was out of sight, he pulled his small sketchbook from his pocket and addressed himself to one of the lions. For the rest of the day he spoke to no one, apart from normal courtesies.

After breakfast on Wednesday morning, Signor Boschini said, 'Is bad news, no?'

'Er...?'

'Your ship. She sink.'

'Ship?'

'Your navy ship. Argentines sink.'

'Oh no!'

'Yes. Bad business. You sink theirs. They sink yours.'

'Very bad business.'

'I hope no war.'

'So do I.'

He went back to his room and started to check what else there was still to complete. He looked closely at the drawings he had done, making sure they contained all the information he would need. Then he went through his list and realised he would easily be finished in time for his planned return on Friday. He'd give Lydia a ring later and let her know.

It was early afternoon when he stood in the hallway of the

305

Giorgione and dialled her number.

'Hullo, Lydia. How are you?'

'Kenneth!' She sounded relieved. 'Are you all right?'

'Of course. Signor Boschini sends you his greetings. And the sun's shining outside. How are things your end?'

'Oh ... everyone's rather on edge.'

'Has something happened?'

'Haven't you heard about the *Sheffield* sinking?'

'Signor Boschini said a naval boat had been sunk.'

'Yes. The *Sheffield*. They don't know how many have died. And you know the *QE2* has been drafted? To take more men out.'

'Oh, God.'

'Maggie's nephew's in the navy. She's afraid he'll be sent. He's only nineteen.'

'The son of the sister I met?'

'That's right.'

It seemed unbelievable. Sending boys all those thousands of miles to ... To what?

Three Dutch tourists he'd spoken to earlier came through the door carrying a white carton of pastries tied with gold ribbon. They smiled at him and pointed guiltily at their purchase.

'It's upset Arthur.'

'Because of Maggie's nephew?'

'I'm not sure he knows about that. No ... you know how he hates the news?'

'Yes.'

'Well, now I can't get him to stop watching it. I think he's worried about you.'

'Me!'

'He looked up the Falklands in his atlas. I think he was checking they were nowhere near Italy.' She gave a faint laugh. 'His geography's hopeless.'

'But he can't really be ...' His words trailed away.

'I'm afraid he is. We're all planning to go over to the house after school tomorrow. Take our minds off it. We thought, if it was fine, we'd have an onslaught on the garden. I hope you don't mind?'

'Mind? I'm delighted.'

He had been planning to go to the Scuola di San Giorgio to see the Carpaccios after speaking to Lydia, and indeed he did set off. But, as he walked the familiar route towards the Piazza, another plan tugged at his mind. When he reached the office of the travel agents he used, he called in.

Yes, the girl said after she had made a 'phone call, they could alter his flight; it would be no problem. He could return to England tomorrow.

The Carpaccios must wait till next time. He hurried back to the Giorgione to get the materials he needed for the one remaining colour sketch.

It was nearly four o'clock by the time he had been through the check-out at Heathrow. He thought of taking a taxi all the way, but apart from the price it would probably also be slower, so he took the Underground to Hammersmith and picked up a cab there.

As they drove over the bridge he looked down the river towards Putney, but couldn't quite see the frontage near Rose-wharf. The water was dark with the reflections of clouds, and it was very cold. Perhaps Lydia wouldn't have gone to the house after all.

'It's a bit longer this way, mate,' said the driver as they sped up Castelnau, 'but the traffic up the Fulham Palace Road is murder.'

'That's okay.'

By the time they turned into Cranstead Rise it had started to spot with rain, and he was sure she wouldn't be there. When he got out of the cab, he looked up at the house for signs of life. A garden fork was propped against the porch. It still had a red trademark label stuck to the handle. Arthur's. He paid the driver and went round to the back.

Arthur was energetically pulling away the weeds from Mrs Williams's fence and heaping them into a big pile. There didn't seem to be anyone else about.

He stood for a moment watching. Arthur didn't just grab the thick stems and yank them up, but knelt to clear away the mats of grass and chickweed too. It must once have been a flower

307

border, for now it was possible to see the clumps of flowering columbines and monkshood.

'Arthur,' he called.

The boy turned as though he'd heard a shot, and then, his arms still full of goosegrass, came running over.

'You're back!'

'Yes.'

For a moment they looked at each other, neither quite knowing what to do next. Then Kenneth put his hands briefly on Arthur's shoulders and said, 'Hi. You're doing a great job.'

Arthur beamed.

'Where are the others?'

'Mum went indoors. When it started to rain.'

He noticed there were dark spots on Arthur's pale sweatshirt. 'Hadn't you better come in?'

'Bit of rain won't hurt. You've got a problem with these weeds.' He returned to the fence, depositing the goosegrass on the way.

Kenneth went to the back door and found that it was open. He looked in all the downstairs rooms, but there was no one there. Then he went to the first floor. The bedrooms were empty, and so was the bathroom.

He climbed the short staircase to Colin's room.

Lydia was sitting on the divan, wrapped in the flowered shawl, reading. She looked up.

'Kenneth!' The colour drained from her face. 'Is something wrong?'

'Wrong?'

'You weren't coming till tomorrow.'

'No, I'm fine. I just thought I'd come early.'

'Oh . . . thank goodness.'

'Where's your father? And Maggie?'

'At home. With Maggie's sister. Jonathan, her son, has got to go.'

'Oh, no.' He leaned down to kiss her.

She stood up, the shawl dropping to the floor, and clung to him. 'I came over because of Arthur. He so wanted to see the garden.'

'He's doing sterling work.'

308

'He would insist on going and getting his fork. And bringing it on the bus.'

'I hope you didn't have to carry it up the hill?'

'Certainly not. He did that ... I started to help him with the weeds, but then it began to rain. I'm afraid I'm not a very dedicated gardener.'

'And I'm certainly not.'

They both went to the back window and watched Arthur for a while.

'I hope you didn't mind me coming indoors. Dad gave me the key.'

'Of course not.'

'And I took that off the shelves downstairs.' She pointed to the copy of Coward's *The Vortex* lying on the divan.

'I haven't looked properly at the books yet. Are there lots of plays?'

'Yes. Marvellous ones. In old editions. With lists of the original casts.'

He looked around the room.

She went to pick up the shawl. 'I haven't disturbed anything else.'

'Lydia, I don't mind a bit if you have.'

'You *will* have it as your studio, won't you?'

'Why?'

'It's such a lovely room.'

He realised suddenly why the idea of letting the front room had made him uneasy. It wasn't the prospect of a stranger, the house was far too big to inhabit on his own. It was because the front room had been Bernard's study, and that was where he wanted to work.

He returned to the back window. There were some paving stones directly below, just outside the french window on the ground floor. Grass had pushed up between them, and there were small drifts of white petals blown from a tree next door. A flurry of wind lifted some of them and, as they settled, a red petal came spinning down to rest on top.

Lydia was standing beside him. 'Now sleeps the crimson petal, now the white,' she murmured. Then, laughing, 'I've a ragbag

309

of a memory. I learned that at school, but I haven't a clue what it is.'

'Do you know what I was thinking?'

'What?'

'About Turner. There's a story that on varnishing day at the Royal Academy he came in, looked at his painting for a long time, and added just one red spot. It completed the painting, but it also killed the ones by other artists hanging next to it.'

'Do you think he did it on purpose?'

'Killed the others or improved on his own?'

'It's not simple, is it?'

At that moment Arthur looked up and saw them. He waved, and then went on attacking the weeds.

Kenneth walked back into the middle of the room.

'Lydia?'

She turned from watching Arthur. 'What?'

'Would you like this to be your studio?'

'My . . . ?'

'Work room. For your costumes?'

'You mean to rent?'

'For God's sake.' He went over to the other window and looked out onto the yellow laburnum and dark lilac. 'I'm wondering . . . wondering if . . . if you would come and live here. You and Arthur. With me.'

28

Due 7 Days From Latest Date

FICTION

Kitchen, Paddy
  Blue shoe